CHARM

Chrys Fey

Charm

Published in the United States of America
First Printing, 2026

Cover Art by Amanda Webb
Cover Design by Chrys Fey
Cover Bracelet from Jewelry By Lady M on Etsy
Scene Break Image by Chrys Fey
Knife Charm from Rsk Supply on Etsy

Dedication

To romance readers who need to read about a *good* tech billionaire who is all heart and treats a woman right.

A huge thank you to MJ Fifield for helping me to make sure my intentions with Thane came across in an *aww* sort of way and not in a "I'm-giving-him-a-massive-side-eye" kind of way. Thank you for being the best critique partner a writer could ever ask for.

And thank you to my readers aka Sparklers for helping me to name characters and restaurants in this story:

Sherry Fundin for naming Sebastion & Astrid Cabot.

Jackie Tanksy for naming The Blitz restaurant, Arden Lebell, and contributing to Sasha Danes' name.

Ryan Clapham for naming Uri Von Dickerson and contributing to Sasha Danes' name.

Rebecca Douglas for naming Detective Engle.

Christine Rains for naming The Ruby Spoon restaurant.

Playlist

"Little Things – Analog Version" by Allie X

"Love Me Wrong" by Allie X, Troye Sivan

"Million Reasons" by Lady Gaga

"Come Back to Me" by David Cook

"Old Habits Die Hard" by Allie X

"Sanctuary" by Allie X

"Forever and For Always" by Shania Twain

"Lionheart" by Demi Lovato

"Til It Happens To You" by Lady Gaga

"Praying" by Kesha

"Crawling" by Linkin Park

"Unconditionally" by Katy Perry

Content Warning

The characters in *Charm* endured traumatic childhoods
that impact their adult lives, including child abuse and
domestic abuse. I treated these moments with care but
did not shy away from them because real life doesn't.

The Bonus Content delves deeper into those traumas to
fully reveal what happened to Letty and Thane leading
up to and just after the Prologue. Originally, the Bonus
Content was at the beginning of the story, but I didn't
want that heavier, darker content to put a shadow over
or delay the love story to come. I decided to move the
chapters from Letty's and Thane's childhoods to the
back of the book. However, there are still flashbacks
and mentions of what happened throughout the story, so
please take care, dear reader.

Child Abuse
Domestic Abuse
Drug/Alcohol Abuse
Harassment
Murder
Night Terrors
PTSD
Rape (Past, Discussed)
Stalking
Threats

Prologue

23 Years Ago

harm woke to the sound of glass shattering. Heart racing, she gathered her blanket to her chest.

Voices shouted.

Shivering, she crept out of bed and inched toward her bedroom door. She strained to make out what was being said.

"I don't want any money," her mom yelled.

Charm frowned. Money? Constantine was upset about money? Didn't he have mountains of riches? She used to picture him hoarding gold and diamonds and rubies in a secret cave like a dragon. Perhaps that was why he sounded so brutish at night in her mom's bedroom; he sprouted scales and a tail and wings.

"Don't. Please, don't!"

Charm paused behind the door.

"Stop."

Bang.

Charm jolted. At seven years old, she knew all about guns.

"Please!"

Bang.

Her mom wasn't shouting anymore.

"Mom!" Charm reached for the doorhandle, but a booming voice halted her.

"You better run, Charm! I'm'll kill you!"

That threat had Charm locking her door. She propped her desk chair under the handle as she'd seen people do on TV. Then she ran to her bedroom window, unlatched the top, and pushed up the pane.

Banging sounded on the other side of the door, rattling it. The chair's legs slid, and it fell with a snap against the floor; she hadn't done it right.

Shaking, she shoved at the screen blocking her escape. She pushed and pushed until the metal frame around the screen bent and she was able to yank it out.

A gunshot sounded.

Charm lifted her body through the opening and hopped onto the dirt. In the next breath, she bolted.

The screen door hit the porch and clattered against the doorframe.

Constantine shouted her name.

Charm's feet carried her though the woods. Sticks stabbed her heels and pinecones pricked her toes. She threw her body into palm bushes. Their teeth ripped at her arms and legs as she followed a skinny path covered with pine needles.

Constantine's shouts and curses followed her

deeper and deeper.

She came out of the woods into the clearing for the Anderson home, but no cars were parked on the gravel driveway. She hit the door with her fists. "Help me! Please!"

But no one opened the door.

Constantine's shouts drew closer.

She flipped the welcome mat, recalling the Anderson children doing the same, and snatched up the rusted key. She had to try a few times to get the key in, all the while afraid Constantine would grab her, until the key finally slid into the lock. She opened the door and locked herself inside. Panting, eyes blurring with unshed tears, she ran into the kitchen and tugged open a kitchen drawer.

Cockroaches scattered.

She grabbed the biggest knife and hurried into the bedroom at the end of the hall, where she slid under the bed to join a horde of dust bunnies. Hitchhikers clung to her nightgown and poked her thighs.

"Charm!"

Footsteps pounded up the front steps to the Anderson home.

A moment later, a great force plowed into the door.

The sound of splintering wood echoed throughout the house.

"Charm!"

Chills tangled with Charm's spine. Clutching the knife to her chest, she listened as Constantine moved through the house to her hiding place.

"Charm. Where are you?" He was in the room.

She held her breath.

His footsteps thumped back to the door.

Her body fell lax, and she released a soft breath. *He's leaving.*

Suddenly, large hands shackled her ankles, and she let out a scream.

He yanked her out from under the bed and tugged her between his legs.

Terrified, she reached up and plunged the knife into his chest.

The blade sliced right through.

She let go of it, unbelieving that she'd done that. *Oh no! Oh no! What did I do?*

Constantine stilled. He peered at the knife sticking out of his chest. Bright red blood spread across his white, button-up shirt. His blond hair had fallen into his eyes. He stared and opened his mouth to speak, but no words came out, only a trail of blood. Then he fell to the floor with a thud.

Charm lay cemented to the spot, panting for breath that fear kept stealing from her lungs. When he didn't move, she pushed away and rose to her feet. A pool of blood spread out from under him. She nudged him with her foot. "C-Con?"

He didn't budge. His chest wasn't rising and falling.

Oh no. Oh no. She ran into the kitchen and reached for the cordless phone on the counter. Huddling in the corner between the oven and a cabinet, she pushed the three buttons she was taught to use in school.

"9-1-1, what's your emergency?"

Hearing that calm voice had Charm sobbing. "I-I-I d-didn't m-mean to."

"What didn't you mean to do, sweetie?"

"I k-killed him."

"Who?"

"My step-father."

Sometime later, a knock sounded on the Anderson's front door.

"Covington Police Department. We're coming in." A police officer stepped inside with a gun pointed at the floor.

Charm hugged her legs tighter and pressed her back into the cabinet.

The officer angled toward her and froze. The hand holding the gun lifted.

Charm squeezed her eyelids shut.

"Sweetie, my name is Officer Lydia Remis."

Charm opened her eyes.

The gun was out of sight.

"I am going to come into the kitchen with you and keep you company. This is my partner, Officer Holland. He's going to check out the rest of the house. Is that okay?"

Charm nodded.

The officer approached Charm and squatted beside her. "Are you hurt?"

Charm shook her head.

From the door, a second officer entered. He headed down the hall with his gun raised. His shoes made soft noises on the floor. Charm listened and knew when he reached the bedroom, because those shoes halted. After a moment, he returned, and the officer hovering beside Charm joined him. As they talked, they kept glancing at her.

She ducked her head.

"Sweetie." The kind officer was back.

Charm lifted her gaze for the first time and noted dark hair slicked into a pony tail.

"How old are you?"

"S-seven."

The officer's mouth parted. "Seven?" She cleared her throat. "Can you tell me what happened?"

Charm told her everything. By the end of it, she was sobbing. "I didn't mean to kill him. I swear I didn't." The officer drew her into a hug, but all Charm could do was cry. "I didn't mean to. I didn't mean to. I didn't mean to."

An ambulance came.

Paramedics cleaned up the cuts on her arms and legs from her frantic trek through the woods. They layered several bandages on her legs and gave her a bottle of water that she sipped with shaky breaths.

Cops and people in funny-looking suits walked in and out of the Anderson home and ventured into the woods, heading in the direction of her home. Thinking about her home, about her mom, brought fresh tears.

My mom is dead.

She wanted to see her mom. Hug her. She wanted her mom to tell her it would be okay, but nothing was okay.

"Sweetie, we're going to take you to the station now."

And now they were going to arrest her. That was what happened if you killed someone. She peered at her hands, imagining cuffs on them. That was how she realized her charm bracelet was gone.

"My bracelet."

"What was that?" The officer leaned closer.

"My charm bracelet. It's gone." Her lips quivered. "I want my bracelet." She didn't have her mom anymore, but she wanted the charm bracelet her mom had given her with the butterfly and flower charms.

"We'll look for it."

They scanned the Anderson home, the woods, and her bedroom, but they didn't turn up her bracelet anywhere. The kind officer assured her that if they found it, they'd give it back to her, but Charm had to leave with them. Right now.

Whimpering, Charm climbed into the backseat of the cop car. She blinked in surprise when the kind officer sat in the back, too.

She looped an arm around Charm and said, "It's okay." They were the exact words Charm had desperately wanted to hear her mom say. "It's okay. I've got you."

1

Letty

*L*etty bolted upright.

Once again, she was that little girl…the little girl she'd fought to lay to rest when she'd changed her name…the little girl who, no matter what she did, would live inside her, homesick for her mom and longing for the bracelet that would give her a piece of her mom back. Except, that bracelet was as gone as her mom was.

Every time she thought that night was behind her, it returned with a vengeance and left her shaken. Even after twenty-three years Constantine wouldn't leave her alone. With a groan, she checked the time to discover she'd slept through her alarm.

Frantic, she snatched the dress off the first hanger in her closet, rushed through her morning routine, and left without even grabbing something to eat. She rode in a taxi from West Village where she lived and hopped out near Lincoln Square when they hit traffic, because of course there'd be more cars than usual when she was running late.

Her phone rang while her heels pounded pavement. She plunged her hand into her purse and dug out her cell phone. It was Lydia, her adoptive mom and the police officer who had been a light in the darkness of a horrid night. Tugging the straps of her purse back on her shoulder, she jabbed the answer icon. "Hello?"

"Hey, sweetie."

Letty hustled across the street on her way to 106 W. 69th with a group of pedestrians. "Hey, Mom."

"I thought I'd catch you at the shop before opening, but it sounds like you're on the street."

"I am on the street. I woke up late." She debated whether or not to add this part, but her mom would probably guess it anyway. "Night terrors."

Lydia sighed. "Have you stopped taking the sleeping pills your doctor prescribed?"

"I didn't like taking them." She slipped around a slow-moving couple. "They gave me daytime drowsiness that made it difficult to work. My doctor gave me a different prescription, but that one gave me night hallucinations, which is the exact opposite of what I wanted them to do."

"I understand. I just wish I could help."

"You've done enough, Mom."

After years in foster care, Lydia had rescued her for a second time when she adopted Letty and gave her a safe home that didn't give her scars—both those psychical and emotional.

"Did something trigger the terrors? You didn't go up town and see Canmore Tech, did you? I told you to avoid that area at all costs."

"No, and it's called All Heart Tech now."

Lydia scoffed. "As if anyone in that family has any heart."

The Canmore family. Letty only knew of the late Constantine Canmore, the reason for her nightmares. She didn't know those he left behind—his ex-wife, daughter, or son. Protecting herself had meant a complete media blackout when it came to the Canmore family. She didn't know their names or what they looked like. All she knew was that his children now owned the multi-billion tech company.

"I don't want to talk about them." She needed to get her mind off that family so she wouldn't have another bad night.

"I'm sorry, sweetie."

"That's okay. You're protective. You lived through the terrors with me." She couldn't blame her mom for loathing anything having to do with the Canmores. If she were as strong as her mom, she'd be the same way, but for her health, she couldn't spend time stewing in hatred.

"I wish you didn't have them, but I wouldn't give those nights comforting you for anything."

Letty smiled. "Same here." She glanced up to see the intersection for Broadway and 69th coming up. "Mom, I have to go. I'll call you after work."

"Okay. Have a good day. I love you."

"I love you, too. Bye." A glance at her phone told

her she was fifteen minutes late already. She paused to send off a quick text to apologize to Yawanda, her assistant manager, and tell her she was almost there.

Yawanda replied back right away: *No prob*.

Grateful for Yawanda, Letty dropped her phone into her purse. She dashed ahead, rushed around the corner onto 69th, and smacked right into a solid body. Her breath fled from her lungs. After a second, she realized she was tipping forward. A cry escaped her lips. Then arms locked around her waist, and she blindly grasped a pair of shoulders as the two of them fell. She lost her breath again when their bodies hit the ground and her knees struck pavement.

The bone-jarring impact had a groan rumbling in her throat. She lay there a moment, stunned, with her cheek resting against a solid chest. That knowledge forced her eyelids wide. A man's chest? Worse than that, their legs were entangled, and their bodies were pressed in a way that was far too intimate.

People continued to walk past them on the sidewalk, not bothering to offer assistance. "Get a room," someone snickered.

"Oh my gosh," Letty said and struggled to get up.

"I'm sorry." The stranger removed their arms. "It was instinct."

"No, it's okay. It was my fault. I ran around the corner." She climbed to her feet and quickly righted her skirt. Where the hell were her shoes?

"I was texting. I'm sorry. I should've been paying attention." The stranger picked up their cell phone while she collected a lipstick tube and tiny bottle of hand sanitizer that had rolled out of her purse. "Here."

Letty peered up at a man wearing a dark gray suit with a matching tie over a black shirt, but it was the man in the suit who had her mouth going dry. He had a lean, athletic body that he could not hide under his expensive threads. Rather, the lines accentuated his muscles and highlighted his height. His amber eyes met hers, and he held out a golden-brown hand. Her shoes dangled from his fingers.

"Thank you." She stepped to the side and flattened a hand on the building to slip her left foot into her heel. Then she leaned her shoulder to the building and kicked back her right leg to try to get on her other shoe. She teetered, and he laid a hand on her arm to steady her. Her eyes widened at the contact. His touch was soft, supportive, warm.

He snatched his hand back. "I'm sorry."

"No, it's okay."

"Damn, that was some collision." A second man, approached them. He wore a black and white suit reminiscent of Will Smith in *Men in Black*. Except, Will had never been so buff. "Are the two of you alright?"

Geez, did the whole city see them run into each other? Burning with embarrassment, Letty managed to get on her other shoe. "Yes, fine, thank you."

The gorgeous man clapped a hand on MIB's shoulder. "We're good, Abbot."

Letty cocked her head to the side. They know each other?

"You can go on ahead."

"But—"

The gorgeous man gave Abbot a look that silenced

12

him.

Abbot peered up and down the sidewalk before agreeing. "I'll see you at work." He gave Letty a nod before leaving.

Letty watched him go. "Co-worker?"

"Of sorts, but also my best friend."

"Well, you didn't have to send him away." She settled her purse on her shoulder. "I think I'm all situated now." Except, her hands were shaking. Why were they shaking so much? Her gaze met his. Oh, right. That's why. Eyes that oozed sex. She hoped he wouldn't notice how she trembled.

"Are you sure? You're shaking."

Damn it.

"Just adrenaline from rushing and...colliding." She brushed her hands over her skirt to disguise their tremors. When she did, though, his gaze shifted to her legs.

His brows lowered. "Are you bleeding?"

She looked, too. Blood streaked down her right leg toward her ankle. She lifted the hem of her skirt to just above her knee, which was scraped and caked with grit.

"Crap. Yeah."

"We need to take care of that." He pointed across the street. "There's a pharmacy there and an outdoor café next to it. I'll help you to a chair and see if I can find first aid supplies."

"No, really, you don't have to." She staunched the bleeding with her skirt and winced. "You were on your way to work. You'll be late."

"It's fine. I can be late."

"Oh. Okay."

"You can take my arm if you want." He held out his arm to her as if they'd be walking into a ballroom for a lavish event.

Hunched over, with her right hand over her knee, she accepted his arm. He stepped up to the sidewalk, checked both ways, and then escorted her across as she limped. Now that she knew her knee was banged up, it hurt like hell.

At the outdoor café, he pulled out a white metal bistro chair with a flower design on it and held her arm until she lowered onto the seat.

A waitress came over right away. "Is there anything I can get you?"

Letty shook her head, but the man said, "Yes, a glass of water. Room temperature, please."

"Right away." The waitress hurried inside.

Letty lifted a brow. A man in a suit can certainly have his way.

"Please, use this." He held out the silk pocket square from his jacket.

"Oh, no, that looks expensive. I'll use napkins." She checked the table. Except, there were no napkins anywhere.

"It's okay. It's black, and I have more. I insist."

"Well, okay..." She took it reluctantly but caught the smile that lifted his lips.

Wow. He has sexy lips. Her cheeks burned, and she bent her neck to hide her face.

"I'll be right back."

She watched him stride to the pharmacy next door. When he disappeared from sight, she peeled her skirt from the bloody scrape. Hating that she'd ruin such a soft piece of silk, she pressed it to her knee.

"Here's your water." The waitress set a tall glass on the white bistro table.

"Thank you. Could I also get a bunch of napkins?"

"Of course."

The waitress returned a moment later with a four-inch stack of napkins.

Letty blinked. "That should do it. Thanks."

"Anything you need."

Curious, Letty watched her leave. Was the waitress naturally intimidated by a man in an expensive suit? Or was it the man in question?

While she waited for the stranger to return, she texted Yawanda.

—*I had an accident of sorts. I'm okay. Just delayed. I'll tell you about it once I get to the shop.* —

—I'm intrigued.—

Smirking at Yawanda's response, Letty set aside her phone. A dark movement in the corner of her eye had her turning back to see him approaching. She swallowed. Damn, he looked good. It should be a sin to look that good in a suit, but she doubted it ended there. Jeans and a T-shirt would be devastating on him. And that was the thing—his long legs and torso, his body carved with defined muscles and plains, his sculpted jawline and cheekbones exuded raw power and sex. More dangerous were the touches that contrasted with those potent features, like his slightly pink, shapely lips. She tore her gaze off him as heat bloomed in places she thought had gone numb.

He stopped at the table. "I have reinforcements."

She tipped her head back to stare up at him. In his hands he held a bottle of peroxide and a box of large flexible fabric bandages. "Thanks. That's really kind of you."

"The least I could do."

What he did next sent shock rippling through her; he knelt at her feet. Her lungs constricted when she held her breath.

He unscrewed the cap to the bottle of peroxide and picked up a handful of napkins. "May I?"

She'd been wrong. His lips weren't his most dangerous feature. His eyes. Her heart skipped a beat. His eyes were lethal. Such an inviting and comforting amber. Beautiful, curled lashes only made them more alluring. Women often said lush lashes were wasted on men, but they'd clearly never gazed into this man's eyes and had him look back. Seconds crawled by before she realized he wanted to assist with cleaning her knee. She jerked back to reality. "Oh, sure." She removed the silk square.

He arranged the napkins below her knee and positioned the bottle of peroxide over the scrape. "This is going to hurt."

She smiled. "I'm acquainted with peroxide."

And yet, he still hesitated.

Her gaze shifted to his hand around the bottle. His fingers were long. Another twinge of lust made her clench her thighs.

The bottle tipped. A stream of peroxide descended. The second it touched her ravaged skin, it exploded into bubbles that hissed. The sting and burn came immediately. She gripped the edges of the chair. "Son of a—" She bit her lip and squeezed her eyelids together.

After a while the sting lessened, and she pried open her eyelids.

The man watched her. "I have to do it again."

She nodded, and he poured more peroxide onto the fading bubbles. When those dissolved, he patted her knee with dry napkins.

"There's still some sand in it." He picked up a fresh napkin. "I'll try to be gentle."

Her leg twitched when he brushed a corner of the rough napkin over her exposed, tender flesh. With tentative strokes, he worked grains of sand out of her scrape.

"I think I've got them all." He held up the peroxide again. "One more time."

She gave him a thumbs-up.

Smiling, he let another thin stream of peroxide loose.

Bubbles formed as the solution killed more bacteria.

"That should do it."

Then he leaned forward, puckered his lips, and blew on the scrape.

Oh, dear lord. She closed her eyes. Not only was it sweet, but he couldn't know how his breath slithered beneath the hem of her skirt and cooled the inside of her warm thighs. The sound of a box opening prompted her to look at him again.

He removed a bandage and tore off the paper

casing. With gentle fingers he smoothed the bandage over her knee. His gaze lowered. "You still have dry blood on your leg." He dipped a napkin into the glass of water. "May I?"

She didn't know if her voice would work or not, so she just nodded. How many men said "May I" before doing something? And this man had asked that twice. How many men were this considerate? She'd never met one until this man kneeling in front of her, cleaning away dried blood on her skin with delicate swoops.

He finished his task, and she realized not once had his hands or fingers touched her leg during the entire process of tending to her wound. Not even a graze. He'd done that deliberately, and it stole her breath. He sat in the chair across from her and gathered the soiled napkins into a brown paper bag.

"Thank you," she said, thinking of so much more than him treating her injury.

His amber eyes met hers. "You're welcome." He bunched up the paper bag and set it aside. "Would you like coffee?"

Part of her wanted to escape his magnetic pull, but the other part of her wanted to stay and let it suck her in. The latter won. "You just dealt with a lot of my blood, so drinking coffee would be the next logical thing to do."

He chuckled and lifted his hand.

The waitress appeared instantly, as if waiting for his cue.

"One black coffee and—" He looked to Letty.

"Black coffee with sugar, please."

The waitress excused herself.

Letty pressed her hands together. "After everything you just did for me, I don't even know your name."

Golden flexes in his eyes sparkled. "And I don't know yours."

She smiled. "Letty."

"Thane."

Of course, he has to have a sexy name. Why couldn't he have a stupid name like...

She studied him but couldn't come up with a name that'd diminish his allure. Her gaze dropped to the table and to his phone. The screen was a spiderweb of cracks. "I broke your phone. I'm so sorry!"

"You didn't do a thing. Texting while walking is clearly dangerous." He glanced at her bandaged knee. "For others. I might've scarred your knee."

She shrugged. "It'll go well with all my other scars."

Thane's brows lowered a fraction, and he tilted his head.

Why the hell did I say that? She could only blame the tormenting dream that still lingered in the corners of her mind. That and his amber eyes had the power to get her to reveal anything about herself.

Luckily, the waitress came back with their coffees, giving Letty a distraction. She tore open a packet of sugar and stirred it into the steaming brew. Her first sip made her taste buds bloom. "Wow. They make excellent coffee here."

"They do. This is my favorite place to buy coffee."

Ah, so that's how the waitress knows him.

They sipped their drinks quietly.

After a moment, she set her cup down. "What is it

that you do?"

He moved his hand in a small flicking motion as if what he did didn't matter. "I fiddle with computer hardware and design apps. What about you?"

"That's neat. I own a small antique gift shop close by."

The corners of his lips lifted. "That sounds nice."

"It is. I love it."

"I can see that. Your face lights up when you talk about it."

Blushing, Letty peered at her coffee. Yes, her shop was her one source of pride and could always get her smiling, but no one had ever pointed it out before.

They made idle chit-chat until their cups were empty. Regretting having to leave, Letty picked up her purse. "Thank you for the coffee, but I should get going."

Thane rose to his feet. "Do you need help?"

"No, thanks. I got it." She rose. The raw skin on her knee protested the movement, though. "I'm really sorry about your phone."

"Not as sorry as I am about your knee."

She held out her hand. "It was nice to meet you, Thane."

His hand swallowed hers. "You, too, Letty. I hope to see you again."

Her heart raced. "Just as long as we don't *physically* run into each other."

He chuckled. "Yeah, let's try to avoid that."

Smiling, she said, "Bye, Thane."

"Bye, Letty."

Tingling all over, she left the café. She tried not to

limp, but she couldn't help it.

Even so, the smile didn't leave her face.

2

Thane

Thane watched Letty go. The breeze fluffed up her dark, short, curly locks and made her skirt dance around her ivory legs. She was the most beautiful woman he'd ever seen, and now she was walking away.

The waitress returned. "Would you like your check?"

"Please. And can I have a small bag, too?"

"No problem."

He paid for their coffees and slipped the soiled silk pocket square into a paper bag with the bottle of peroxide and box of bandages. Then he walked across the street to the spot where they'd collided. Droplets of blood gleamed on the concrete in the sunlight. He frowned; she'd bled a lot. He hadn't seen that much blood gush from a knee since he was a kid and scraped himself up trying to ride his bike without hands.

His gaze landed on a business card, and he bent down to pick it up. The thick cardstock was eggshell white with a Victorian-styled border of pink and red roses. Elegant blue cursive letters spelled out Letty Remis. His gut twisted while he studied her name. He flipped the card over, fashioned like a calling card, and found the information for her antique gift shop—Let It Charm You. The address, telephone number, email, and website for the store were listed beneath the shop's name.

Thane stared off in the direction Letty had gone, although he couldn't see her anymore. Fingers aching with the need to touch her; heart racing, telling him to run after her, he slipped the card into his pocket and left to go to work.

He arrived at All Heart Tech fifteen minutes later and rode the elevator up to the top floor. When he stepped off, Rebekah beamed.

Rebekah had been his father's assistant when Thane was a boy. Back then, she'd been a motherly figure for him when his own mother was in rehab for drug and alcohol use. Rebekah was the only one who'd looked after him and hadn't pretended that she couldn't see his father's abuse. In many ways, Rebekah had been his savior.

"Good morning, Thane, I pushed the board meeting to after lunch."

"Thank you, Rebekah. Sorry I didn't call. I busted my phone." He removed his cell phone from his inside coat pocket and set it on her desk. "Can you have someone run out to get me a replacement?"

She eyed the shattered screen and pursed her lips. Hairline wrinkles formed around her mouth. "Yes, I can."

"And can you have this dry cleaned?" He removed the peroxide and bandages from the paper bag and showed her the silk pocket square. "There's...um...blood on it."

She blinked at it through her thick lenses. "Are you okay?"

"Yeah. It's not my blood."

Her gaze flicked to him and then back to the paper bag with the silk pocket square in it. "Are you sure everything is okay?"

"Positive. It's not like that. I..." His voice trailed off. Although he knew Rebekah wasn't hinting at where his mind went to, he couldn't stop his deceased father's reputation from sneaking up to shame him. He set the bag next to his phone. "Never mind," he muttered and headed into his office.

He shut the door at his back and leaned against it a moment. Would his father's crimes ever leave him alone? Rebekah would never accuse him of being like his father, but what about everyone else? Were they waiting for the time when he'd crack and become just like him?

Thane's hands shook with nerves, and he gripped them. That wouldn't happen. He wasn't anything like his father. Constantine Canmore had been a wifebeater and a child abuser, and he had died a murderer. Thane didn't want anything to do with the monster or with the monster's memory, but he was Constantine's only son, and he now ran the company his father had built.

To everyone's surprise, especially Constantine's best friend and CEO at the time, Alec Danes, his father had left the company and most of his wealth to Thane. He had only been twelve, so Alec kept the company going until Thane turned eighteen. Alec was his mentor, but Thane had made decisions Alec didn't agree with, like taking the company as far from Constantine's toxic memory as possible. That was how Canmore Tech became All Heart Tech, with a focus on helping others. He succeeded with the company, but he wondered if he'd ever fully succeed with himself. He didn't want his father's shadow to follow him the rest of his life, but how could he escape it when he bore the name Canmore?

At his desk, he removed Letty's business card from his pocket. Staring at her name, he wondered what she'd think when she found out he was the devil's son.

He set the business card aside and powered on his computer. Throughout the rest of the morning, he thought about Letty while he made his runs to the innovation labs where prototypes were created and ideas fleshed out. Those labs and the people who worked there were the hub of his company. Everything relied on them to think outside-the-box and usher the future to the present. He loved to spend time with the techs and to pitch in, just like when he was a kid. He often removed his jacket, rolled up his sleeves, and picked up a screwdriver or wrench to help tinker on new tech that had a few kinks. It cleared his mind and was the one place he felt free of his father's impending cloud. Today, though, Letty was on the fore of his mind, even as he fixed a computer bug.

During lunch, he ate at his desk with Letty's business card in front of him. Too long he'd denied himself relationships with women because they either wanted him purely for sex—or sex and money—or were intrigued by the man spawned by a murderer, which usually involved the first two things as well. Others eyed him out of suspicion and fear. They edged around him, trying not to get too close.

Letty was the first person who'd met him and didn't seem to know who he was or his story. She hadn't even reacted to his first name, which was a rarity.

He set aside his lunch and typed in the website for Let It Charm You. The webpage matched her business card. He scanned the pages, checking out the photos of the display cases. The antiques were tasteful. She had a good eye.

On the About page, he stared at a headshot of Letty. Her short curly hair, her dimples framing red lips, her cheeks flushed with happiness, and her green eyes sparkling with the camera's flash—everything about her captivated him. He wanted to caress her delicate jaw, kiss each of her dimples, and dive his hands into her hair.

Closing his eyes, he rubbed his palms over his face.

His intercom beeped.

"Mr. Canmore, the board members are in the conference room."

He pushed a button on his console. "Thanks, Rebekah."

For two hours they discussed the next steps for buying A Dawn of Technology. The whole time, he held Letty's business card in his hand.

The last one to leave, as usual, Thane closed up his office and sent a text to Abbot, his best friend turned bodyguard. He rode the elevator to the garage where Abbot waited. No matter how early or how late, Abbot always presented himself the same way in a sleek black and white suit, with a large platinum watch on his brown wrist. His shaved hair always had the sharpest edges, and his brown eyes were always clear, as if he didn't get tired. Unlike Thane.

"You look like you have something on your mind," Abbot said. "But this time, it doesn't look like work. It's that woman you ran into this morning, isn't it?"

Thane leaned against the door of his black sports car. Although he liked to walk to work most mornings if he could, he always kept a car in the garage to travel home quickly after a long day.

"I can't stop thinking about her," he admitted and stared off into space. "She's gorgeous. She didn't treat me like a billionaire celebrity. I felt human. I've never felt that with another woman. I want to know her."

"Do you know her name?"

"I do. I actually have her business card. She'd dropped it."

Abbot tilted his head. "Then get to know her, man. Don't let Cinderella get away. That business card is your glass slipper."

Thane laughed. "Alright, Fairy Godfather, I'll see

you in a bit." He unlocked his car door and climbed into the driver's seat. Zoned out from the mundaneness of routine, he drove to his penthouse. The entire way, Abbot followed. They parked side by side and stepped into the elevator together. A moment later, they gave each other a parting fist bump when the elevator stopped one floor below Thane's. Abbot got off, and Thane finished the ride to the top floor.

His penthouse felt empty, even with the electronics, paintings, and furniture. He stood in the entry way for several minutes, just staring. Why did he feel as though Letty belonged in his life? He'd been content with his life up until the moment his arms instinctively came around her, shielding her.

Sighing, he dragged his feet to his bedroom. He stripped out of his clothes, scrubbed down in a steaming shower, and then crashed on his bed.

The next morning, he dressed in a navy-blue suit, white shirt, and blue-gray tie. Where he'd run into Letty, he paused. More than anything he wanted to see her again. Glancing up and down the sidewalk and around the building, he searched for her flouncing curls.

Abbot caught up. "Hoping she'd still be here? A day later?"

"Mind your own business."

"As your bodyguard, you are my business."

Thane glared.

"I'll wait up ahead for you."

Thane stayed there a full five minutes before admitting defeat and continuing to work. When he exited the elevator, Rebekah covered the microphone to her headset and told him, "Your pocket square came back from the cleaners. I set it on your desk."

"Thank you."

He made a beeline straight to his desk and clutched the silk in his hand. It wouldn't have the smell of her perfume on it, but she'd used it. Feeling like a sentimental fool, he slipped the square into his pocket and removed her business card. He didn't know why he'd slipped it back into his pocket that morning. Why hadn't he just added it to the pile of cards in his kitchen junk drawer? All he could come up with was that he wanted it close. He placed it back on top of his desk where he glimpsed it throughout the morning during two back-to-back meetings. By lunch, he'd signed all the papers and made the appropriate transaction to acquire A Dawn of Technology.

Rebekah stepped into his office carrying a container. "Your lunch."

"Thank you." He accepted it and lowered it to the desk, but Letty's business card caught his eye once more. "Actually, can you put this back in the fridge? I'm going out."

He snatched up the card and his new cell phone. After texting Abbot his plan to drive one of his cars from the garage to go somewhere alone, he was off driving downtown. He parked his car a few storefronts down from Let It Charm You. His hands were sweating when he twisted the golden knob and stepped inside.

"Just one moment!" came a voice from the backroom.

He glanced around the space. Antique furniture positioned around the room held a wide variety of merchandise. On bookcases, Victorian plates, vases, and tea cups mingled with crystal vases holding real red and pink roses. A vanity held perfume bottles with elegant atomizers and vintage picture frames. Atop an oak wash stand he found a display of vintage jewelry.

The sound of heels on hardwood drew his attention to the door of the backroom.

Letty stepped out and froze when she saw him. Her jaw dropped.

Although he hadn't been moving, he became rooted to the spot, too. Seeing her again sent a rush of excitement through his body.

She wore a long-sleeved black shirt and a white skirt with black roses that covered her knees. "I—" She closed her mouth and then tried again. "How'd you find my shop?"

"You said it was close by." He dug her business card out of his pocket. "You also dropped this. I found it after you left."

Her cheeks brightened to match the shade of red on her lips. "Oh, well, welcome to Let It Charm You. Did you come here to check on my knee or are you interested in buying something?"

"Honestly, I wanted to see you again." She blinked, and he hoped he wasn't making a huge mistake. "I'd really like to get to know you more."

She continued to stare.

Shit. I've completely freaked her out. Who just went to someone's place of work after running into them on the sidewalk and expressed their desire to see them again?

He did.

"I'm sorry. I wanted to be honest with you."

She nodded. "I appreciate that…your honesty."

Thane exhaled. At least she wasn't running. That was a good sign. He'd take it, although he yearned for more. His gaze roamed around the shop, hoping to extend this moment longer. "Your shop is amazing."

"Thank you. Would you like a tour complete with antique nerd facts?"

He wanted to spend as much time with her as he could manage, and a tour while listening to her talk sounded perfect. "I'd like that."

She led him from display to display, telling him about the pieces she prized the most. After working their way through half the shop, they came to the counter and a cluster of vintage jewelry boxes that were opened to showcase specific pieces. A gold locket caught his attention. He picked it up to look at it closer. Out of the corner of his eye, he noticed Letty's shoulders lift and then instantly fall. She shifted away.

"Is this locket special?"

She rotated back. "It is. Well, it is to me. This is a simple, round, ten karat yellow-gold locket with an engraved star in its center, which is set with a single diamond. It reminds me of the North star. And on the back—" Her fingers brushed his when she took the locket and flipped it over. "On the back are the initials CMS. I saw it online and bought it right away because it's…"

"Charming," he finished.

She beamed. "Exactly. I don't know who CMS is, but I can't help but feel whoever engraved it loved them with all their heart."

Thane met her gaze then, and they stayed like that

for several seconds, staring at each other. His chest constricted. He yearned to touch her, but it was too soon.

A throat cleared, and Letty jolted.

Thane rotated to see a tall Black woman in the doorway to the backroom. She was leaning her shoulder against the doorjamb and apparently enjoying what she'd been spying on if her grin was anything to go by. "Do you need my help out here?"

"Nope. We're good," Letty said.

But the woman didn't retreat.

Letty released a sigh. "This is Yawanda, my amazing assistant manager who I don't know what I'd do without. Yawanda, this is Thane, our customer." How she said the final word had Thane turning back.

I want to be so much more than a customer, Letty.

But she didn't look at him. Her gaze was trained on Yawanda. Her eyes widened.

He twisted back around.

Yawanda was biting her bottom lip and wagging her eyebrows up and down. Caught, she froze. Then she gave him a wide, toothy smile. She lifted her hand to her face and ran a finger above her right eyebrow. "I suffer from sporadic eye twitches."

Unable to resist, Thane said, "That's unfortunate."

"It is. People always get the wrong idea."

"I bet."

The shop's phone shrilled.

"Yawanda, could you get that please?"

"Damn it," Yawanda mumbled and disappeared into the backroom.

The ringing stopped.

"I'm so sorry about that," Letty said.

"Don't worry about it." He set the locket back in the jewelry box and faced the rest of the shop to examine each display from there. Every piece she'd told him about, she'd spoken about them as if they were her own personal tressures, and yet, these were items she was willing to sell, so he wondered...

"If you could own anything in this shop, what would it be?"

"That's easy." At a dark oak china cabinet, she twisted a gold key already in its lock and opened the glass door. From the middle shelf, she removed a small box. "This is a 144-Note Reuge Music Box. It plays 'Canon in D,' composed by Johann Pachelbel. Myrtle burl and rosewood with brass hardware. The exterior is natural light wood with lacquer trim." The tip of her finger curved around the dark edges. "On the lid is a delicately painted floral arrangement and two butterflies." She lifted the lid. "The inside is painted with black lacquer, and a glass panel protects the instrument. There's even an on and off switch." She flicked the switch, letting "Canon in D" play for a moment. "It's twelve thousand."

He lifted his brows.

Letty laughed as she switched off the music. "I know. Steep for a music box, but I'd never had a Reuge Music Box before, and music boxes are a big hit with my customers. It's also one of my favorite songs. Kinda sappy considering it's the most popular wedding song in existence." She shrugged and reached up to set it back on the shelf.

"I'll take it."

"Really?"

"You sold me."

Behind the counter, Letty placed the music box gingerly in a cardboard box and taped it up. Watching her prepare his purchase, her words came back to him, like a punch to the gut. Customer. He stared at the box as he spoke. "What I said before is true. I want to get to know you, Letty."

She stilled.

That reaction wasn't exactly what he'd been hoping for, but he plowed on because he had to know if this was one sided. "I want you to be more than a stranger I met on the sidewalk. More than an acquaintance. More than a friend. And I definitely want to be more than a customer to you." He inhaled. "You have me at a disadvantage, Letty. You know what I want, but I don't know what you want." And he desperately needed to know.

When she spoke, her voice was soft. "How you took care of my knee yesterday...you were attentive and polite. I want to date a man who can be that attentive and polite to a woman he doesn't know."

Thane braced his hands on the counter. He bent his neck while saying a quick, silent prayer of thanks.

"Especially one who can look that relieved after hearing me say that."

He gazed at her. "Would you like to have dinner with me tomorrow?"

She blinked. "Tomorrow?"

"It's Friday, a good day for a dinner date. I know it's fast, but I really don't want to wait. It's up to you, though. We can wait. We can take all the time you

34

need. We can get more coffee. I love coffee."

The smile she gave him warmed him inside and out. "Tomorrow." Her cheeks were the prettiest shade of pink when she checked the register and told him the total.

He passed her his credit card.

"For large credit card purchases, I always require an ID."

"Right, of course." He extracted his driver's license.

She examined them. Her body stiffened, and her lips trembled apart.

Thane's eyelids lowered. And the Canmore name strikes again. He opened his eyes and hated seeing the horror stamped across her face. "Is something wrong?" he dared to ask.

"No." Despite her answer, her hand shook when she returned his ID. She swiped his credit card and slid it back to him over the countertop.

He signed the receipt.

"Um." She scratched her forehead. "Is this a gift or a personal purchase? I offer free gift wrapping."

"A gift."

"I have an assortment of paper you can choose from."

"I'm more of a gift bag and tissue paper kind of guy. Why don't you choose?"

"Sure." She wrung her hands while checking out the rolls. After a moment, she selected a dusty rose paper that matched one of the flowers on the lid. Her hands still trembled as she made neat creases in the paper, although she attempted to hide it. "All done."

She placed the wrapped box before him. "I hope the receiver likes their gift."

"I think they will." He settled a hand on the box, and his gaze caught sight of a gold-framed, black and white portrait hanging on the wall behind the counter. "Who is that?"

While her back was to him, he slid the wrapped box toward her.

"That's my mom. It was taken a couple of years before I was born."

"She's beautiful. You look like her."

"Thanks. I…lost her when I was a child."

"I'm sorry."

She faced him but avoided his eye. "Me, too."

An alert on his phone reminded him that he had a meeting in thirty minutes. He peered at Letty with regret. He didn't want to leave, but she was obviously uncomfortable, and he didn't have the courage to ask her if their date tomorrow was still on the agenda. He didn't even have it in him to ask for her number. She'd been willing to go out before she'd read his full name on his credit card, but once people knew who he was, everything always changed. He'd been regretting that with Letty, hoping things would be different this time. Seeing it happening now…with her…all but gutted him. "The next time I need a gift for someone special, I know where to come."

She gave him a small smile. "I appreciate that."

He wanted to say that he hoped to see her again, but that look in her eye stopped him. Just like that, it was over. "Take care of yourself, Letty."

"You, too, Thane."

Wishing he wasn't his father's son, he left the shop.

3

Letty

*L*etty gaped after Thane. The man she'd run into and couldn't stop thinking about, the man who'd prompted stirrings in her that she'd never felt before, the man oozing sensuality but didn't abuse that, the man she'd just admitted to that she wanted to date someone just like, the man she'd agreed to have dinner with tomorrow, how could he be the son of the man she'd killed?

How could this have happened?!

She peered at the countertop and gasped. He'd left the gift-wrapped box. Instead of it being on his side of the counter, it sat inches from her hands. She grabbed it and ran onto the sidewalk, but Thane was gone.

Back in her shop, she stared at the box. Her heart pounded. He'd asked her what she wanted to own in her shop, and then he'd bought it. When he did, a part of her heart had broken. He'd said the music box was a gift, hinted that it was for someone special, and then he'd left it at her fingertips. She set the box down and covered her mouth. Twelve thousand dollars. Twelve thousand dollars!

"He can't do this."

She wouldn't let him.

Sinking onto the stool behind the counter, she canceled the transaction immediately. Once that was done, she hurried into the backroom.

Yawanda glanced up from the computer.

"Can you watch the shop for me? I have...I have something..." She held up the gift-wrapped box. Her hands shook.

Yawanda sprang to her feet. "Is it a bomb?"

"No. I have to...I have to go."

"No. You need to have a seat and tell me what's going on." She guided Letty to the chair behind the desk and handed her a bottle of water. "Drink. You look as though you're about to collapse."

Letty gulped down water.

"Now tell me what's up."

"You remember the man I ran into yesterday?"

"You mean the man who aroused you without so much as touching you? Hell yeah."

"That was him."

"Well, that explains the heat the two of you were emitting like ultra violet rays, but that doesn't explain why you look so freaked out right now."

Letty peered at Yawanda and grimaced. "Do you remember Constantine Canmore?"

Yawanda's shoulders jerked back. "No."

"His son."

Yawanda's face became slack. "Oh my God. I thought his name sounded familiar, but I couldn't figure out where I'd heard it." She caught the edge of the desk. "Now I think I'm going to faint. How could this happen?"

"I don't know. Whenever I heard the Canmore name I looked away. I didn't want to see any of them. I didn't even know any of their first names. Only Constantine's. I don't even know his ex-wife's name. And Thane didn't seem to recognize me, either. How could he? I was only seven when it happened, we'd never met, and I'd changed my name."

A silence descended over them, and then Yawanda laid a hand on Letty's shoulder. "You have to be careful. I've heard stories about people going after their loved one's murderers by faking accidental meetings, pretending to fall in love with them, and then attempting to kill them. Or stalking them in order to run them over with a car. Or—"

"Stop. I get the picture." Letty rubbed her arms as goosebumps developed. "But I have to return the Reuge music box. I have to."

"Wait. Hold up. He bought the Reuge?" Yawanda pointed at the gift-wrapped box. "Is that it?"

Letty nodded.

"Then why do you have it?"

"He...he left it for me."

Yawanda gasped. "Stop. Shut up. He didn't."

"He did."

"Holy shit."

They fell quiet again, staring off into space, thinking.

After a moment, Yawanda tapped her metallic purple nails on the countertop. "How exactly did he come to purchase the Reuge? The most expensive item in the shop?"

"Um…well, he asked me what I'd want if I could own anything in the shop, so I showed him the music box."

Yawanda pressed a hand to her chest. "Let me get this straight. He cleans up your blood and patches up your knee in the most careful way possible, and the next day he wants to see you again so badly that he tracks you down—"

"I told him I own a shop close by, and he found my business card on the sidewalk where we'd fallen. I didn't see it when I was getting my things."

Yawanda waved that information away. "—and he asks you what your most beloved item in the shop is, bought it, and leaves it for you?"

"Yeah."

Yawanda's burgundy lips stretched.

"What?"

"That was romantic."

Letty groaned. "What happened to all the scary talk about what people do to their loved one's murderers?"

Yawanda shrugged. "Your files are sealed. There's no way anyone could find out Letty Remis is Charm Ambrosia. And everything he did, unless he's a sociopath or something, was incredibly sweet and thoughtful. He sounds sensitive to women, which, I admit, is astonishing considering who his father was."

Letty's stomach clenched. "Doesn't matter. I can't have feelings for the son of the man I killed. Just…can't."

"Feelings?" Yawanda tilted her head.

Letty squeezed her eyelids shut. Yes, feelings. He had awakened her body like never before without even touching her. He had dominated her mind from the moment she left the café yesterday. So. Many. Feelings.

She shoved to her feet. "Doesn't matter," she repeated. "I'm going to give him back the music box and that will be the end of it."

And she would make damn sure that her feelings didn't matter.

Twenty minutes later, she stormed inside All Heart Tech. She intended to go straight to Thane's office, but security was tight. They wouldn't let her past to the elevators, so she waited while they called Thane and spoke to him directly.

She tapped her foot nervously.

The guard hung up the phone. "Mr. Canmore said you can go right up."

That name made her wince.

During the elevator ride, she gripped the railing, worried that her knees would give or that she'd vomit. A ding announced her arrival, and the door opened.

An assistant with gray-streaked hair sat at a mahogany desk beside a door with Thane's name on it.

Letty stepped up to the desk. "I'm here to see Thane…I mean…Mr. Canmore."

"Yes, I know, dear. I'm Rebekah." She pressed a button. "Thane, she's here."

The words had barely come out of her mouth

before the door beside her desk opened. Thane stood there, framed by the doorway, looking imposing with his height and build, but damn sexy.

"Letty, please come in." He stepped back to allow her to pass.

"I'm not staying. I just wanted to give you this back." She pushed the wrapped box toward him.

"I don't want to take it back. It was a gift."

"For me? You bought it for me?"

He slipped his hands into his pockets but didn't break eye contact. "Yes."

She gawked at the box still in her hands. "I can't accept it." She tried again to give it back, but he still wouldn't take it, so she placed it on the corner of Rebekah's desk. "I'm not a charity case. I don't need your gifts or money."

"I didn't intend for you to feel that way. I wanted to give you something."

"Why?"

"I don't know." He made a small step toward her but immediately halted. His gaze shifted to Rebekah, who was pretending to be immersed in work. He lowered his voice. "Since we met yesterday, I haven't been able to stop thinking about you. That's the truth. I want to get to know you. I'm sorry for any unease I've caused you, and it's clear I've caused you a lot. I didn't want any of this to happen. I saw how much you loved the music box, and I wanted to give that to you. That happiness. It was selfish. But I could see it…that music box is your heart. You should have it."

She shook her head. "I can't accept it from you.

I'm sorry. I canceled the transaction, and everything else doesn't matter because we're not going to see each other again."

The look on Thane's face made her feel as though she'd shot him in the gut. "What?"

Letty's heart shattered because he didn't know, and he had the right to know. She flattened a hand on Rebekah's desk when her knees threatened to buckle.

What sort of sick game of fate was this? Why in the world did she have to run into him? Why did she have to feel an attraction toward him? And why, oh, why did he have to be related to that monster?

She opened her mouth to say the one thing that would change everything—I'm Charm Ambrosia—when a woman's voice carried from down the hall.

"Oh, hell, no!"

Letty jerked around to see a woman in a sleek pant suit, with golden-blonde hair, stomping toward them. She pinned Letty with eyes full of rage and hate. "You?! What the hell are you doing here, you gold-digging, white trash, daughter of a whore?"

4

Thane

"What the hell, Jess?!"

Letty scrambled back when Jessalyn came toe to toe with her. "Get the hell out of here before I call security to throw your ass on the pavement where you belong."

Rebekah rounded her desk and drew Letty away from Jessalyn.

Thane stuck an arm in front of his sister. "What is the matter with you, Jess? You don't even know Letty."

Sneering, Jessalyn edged closer, fighting against Thane's arm. "I apparently know more than you, little brother." She eyed Letty. "When were you planning to tell him, Letty?" She said Letty's name as if it were a vile word. "*Were* you going to tell him? Thought you'd get away with it?"

"With what? You're not making any sense." Thane shifted to Letty to ask if she knew what Jessalyn meant, but the tears shimmering in her eyes made his heart stutter.

"I'm sorry." She whirled on her heels.

Thane sprang forward and caught her hand, pulling her to a stop.

She met his eye just as her tears broke loose and streaked down her cheeks.

Jessalyn didn't let up on her attack. "Fuck your apologies!"

When she lifted her hand as if to strike Letty, Thane released Letty and grabbed his sister. He stepped between them. "What is wrong with you?!"

A ding had him spinning back to see Letty fleeing inside the elevator. "No. Letty, don't go." He took a step as the elevator closed, taking Letty away. Anger boiled high in him, about to erupt. He whirled to Jessalyn. "You better explain yourself. Now."

"That was Charm Ambrosia, the little bitch who murdered our father."

Thane's head knocked back. Never had he expected to hear those words. He glanced back at the elevator. "How do you even know that?"

"Because I have a PI following her."

Thane's spinal column stiffened like a steel rod. "How long?"

"Since she killed Daddy."

His jaw clenched. "For twenty-three years?" Seething, he marched to Rebekah's desk and picked up the phone to call the guard downstairs. "This is Thane. Letty will be coming down any second. Please ask her

46

not to leave. If she doesn't want to stay, ask Abbot if he wouldn't mind bringing her wherever she needs to go."

"Yes, sir."

Thane hung up. He flattened his fists against the desk and spoke without looking at his sister. "You've had her stalked by a PI for twenty-three years? You've taken away her privacy for twenty-three damn years?"

"Absolutely. I wanted to keep close tabs on that murdering bitch."

He whipped around. "She was seven years old!"

"I was fifteen. And you were twelve. We lost our father because of her."

"And she lost her mother. He killed her. Then he attempted to kill Letty. Or did you forget that?"

"That's the rumor."

"Facts."

"Facts from a seven-year-old girl? That's hardly credible."

"The police thought so."

"Oh, you mean like the police officer who adopted her three years later?"

"Is that something your PI dug up?"

"Of course, it is."

The phone rang.

Thane held up his hand.

In response, Jessalyn crossed her arms and let out a huff.

He plucked up the receiver. "Yes?"

"Mr. Canmore, she left. She refused Abbot's offer to drive her."

Thane clenched his jaw. "Thank you." He slammed the receiver down. "I want to see everything." He glared at Jessalyn. "Everything you have on her."

"It's in my office safe."

He held out a hand.

"Now?"

"Yes. Now."

With a grumble, she spun on her heels. Thane followed her to her office at the other end of the hall. She lifted a Chagall painting off the wall and pushed in the code to her safe. When the lock beeped, she swung it open. From inside, she hefted out several files. The stack was four inches thick. She dropped it into his waiting hands.

"What the fuck?"

She crossed her arms. "I like to be thorough."

"No kidding." He started back toward his office.

"I want all that back," she shouted.

He slammed the door to his office at his back. Then he wrestled out of his jacket. He tossed it at the wall, and it crumpled to the floor. After it, he threw his tie.

Behind his desk, he flipped open the first file. He found the transcripts to the detectives' line of questioning. There were pages and pages. They'd asked Letty the same questions over and over again, after asking her to be even more detailed. His heart shredded as he read a child's replies to what she'd heard and seen. She'd heard them fighting. She'd heard the struggle. She'd heard the gunshots that stole her mother's life. Her recounting of climbing out the window to escape his father had him holding his head. He couldn't imagine how terrified she had been running through the woods. She had only been a child.

Thane inhaled and exhaled slowly. His father had

beaten him plenty of times growing up. He'd heard the sounds of Constantine abusing his mother in their bedroom, knew the kinds of noises Letty had heard echo throughout her own home. He knew all too well what his father was capable of, but Letty knew more than anyone.

The second file contained her childhood medical records, which detailed a broken arm she'd received shortly after Constantine had married her mother. The break had been so bad that she'd needed surgery to put in a metal plate and pins.

The third file held foster care documentation, including reports from psychiatrists and her social worker, as well as a list of the homes she'd been in—six in three years. She'd been pulled from those homes due to inadequate conditions and allegations of abuse that curdled his stomach.

Alec Danes, his father's best friend, and his wife, Sasha, had been her first foster parents. While she had been with them, Alec had used a riding crop to beat Letty whenever she was "bad."

Thane shoved away from his desk. "Goddamn, that son-of-a-bitch."

Thane'd had no clue that Alec and Sasha had ever fostered. They'd taken in Letty for pure vengeance. There was no mistaking that.

Another rich family, the Cabots, had taken her in after that. Sebastian and Astrid, while not tied with his company, were close friends to his family. Letty told her social worker that they'd sent her to bed four nights in a row without dinner. Then they'd sent her to school without breakfast. She passed out on the fourth day during class.

Thane couldn't believe this family would do that. They had a kitchen full of food and personal chefs. They had the money. How dare they starve a child. Like with Alec and Sasha, he never knew they had fostered a child. And maybe that was the point. It was purposeful. Evil.

At the age of ten, Officer Lydia Remis came and quite possibly saved Letty's life when she adopted her.

The file after that showed proof of Letty's name change.

About ten years ago, Thane had done everything to find the girl his father had almost killed. He had wanted to talk to her—if she'd let him—and make sure she was okay, but he'd been told that Charm Ambrosia's case was sealed. He couldn't find out a thing about her and decided it was for the better. Turned out his sister had known all along.

Jessalyn's PI had tracked Letty everywhere she had lived. A single file was devoted to bank statements for Let It Charm You. He didn't know how the hell the PI had acquired those, but the bastard had used illegal tactics to do it. Apparently Jessalyn had wanted close tabs kept on Letty's business, too.

The final folder was all about Carmen Ambrosia, Letty's mother. School transcripts, job applications, rental agreements, bank statements, government aid documentation, as well as Letty's birth certificate, which listed her father as Michael Walsh, a man who'd died in a car accident before Letty was born.

Thane read through the files for two hours. When he finished, he hadn't found one shred of incriminating evidence against her. She hadn't done a damn thing wrong. All she had done was survive his father and build a life for herself.

He lifted a bottle of scotch and a glass from his bottom drawer and poured himself two fingers. In one swallow, he knocked it back. He could only imagine how much his father haunted Letty. The bastard haunted Thane every day, too.

One memory in particular returned more than he'd like, because of what he'd overheard his father saying about Letty...about Charm. It'd sickened him then, and like a parasite it came to him now.

A car whisked Thane and Jesselyn off to Canmore Tech for the holiday party. Thane wore a black tux with a red tie. Beside him, Jessalyn wore a short, red velvet dress and black heels. Her vanilla and jasmine perfume filled the back seat of the car and choked Thane.

"Do you think they'll be there?" he asked while fooling with a silver cuff link.

Jessalyn inspected her red, glossy fingernails. "Who?"

"Dad's new wife and kid."

Her eyes flashed with anger. "The bitch better not step foot in Canmore Tech."

Thane clenched his jaw. "Don't call her that."

Jessalyn's laughter rang. "I'll call her exactly what she is, little brother."

Thane balled his hands into fists. "You don't even know her, but you know Dad. You know what he's like, how he treats Mom..." He ran a finger over the small

*scar that cut over his jaw from a 9 iron to the face.
"How he treats me."*

Jessalyn looked away.

"He could be that way with them, Jess."

She didn't say a word.

*The largest conference room in Canmore Tech had
been transformed with a nine-foot Christmas tree
decked out with silver ribbon and ornaments. Twinkle
lights lined the ceiling, creating the illusion of a star
scape. Along the walls, massive tables overflowed with
expensive hors d'oeuvres.*

"There's Daddy."

*Jessalyn headed off toward their father who stood
beside Alec Danes. Alec wasn't as tall as Constantine,
but he was still imposing because he had power and
knew it. He wore that power like a cape. Constantine
and Alec resembled two men who believed they were
immortals among mortals.*

*Dutifully, Thane followed Jessalyn to greet their
father.*

"Alec, you remember my daughter, Jessalyn."

*"Yes, I do." Alec smiled. "I found this in an
oyster." He presented Jessalyn with a smooth, round,
white pearl. "You can have it."*

*"Thank you." Jessalyn accepted it with a blush on
her cheeks. "It's pretty."*

"As pretty as you."

Jessalyn lowered her eyes. That blush deepened.

*"And you remember my son, Thane." Constantine
held a hand out.*

*"Of course." Alec shifted to him. "The prodigal
son."*

Thane clenched his jaw.

Jessalyn excused herself then and headed toward the group of teenagers who had congregated in a corner. Thane gazed off in their direction, wishing he could join them and be a normal kid for once. His father had to dismiss him first, though, and he doubted the teenagers would want to hang out. Not only was he younger than them, but they called him ConstaClone behind his back because they knew his father was grooming him to take over one day.

What if Thane didn't want any of it? What if he refused? What would his father do then?

Thane returned his attention to his father and Alec in time to hear his father say, "Carmen's daughter is a pretty little thing. She'll grow up to be as beautiful as her mom." He held up his cell phone. "This is them."

Alec licked his lips while viewing the photo. "I see what you mean."

"When she's of age, I'm going to give her to the highest bidder."

His father couldn't mean that. Thane backed away, but that movement didn't go unnoticed.

"What are you doing?" Constantine snapped.

"I..." Thane swallowed. Before he could get another word out, a voice lifted.

"Time for the group photo."

Little did he know then, he would relive that night a lot. Still, he imagined it was nothing like the night Letty survived. He couldn't have done anything about that nightmare then, but he could do something about it now. He made a phone call. When he finished that one, he made another. With that done, he poured a second glass of scotch, sat on his office loveseat, and sipped on it while staring into the fireplace.

Jessalyn burst into his office unannounced. "Riveting read, huh? So, where is it? I want it back."

"It's right there." He pointed his glass at the fireplace. Inside, flames feasted on the four-inch stack of files.

Jessalyn let out scream. "You bastard!"

He glared. "You think I'm a bastard? You think I'm a despicable person? What you did was despicable. How could you read those things and not feel for that child? She went through so much."

"What about what I went through? Years of therapy and rehab because of what she did to us!"

"She didn't do a thing to us. He did. I don't know how you can't see that."

"What about the ten million dollars?"

"What ten million dollars?"

"In Daddy's will. You got his company and almost all his money. Mama got the house. I got a measly mil, and he left her white trash mother ten million dollars."

Thane set his glass on the small coffee table. "Need I remind you that he killed her mother?"

"Need I remind you that money would've gone to her daughter?"

He rubbed his hands over his face. "She was seven years old. She wouldn't have received a dime of that until she was eighteen, and, according to the bank records your PI acquired illegally, she never had ten mil."

"That we know of yet. My PI is looking into it, and he's looking for proof that her white trash mother planned to off Daddy for that money. Ever strike you as odd that he was killed two months after he added her to his will? Daddy defended himself when she made to kill him and shot her in self-defense. That little bitch lied, because it was what her mother had wanted her to do."

"That's crazy."

"Don't you dare call me crazy!"

"The *theory* is crazy."

"I'll prove it. And it doesn't matter that you burned all that." She flicked a wrist at the fireplace. "I'll get copies from my PI."

Thane stood. "No, you won't."

"Watch me." She whirled on her heels.

"Your PI doesn't work for you anymore."

Jessalyn spun back around. "What are you talking about?"

"I paid him off. He won't ever do a thing you ask, and he's destroying whatever he found for you as we speak."

Jessalyn's face burned red.

"I also hired him to make sure you never hire another PI to look into Letty. If you try, I'll pay them off, too. I have more money than you." He advanced a single step. "And if you go after Letty in anyway, so help me…" He let his words fade into the tense air between them.

"You'll regret this," she hissed and stormed out.

Thane headed to his opened door and saw Rebekah sitting at her desk. "I called Alec in to speak to him," he said. "When he gets here, let me know."

"Of course, but, Thane, there's one more thing." She pointed at the wrapped box sitting on the corner of her desk, right where Letty had left it.

His heart clenched.

"She cancelled the transaction."

He frowned. "What?"

"Letty said she cancelled the transaction. She must not have realized what she'd done. If you keep this—"

"I'll be stealing a lot of money from her."

Rebekah nodded.

He sighed. "I'll find a way to return it." He picked up the box and carried it to his desk. Sitting in his chair, he stared at it, wishing he knew how to fix this. All of it. After everything he'd read, he wanted to get to know Letty more than ever, but he figured it'd take a miracle to bring her back into his life.

Beep.

Rebekah's voice: "Alec is here."

And just like that, anger replaced grief. "Send him in."

Alec strutted through the door as if he owned the goddamn building. His hair was slicked to the side. He wore a black tie and a black, full-length trench coat.

"You're always working," Alec said and laughed. "Nothing like your father."

Thane pushed back his chair. "No. I'm nothing like my father." He made his way around the desk, eyeing the man who had abused a young, defenseless little girl after she'd lost her mother and suffered in the system. He could only be thankful that she'd been taken out of that home. If she had stayed and became of age while living in Alec's house…he couldn't think about what might've happened then.

From his desk, Thane picked up a piece of paper. "Do you recognize this?"

Alec took it, read it. His gaze flicked up to Thane. "How'd you get this?"

"A private investigator."

"You were looking into me?"

"No. Charm Ambrosia. And then I stumbled across this. I had no idea you fostered. How did you happen to foster the little girl who killed my father?"

"My wife and I, as well as other friends of Constantine's, had your father's back. Even in death."

Thane gripped his hands into fists. "You had his back by whipping a child's back?"

"Women are like horses. You have to break them young."

After the memory of his gross words from the holiday party echoing in Thane's head, this was the final straw. Thane's carefully checked anger snapped like a fishing line attached to a one-hundred-pound weight. He swung his fist at Alec, cracking his knuckles against the man's face.

The blow sent Alec to the floor. "I will sue you for that!"

"Go ahead and try." Thane towered over him. "You are a sick son-of-a-bitch for what you did. The fact you did it in honor of a wife-beater and murderer is disgusting. You're fired. Pack up your office and leave within the hour. And you better pray I don't decide to let the world know about this."

Alec clambered to his feet, leaving the piece of

paper on the floor.

Rebekah hurried into the office a moment later. "Are you okay?"

"Fine." Thane flexed his hand.

Rebekah hurried to the ice bucket on a stand in the corner where glasses and a pitcher of water waited for guests. She opened a linen napkin, scooped ice cubes into it, and then hurried back.

When she handed it to him, he smiled at the motherly gesture. "It's not that bad."

"I can't help it." She clasped her hands together. "I watched you grow up and took care of you as much as I could...when I was allowed to, and I have to say, Thane, I am so proud of the man you are. I really am."

With memories weighing heavily on him, her words filled him with gratitude. "That means a lot to me."

She smiled. "I have to say something else..."

He nodded for her to continue.

"I hope Letty hasn't been scared off."

"I hope so, too."

She squeezed his arm before closing the door to his office.

Behind his desk, he thought about Letty and wondered if there was something he could do to make right everything that had gone so horribly wrong today. The one way he could think of doing that was by continuing to tell Letty the truth. She deserved that. She deserved to know what Jessalyn had done. She deserved to know about Alec. She deserved to know it all, including his truth, which was that nothing had changed. Strike that. Everything had changed; his feelings and needs had intensified.

He picked up a pen and a note pad with All Heart Tech's logo on it and, ignoring the ache in his knuckles, wrote out everything he needed to tell Letty.

5

Letty

Letty deserved what had happened, every awful thing that Jessalyn had said. Thane hadn't been brought into her life for anything other than to remind her of what she'd done and what she deserved. Or didn't deserve.

In the lobby, a figure stepped in front of the glass door, blocking her way. She recognized the man from the sidewalk. Her feet skid to a stop. "You're not just his best friend, are you?"

He shook his head. "No, I'm also his bodyguard, Abbott. He's asked me to make sure you get to wherever you want to go safely."

"I just want to get out of here, and I don't need your help." She met his eye. "Please."

After a heartbeat, Abbot stepped aside.

"Thanks." She barreled through the door and walked two blocks in tears before hailing a cab. By the time she arrived back to Let It Charm You, the scab over her knee had broken open and leaked a gross yellow ooze, soaking the bandage. She entered through the backroom to avoid any customers. Alone, she peeled away the soiled bandage and smoothed a fresh one in its place.

The bell at the front door jingled.

A moment later, Yawanda stepped into the backroom. "I thought I heard you come in. I had to wait for the customer to leave. How did it go?"

Letty gazed at her with puffy eyes.

"Oh shit. What happened?"

Letty recounted the events.

"Wow. Isn't his sister a horrible witch?"

"I deserved it."

Yawanda slammed a hand on her hip. "Excuse me? No, you didn't. She doesn't know how you met. She doesn't know you were planning to tell him right at the exact moment she waltzed in on her high horse. She doesn't know a damn thing about you."

"She knows what I did, what I feel awful about, what gives me nightmares to this very day."

"No, she doesn't. She only knows what she wants to know."

"Whatever. It's done. I just want to get back to work and forget this ever happened."

Customers distracted her. She helped rich people find the perfect gifts for their loved ones, or for themselves. During lulls, she scanned catalogues and websites, flagging items she considered buying for the shop. When a delivery arrived, it gave her busy work that kept her mind from straying.

From one box she discovered the replica of the famous Tiffany wisteria lamp that sold for auction at 1.56 million dollars. Many replicas existed, some as little as two hundred dollars. Others with price tags in the thousands. A few nearing ten thousand dollars. She'd found an exquisite table lamp reproduction for eight thousand. On her price tag, she tacked on another five hundred. She screwed a bulb into it, set it on the antique oak desk, and switched it on. Nearly two thousand pieces of blue and green glass lit up. Letty sighed. "Beautiful."

Two of her best customers had expressed their desire to own one. "Hey, Yawanda," she called into the back. "Call Dolly and Vera. Let them know the wisteria lamp is here."

Yawanda poked her head around the doorjamb. "Oh, this is going to be good."

Dolly and Vera raced into the shop and held their own private auction for the Tiffany lamp. Dolly and Vera were sisters, Black women, and held prominent positions in society. They loved each other, but they had a hilarious feud that stopped the other from getting what they wanted if they could help it. Letty ended up getting five hundred over asking price.

"Thanks for my new lamp, Letty," Dolly said as she strutted out the door with her purchase.

Vera rolled her eyes. "Next time I get here early, I'm locking the door after me."

Letty laughed.

"Bye, dear."

"Bye, Vera."

While Yawanda called in orders in the back, Letty rearranged displays to hide the holes from where merchandise had been and carried out a few items in stock. In the middle of the floor, she held a unicorn statue. Turning slowly, she scrutinized the displays, trying to find the right one for it.

"Hmm." She stepped up to a vanity. Smiling, she situated perfume bottles around the unicorn, adding a touch of whimsy to the vintage beauty supplies.

The bell gave a soft warning as a customer entered. She glanced over her shoulder. Her fingers chilled around a vase.

The gray-haired woman who had sat at the desk outside Thane's office stood there. She held the cardboard box in her hands, only this time it wasn't wrapped.

Letty nearly dropped the vase but caught herself in time.

"I didn't mean to startle you."

"It's okay," Letty whispered and set the vase on the shelf. She faced the woman. "Rebekah, right?"

"Yes. I'm Thane's assistant. Before him, I was his father's assistant."

Letty's eyes widened.

Rebekah nodded. "I know all about how his father had been, but Thane is nothing like his father, which is why he sent me here to return this." She moved closer, extending the gift box. "He knew you wouldn't want to see him."

Letty held up her hand. "I can't take that back."

"Yes, you can, and you have to. You canceled the transaction."

"Huh?"

"You said you cancelled the transaction, so Thane can't keep this."

Letty's jaw unhinged. She had wanted Thane out of her life so badly that she hadn't realized her mistake. She'd cancelled the payment *and* given him the music box back in her desperate attempt to undo what he'd done. "I am such an idiot." She accepted the box and carried it to the counter.

"You're not an idiot. Anxiety can do that to us. Fear, too."

Letty set the box down, opened the flaps, and pulled out the music box. Having it back was bittersweet. She was glad it was in her possession, but now, whenever she looked at it, she'd think of Thane. "Can you thank him for me? For being honest?"

"You could always thank him yourself."

Keeping her back to Rebekah, Letty shook her head.

"Okay. I'll thank him for you, but there's something you should know…something Thane doesn't know I'm going to tell you."

Letty squeezed her eyelids shut, bracing.

"I heard a lot of what happened after you left. Does the name Alec Danes ring a bell?"

Letty whipped around. Horror roped through her.

Sadness masked Rebekah's kind face. "Alec held a seat on All Heart Tech's board. He was Constantine's best friend."

Letty's breath hitched.

"After the things Thane found out today, he fired Alec. Actually, he did more than that. He punched him."

Letty's jaw unhinged.

"Thane would never hit a woman, but he would defend one without a second thought. The saying 'the apple doesn't fall far from the tree' couldn't be further from the truth when it comes to Thane and his father. Thane fell lightyears away from that rotting tree. He escaped that rot."

Throat tight, Letty nodded. She believed her. "Thank you for telling me that."

Rebekah pointed at the box. "Thane wanted me to tell you that he left something in the music box for you, whenever you're ready. No pressure. His words, not mine. He just didn't want you to be caught off guard when you found it."

"Found what?" Letty's voice was a rasp.

Rebekah shrugged. "That's for you to find out." She gave Letty a parting smile. "I truly hope I see you again." With that, she left.

Letty rotated toward the Reuge.

Yawanda stepped out of the backroom and joined her at the counter. "I was totally eavesdropping." She studied the Reuge. "What do you think he put in it?"

"I have no idea."

Yawanda nudged her with her elbow. "Open it."

Heart thudding, she raised the lid. "Canon in D" emitted from the gears. Folded sheets of white paper rested atop the glass plane. Blue ink crawled across them in fancy cursive. She stared at the stack with a dry mouth while the tune played. Then she switched off the music, removed the pages, and shut the lid.

Three sheets. He'd hand-written her a three-page letter.

She unfolded them, hating how her hands trembled.

Letty,

You didn't deserve what my sister said to you. I don't have the same sentiments toward our father as she does. Constantine's actions have dogged me my entire life. Haunted me. I see it in everyone's eyes, as if they expect my father's evil to be lurking just beneath my skin and they're waiting for it to break loose. I've fought to rid myself of his shadow, but his crimes are something I'll never escape.

I am so sorry for what my father did to you and to your mom. Although, I know my apologies don't mean a thing and won't bring her back.

After you left, I found out that Jessalyn had a private investigator following you all these years. Twenty-three. She had everything on you. I'll never make right this invasion of your privacy, but I did burn everything she had and fired her PI. Actually, I hired him myself to make sure she never does this to you again.

In one of her files, she had information about your foster homes. Two of them were close friends to my father. They fostered you on purpose. To hurt you. Up until a moment ago, Alec Danes had been a board member at All Heart Tech. He admitted to hitting you with a riding crop, and I fired him on the spot.

These people did these things behind my back—my own sister, employees of my company, and so-called family friends.

Jessalyn believes you and your mom conspired to kill my father for the ten million dollars he had willed to your mom, which he'd reportedly added to his will two months before his death. I had never heard of this. I called my father's old attorney, the executor of his will, but my father's Will is nowhere to be found. Without that, I can't disprove Jessalyn's claim. She believes our father killed your mom in self-defense and that you lied about what happened. I know this is ludicrous, because I knew my father. I wasn't jaded by him. I didn't hold him on a pedestal. I saw him for what he was. He beat my mother, and he beat me. The only one he didn't beat was his precious daughter.

If there is anyone else in my company who still supports my father, who believes Jessalyn, I'll find out about it. I'll make sure they never hurt you again. You may not want to see me again (I get it...I'm a Canmore), but I won't stop looking out for you.

But I have to tell you, Letty, I still want to get to know you. I still want what I said I wanted earlier today, but I'll respect your wishes and stay away.

If you ever change your mind, this is my number.

Thane

Stunned, Letty hurried around the counter and sat heavily on the stool.

"What did he say?"

Letty held the letter out to Yawanda. She didn't have the energy to speak, didn't know what to say if she did. A PI had been following her for twenty-three years? Spying on her? Violating her privacy? And all because Jessalyn Canmore believed a seven-year-old child could manipulate the police department, evidence, and whatever else?

Letty hadn't lied. She had lived through it. Every horrendous second. Her mother had been a good woman. Honest. Sweet. She didn't care about money. Perhaps her mother had been naive and gullible, because she'd believed that Constantine Canmore had loved her, even as he beat her black and blue, but she certainly didn't try to kill Constantine for money. Nor had she groomed her child to help her with her con.

And the rich couples who had taken Letty into their mansions? Not once had she fathomed that those people could be Constantine's allies. She couldn't believe the man who'd left scars on her back had done it to avenge his deceased, monstrous friend.

Would she never escape what she'd been forced to do at such a tender age?

Yawanda laid the pages on the counter. She tilted her head. "So, what are you going to do now?"

"I...I don't know. I have to think."

And Letty did just that. She spent days thinking about Thane's letter. The things he revealed to her rattled her core. Who else was out to get her? The thought scared her. Late at night, she wondered if Thane was in on it. Could he be secretly working with his sister, luring Letty in, hoping to make her spill her guts so they could lock her up in prison? Men did things like that. They trapped women with fake offers of love and security only to swoop in for the kill once their unsuspecting targets were comfortable, blinded, deceived. Just as Constantine had done.

Several nights in a row Letty woke up in a panic, soaked with sweat. The nightmares were coming back stronger than ever, awakened by the Canmore name.

Daily, hourly, she thought about Thane. Couldn't help it. Her mother hadn't been a good judge of character—and maybe Letty took after her—but she believed the things Thane had told her; that his father's sins haunted him and how he couldn't escape them, though he tried. The two of them were in the same boat. Could they get free of Constantine Canmore together? Was that what it would take? The idea clenched her stomach with longing and apprehension. They were linked by what happened twenty-three years ago. Had they been brought back into each other's lives to cure each other of the things they hadn't been able to heal on their own?

She had added Thane to her contacts and considered calling him every day, but the unknown stopped her. Possibilities halted her. Her own confused thoughts held her back. A coward, she called herself, but she knew why it was so hard for her to take even the tiniest of steps toward him. *He's a Canmore. He's the Canmore now.*

A week dragged by. Then a second.

She remained silent. Eventually, life would go back to normal. It had twenty-three years ago, and it would again.

On her way to work one day, she walked on the sidewalk, hugging the building, and following the flow of pedestrians. She rounded the corner across from the café. The couple in front of her stepped out of her way toward the curb, and she came to a standstill. Behind them emerged Thane.

He steered around them right into her path. His gaze landed on her, and he stopped as if he'd collided into a wall. "Letty." Her name came out on his breath.

To her surprise, she found that she didn't want to bolt in the opposite direction. Instead, she wanted to go to him. He was magnetizing. More than ever. He wore a burgundy suit that made his amber eyes hypnotic.

She gave him a small smile. "I wasn't running."

"And I wasn't texting."

"Seems we've learned our lessons."

He dipped his head. "I'll take another route to work from now on."

"That's not necessary." She glanced toward the café. "Do you want to have coffee?"

Thane studied her. "Yeah. I would."

She peered past his shoulder, knowing she'd see someone not far behind. "Abbot can join us."

But Abbot didn't slow. He walked right around them as if not registering they were in the middle of the sidewalk, blocking the flow of pedestrian traffic. "Minding my own business," he said as he passed.

Letty pressed her lips together. "Awesome best friend."

"He is." Thane shifted toward the curb. "Shall we?"

Smiling, she gave a nod. When she stepped up beside him at the curb, her pulse elevated. The second a break in the traffic appeared, they made their way across the street to the café. At the same table as before, they sat across from each other.

She set her purse on the table beside her and immediately regretted it. Her hands needed something to grip, to divert energy to.

"Your knee has healed."

Letty followed his line of sight. The blue ruffle hem of her pencil skirt had risen to expose her knees. On her right knee, a fresh patch of skin shone pink.

"It has. It's just very pink now."

Thane closed his eyes briefly. When he regarded her again, he said, "I wish none of this had happened to you, Letty."

A waitress, a different one from last time, came to

her rescue right then, so she didn't have to worry about coming up with a response to such a heartfelt declaration.

"Would you like to order?"

"Coffee, black, please," Thane said.

"And you?" the waitress asked Letty.

"Same but with sugar."

After the waitress left, they didn't speak for a while. Not even when their coffees came and they'd tasted them. Letty lowered her cup to the table.

"When you look at me, do you see him?"

Letty's neck snapped up.

Shame, regret, and a dozen other emotions lined Thane's face. His eyes reflected sadness, and his body language told her he was braced for the worst.

"No."

Thane's shoulders dropped.

She leaned forward. "From the moment we met, I knew you were nothing like him. I never would've agreed to go out to dinner if I thought you were. You..." She paused and licked her lips. "You are tentative when it comes to touching a woman. You avoid it at all costs. I understand now that's because of him. You don't want to do anything without a woman's consent. I ran into you and you apologized to *me* for having your arms around me when we fell. You took care of my knee and not once did you touch my skin. You didn't chase me down when you realized I left the music box after already cancelling your transaction. Even in your letter you said you'd stay away, if that's what I wanted. And you have. You've stayed away.

"Do you know how many men would've taken

advantage of the conditions for how we met? There are men who would've purposefully brushed my curves while getting up or touched my leg. Heck, most would've made me clean up my own damn blood."

He cracked a smile at that.

"Do you know how many men would've shoved their arm into the elevator to stop the door from closing? Or restrained me so I would listen to what they had to say? Too many. You are not your father's son. No, I don't see him when I look at you."

He met her eye.

"Frankly, you don't look anything like him." Constantine had been a white man with blonde hair. Thane was mixed, with golden-brown skin and shaved black hair.

He chuckled softly. "I take after my mom." His fingers closed around his cup of coffee. "I'd seen my father bar my mother's way in arguments and physically restrain her. I'd seen him grope assistants. I learned what not to do by watching my father."

She nodded. "You are a good man. That was clear to me from the beginning."

Thane stared at his coffee. The pain from his past and from his present with people assuming he was like his father—or would turn into him—made her want to hold him. Her chest constricted with the need to soothe that pain. That urge spiraled out. Every time she saw him, he caused reactions in her body that he didn't mean to do, that he probably had no idea he caused. For the first time, she wanted him to know, without a shadow of a doubt, that she did have those compulsions. He didn't even have to touch her to draw them out, either. His body, no lie, was the biggest culprit, as well as his chiseled but sensual features. It was his eyes that did her in, though. But his mannerisms were the clencher.

"Thane, when we met, you took care of me without touching my leg." She met his eye. "I want you to touch my leg."

His chest rose. He checked the rest of the outdoor café. They were alone. "Now?"

"Right here. Right now."

Holding eye contact, he rose from his chair and knelt in front of her. She shifted so he'd have easier access to her leg, but he didn't lift his hands to touch her.

"I give you full permission," she said. "I won't take it back. I want you to touch me." She was close to begging.

That was apparently what he had needed to hear. He molded his hands around her calf and dipped his neck. His lips touched the pink scar on her knee. She bit her bottom lip, and he peered up at her. "Was that okay?"

With the bit of flesh still caught between her teeth, she nodded.

He leaned down again and kissed a trail down her shin to the strap of her shoes. She closed her eyes. How could his kisses make her feel as though he thought she were precious? Because, damn, that's what she felt each time his lips touched her skin. He did it softly, a mere brushing of his lips, but it spoke volumes.

When he finished with his lips, his hands caressed her calf all the way down to her ankle. Then he raised his hands, so that the pads of his thumbs journeyed along her shin bone. His fingers skimmed over her kneecap, drawing out shivers.

She grasped the chair. Her breathing became shallow.

His touch electrified her. She bit her lip again when a warm throb bloomed between her legs. Her heart pounded so hard that she was sure he could feel it at the tips of his fingers. How could he not? Her pulse was everywhere. It was erratic. It was deafening.

His palms weren't soft as she'd imagined a pampered business man's hands to be. The strong skin of his hands was slightly roughened by work, by passion, but his touch was gentle, arousing. His fingers stroked the back of her knee, and his hand cupped her calf muscle again while his other hand curled around her ankle. The tips of his fingers fondled her ankle bone before slipping beneath the leather strap. Her foot jumped when he teased the delicate skin on the inside of her ankle.

She caught his other hand as it grazed up and down her calf. "Okay," she said, breathless. "That's good."

He pulled his hand from hers.

She still hadn't opened her eyes, not even when she heard him take his seat. When she managed to peel her eyelids apart, she found him staring and breathing just as hard as she was. They sat like that, inhaling and exhaling, feeling the fire in the air between them. It was potent.

Undeniable.

She wanted to say something, but no words came to mind. Thanking him for arousing her like that felt silly, but her body desperately wanted to thank him. With hands clasps. Knees bent. Hell, yes, her body was oh-so-very-thankful, and all he'd done was kiss and touch her leg. Half her leg. Delicious flashes of heat exploded inside her with curiosity. What would it feel like if he kissed and touched her entire body?

She hummed with desire.

Thane's phone sounded. He didn't move. Only his gaze did. "That's Rebekah reminding me I have a meeting in forty-five."

She licked her lips. "I should go, too."

Thane dropped bills onto the table.

On the sidewalk, they faced each other.

"Bye, Letty."

"Bye, Thane."

And he turned away. She hadn't told him she wanted to see him again. For all he knew, she didn't. He didn't peer back, either, but continued on his way.

Watching him, she dug her phone out of her purse and called him.

Thane's phone rang. His head lowered as he checked the screen. Then his hand lifted it to his ear. "This is Thane Canmore."

"You probably shouldn't talk on the phone and walk, either."

He ceased walking and wheeled around.

She smiled. "Don't hang up."

"I wouldn't dare."

She resumed walking to her shop. "This will be easier to tell you when I don't have to look at you." She exhaled. "I'm sorry for not calling you until now. Obviously, I've had your number in my phone. I almost called you a few times, but I lost the courage."

"Why?"

"Because the things you told me about your sister and my foster parents scared me. A lot. Your sister thinks my mom and I conspired against Constantine. My mom wasn't like that. Constantine was rich, and we had nothing. That night, I heard her screaming, 'I don't want any money.' She wouldn't have done what your sister claims. And I wouldn't have, either. I was seven. My concept of money was a few bucks to spend at the dollar store. I didn't lie, either. I swear."

"Baby, I know. It's okay."

The endearment made her heart soar, right before it plummeted. "It's not okay, Thane. Apparently, the Danes and Cabots thought I was in on a plot against Constantine. Or, at the very least, my mom's tool to get the police to believe her self-defense plea. Why else would they do what they did to me? There could be countless people close to you who think that and you don't even know it."

"If there are, I'll find them. They won't ever hurt you again."

"And the ten million dollars. I had no idea about that until I read it in your letter. No one ever told me. I never got a phone call or a letter. Nothing. I don't have it."

"I believe you. Seconds after Jessalyn told me you're Charm, I didn't care. All I cared about was you. I wanted to make sure you were okay. I called my security downstairs to have them ask you to please not leave. If you didn't want to stay, I wanted Abbot to drive you home or back to your shop. Please don't tell me you walked all that way."

"I walked for two blocks, and then I hailed a cab." She stared at her shoes as she walked. "Thane...when you look at me, do you see Charm?"

The silence on the other end was like a knife to her side.

Finally, he said, "When I look at you, I see the most beautiful woman I've ever met, who I ran into on the sidewalk. I felt something in that instant, as if the universe was slapping me awake, and it needed us to slam into each other to do it. It literally had to knock me down."

Letty smiled but didn't say anything.

"Now that I know you're Charm, none of that has changed, but something has been added. I look at you and marvel at the strength you must've had to go through what you did at such a young age and to survive it all." He paused. "I wonder about your scars."

Her hand lifted to her left arm. She wore quarter sleeves to hide the surgical scar on the side of her bicep, from her broken arm Constantine had caused.

"Ten years ago, I tried to find the young woman who had survived my father."

Outside her shop, Letty clamped a hand to her mouth as tears formed.

"I wanted to make sure she'd had a fair shot at life, and I wanted to meet her, if she felt comfortable with that. I couldn't find her, though. There were no records of Charm Ambrosia anywhere. What did exist were protected by the courts and sealed. I didn't press. I let her be, and I just prayed my father hadn't ruined her chances."

She swallowed. "When I was adopted, I accepted my adoptive mother's last name, and I asked the judge if I could change my first name, too. I wanted to leave Charm far behind me." She unlocked her shop door and stepped inside. "The past couple of weeks were difficult. I thought about you all the time. Every time I did, though, I told myself that it's not meant to be."

"Why not?"

"Because Constantine is between us. Not only as the burden we share, but as a barrier. No one is going to want us to be together. Not your sister. Not your family's friends. And certainly not your mother."

"My mother is in rehab. She's still dealing with his trauma. And I am done with letting Constantine have his way. I want you, Letty."

She collapsed into the shop's door.

"When I asked you what you wanted, you said you wanted to date a man who can be attentive and polite to someone he doesn't know. Do you still want that?"

"Yes."

"Then forget about everyone else. Don't let anyone stand in the way from you getting what you want. And if that man ends being the man who comes after me, then I won't stand in your way, either."

Letty smothered a sob as it broke loose. She squeezed her eyelids shut, causing the thick wall of tears over her eyes to shatter.

"What do you want, Letty?"

She bent over. All the emotions inside her poured forth, prompted by his words, his voice, his sincerity. She covered the phone's speaker, not wanting him to hear her breaking.

"Letty?"

She lifted the phone. "You. I want you."

Thane exhaled on the other end. That rush of relief told her all she needed to know; he'd been waiting to hear her verdict.

"I'll let you decide when you're ready to see me again."

Pressing her hand to her chest, she said, "Sunday?" It was two nights away. She wanted to see him soon, but she also needed time to compose herself.

"Sunday sounds good."

She swiped her wet cheeks with her finger. "Can you pick me up?"

"Absolutely."

6

Thane

Thane parked in the back of Letty's apartment building per her instructions. He had to restrain his urges from pushing him to race up the stairs two at a time. The fact Letty had agreed to go out on a date was a miracle. Nor had she called or texted to cancel. Good signs. More than anything he wanted this date to go well, and he wanted many, many more dates with Letty afterward.

Thane paused outside her door. His heart pounded with excitement. He ran his hand down the length of his skinny black tie, rebuttoned his jacket, and breathed deep to settle his nerves. Never in all the times he'd gone out with someone had he ever felt this nervous or happy. Letty was different. He'd felt that the instant he'd gazed into her eyes. She was special. The pounding of his heart intensified with the mere thought of her sparkling eyes and dimpled smile.

Another deep breath, and then he knocked on the door. A moment later, it opened to the most stunning woman he'd ever seen. Letty wore a black, off-the-shoulder, quarter sleeve, knee-length dress that highlighted her smooth, shapely shoulders and her slender collar bones. The temptation to lavish kisses over the curve of her shoulders and follow the cut of her collar bones with the tip of his tongue jabbed him in the pit of his stomach. His gaze followed her legs down to nude heels. Her lips were painted nude, too, but that didn't make them any less sensual. On the contrary, he yearned to kiss them, suck them, nibble them more than ever before.

He cleared his throat. "You look gorgeous, but then again, you always do."

Her nude lips lifted into a smile. "Thank you." She stepped out of her apartment and pivoted to lock the door. When she did, he caught a whiff of her perfume. Was that rose? He inhaled. Patchouli, too? He didn't know, but he liked it. The scent was uniquely Letty.

She faced him. Her curls bounced with the movement. He wanted to feel their feathery-softness, run his fingers down a curl to watch it smooth out and then spring back into place. My God, he wanted so much, but none of that was for him to take. Except for her scent. He could indulge in her scent all he wanted while breathing. Taking in oxygen, at least, didn't require permission. It was actually very much a recommended thing to do...to stay alive and all that.

Yes, breathing was innocent, so he inhaled a lungful, allowing his senses to get drunk on her perfume.

At the stairs, he held out his hand to assist her. She grasped it. The moment of contact sent fireworks of awareness throughout his body, from his palm all the way to his scalp. Her heels clacked on the steps, matching the beat of his heart. Thank God her heels were loud enough to drown out his heartbeats, because he was sure the excited thumps would've echoed in the space.

When they reached the base of the stairs, she didn't release his hand, as he'd expected her to, but continued to hold onto it. If only they were walking to the restaurant, because then he would've had the opportunity to hold her hand for blocks. The walk across the parking lot to his car wasn't long enough.

He opened the passenger's door. His gaze immediately lowered to her knees, uncovered by the hem of her dress when she sat down, and that sweet scar that called out to him to kiss, as he had the other day. The memory of that moment was fire in his belly. She'd allowed him to touch her intimately, and his passionate instincts had taken over. If he could repeat that moment, he'd do it all over again.

And so much more.

She released his hand, though, bringing him back to reality.

He shut the door, moved around to the driver's side, and slid behind the wheel.

"No Abbot?" she asked.

"Abbot and I have a new agreement that anything that has to do with you, I do alone."

Letty snorted out a laugh, and Thane replayed his words in his head.

"That didn't quite come out right."

Letty smirked.

The close quarters and her perfume softly circulating in the air exhilarated him. He started the engine. "I have reservations at The Blitz, but if you'd rather eat somewhere else, I can make the call. I'm sure we could get in last minute."

"No, that's okay. The Blitz is fine. I've never eaten there before."

"They're excellent. I think you'll like them." Or, he hoped she would. He hadn't had the chance to ask her what kind of food she liked, but the chef at The Blitz crafted many dishes from simple steak and lobster to pastas that blended many amazing textures and flavors. He was sure she'd find something she'd like on the menu.

The ride to the restaurant was quiet. Thane kept wondering if he should speak, ask a question, but he didn't want to use up all conversational talking points now and not have a thing to discuss during dinner. Still, he couldn't shake off the feeling that Letty wasn't just nervous. She was more reserved now than she had been before, and he could guess why. Not only had the last time they'd spoken been emotional, but the last time they'd seen each other had been steeped in hormones.

Arriving at the restaurant was a relief. He opened the car door for her, and she clasped his hand again while they walked into the restaurant. "Canmore," he said to the host inside the door. With a discreet nod, they were led to the chef's table in front of the kitchen.

Thane pulled out the chair for Letty and pushed it in as she scooted closer to the counter. Then he sat in the chair beside her.

"Wow. The chef's table," she said.

"I…um…didn't request it."

"I suppose you don't have to. Your name does."

Yes, his name. The infamous Canmore name.

"Not that that's a bad thing," Letty added quickly.

"It's okay."

"No, it's not." She peered at her lap. "I shouldn't bring up your name. You're much more than your name and your status. So much more."

Hearing that from her lips tightened his gut. He wanted to reach out, touch her chin, turn her head toward him, but he didn't. Instead, he leaned closer, catching a hit of her perfume. "I know this isn't normal. Our histories aren't normal. How we're connected isn't normal. My name and status aren't normal, and what's happened since we've met isn't normal, but…" He paused, unsure of where he was going with this.

"Normal is overrated," Letty finished.

Grinning, he nodded. "Exactly."

"I want to see where this is leading us," she whispered.

"So do I."

She gave him a pretty smile topped with blushing cheeks.

My God she's perfect. He cleared his throat and handed her a menu.

They fell into a lapse of silence while looking over their menus. The waiter came and took their orders: avocado, grapefruit, and fennel salad for their appetizers, beef wellington for two with truffle brie mashed potatoes and asparagus drizzled with hollandaise sauce for their entrees, and a bottle of pinot noir to enjoy throughout their meal. In minutes they were given their salads.

"How did you get into antiques?" Thane asked while piercing a slice of creamy avocado, crisp greens, and a plump piece of red grapefruit with the prongs of his fork.

"My adoptive mom. Her home was…is…filled with amazing antiques. I had never seen anything like it. She told me the history behind each piece, the date it was made, who made it, where, and the materials. I was fascinated. More so by the fact that it was an activity that people did…antiquing. She showed me a massive antique mall during our first weekend together, and we spent hours hunting up and down every aisle and booth. I couldn't believe that people not only bought antiques but that people made a living selling them. At first, it was a way for the two of us to bond, but I was a sucker immediately. It became my passion."

Thane smiled. Her enthusiasm for antiques lit her up from the inside out. He asked her more questions until he no longer had to encourage her and her story poured freely from her lips. She told him all about her first booth selling antiques at a flea market on the weekends and her job at an antique mall during the weekdays. Two years later, she opened up her own shop. A tiny thing in a strip mall. That was how she'd met Yawanda, who came in to apply for a job. Together, they made Let It Charm You a success in their small town. Through social media and ads, their website also kicked off, pushing them to expand. They took a big chance picking up and moving to New York, where their largest clientele base was located, and that chance had paid off more than they ever could've foreseen. They had loyal customers who came in weekly, and they even shipped internationally.

Thane could listen to her talk about her shop and antiques all night long. He loved how the subject relaxed her, opened her up. "Your shop is amazing."

"Thank you."

"You've been through a lot and made yourself into a successful business owner."

"Coming from you, that is a compliment."

He shook his head. "I didn't build a business from nothing."

"No, but you did rebrand it and made it into something inspiring and incredible."

"I appreciate that."

"I speak only the truth. From what I hear, it's never been more successful than in your hands."

Talking about All Heart Tech did the complete opposite to him that talking about Let It Charm You did to Letty. He gazed into the kitchen, searching for something to say that did not have to do with his father, but in trying so hard to avoid thinking about his father, there was Constantine Canmore towering over his thoughts.

"I see the benefit of the chef's table now," Letty said. "During a lull in conversation, we have something entertaining to watch and it looks completely normal."

"It'd be more entertaining if it was *Hell's Kitchen* during a taping."

Letty laughed. "True."

Their entrees came a minute later. They cut into their beef wellington, and Letty released a moan that had Thane's body reacting instantly. He wondered how he could get her to make that same sound.

"Oh my God."

And to say that.

"Wow."

And that.

"This is amazing."

Definitely that.

"I've never had beef wellington before. I can see what all the fuss is about. This is delicious."

"It is." Although he wasn't thinking about the meal.

They resumed eating. This time, their silence wasn't awkward while they cleaned their plates. Thane didn't feel pressured to initiate conversation, either. The food received their full attention, and neither of them appeared to feel bad about that. But at the back of Thane's mind, a thought still lingered. When their plates were taken away, that thought became an irritating itch. He had to know.

"Letty..."

"Hmm?"

"When we first met, you said something about scars. You said the scar on your knee would go well with all your other scars..."

She lowered her gaze.

"That was before I knew who you were. Now that I do, I need to know something else." He leaned closer. "Did my father give you any of your scars?"

Lips compressed, she nodded.

"How many?"

"One." Her voice was soft. She tapped a finger to her left arm. "Here. From surgery. When I broke my arm."

Her quarter sleeve completely covered the scar. Not even a sliver of it peeked out from beneath the fabric. His fingers ached to roll that sleeve up, to skim his fingertips down the length of the scar. To relieve that ache, he flexed his hand beneath the counter. Then he curled his fingers into his palm and clenched his hand.

"I was on the porch railing, pretending it was a balance beam. Constantine pushed me off it, and I fell on my arm, on concrete garden edging. He threatened me into saying I fell on my own."

"I'm sorry." Thane laced his fingers with hers. "I'm so sorry for everything my father did to you, and to your mom. Nothing I can ever say or do will make up to you for what you lost."

She shifted toward him. "That's not your burden, Thane. You have nothing to make up to me."

"He was my father."

"That doesn't mean that his wrongdoings are yours."

"It feels that way." He peered at their hands, realizing he still held hers. "He gave me a scar, too." He tilted his head to the side and ran his thumb over the scar on his jawline.

Letty leaned closer. "I never noticed that before."

"I was lucky. One, that the 9 iron hit my face low enough. Two, that it didn't break my jaw."

She gasped. "A 9 iron? He hit you in the face with a golf club?"

"I stood up to him when he went after my mom. I was twelve."

"Oh my God." She covered her mouth with her free hand. "I'm so sorry, Thane."

"It seems he's given us many scars. The worst of which aren't even visible."

She swallowed. "Yeah...but maybe..." She trailed off.

"Maybe what?"

"Maybe we can help each other heal. Finally. Once and for all."

He squeezed her hand. "I'd like that."

Their dessert, a pear and chocolate frangipane tart, arrived, giving them a chance to focus on something else until it was time for them to leave. Before Thane knew it, though, they were back at her apartment, right outside her door. He watched her unlock it. How'd they get here already? He didn't want the night to end, but he knew better than to invite himself into her home. More than anything, he wanted to take things slow with Letty. He was never the kind of person who believed in one-night stands, and he certainly never assumed that walking someone to their door meant he'd get inside for drinks and then one thing would lead to another, which would lead to a bed or some other solid surface. Except, Letty didn't know that he wasn't that kind of person.

She cracked open the door to her apartment. Then she glanced at him and quickly looked away.

"I just wanted to walk you to your door, make sure you got in safely."

"Thank you," she said. "That's really sweet of you."

To keep himself from touching her as he desperately yearned to do, he slipped his hands into his pockets. "Would you like to do this again?"

"I would."

His heart leapt at her words. "How soon?"

"Soon."

"Friday?"

She nodded. "Friday is good."

"I can call you tomorrow to set everything up."

"Okay."

Say goodnight now and leave, he told himself, but his feet weren't moving and he couldn't make them. "Letty…"

She gazed at him in the hall's dim lighting. "Yeah?"

He breathed long and slow and shook his head. "I really want to kiss you."

She continued to look at him. Only now, her eyes were wide, unblinking. Had he scared her with that statement? Was it too soon? Should he bow out?

"I really want you to kiss me, too."

If his feet weren't as good as cemented to the floor, her words would've knocked him over. He pulled his hands from his pockets, closed the small gap between them, and cupped her face with his hands. When he would've swooped in to cover her mouth with his in a passionate kiss, he yanked on his hormones, reining himself in, and came to an abrupt stop a mere inch from her face. Everything about his body screamed to go, go, go, but he ignored that temptation.

His gaze flitted from her mouth to her eyes. She stared, probably wondering what the hell he was doing. The urge to kiss her was so intense that he knew if he did it right this second, it'd be fast and hard and hot. Sure, it'd be phenomenal, but he wanted to ease into it, build up to it, not just plunder her mouth as if he was taking something, stealing. Men always took, and women often felt they had to give, even when they didn't want to, but he didn't want that this time. Or ever. Not with Letty. No. With Letty, he wanted to be the giver, to let her take.

So, he skimmed his lips over her forehead. Back and forth. The softest of kisses. No pressure, just the skin of his lips grazing the skin and baby hairs on her forehead. Then he did the same thing to the apple of her cheeks before tipping her head back to rub his lips over hers. He paused, with their mouths touching, and felt the warmth of her breath from her barely parted lips. He closed his mouth around hers, finally applying gentle pressure. First, her top lip, then her bottom, and then back to the top.

Ready for more, he licked the space between her parted lips with the tip of his tongue, hinting at exactly what more he craved. Her mouth opened, and when the tip of her tongue touched his, he didn't slide his tongue fully into her mouth. Instead, he used just the tip of his tongue against the tip of hers. Soft, small, silky strokes. Tip to tip. Side to side. Up and down. The eroticism of it ignited him. He had no idea doing this would be that powerful. All he had wanted to do was go slow. Inch by inch. But by God, this was unraveling him more than a fast and hard kiss ever had. Overcome by it, he wrapped his lips around the tip of her tongue and sucked.

A sound escaped her. It was small. Not desperate. Or at least, not desperate in wanting him to stop, because how her hands gripped his sides and tugged him closer told him that wasn't the case. He wasn't sure exactly when she had raised her hands to his hips, but he liked it.

He released the tip of her tongue and stroked it again with his before slipping his tongue leisurely and fully into her mouth, along the entire length of hers and back again. Her tongue melded with his, and their lips molded. He gradually increased the pace and heat until she let out a moan equivalent to the one she'd made when she tasted the beef wellington. Except this one was of pure passion.

He eased back so he could rest his forehead against hers. They panted as their heartrates settled back to a semi-normal rhythm.

"Oh my God."

Check.

"Wow."

Check.

"How…?"

Well, two out of three wasn't bad.

Smirking, he inched back, still holding her face with his hands. "How?"

"I guess I was going to say, 'How'd you learn to kiss like that?' But now I really want to know if you kiss everyone like that."

"No." He skimmed the side of his thumb over her cheek. "Only someone I really care about." He paused.

"Actually, you're the first person I've ever kissed like that."

She gaped.

"I care about you, Letty."

"Now I'm going to ask how. How can you care about me so soon?"

He brought his lips to hers again in a soft kiss. "I don't have an answer for that. All I know is that I do."

"All I know is that I do, too." Then she did something that he hadn't anticipated. She trailed a fingertip down the scar on his jaw. That gesture alone would've struck him, but she topped it off by pressing a kiss to it that made his heart skip a beat. A literal heartbeat skipping moment. He had never believed those were real, but he'd had one.

"Goodnight, Thane."

He forced himself to release her. "Goodnight, Letty."

He waited for her to close the door and to hear the sound of the dead bolt clanking before turning away. Walking down the hall, he smiled from ear to ear. He couldn't wait to see Letty again, to kiss her, hold her hand, inhale her scent. Friday wasn't soon enough.

The two of them dating wouldn't be easy once it became public knowledge, but he vowed to keep their relationship private for as long as he could.

Letty deserved that.

They both did.

7

Letty

etty walked to work the next day on a high. Their date had gone better than Letty ever could've imagined, and the kiss at her door had been knee-quaking, head-spinning, mouth-watering. Lips still tingling, she went to bed. There had been inches between their bodies, but that space might as well had been tissue paper, because she had felt him as if they were pressed together. She fantasized about what that would be like, to be flat against his chest, with his arms around her waist and his heart beating against hers.

When she approached her shop, she found twenty or thirty people crowded in front of the windows and doors. She gaped at them. What in the world was going on? She'd never had a line of people waiting to get in before. She'd never even had one person waiting. Was the shop on fire? Craning her neck, she checked for signs of smoke pouring out of the roof, but she didn't see anything.

One of the men on the outskirts of the crowd glanced at her. He did a double take. "It's her!"

Suddenly, everyone was staring. Then they were rushing toward her with video cameras, digital cameras, and cell phones. They called out her name. The wrong name.

"Charm!"

"Charm!"

"Charm!"

She retreated. *No. That's impossible. They can't know that name.*

"Charm, how was your date with Thane?" a man with a video camera perched on his shoulder asked. He wore a T-shirt with the name of the most popular celebrity paparazzi group printed on it.

Cameras flashed in her face.

How did they know who she was? Where she worked? How did they know she'd gone on a date with Thane?

She shoved her way through the crowd to get to the shop. Everyone followed on her heels. The name that she had put behind her surrounded her on the lips of strange men snapping pictures and capturing video. The sound of the cameras going off filled her ears, mixing with their many voices.

"Charm, how'd you meet Thane?"

Their bodies closed in on all sides. They reached

around her shoulders and over the heads of each other to catch a good shot.

Her hands shook as she pushed the key in the doorknob.

"Charm, what was it like having dinner with the son of the man you killed?"

Jaw unhinged, she spun around. "What did you just ask me?"

"You heard me."

The door behind her flew open and hands grabbed her. "Leave her alone," Yawanda shouted. "Hurry. Get in."

Yawanda yanked her inside and blocked the paparazzi with the door, so they all flocked to the display window. Camera flashes bounced off the glass.

Letty turned her back on them.

"I got here right after you and ran to the back," Yawanda panted. "Are you okay?"

Letty swallowed. "They know who I am. They know I'm Charm. A man asked me what it was like dating the son of the man I killed."

"Oh my God. What do we do?"

Letty peeked at them. They raised their cameras again. "We can't do anything about them. This is their so-called job, but they're not allowed to set foot inside, so we'll just have to ignore them and do our jobs."

The crowd outside doubled in size, though, as Letty and Yawanda prepared to open. Someone banged on the front door, but with the fabric panel covering it, they couldn't see who had done it.

"Are you sure about this?" Yawanda asked.

"Yeah." Letty clasped her hands behind the counter. "Unlock the door."

Yawanda retracted the fabric panel, flipped the sign, and whisked the deadbolt. As soon as she did, a customer in a pink, tweed jacket plowed inside. "Whoa." Yawanda's back was plastered to the wall as a stream of people burst through the door. They weren't paparazzi, but normal people, and they flocked around the counter.

A woman in a tweed jacket, who led the pack, slammed a tabloid down in front of Letty. "A gold-digging hussy caught in the act."

On the cover of the tabloid was a photo of Letty and Thane sitting side by side at the chef's table at The Blitz. Their fingers were twined, their gazes locked. The headline above the photo read, "Thane Canmore Dating His Father's Killer."

"What'd you do to snag him? Spread your legs?"

Letty's face flamed. "Excuse me?"

"He probably didn't even know who she was when they were on that date," someone else said. "But you can bet he knows now."

Tweed Jacket shoved the paper toward Letty. "If you thought Constantine was rough, wait until you meet his son's wrath. Constantine groomed Thane. You'll need a bigger knife."

Letty's legs weakened. She gripped the counter for stability.

"That's your plan, isn't it?" A woman in a tan, plaid coat came forward. She sneered impossibly white teeth. "Remember me?"

Vile rose up Letty's throat. She swallowed it down. The woman before her was Sasha Danes, Alec's wife.

"Good. You do remember me." Manicured hands shackled Letty's wrists when she attempted to back away, and Sasha leaned forward. "I knew you weren't only after Constantine. Sooner or later, you were going to come after them all. That was your mother's plan all along, wasn't it? Thane might've been fooled by your charm"—she bared her teeth like a lion at the clever use of Letty's given name— "and he might've fired my husband from the board, but there are more of us out there than you could possibly imagine. We won't let you get away with it this time." Her fingernails dug into Letty's skin, making her wince. "You and your mother never deserved the Canmore name. You will never belong here. Leave Thane alone and go back to the Dumpster where you belong." She tossed Letty's hands aside as if they were filth.

"Okay, everyone, out. Now! The shop is closed." Yawanda wrangled the customers out the door and slammed it at their backs.

Free of their harassment, Letty dashed into the backroom. Tears blurred her vision.

Once the cameras couldn't see her anymore, she dissolved into a puddle on the floor. She tucked her knees to her chest and covered her head with her arms. Sobs wrenched out of her body. Her lungs shook. She couldn't catch her breath. The last time she'd cried like this, her back had been raw from a fresh beating.

The insulting things those people had said to her, the paparazzi's prying questions, the invasive tabloid, and Sasha's torment tossed Letty back to the years after her mother's death when reporters begged for exclusives and random strangers all had opinions. They either praised her for her bravery, stared at her with pity, or held unveiled animosity toward her for killing one of the richest men in the world. How could a weak child such as herself do it? That was what everyone, regardless of where they stood, wanted to know. Was it luck? God's will? Or had someone helped her? The questions had scared her as a child. She didn't know what they meant or what they wanted. Over and over again, she'd told them what had happened. Every time she did, she had lost a piece of herself.

Now, huddled in a ball, she was back in pieces.

She thought she had escaped all that, but you can't get away from people who want you to pay. No matter what you do or what you change your name to.

Yawanda hurried into the backroom. "Letty, you're okay. Ssh." Her comforting hands touched Letty's arms. "Oh my God. You have claw marks on your wrists." She tried to take one of Letty's hands to inspect the scratches, but Letty yanked her hand away and tucked her arms behind her thighs, over her stomach, hiding them. It was what she'd done in school when teachers had asked her about her bruises.

"Letty, Letty, what do you want me to do?" Yawanda wrapped her arms around Letty and rocked her, which only made Letty cry harder. "I don't know what to do, Letty. Do you want me to call Thane?"

"No," Letty choked. "No. No. No."

"Okay. Okay, ssh." She ran a hand down Letty's hair. "You're safe now."

"I'll never be safe."

Safety was not a luxury afforded to murderers of rich men.

8

Thane

A knock sounded on Thane's office door while he read over the details for their new security software release in three days. "Yeah?" he called out without looking away from the recent data reports.

Rebekah poked her head inside. "Sorry to disturb you, but you have a call on line one. Her name is Yawanda. She says she works with Letty and that it's urgent. She sounds frantic."

"Thank you, Rebekah." He snatched up his phone and hit the button for line one. "Yawanda? This is Thane."

"I don't know what to do." Yawanda's voice trembled. "Letty told me not to call you, but I don't know what to do."

Thane pushed to his feet. "What happened?"

"There were a ton of paparazzi outside when I got here. Letty was trying to unlock the front door, and they were surrounding her. Before I whisked her inside, one of them asked her what it's like dating the son of the man she killed."

His hand flexed around the phone.

"Letty was visibly shaken, but we still opened the shop because paparazzi can't come in. A whole bunch of people came in as soon as I unlocked the door, though. They said the most awful things. One said that you're rougher than your father and she'll need a bigger knife."

Thane closed his eyes.

"And someone grabbed Letty. She has claw marks on her wrists, Thane. Actual claw marks. I kicked them out. When I found Letty in the backroom, she was curled up on the floor, crying. I've never seen her like that. It took me an hour to calm her down. Then she snuck out the back to go home. We were lucky none of the reporters thought to station in the back alley. I've stayed behind to make the paparazzi believe she's still here, but I haven't heard from her. I've tried calling to make sure she got home safely, but she's not answering her phone. I don't know what to do."

"Stay there. I'm going to her apartment. I'll call you when I know she's safe."

Yawanda sniffed. "And, Thane...I know you respect women and do what they ask, so I'm asking you to do what I'm going to tell you. Letty will want you to leave, but you can't. Don't leave until you see her and know she's okay. She'll tell you she's fine, but don't listen. She's not fine. She needs you whether she wants to say it or not. Stay. No matter what she does or says. Stay."

Thane swallowed. "I will. I promise."

"Thank you."

Thane hung up his phone. Still standing, he opened a new browser and navigated to a celebrity gossip website. He dropped into his chair when he saw a picture of the two of them having dinner plastered on the home page. "Thane Canmore on Intimate Date with His Father's Killer" headed the site in bold, black letters. The article provided both of Letty's full names and the name of her shop.

He powered on his TV and found one of the entertainment shows devoted to celebrities. The same photo from the website was propped up in the corner of the TV screen. "Are Thane and Letty dating? And how did that come about? We don't know the details yet, but we will stay on top of this juicy story as it unfolds."

He switched the channel to a late-morning talk show.

"We don't know what this dinner was about or what happened between them before now," one of the hosts said, trying to be reasonable and civil.

"We know what happened before now," another host said with a cool eye pointed at the cameras. "There was a lot of blood."

Half the audience "oohed" in disapproval while the other half laughed.

Thane shut off his computer and stalked to Jessalyn's office. She lounged in her chair with her bare feet crossed on top of her desk, watching a news program.

"You have to wonder why a woman who survived Constantine Canmore's abuse and attempted murder would be on a date with his son, twenty-three years after the fact," the female host said.

"And you have to wonder why a man would have such an intimate dinner with that same woman who killed his father," the male host added.

Jessalyn eyed him. "Yes, you do."

Thane braced his hands on her desk. "You did this, didn't you?"

"You mean, did you I tip off a papper about your date? Why, yes, I did do that."

"This isn't going to stop me from seeing her."

"Oh." Jessalyn made a hissing sound between her teeth as she inhaled. "But it might stop her." She pointed a finger at the TV.

On the screen was footage taken through Let It Charm You's shop windows. A throng of customers swarmed the counter, and a woman held Letty captive. Anger seared through him when he recognized Sasha Danes.

Without taking his eyes off the TV, he said, "All Heart Tech doesn't condone this kind of behavior. You no longer work here."

Jessalyn sprang to her feet. "You're firing me for alerting a papper to your date?"

His gaze cut to her. "No, I'm firing you for exploiting an innocent woman who has gone through things that you don't understand, and that you don't care to understand. I'm firing you for taking away her rights as a survivor."

Jessalyn snorted.

Thane leaned closer and lowered his voice. "I'm firing you because telling the world about her and opening those floodgates, purposefully setting those people after her for your own sick amusement, was a gross play of abuse to get what you want. I'd think by now you'd know I don't forgive any form of abuse." He turned his back on her.

"Are you going to fire everyone who picks on her? Who wants to see her fall for what she did? If so, then you're going to have to fire half your board."

Thane didn't pause. Hands in fists, he continued to his office. It shouldn't have surprised him after his recent discovery about Constantine's old pals putting Letty though hell, but hearing that even more board members of All Heart Tech had a vendetta against Letty seared his veins. Those men had been on the board when his father was alive. They'd kept the company afloat until Thane became of age to run it. They'd helped him learn the ropes. He never thought they were cruel like this, but then again, any close friends of Constantine Canmore had to be as cold-blooded and vicious as him. It only made sense. And Thane had been a fool to not see it sooner. What disturbed him even more was that he might not have ever found out.

At Rebekah's desk, he lowered his voice. "Jessalyn no longer works here. Make sure she doesn't take any All Heart Tech property. Then call Arden, Mitch, Jeff, and Mark. Set up a meeting first thing tomorrow morning. Tell them it's about...continuing my father's work. I'll text you more details after I check in on Letty."

"Right away."

Thane held up his hand when she popped out of her chair. "One more thing. I need to get out of here without being seen. Can I borrow your car? I'll have a car drive you home and pick you up tomorrow morning."

"Of course." She dug out her keys from her purse.

"Thank you."

He headed to the underground parking garage and found Rebekah's nondescript vehicle, perfect for a sneaky getaway. Classical music came through the speakers when he twisted the key in the ignition. He lowered the volume before backing out of the parking space. Creeping up the ramp toward the street, he glimpsed a horde of paparazzi staking out on the sidewalk in front of All Heart Tech. Thankful the windows were tinted, he slipped past them. During the drive, he called Letty, but each attempt rolled to voicemail.

From the street he spotted a crowd camped out on the sidewalk in front of Letty's apartment, so he pulled up to the curb a couple of buildings away. He called Rebekah.

Rebekah answered after two rings. "Thane, is Letty okay?"

"I don't know yet. Can you leave a tip with a few tabloid journals that Letty was spotted in Central Park or somewhere far from her apartment?"

"No problem."

"Thank you."

After the call disconnected, Thane waited. He used that time to text Rebekah exactly what he planned for Constantine's old board members. Five minutes later, the reporters checked their mobile phones one at a time, and like a chain reaction, they packed up their things and raced in the direction of uptown. A small group even hustled out of the alley, no doubt guarding the back of the apartment building.

Thane waited another couple of minutes to be sure no one was lingering before hurrying out of the car. He jogged up the sidewalk, raced up the stairs two at a time, and rapped gently on Letty's door, not wanting to scare her. Seconds ticked by. After a moment, he sensed her on the other side of the door, peeking through the peephole. She didn't saw a word. The chain didn't slide free. Nor did the door handle rattle. He placed his hands on either side of the doorframe, shifted back, and lowered his head. "Letty, I know you're there. I can feel you."

Her voice came out in a whisper. "How?"

"I don't know. I just do. Please open the door and let me in."

"No."

Thane lifted a hand to his forehead and rubbed his eyes. "It wasn't me, Letty. I didn't do it. Jessalyn admitted to contacting the paparazzo who sold that photo of us. I'm so sorry this is happening to you. Please let me in so no one else has to hear this."

"I'm fine, Thane. Please go."

He shook his head. "You're not okay, and I'm not going anywhere."

"Thane, this isn't going to work. Us. It's clearer

than ever before that we don't belong together, that I don't belong in your world."

His heart plunged to the pit of his stomach.

"Just look at everything that's happened so far. We can't even start a relationship."

He raised his gaze to the peephole. "I can't change who fathered me." And that hurt, because he wished he could. "I don't want us to be anything other than who we are, but I do want us to be together. We're connected by our screwed-up pasts, but there's more. I know it. You know it. We can get through this together." He paused. "I'm in. Are you?"

She was silent for a while, and he didn't budge from where he stood.

"You think the universe brought us together," she finally said, "but I think it's trying everything in its power to keep us apart."

Thane laid his hand to the center of the door, wishing he could see her, hold her. "If you need one reason to stay in this...you deserve so much good and I want to give you everything." Beneath his palm, the metal door blazed. He stared at it, wondering if she was touching it on the other side. "I want to be the person who proves to you that you are worthy of all the things you deny yourself, especially love."

The door suddenly fell cold.

He moved his hand back to the doorframe.

"Is that your reason for wanting to be in this, too?" she asked.

"Part of it."

"What's the other part?"

"I have feelings for you that I can't ignore. I don't

want to." He shook his head. "We can talk more inside."

"I can't let you in, Thane. If I do…" Her voice faded.

"I won't touch you. I swear. I just want to see you."

"That's not what I'm afraid of."

"Then what are you afraid of?"

"Myself," she whispered.

"Letty." He stepped closer to the door. "You're not what they claim you are. And if it's your feelings for me that you're afraid of, let them be. We could be something amazing."

He couldn't see her, but he sensed her putting distance between them.

"I promised Yawanda I wouldn't leave. More than that, I promised myself. I'll be here for you when you're ready to let me in." And he didn't just mean through the door. He meant in her heart.

He backed away and leaned against the far wall. As minutes passed, he texted Yawanda to reassure her that Letty was safe in her apartment and he was there. Outside, but there. And he kept an open conversation with Rebekah while the plan for the board meeting tomorrow unfolded. Once that was done, the only thing he had left to do was wait.

9

Letty

*L*etty had run home.

Her phone wouldn't stop ringing. She'd made the mistake of answering it. A reporter for a well-known magazine wanted to ask her questions about her date with Thane. She hung up. The next call to come in was from the most influential news channel in the world. They wanted her to come to their studio for an exclusive live interview.

"Not interested," she said.

Her phone rang again the second she ended the call. That time, she shut down her phone. She peered over her shoulder every few feet. Any of the people she passed could know who she was. Nearly everyone had their phones out. Were they recording her? Taking pictures? The thought gave her chills.

She flew up the stairs to her apartment. Once safely inside, she locked and chained the door. Then she lowered the blinds and drew the curtains. In her bedroom, she stripped out of her shirt dress and belt. She tugged on an over-sized sweatshirt and rushed into her bathroom. With the sleeves pushed up to her elbows, she ran cold water over her wrists. Crescent-shaped marks marred her skin. Sasha's nails had drawn blood.

Letty splashed peroxide over the cuts. As they bubbled, she bent over and laid her head against her outstretched arms. Tears filled her eyes.

Her other mistake was turning on the TV. She was on every entertainment and celebrity talk show. Not only were they speculating about her relationship with Thane, but they also dredged up details about Constantine's case. Even going so far as to show images of her from when she was seven. She switched off her TV and curled up in the corner of the couch, in her dark apartment, and cried.

The knock on her door made her jump. She tiptoed to it. Had the paparazzi discovered where she lived? Was it a reporter? She didn't touch the door when she peered through the peephole, not wanting to tip the person off on the other side that she was home. Seeing Thane gave her a mixture of reactions. Her hand lifted to the door handle, but she stopped herself from opening it. She wanted to throw her arms around him. At the same time, she wanted to push him away.

"Letty, I know you're there. I can feel you."

She gaped through the tiny device. "How?"

"I don't know. I just do. Please open the door and let me in."

She stuck her hands behind her back. "No."

The things he had said to her conjured more tears, but she didn't want to give in to her feelings. She had done that already by agreeing to go out to dinner. And now she was paying for that. This wouldn't work. People would do everything in their power to tear them apart. Letty and Thane should end this now before it was too late.

When Thane had moved his hand to the door, she put hers to it. Despite every rational thought in her head, she couldn't tamp down her urges. They weren't just physical. They were emotional.

"...especially love," he said.

She yanked her hand back. This was too new to be love. Right? Then why did her heart beat like this? Why did her head swim? Why did her knees shake?

"We can talk more inside."

She shook her head. "I can't let you in, Thane. If I do..."

If she did, she'd give in to her longings. She'd draw him close, and she wouldn't want to let him go.

"I won't touch you. I swear. I just want to see you."

Her chest tightened. "That's not what I'm afraid of."

"Then what are you afraid of?"

She leaned against the door. Her fingers touched the crack between the door and the frame. "Myself."

"Letty."

He knew how to say her name in a way that tore her in half.

"We could be something amazing."

She flinched from the door and backed away. He

was right. How could they not be something amazing when they could do what they did to each other with no physical contact? Her body reacted just by seeing him. Just by hearing his voice. And it wasn't merely sexual. Her heart and soul responded to him.

"I'll be here for you when you're ready to let me in."

Every once in a while, Letty stole a peek. He leaned against the wall, paced in front of her door, and then he sat with his legs stretched out and his ankles crossed. Hours went by. She felt damn guilty for leaving him out there, but she'd told him she wasn't going to open it, and she had meant it. Apparently, he had meant it when he said he wouldn't leave.

Her guilt doubled when she fixed herself something to eat. Apartment growing darker, buzzing with silence, she laid down on the couch. She drifted to sleep while thinking about Thane outside her door, figuring he'd eventually give up.

She jolted awake when her landline shrilled. Most of the time, she forgot she had it. Telemarketers and Lydia were the only ones who ever called her on it. This could very well be her mom. Or the media discovered that number, too.

She stumbled through the darkness as the phone rang again and plucked it up. "Hello?" she said, voice drenched in sleep.

"Letty, this is Ida from next door."

So, not Lydia. The fact her mom hadn't called yet meant she had likely slept all day in order to pull a twelve-hour night shift on her beat. As soon as she clocked out and plugged back into the virtual world,

Letty would have Cop Mom on her case.

"Oh, hi, Ida."

Ida was a sweet older woman who always cooked too much food, so she could give Letty leftovers.

"I called your cell phone, dear, but it rolled to voicemail."

"I'm sorry. I turned off my cell phone. Is everything okay?"

"Well, I thought you ought to know that a sexy man is asleep outside your door."

Letty blinked. "What?"

Thane hadn't gone home?

"What part do you need me to repeat? The 'sexy' part, the 'man' part, the 'asleep' part, or the 'outside your door' part?"

Letty blinked. "I understood every word. Thanks for letting me know. I'll handle this."

"Lucky duck," Ida said before hanging up.

Letty checked the time on her oven. It was ten o'clock. She'd been asleep for four hours. At her door, she peered through the peephole. Sure enough, Thane was there. He'd removed his jacket. It was draped over his crossed arms, and his neck was bent at an uncomfortable angle.

She unlocked the door as fast as she could.

His head jerked up the moment she opened it.

She waved her hand. "Come inside."

Thane rose to his feet and stepped in. She locked the door, and he set his jacket on the back of the chair at the kitchen bar. When he faced her, she threw her arms around him. He held her close. Relief emitted off him and warmed her skin.

"I didn't know you were really going to sleep out there," she muttered.

"I meant it when I said I wasn't going to leave."

"No kidding."

He eased back to frame her face with his hands. "Are you okay?"

She shrugged a shoulder.

"Can I see?" He held out his hand for hers.

She lifted her left hand. His touch was incredibly tender as he examined the small cuts. Then he lifted her hand to his mouth and kissed the skin on the inside of her wrist. Flutters dominated her stomach. He picked up her right hand to kiss that wrist, too. Those flutters became a series of explosions.

"What you said out there...that we could be something amazing." She laid a hand against his chest, felt his heart beating. "We already are."

Thane drew her in for a kiss. His lips sucked hers, leaving her weak-kneed. She opened her mouth for him, and the tip of his tongue touched hers. He slid a hand to her neck and tipped her head to the side with his thumb against her jaw. His tongue slipped into her mouth and curled around hers. She moaned, and he inched back.

"This is insane," she said, with her nose touching his. "I don't understand how I

can feel this way for you already."

"There's a lot between us."

"That's what they said on TV."

His fingers skimmed along her jawline, and he raised her chin. "You heard that?"

She nodded. "Yeah. A whole lot of blood. More than they know."

He tilted his head.

"My knee."

He smiled.

"Are you hungry?"

"Actually, yeah."

While making him a sandwich she wondered if billionaires ate sandwiches like common folk. She only had plain white bread and cheap condiments. She didn't even have a toothpick to stick into it like they do at restaurants. Self-conscious over the sad meal, she joined him at her small kitchen table and handed him the plate. He didn't show any signs of disgust or disappointment but instead picked up the sandwich and took a big bite. While he ate, she scrutinized her tiny, comfy apartment. There was no dining room. The kitchen had three cabinets. Her living room could barely fit her couch, and her bedroom was a few feet away. What did her apartment look like to a man who probably had never lived in something so small?

Moments later, he'd eaten every bite of the sandwich.

She set the plate in the sink and then curled her legs beneath her on the couch. Thane stared quietly. His gaze called out to her from the table.

"Thane," she said. "Come here."

He rose onto his long legs and walked toward her, making her mouth go dry. Instead of sitting close, he sat on the other cushion. She smiled. Even when they'd kissed a moment ago, he hadn't moved his hands past her neck. Still so polite even with whatever he felt inside raging at him, and if it was a fragment of what she felt, he should be praised for his restraint and chivalry.

She scooted over the couch to him so that she was cuddled against his side. "I appreciate you and how you are, but I don't want you to have to ask if you can touch me anymore. From now on, you have my permission."

"Thank God," Thane said and held her hand. Her arm rested on his chest as his fingers stroked her wrist. His touch lured her to sleep.

But Letty's landline pried her awake once again. She eyed Thane groggily. "Well, you're here, so it's not my neighbor calling to tell me you're asleep outside my door."

She shuffled to the phone.

"You have a landline?"

"For my mom, mostly. Once, she went all Cop Mom when I had my cell off." And her cell phone had been off for hours. Night shift wouldn't be over yet, but if her mom heard the news from another cop or on the radio, this could be her right now, which would be an awkward conversation in front of Thane.

Letty answered as if bracing for an attack. "Hello?"

"Good evening, this is Brianna from Day to Night Security. Is this Letty Remis, the owner of Let It Charm You?"

"Yes, it is." Letty pivoted on her feet to look at Thane with wide eyes. "I'll be right there."

Thane stood. "Who was that?"

"My security company. Someone broke into the shop. I have to go."

"I'll come with you."

Before they left, she powered up her phone long enough to send Yawanda a text message about what was going on.

—I got a call from our security company. Someone broke into the shop. If you see this before you get up in the morning, try to relax and go back to sleep. I'm on my way there now. I'll let you know what I find when I get there. I'm going to turn my phone off again, but you can call the shop if you need to. Fingers crossed everything is okay.—

Letty sent the text, hoping she wouldn't wake Yawanda. Right now, only one of them needed to be awake and worried and talking to their security and the police on the scene. Dealing with the aftermath together would come later.

Thane led her to a normal-looking sedan parked in the back of the complex. Like a real gentleman, he held the door open. "Is this your car?" she asked.

Thane flashed a grin from behind the wheel. "It's Rebekah's. I borrowed it to get here without anyone noticing."

"Do you think there will be paparazzi at my shop now?"

"They shouldn't be. It's after three in the morning."

Paparazzi didn't clog the sidewalk, but two police cars and a security truck did. Three men in uniforms stood on the sidewalk in front of her shattered display window. The back of her neck burned. She owned tens of thousands of dollars' worth of merchandise. Burglars could've made out with everything, including the Reuge music box. What that meant for Let It Charm

You would be devastating. Sure, she had insurance, but if the police couldn't get all of her merchandise back, she'd lose out on more money than she could afford.

She showed her ID to the cops on scene. After they checked her credentials, she unlocked the door and flipped the light switch. She expected to see the shelves stripped and valuable items smashed on the floor, but everything appeared just as it always did.

Her brows lowered. Glass crunched beneath her shoes. She hurried to the counter and opened the jewelry boxes that they ritually locked every evening. All of it was there—the gemstone rings, Victorian pendants, and stringed pearls. She touched the gold locket with the single diamond, glad that it hadn't been stolen.

At the window, she checked out the display. The Turkish rug, French curved mirror, and ornate candelabras hadn't been lifted, either, and they were the closest to the sidewalk, within easy snatching range. Not even the chiming Howard Miller grandfather clock had been damaged.

"Does anything look to be missing?" an officer asked.

"No. Everything's here."

Why would someone break in and not steal anything? Or at least not trash the place?

"I found something." Thane pointed to a brick on the floor. "What does 'ER' mean?" A piece of paper stuck to the brick with a rubber band. Printed in black from an ink jet printer were the letters "ER" and three exclamation points.

Letty followed the blast of glass to behind the

counter where she discovered two more bricks. Rubber bands stretched around their middles, too. She bent down to turn them over. In all caps, "MUR" and "DER" stared up at her.

"It doesn't say 'ER,'" she said. "It says 'murderer.'"

10

Thane

Thane helped board up the smashed window with two large sheets of plywood. Letty planned to call a window repair shop when they opened. The drive back to her apartment was fraught with exhaustion and worried silence. Thane's mind spun. Who would throw bricks into her shop? Who would call her a murderer? The fact it happened wasn't unthinkable. What disturbed him was that anyone could've done it—Jessalyn, Sasha, any one of the customers who had terrorized Letty, and an unknowable number of people who'd read about Letty online, in a tabloid, or saw something on TV.

The security camera inside her shop didn't show anyone on the street. One second, everything was calm, and in the next a brick sailed through the glass, quickly followed by two more so the entire window was decimated. The feed didn't show a partial body or even the tires of a car as the culprit sped off.

Thane eased Rebekah's car into a parking space behind Letty's apartment complex and shut off the engine. The silence expanded until it bore down on his shoulders.

"You've had a bad night," she said.

"So have you."

She tugged the hem of her sweatshirt's sleeves into her palms. "Do you want to come up?"

Her question had him contemplating her face. He knew very well she wasn't inviting him up for anything other than to rest. The alternative wasn't even on his mind. Not so soon, and not after what had just happened. Shadows darkened her eyes. Her face appeared paler from a lack of sleep.

"No. I should get home, but I'll walk you up."

At her door, she unlocked it, pushed it open a crack, and then faced him. Wordlessly, she drew him to her. Her arms locked around his middle, and she snuggled her head in the crook of his neck. He cradled the back of her head with one of his hands. His fingers tangled with her curls as he caressed her scalp. His other hand stroked her back.

She became still and languid in his arms. Her body leaned against his. He supported her and continued to soothe her. His own eyelids drifted close. The softness of her hair, the curve of her back, the feel of her arms looped around him, her body heat seeping through his

Charm

shirt, and the steady blast of warmth from her exhales against his neck—it all felt right.

God, she belongs in my arms.

She hadn't moved in a while, though.

"Did you fall asleep?" he whispered.

Her arms, which had loosened, tightened their hold. "Mm. Yeah. For a second there." Fatigue deepened her voice. "I could sleep in your arms." She shifted back slightly, but not far enough for him to see her face. "You shouldn't have to drive home to catch a couple hours of sleep. Stay here. You can sleep on my couch."

He shifted farther back to hook a finger beneath her chin. "Are you sure?"

"Yes. I don't want you driving tired." Her hands grasped his elbows. "Stay."

He flattened his palm to the side of her face and rubbed his thumb over her cheek. "Okay."

In her apartment, she set a pillow and blanket on the couch. She hesitated before telling him goodnight and retreating into her bedroom where she closed the door as soundlessly as possible. Smiling to himself, he stretched out on the couch. He closed his eyes and tried to fall asleep, but he was all too aware of Letty lying in a bed on the other side of that door. Several minutes later, he couldn't calm his mind, he cursed and threatened himself.

You better fall asleep now. You have things to handle. You need to sleep.

A while later...

Dammit. Go to sleep!

Then Letty's bedroom door creaked.

His eyelids sprang open.

She stepped out, twisting the sleeves of her sweatshirt in her hands. "This is going to sound incredibly needy. It'll probably give you the wrong idea, but...I feel like I'm not going to fall asleep without your arms. That sounds silly. I know it does. I've never needed anyone to hold me so I could fall asleep but..." Her words trailed off.

"It may be silly," he said, "but I feel it, too." He sat up. "I don't have the wrong idea. I know what you mean because I want you in my arms, too. Nothing more. No strings."

She approached the couch, and he rotated onto his side and pushed up against the back cushion. Biting her bottom lip, she lowered onto the couch in front of him.

"How do you want to do this?" he asked, not sure how she wanted to be held.

She scooted closer, settled her head below his, grabbed his arm, and draped it over her side. Then she curled her arms between them, so that her hands were against his chest. "Like this," she whispered. "And don't be afraid to hold me."

With her blessing, his arm flexed, and he held her more securely.

Falling asleep was swift, like slipping into cool waters. All too soon, though, his phone chimed with his alarm. He woke with Letty still in his arms and their legs knotted together. She let out a sigh as his alarm grew louder.

"I'm sorry," he said and kissed her temple.

Scrubbing her eyes, she peeled herself from him.

He sat up and switched off his alarm. The blinds

clattered against the window when Letty, kneeling on the couch, peeked outside. "I see a few paparazzi down there."

"Don't worry about that. I have a way to slip false tips to them that'll have them leaving in minutes. What about you? Are you going to open the shop today?"

Letty plopped back onto the couch. "I have to. I can't afford to stay closed, but I'm not looking forward to being bombarded again and asked prying questions."

And she shouldn't have to deal with that. He'd long accepted he'd be photographed by strangers because of who he was, but this was new to her. Jarring. Unfair. She hadn't signed up for this as he had. Actually, he'd been born into it.

An idea popped into his head. "I'll take care of them."

"How?"

"I have my ways."

She arched a brow.

"Trust me." He kissed her on the forehead. "I have to go, but I'll call you soon."

First, he tipped the paparazzi off that Letty would be at Let It Charm You soon, which really wasn't a lie. While they flocked there, Thane drove to All Heart Tech rather than go to his penthouse. He showered in his private bathroom, skipped a shave, and put on a fresh suit from his office armoire. In the parking garage, he left Rebekah's car and climbed into his own. Then he went straight to Let It Charm You. A sea of paparazzi and reporters had congregated already, practically frothing at the bit to harass Letty as soon as she arrived. Thane maneuvered to the side of the road.

The roar of his engine had them whipping around with their cameras. When he climbed out, they shouted his name.

He stepped onto the sidewalk.

They closed around him, jostling for position and a clear shot.

"Thane, are you here to see Charm?"

"Thane, what happened on your date?"

"What does your family think about you dating your father's killer?"

Thane curled his hands into fists. He struggled not to clench his jaw and speak through his teeth. "I'll answer your questions, but not here. You can camp out in front of All Heart Tech night and day, but you're going to leave Letty and her shop alone. Get in your cars, follow me there, and I'll give you what you want."

Like the paparazzi pied piper, Thane led a stream of pappers on motorcycles and reporters in news vans to All Heart Tech. He even held the door open for them himself, letting them into the lobby. "I'll give you twenty minutes," he told them. "Contact everyone you know. Tell them to get here."

They ripped out their phones, texting in a frenzy.

Thane paused beside security. "Make sure they don't leave the lobby."

"Yes, sir."

Thane rode the elevator up to his office. No one else occupied the floor. It was still too early for anyone to be there. He kept the lights off while he patrolled the length of the hallway, back and forth.

Letty occupied his mind. He wanted to do right by her, make up for everything his father and Jessalyn had done. What he felt for Letty made no logical sense, but he didn't care. Nor did he give a damn what anyone else thought. That was one of the paparazzi's questions, he realized, but he was used to ignoring what his family thought and went against their wishes all the time. He had done it when he decided to rid the company of his father's presence. He did it when he donated money to domestic violence and child abuse awareness charities every year.

When the twenty minutes lapsed, he returned to the lobby with Abbot at his side. About forty paparazzi and reporters waited. They scurried to get their devices ready. Thane waited calmly for them to point their devices.

Everyone held still.

"My name is Thane Canmore. I am the owner of All Heart Tech and the son of the infamous late Constantine Canmore. Yesterday, a photo of me and a woman circulated in the media. The woman in the photo is Letty Remis. When she was a child, her name was Charm Ambrosia."

Questions exploded.

"How long have you known Charm?"

"When did you meet Charm?"

"What led to the dinner?"

Thane held up his hand. "I'll explain everything, but first, no one better use the name Charm anymore. Her name is Letty."

"Apologies, Mr. Canmore," someone said.

He nodded. "I met Letty a few weeks ago on accident. We ran into each other on the sidewalk. How we met, it wasn't as romantic as it sounds. She got a scraped knee out of it. She didn't know who I was, and I didn't know who she was. All I knew was that I was head over heels for a woman I had met on my way to work." He smiled when several of them chuckled at his use of the phrase "head over heels."

"She had told me she owned an antique gift shop. I wanted to get to know her more, so I found her shop, hoped she wanted to get to know me, too, and prayed that I wouldn't screw it up. When I gave her my credit card to pay for a gift, and that was when she found out my last name. Her reaction was what I've gotten used to when people put two and two together, linking me to my father. And yet, she agreed to have dinner with me. Before our dinner I'd learned she was the little girl who survived my father. That knowledge didn't change anything for me. As a matter of fact, it made me want to get to know her even more. I was drawn to her for a reason, and I finally knew why.

"Letty is an amazing person. I want the chance to get to know her more. I want the chance to make her happy. To do that, I ask you not to stake out in front of her place of business or where she lives. Stop taking pictures of her. Stop asking her questions that dredge up a painful past. Leave her alone. She doesn't deserve the harassment. She's already gone through enough. You can camp out in front of All Heart Tech and my penthouse all you want. I will stop and answer your questions." He held up a finger. "But not all of them."

Snickers.

"I hope you can do this, not just for me, but for her. She's innocent." He paused. "As for everyone else…a well-known socialite had physically harmed Letty in her shop yesterday. And someone had vandalized her shop last night. I won't tolerate these attacks on her." He stared into the camera in front of him. "Action will be taken." Then he addressed the people in the lobby. "Thank you for your time. Help yourself to whatever you want from the breakfast bar." He indicated at the spread of donuts, bagels, croissants, fresh cut fruit, orange juice, tea, and coffee.

They shut off their cameras and stashed their cell phones. "Thank you, Mr. Canmore," several of them said as they headed for the breakfast bar.

Thane turned to see Rebekah waiting for him by the elevators. While Abbot stood guard, making sure no one moved past the breakfast bar, Thane joined her.

"What you said about Letty was very sweet," she said.

He stared at his shoes. "I meant every word."

"I thought you did."

"Is everything set up for the board meeting?"

"Just as you specified."

"Good. When they get here, let me know."

"Of course."

Thane called Letty the moment he arrived at his office. She answered on the second ring. "Hey, your cell is on."

"I figured I had to turn it on eventually. I blocked all the numbers that had called me yesterday, and my voicemail was full."

"Don't even listen to them. Delete them all."

"Already did."

"Good. And hopefully the media won't be stalking you anymore. At least not outside your apartment or shop."

"Are you going to tell me what you did?"

"I'm sure you'll see it on gossip websites and celeb gossip channels soon."

"Uh-oh."

He smiled. "It's not like that."

Rebekah knocked on the door. "They're here."

"Letty, I have to go. I have an important meeting. Call me if anything happens."

"I will. Bye."

In the boardroom, four older white men occupied one side of the table. Thane lowered onto the chair at the head of the table, in front of the intercom connected to Rebekah's desk. He folded his hands.

"Thank you for coming here on such short notice."

"I noticed that the other half of the board isn't present," Arden Lebell, his father's favorite golf buddy, said. By the way he said "other," made it clear he meant "lesser," because they were women. Four were women of color. One was transgender. All five were far more valuable to Thane and All Heart Tech than the four white men before him.

"Very astute of you, Arden. I only requested the four of you so no one outside this room will know what we're really discussing." Thane paused for effect. "Charm Ambrosia."

The men exchanged glances.

Thane didn't budge under their stares.

"Didn't you fire your sister yesterday for tipping off a paparazzo about your date?"

Thane cut his gaze back to Arden, the apparent spokesperson for the group. "I let her believe that, but I really fired her for ruining my plans. I wanted to seduce Letty and take her down quietly, without the world watching. Jessalyn blew that, and she has to learn her lesson. Why do you think I've changed the company's name and rebranded it? It's all a ruse."

"What about the things you said to the media?" Arden lifted a brow. "I was there. I heard every word."

Thane kept his face calm and his tone cool. "I played it up to the media to make sure no one will later suspect that I and All Heart Tech had anything to do with her downfall. And Letty, most of all, won't see it coming." He considered each of them. "Before you ask, I fired Alec because we can't have someone on the board with his record involving Charm. It would shine a light on us if it leaked. I had to be proactive."

"You had to punch him to do that?"

Thane waved a dismissive hand. "Again, I had to make it convincing."

One at a time, the four men nodded at each other.

"Your father taught you well," Arden said. "We all hoped you would come around and pick up his mantle."

Thane forced a smile that felt too much like a sneer. "It's all a matter of timing and manipulation, my friends. I've been working toward this since my father's murder, and now the time has come for revenge."

"What do you have in mind?" Arden said.

Fucking gullible pieces of shit.

"I actually called this meeting to brainstorm. My plan got me this far, but I could never decide on how exactly to ruin Letty's life. Do any of you have ideas?"

Grins formed on their faces.

"We know someone who can get stolen goods into

her shop. We'd then give the police an anonymous tip. When they find the stolen goods, she'd be arrested and charged with possession of stolen goods with the intent to sell. Her reputation as an honest business person would be ruined. The goods we have in mind would make her a felon. Her clients will worry that they have stolen goods in their homes. She'd lose her business."

Thane nodded, keeping his anger in check. "I like it, but how do we get justice for my father?"

Arden leaned forward. "I have a graphologist who has studied and learned how to reproduce Carmen Ambrosia's handwriting. On appropriately aged paper, she'll write out a letter as Carmen to Charm."

"And what will this letter say?"

"That Carmen planned to kill Constantine for the ten million dollars that would set them up for life, and apologizing for using her daughter to get the deed done."

"Which will finally prove what we all know," Thane said, "that my father was innocent, Charm's mother was a gold-digging bitch, and Charm's self-defense story was a lie."

The men nodded eagerly.

"When can we get started?"

"Whenever you say."

"Let's wait until after the launch of our security software. This could give us a boost in sales, and I need to make sure things die down so Letty won't see it coming."

"Sounds good. We'll finalize the details and get everything ready."

"I have every faith you will." Thane stood. "I have

a few people who could help us out in the meantime." He pushed the button on the intercom. "Rebekah, please send in our guests."

A second later, the door opened and six officers marched inside the conference room. They removed their handcuffs.

Arden shoved back his chair. "What the hell is this?"

"You gentleman are under arrest for conspiring to commit a frameup, involving conspiracy to move stolen goods, tampering with evidence, fraud, and defamation of character," an officer said as he slapped cuffs on Arden's wrists.

Thane smirked under the glares he received. "You're also fired."

Arden seethed. "You won't get away with this."

Thane didn't say a word, just watched his father's old friends get hauled out in handcuffs. Alone, he lowered into the chair and propped his head in his hand. He hated pretending to want to set up Letty, hated calling Letty's mom a gold-digging bitch. Not once in his life had a degrading word against a woman left his lips—he could still hear his father screaming in a rage, calling his mother a bitch—and saying that about Letty's mom had sickened him.

Rebekah sat in the chair adjacent him. "Are you going to tell Letty about this?"

"Yeah." He lowered his hand. "I'm not going to keep anything from her. Ever."

11

Letty

Soon after she spoke to Thane, Letty's phone rang with a video call from her mom. On the screen, her mom's brows were drawn together. Her lips were flat. Growing up, Letty grew accustomed to that look. It meant anger, parental disapproval, and worry. Grimacing, Letty answered the video call.

"Hey, Mom."

But Lydia was not in the mood. "Tell me why, after I got off a twelve-hour night shift and turned on the TV, I saw a table of very opinionated women talking about my daughter and Constantine's son going on a date? A pretty intimate date, by the looks of it."

Shit.

"Mom, it's not what it looks like. Well, it is. In a

way. We were on a date. But it's okay—"

"How? How exactly is this okay? I did everything I could to protect you from those people. When you moved to New York, I knew it would be a bad idea, that there'd be a chance they'd discover you were there and make your life a living hell, try to run you out of the city and back to Georgia, but I supported your decision because that's what a parent does. But I never, not in a million years, thought that after all I did to keep you safe that I'd find out you were keeping something like this from me. Are you in a relationship with this man?"

Letty winced so hard throughout her mom's spiel that she thought her body would never straighten out of the hunched posture of a child being scolded. She met her mom's eye through the screen. "Yes. I am in a relationship with Thane."

Her mom sucked in a hiss that had Letty flinching. "How could this happen?"

"I asked myself that so many times, Mom. You did a great job of making sure I was sheltered from everything that had to do with the Canmores. Too good, in fact, because I learned how to protect myself from any mention of them. I didn't know what any of them looked like, or their first names. If I had, I would've recognized Thane right away and my fight-or-flight would've kicked in. I would've gotten the hell out of there, far away. If I had even just known his first name, I would've realized who he was and shut down what was happening so fast. But, Mom, I'm glad I didn't know. If I had, I wouldn't have met the most respectful, caring, and protective man I have ever known."

Her mom scoffed.

Letty shook her head. "Don't do that. Don't do what everyone has done his entire life and lump him in with the monster who was his father. He was stuck with Constantine, too. He survived Constantine, too. His father abused him, and he's had to deal with that trauma on top of his father's crimes, and it's not fair. Thane is good. So incredibly good. He's never hurt me or abused me, and he would never."

"You don't know that."

"Yes, I do."

Her mom only shook her head.

"I know. I know what this looks like. You see a giant red flag over Thane's head, but he's not the one holding that flag. Look behind him and you'll see that flag is in his father's hands. Do you want to hear how we met and what has happened so far?"

"Yes."

While Letty detailed their meet cute and everything that had transpired after that, she watched her mom take it all in like a cop listening to a witness statement. Although she wasn't taking notes by hand, Letty could see it in her mom's eyes that she was keeping detailed notes in her head. And because she knew it would help Thane's case, Letty revealed how she felt about him, the connection they had, the chemistry.

"I want to be with him, Mom. I truly do. I believe we're meant to be together. Just as long as the world doesn't tear us apart." She met her mom's probing stare. "He's gotten behind my security walls with who he is on the inside. With his gentleness and kindness. He's nothing like his father. Nothing."

Her mom turned her head away, and Letty waited.

"I believe you." Her mom's words, spoken softly, lifted a thousand-pound weight off Letty's shoulders.

"You do?"

Her mom angled her head back and nodded. "Everything you've told me makes that clear, but I'm still going to keep tabs on them."

"I wouldn't expect anything less from a loving and protective mom."

"And, one of these days, I'd like to meet him."

Letty didn't doubt that that meeting would turn into her mom grilling Thane, but as she'd said: she wouldn't expect anything less.

"It's still early in our relationship, but that could be arranged when things calm down." She glanced at the time. "Hey, Mom, I have to start getting ready for work, but before we go, do you have any idea what Jessalyn meant about the ten mill that Constantine willed to my mother and I should've received as her only living relative?"

"I was wondering about that and plan to look into it, but as far as I know, that never happened. And the fact that Thane said his father's last will and testament is mysteriously missing is quite convenient. That tells me that someone either stole it or destroyed it to cover up their story."

"Like Jessalyn?"

"Well, innocent until proven guilty, but she would be one suspect, as well as anyone who could've had access to it, like Constantine's attorney."

Letty nodded. "If you find anything out, let me know."

"I will, and, Letty, be careful. The coverage on this

story is already ugly, and I don't want you to get hurt."

"I'll do my best. I love you, Mom."

"I love you, too."

She blew her mom a kiss before ending the video-call. Setting her phone down on the counter, she exhaled. If she could convince her mom that Thane was good and cared about her, then there was hope for them after all

Letty arrived at Let It Charm You to find the sidewalk blissfully clear. Thane had helped her clean up the glass after the cops left, but the board was still in place, casting the shop in a gloom. She called a window repair company and scheduled them to come out when she closed for lunch.

Yawanda came in through the backdoor moments later and placed her purse on the counter. "Are you okay? Is the shop okay?"

"Yes and yes. I'm so sorry for not texting you again after we boarded up the window. It was a long night…morning..." She shared with Yawanda everything that had happened since she left the shop yesterday.

"Let me get this straight…" Yawanda leaned over the counter with her chin in her hand. "He was asleep outside your apartment?"

"Did you not catch the part about someone throwing bricks into the shop?"

"I did, but I was still hung up on that detail about Thane." Hands on hips, Yawanda inspected the shop. "Did they take anything?"

"No. They just wanted to give me a message."

"What message?"

"'Murderer.'"

Yawanda's lips flattened. "Don't listen to them."

What Yawanda and Thane couldn't understand was that it was impossible for Letty not to listen to them when her own thoughts chanted the same word. Murderer. *Murderer*. *Murderer*. She'd heard that chant in her head ever since she was a child.

Many people had defended her. A child couldn't be a murderer, they said. Others stated the case that anyone could be a murderer, even children, especially if they were hiding psychotic tendencies. In this day and age, in this twisted and cruel world, children could very well commit murder, knowing exactly what they were doing. Countless people believed she fell in that latter category. Now, as an adult, they believed she got away with it and would do it again to Thane.

While she prepped the cash register for the day, a thought circulated in her mind. She paused in counting bills. "Did you really ask Thane not to leave until he knew I was okay?"

"I made him promise he wouldn't. It's nice to know he takes promises seriously."

Letty couldn't agree more.

Thirty minutes after opening, the shop was full of curious people all wanting to get a look at the woman from the news. She was a spectacle, and it made her hands sweat. Customers with designer bags on their arms, expensive sunglasses perched atop their heads, and silk scarves around their necks eyed her up and down while pretending to scope out the merchandise.

Their manicured fingers held their cell phones at hip level, and they pointed the camera whenever they could. The other half of the people in the shop wore jeans and had no problem lifting their cameras in her direction. They were young. Most likely students. Some even had packs on their backs; probably stopped in on their way to school.

Letty's phone dinged non-stop with social media notifications. The people in her shop at this very moment were posting photos, videos, and updates of her and tagging the shop's social media accounts. She picked up her phone. A notification caught her attention. A photo of her with the caption:

What do you guys think? Does she look like a murderer to you? @LetItCharmYou #CharmAmbrosia #KillerKids #LettyRemis #ThaneCanmoreGirlfriend #ConstantineCanmoreKilledHerMom #ThenSheKilledHim

The post came from a young person with a brunette bob. The user's handle included the pronouns "they" and "them." That same person stood a few feet away in a leather jacket and long, pink nails.

Their gazes locked.

They smirked, shrugged, and walked out of the shop.

Letty thrust her phone at Yawanda. "Can you remove my social media apps?"

Yawanda took the phone. "Oh, hell no," she muttered when she saw the notifications coming through. One right after the other. Yawanda's fingers jabbed the screen. The dinging and buzzing disappeared. Then she slapped the phone down. "Okay, everyone, listen up! From now on, this shop has a no cell phone policy. If you need to call or text someone, step outside. If you have a cell phone out, you will be asked to leave. If I see one pointed at Letty, I will remove you myself. This is a matter of privacy and decency. Have some respect, people." She glared at them. "Put those phones away. Now."

Grumbling, they dropped their phones into their designer bags or stuffed them into their back pockets. A few stomped out, grumbling about their rights.

"We have rights, too," Yawanda snapped back. She scowled at the people who remained. "I hope that means you're here to shop, because that's what this place is. A shop."

At her words, they faced the shelves or stands before them and picked up items at random to fake admire them. A customer neck-deep in pearls came up to the register and set a French perfume bottle with an attached music box on the countertop. "I'd like this."

The whole time Letty rang up the perfume bottle, the customer eyed her.

Letty handed over the bag. "Thanks for your purchase."

"Mm-hm." Two manicured fingers plucked up the bag.

Another customer stepped forward. This one wanted a jeweled hand mirror.

"Enjoy the mirror," Letty said.

"Sure."

Suddenly, a line of people waited to purchase

something. Letty knew perfectly well what they were doing. Buying something meant they could get close, stare unapologetically, size her up, try to get a vibe off her.

She let them.

Yawanda offered to take her place, but Letty declined. These people wouldn't be happy unless they could gawk or get a good look. Most of them wanted to glare into her eyes, passing whatever they thought about her with their burning looks.

She let them.

Several scribbled offensive notes onto her copies of their credit card receipts. Things like: whore, murderer, trash, bitch.

She let them.

A few weren't shy. Leering wasn't enough. Writing what they thought about her on a receipt wasn't enough. During their minute or two, they let her have it verbally.

"You're not fooling anyone with your little sweet act."

"Who do you think you are dating Thane Canmore? Huh?"

"We see right through you. We won't let you get away with it again."

She let them.

She let them.

She let them.

Come lunch time, Letty and Yawanda weren't able to close their doors as they usually did. There were too many people in the shop, so Letty was forced to eat her chicken and apple salad in between customers. The window repair crew came. Instead of talking to them herself, Yawanda had to. The sound of a drill removing the plywood didn't bother anyone in the shop. They weren't there for peace and quiet. They were there for scandal and intrigue. The racket actually gave them a chance to whisper to each other while darting looks at Letty.

She let them.

Sunlight came through the airy display when the boards came down, lighting up the shop and placing Letty in a bright spotlight.

She continued to ring up their purchases. They snickered when they snatched their bags. Some even whipped out their phones and snapped quick pictures of her as they left. One did it right there at the counter, putting their phone right in Letty's face.

She let them.

"So, you're little Charm?"

Letty jolted.

Dolly stood there in a lavender tweed jacket. Inside, Letty winced. This woman was one of her biggest spenders, and now Dolly knew she'd given thousands upon thousands of dollars to the woman rumored to have wanted to murder a rich white man for ten million dollars.

"Yes," Letty whispered.

"I always liked you."

Letty wrung her hands.

"And now I like you even more."

Letty's neck snapped up. "What?"

"I always thought that little girl was the bravest

little girl. I am happy to see she had grown up into a lovely young woman."

"Thank you."

"I never believed any of the cockamamie things Emma said."

Letty frowned. "Emma?"

"Constantine's ex-wife. After that night, Emma spread rumors about your mother. Horrible things. She was drunk on gin, full of antidepressants, and coked up. I didn't believe a word of it. She was clearly out of her mind, but many people believed her. They didn't like your mother from the get-go. Not from the same class, a social ladder climber. Yada-yada-yada. They are despicable people who look down their noses at everyone else. But Emma riled them up." Dolly pointedly looked around. "They are still riled up."

Letty looked, too. The closest person sneered at Dolly, having heard her words.

"Don't worry, dear. I'm not afraid of them."

Should I be? She thought but didn't ask.

Dolly gestured at the window repair crew. "What happened?"

"Someone threw bricks into the shop last night."

Dolly shook her head. Then she removed her checkbook. "How much do you need?"

"Oh no." Letty waved her hands in the air. "My insurance will take care of it."

But Dolly still filled out a check. "Then consider this a donation to my favorite antique gift shop." She ripped off the check.

Letty's throat tightened when she saw it was written out for a thousand dollars. "You don't have to do this."

Dolly glanced around at the crowd watching disapprovingly. "Yes, I do."

"How much did she give you? I'll double it." Vera stepped forward. She dropped her black crocodile bag onto the counter and rifled through it.

"I gave her fifteen hundred, Miss Nosey Pants."

Letty opened her mouth, but Dolly laid a finger to her dark, matte red lips and winked.

Vera gave Letty a check for three thousand dollars.

Gawking at the checks in her hand, Letty said, "Thank you, but I can't accept them."

She attempted to return them, but they refused.

"Yes, you can," Vera said.

"At least let me give you something." She slid a jewelry box closer. Her fingers skimmed over the gold locket. She adored these women, but her heart quivered at the thought of losing that locket. Silly, since she had it for sale.

She found a gold, pear-shaped amethyst pendant. "This would look beautiful with your jacket," she told Dolly.

Dolly immediately read the price tag for one thousand, four hundred. "This is more than what I gave you."

Vera snuck a peek. "Hey, I thought you said you gave her fifteen hundred."

"I lied." Dolly stuck out her tongue.

Letty passed a pair of 14K rose gold onyx and diamond drop earrings worth one thousand, eight hundred to Vera. "And I want you to have these. They'll match your bag."

Vera pursed her lips. "This will only leave you eight hundred from what we gave you."

"You're good at math," Dolly said. "I'm impressed."

Letty grinned. "I won't accept these checks unless you accept these gifts."

They glanced at each other. "I suppose she has us," Dolly said.

"I suppose so. We should probably admit defeat."

"You first."

Rolling her eyes, Vera slipped the earrings on right there in the shop. Following her example, Dolly accepted the necklace and hooked it around her neck.

"Beautiful," Letty said with an approving nod.

"Money well spent," Dolly said.

"Agreed," Vera added.

"If any of these rich housewives give you a problem, let us know. The two of us have more sway in society than any of them do," Dolly said.

"Thank you both. You're by far my favorite customers."

"But I'm your number one favorite costumer, right?" Vera pointed at her chest.

"Oh, hush." Dolly pushed her sister toward the door. "She likes us equally." While ushering Vera out, she angled toward Letty and mouthed, "I'm your favorite."

Letty laughed. It felt good to do that after spending the morning tense, taking the abuse from an endless stream of strangers and enduring it with a silent grace that required all her courage to maintain.

Two hours later, new glass covered the window

display.

Yawanda hurried out of the backroom. "Letty." She waved her from the counter. Close to her ear, she whispered. "I was checking to see if anything new came up about you and Thane. There's something you need to see on the computer."

Letty stiffened. "Do I really want to see it?"

"Yes. Believe me." She shoed Letty toward the backroom. "Go. I'll handle things out here."

Letty approached the computer cautiously, as if it would explode and pierce her with chunks of plastic and metal. A prominent gossip website was displayed on the monitor. On the Home page, right at the top, was a video with a thumbnail of Thane. The header read: *Thane Canmore Gives Exclusive About His Relationship with Letty Remis.*

Her heart thundered like a raging lightning storm. She pressed the play button. Thane stood, tall and magnificent, inside All Heart Tech's lobby. The camera zoomed in, framing his shoulders.

"Yesterday, a photo of me and a woman circulated in the media. The woman in the photo is Letty Remis. When she was a child, her name was Charm Ambrosia."

Bracing, she closed her eyes, but that didn't shut out Thane's voice.

"No one better use the name Charm anymore. Her name is Letty."

She opened her eyes. Protectiveness vibrated in his voice. Her breaths became shallow. That level of protectiveness was a foreign concept. She'd dreamt of it, wondered what it would feel like to have a partner care that much. The few men before Thane couldn't handle her night terrors, her anxiety, her fears. Her emotional problems suffocated them, they said. One ex-boyfriend would go so far as to get up and sleep on the couch after she'd wake him up from a nightmare. He'd leave her to deal with the aftermath alone. So, she resigned herself to never having another intimate partner.

"How we met, it wasn't as romantic as it sounds. She got a scraped knee out of it."

Scraped knee aside, he didn't realize how romantic he had been? What he did for her that day had been the most romantic thing any man had ever done for her. And he had been a stranger. That was unheard of. At least for her.

"Letty is an amazing person. I want the chance to get to know her more. I want the chance to make her happy."

Why? Her mind asked it.

Her heart cried it. *Why*?

She couldn't understand his desire, even with her own intense desire to be near him. He was arresting, immense, magnetic. But that didn't explain why they wanted to be with each other as much as they did. Shouldn't their history divide them? Put barricades in front of them? Make them not want to have anything to do with each other? She stared at the monitor long after the video had ended.

Yawanda came to check on her. "Are you okay?"

Letty nodded.

"He's really something."

"Yes, he is," Letty whispered.

During the rest of the day, it became clear that everyone who came into the shop had seen Thane's exclusive announcement, and even they were heeding his words. They didn't scribble derogatory remarks on their receipts or tell her to her face what they thought of her anymore. They did, however, give her the stink eye.

She let them.

They closed the shop fifteen minutes past closing because they had to clear out the people who were there. That was a first for Letty. Curiously, everyone decided to buy something. What did that mean? She didn't quite know. Before they had done it because they wanted the chance to humiliate her, measure her up. Now, after Thane's threat, she could only assume they had actually found something they liked and were willing to give her money for it. And it wasn't just the wealthy, but every-day people were spending ten, twenty, thirty dollars on items. Maybe they all just wanted to say they owned something from the infamous Letty Remis' shop, but that didn't bother her.

Letty carried the full money bag into the back to lock it in the safe. That day they'd made more money than any other day in Let It Charm You's existence.

Yawanda lugged out stock to replenish the shelves. Fortunately, a shipment would be coming tomorrow.

Letty input the day's income into the spreadsheet for the month. The total staggered her. Was this the advantage of being in the spotlight? As good as the numbers were, she didn't like everything else that came with it.

"Hey, Letty! You have a customer," Yawanda shouted from the front.

Letty made her way to the doorway. "What are you talking about? We closed the—"

Thane.

Seeing him in her shop still gave her butterflies. "Hey."

"Hey, beautiful."

She melted.

"Damn."

They peered over at Yawanda, who stood behind the counter, elbows on the glass, chin in her hands, watching them. "What? I'm just admiring the vibes."

Thane directed his grin at Letty. He gestured at the barren shelves and cases. "What happened in here?"

"Um…we happened. A lot of people came in because of yesterday. They bought things after Yawanda laid down the law about their cell phone usage."

"And they were still rude as hell." Yawanda picked up the Manilla envelope of receipts Letty had yet to file. "You should see the things they—"

Letty shook her head, and Yawanda stamped her lips together.

Thane glanced between them. "I should see what?" He strode up to the counter. "Can I see that?"

Letty leapt forward, putting her body between him and the envelope. She stole it from Yawanda's hand before Thane could get it and gripped it behind her back. "That's not necessary. It's nothing."

Thane's gaze met hers. Their bodies were inches apart. "It doesn't sound like nothing."

"Yawanda is just over-reacting."

"I am?"

Letty shot a glare over her shoulder and spoke between clenched teeth. "Yes. You. Are."

"Right. I am."

Thane squinted his eyelids at them. "Very convincing."

Movement caught Letty's attention. She turned her head toward the new window. A young person, who had been walking by, skid to a stop and then lifted their phone.

Letty laid her hand on Thane's arm. "Let's go to the backroom."

So Thane wouldn't be tempted to get it, she shoved the envelope of receipts into the filing cabinet. Then she faced him. He dominated the small space. She stayed by the filing cabinet so his magnitude and allure wouldn't crush her.

"You said something to the media today...You said that how we met wasn't very romantic. You're wrong. It was extremely romantic. When you blew on my knee...my God, Thane..."

He inched closer, but she held out a hand.

"Don't. If you come closer, we'll need privacy."

He nodded, knowing exactly what she meant.

"Not that I don't enjoy you being here, but why did you come?"

"Other than to see you? I wanted to tell you what happened today." He inhaled. "I fired four members of my board."

She blinked. "Why?"

"Because they were conspiring to set you up."

12

Thane

Sitting at the desk beside Letty, Thane explained how he'd gotten them to confess to their plans. He waited for her to digest the information and say something. His hand itched to touch her cheek, but he didn't give in, didn't want to pressure her into speaking before she was ready.

"I'm really making things difficult for you, aren't I?"

He hadn't expected her to say that, though. "What? No. If I had known about this when I came on, I would've fired them then. If we had never met and I learned about this today, I would've done the same thing. I don't stand for that kind of behavior."

"I still feel like I'm causing you problems."

He picked up her hand and rubbed his thumb over

her knuckles. "It's not you. It's everyone else."

"But because of me."

He kissed the back of her hand. "Don't think that. I don't." Standing up, he drew her to her feet. "I'll drive you home."

They came out of the backroom to see Yawanda had made a quiet exit through the front. Thane didn't fully trust the media, so they left through the back to where he'd parked his car. This time, he'd driven a car of his own, but a normal every-day car that no one in the media would expect him to be driving.

In the parking lot of her apartment complex, Letty fiddled with her fingers. "You probably shouldn't walk me up. If you do..." She didn't finish that sentence, and she didn't have to.

"I won't, but tomorrow I do want to have lunch with you."

"Lunch?" Her lips meshed together.

She hesitated, and he knew why.

"We don't have to go out anywhere. We can have lunch in your backroom."

"That might not work. There were so many people in the shop today that I wasn't able to have a proper lunch break."

"That should die down soon, but we could have lunch in my office instead."

She addressed her hands when she said, "Your sister..."

"Don't worry about that. I fired my sister, too."

Her eyes widened.

"Did I forget to tell you about that yesterday?"

"Yes, yes, you did."

"I spaced on that. I should've told you. Jessalyn was the one who tipped off a paparazzo about our date. She admitted it."

"How'd she even know?"

"I don't know, and I'm sorry." Gripping the steering wheel, he stared out the windshield. "Really it's *me* and the people around me causing *you* trouble." They were silent a moment as he thought about all the trouble he had brought into her life.

She surprised him when she leaned over and kissed his cheek. "I do want to have lunch with you, but All Heart Tech is going to be swarming with paparazzi."

"If it's not too much, and if you trust me, I have ways to get you in unseen."

"Mm. Mysterious."

If only. He meant Rebekah would sneak her in with a non-descript car. Eventually, though, the reporters would catch on to that trick.

Letty cupped his cheek, and her lips touched his. "I'll see you tomorrow."

"I'm looking forward to it."

"So am I." With a smile, she departed from the car.

He waited until she made it safely inside the building before driving away.

The next day, when Letty said she liked to eat everything, Thane ended up ordering a few dishes from nearly every cuisine. He was arranging the containers on the coffee table in his office when a knock sounded on the door.

It opened, and Letty stepped in. "Hey, Rebekah

said I could come in."

"You can." He held out his hand to her and was pleasantly thrilled when she came right to him, laid her hand in his, and kissed him.

"Is that all for us?"

He studied the full coffee table. There were eggrolls, a hot pot of veggies and seafood, and chow mein next to a platter of sushi and sake, which sat beside a margarita pizza. In the middle of the table were tamales, Spanish rice, and enchiladas tucked close to Greek salad, stuffed grape leaves, and gyros. At the other end of the coffee table was tandoori chicken and naan with ghee beside jerk chicken, gumbo, and beignets. He chuckled. "It is. I wanted to make sure I ordered something you liked. And
then I couldn't settle on which cuisine."

"Well, you're in luck. I like it all."

They sat side by side on the loveseat and sampled each dish. Letty let out a satisfied sigh when she leaned back. "That was delicious, but I have to say my favorites were the eggrolls, gyros, and beignets."

He smiled. "I'm glad you liked it."

"What's not to like? You must've spent a fortune. And this was just lunch."

"It's not just lunch when it's with you."

Her cheeks brightened to a pretty shade of pink. He liked how she still felt shy around him because of the things he said, but he wondered when she'd get used to it...to him.

He sat back, too, satisfied with her just being there.

Letty's legs were crossed, her body was turned slightly toward him, and her skirt revealed her knees.

His hand lifted to her knee, and he rubbed his thumb over the pink scar. "I'm going to be launching new software tomorrow. There will be a panel exclusively for select members of the press and then an unveiling on the stage for our shareholders. Would you like to be there? You can stay backstage with Abbot. Only my team will know you're there." He gazed into her eyes, looking for a clue as to what she thought of his invitation.

"I'd love to be there."

Sitting in silence, he indulged in the feel of her knee and the pink scar he had unwillingly helped in creating. After several minutes, he looked up to see Letty's eyes closed, her brows lowered, and her bottom lip clamped between her teeth. His thumb stilled, and he lifted his hand. "Does that bother you?"

Shaking her head, she opened her eyes. "No. It feels good. You're really good with your hands. You have no idea what you were doing to me when you were touching my leg at the café, do you?"

Staring into her eyes, he lifted her leg to his lap and ran his hand from her ankle to her knee. She instantly closed her eyes.

"There it is," she said on a breath.

Smirking, he shifted closer.

He curled his other hand at the back of her neck and caught her bottom lip, which she was biting again, with his own teeth, applying the gentlest of pressure. She gasped against his mouth and released her lip. He sucked on it, tasting the flavors of the many cuisines. She reacted to his touch and his kiss by inching even closer. Her arms looped around his neck, and then she leaned back, pulling him down. Lying on her back, she propped her left heel on the couch so that her leg was bent.

His hand slipped down silky skin from her knee to thigh, beneath the fabric of her dress. Feeling the heat of her hidden skin invigorated him. He paused his hand on the middle of her thigh, not wanting to go any farther, not wanting anything to happen too quickly, although his fingers ached to keep on going, to continue exploring.

They kissed hungrily, as if they hadn't just filled their appetite with food. And that's because their appetite for each other hadn't been filled yet. Thane wondered if he'd ever get his fill of Letty. Frankly, he didn't ever want to.

A loud beep sounded, causing them to flinch apart.

Rebekah's voice filled his office. "I'm sorry to interrupt, but Jessalyn is here to see you."

Letty's body tensed beneath him.

In the background, Jessalyn's voice came through. "And tell him I'm not leaving."

Cursing inside, Thane sat up. Letty shot to her feet, and he stood, too, taking her hand. "It's okay. You don't have to be afraid of her."

"I'm not afraid of her. I'm afraid of the people she knows."

His jaw tightened at that because he was, too. "I'll take care of her. You can step into the bathroom. I'll lead her to the conference room, deal with her, and then come back to you. I promise."

She nodded and retreated to the bathroom. As soon as the door closed, he stepped out of his office. Jessalyn stood there, fuming. He gripped her arm and led her toward the conference room at the other end of the hall.

"What are you doing? Wait. She's in there, isn't she? You have that whore in your office, don't you?!"

Thane rounded on her and growled, "Keep your voice down. And you better not ever call her that again." He pushed open the door to the conference room. Once inside, he shut it. "What do you want, Jess?"

"Well, I came to ask for my job back, but I don't want to be here if that—"

He glared.

"...woman"—she corrected between bared teeth—"is going to be here all the time. I refuse to be near that murderer." She arched a brow. "Or am I not allowed to call her that, either?"

"Not around me."

She sneered. "Yeah? And if I call her a murdering whore to your face again, what are you going to do about it?" She pressed her fingers to her lips. "Oops. I guess I just did." Now she eyed him. "So, what are you going to do about it? Are you going to hit me?" Her voice deepened. "Find out that you like it?"

Thane inhaled. Inside his chest, it felt as though a volcano was erupting and spewing lava. "I'm nothing like him."

"Keep telling yourself that, little brother. One day, you may snap and hit a woman. I pray that woman will be Letty."

He took a step toward her.

She inclined her chin.

"Dad never hit you, but he hit me loads of times.

160

Maybe if he hadn't doted on you so much, you wouldn't be this way. You're my sister, and I love you, but by God if you keep up with this, you'll regret it. I won't just fire you, I'll cut you out completely. For the sake of our relationship, learn some damn compassion." He stalked to the door and opened it. "Leave. Security will be informed to not let you into this building again."

Jessalyn stomped to the elevators.

At Rebekah's desk, Thane watched her get on the elevator. He didn't turn until the door slid shut.

"She left," Rebekah said.

Thane glanced at the elevator. "Yeah."

"No, not Jessalyn. Letty. She left a few minutes ago. She told me to tell you that she enjoyed lunch and that she was sorry for leaving but she had to get back to work."

In his office, he walked to the couch. A note sat there. He picked it up and read:

Dinner tonight? My place? All of this would make great leftovers.

He smiled, thankful that she wasn't running.

13

Letty

etty stayed late at the shop while her security company installed a new camera behind the checkout counter and under the eaves, in the corner. The goal was to catch the next person who dared to vandalize her shop. Then she rushed home to freshen up before Thane could arrive with their leftovers. Outside her apartment she found a cardboard box waiting. She unlocked her door and picked up the box. Using box cutters, she slit open the strip of tape. Beneath the flaps, she found foam packing peanuts. She stuck her hands inside and searched through the bits of foam. When you buy expensive breakables, you can't just dump a box over to find the contents.

Her fingers bumped into something plastic, and she

curled her fingers around it. When she unearthed it, she let out a gasp. Her grip went limp, and the object fell. It clattered onto the counter. She stared down at a butcher's knife like the one she'd used to defend herself with from Constantine. It was identical down to the brand.

In black letters, a message was scrawled over the blade: UR NXT.

Her mouth became dry. Her heart crashed against her ribcage. Memories of curling her fingers around the handle of a knife just like that one flooded her. She fumbled for her cell phone and dialed 9-1-1.

"9-1-1, what's your emergency?"

"S-someone left a package at my door. There was a knife in it. I...my name is Letty Remis...I think this has to do with Constantine Canmore."

Two male police officers came to her apartment. They inspected the box and the knife, asked her a bunch of questions, and wrote notes in their small notepads. She was sitting on the couch, talking to one of them while the other stood at the opened door, guarding the scene with his arms crossed.

"And you believe this has something to do with the deceased Constantine Canmore?" Officer Kevin asked.

"I know it does. I'm..." She winced. "I'm Charm Ambrosia. I was the little girl who killed him in self-defense." She pointed toward her kitchen counter. "With a knife just like that one."

Officer Kevin scribbled notes. "How old were you?"

She dropped her head in her hands, aggravated. "Seven. I was seven."

"Who do you think would leave that package for you?"

"Anyone who knew Constantine. Any of his friends, his old employees, his family. His daughter has a personal vendetta against me."

"What's her name?"

"Jessalyn Canmore."

He jotted down her name. "Why do you say she has a vendetta against you?"

Letty stared. "I killed her father."

The officer nodded.

"What's going on?" A commotion from the hallway caught her attention. "Letty? No, that's my girlfriend! I want to see her."

Letty jumped to her feet. She ran around Officer Kevin and the coffee table to see Thane wrestling with Officer Wolfgang at the door, who had his hand on his firearm.

"No, it's okay." She rushed forward. "He's my boyfriend. He's okay. We had plans to meet tonight."

Officer Wolfgang reluctantly released Thane, who immediately came to her side. He laid a hand on her cheek. "Are you okay? What happened?"

"I'm fine."

Before she could say more, Officer Kevin stepped forward. "Sir, what's your name?"

Thane secured an arm around Letty. "Thane Canmore."

Officer Kevin's head jerked up. "Canmore?" He peered at Letty. "Seriously?"

Her cheeks burned. "Yes."

Thane glanced from her to the officer. "What's

going on?"

Officer Kevin lifted his hand. "Sir, move to the other side of the living room for me. Away from Ms. Remis."

Thane's brows lowered. "Why?"

"Just do what I say."

Thane retreated without another word. He had no idea what was going on because she hadn't had time to tell him. From across the way, he stared. His face was drenched with worry.

"I'm okay," she mouthed.

He exhaled, but he didn't look convinced.

The two officers spoke in hushed tones between them. Then Officer Kevin stomped over to Thane, and Officer Wolfgang came to stand beside her, resuming his crossed-arm stance. She shifted away; his quiet, aggressive manner bothered her. What the two officers were doing didn't escape her. One was at her side to "protect" her, while the other questioned a potential suspect.

She strained her ears to hear what was going on across the space and heard Officer Kevin ask Thane where he'd been today.

She swallowed. *Oh, God, they think Thane had something to do with this, and all because he has the Canmore name.* And she hadn't had a chance to tell them any different. She'd told them about Jessalyn and that anyone who knew Constantine would send her a box with a butcher's knife in it, but she'd failed to omit Thane from that suspect pool. Fidgeting in place, she watched Thane and Officer Kevin talk. Every once in a while, Thane glanced her way.

I'm so sorry, she thought.

After several minutes, the officers switched places. "Mr. Canmore says he was at work all day and has witnesses to corroborate that."

"Thane wouldn't do this." Her gaze connected with Thane's over Officer Kevin's shoulder. "I know he didn't do this."

"Can you do me a favor and come here so your back is to Mr. Canmore?" He pointed to where he stood.

Letty stepped forward and turned. Officer Kevin now stood at the doorway, facing Thane and his partner. Letty knew why. He thought Thane was intimidating her, keeping her quiet, making her say what he'd want her to say with nothing more than a look. Her hands began to sweat.

"Ms. Remis, has Thane Canmore ever hurt you?"

Her eyes widened. "No."

Officer Kevin lowered his voice. "If you don't want to say, you can give me a signal. Blink twice to let me know if you fear you're in danger with him."

Letty stared at the officer, trying desperately hard not to blink. Not even once. She shook her head. "You don't understand. He is a Canmore, and he is my boyfriend, but he's not like the others."

Officer Kevin didn't look convinced. Even to her own ears it sounded ridiculous.

"He's only ever treated me with respect and kindness. He's the nicest man I've ever met." She squirmed in place, wanting to look over her shoulder. "Our relationship is new. There are many people who are pissed off that we're together. Like his sister,

Jessalyn. And old friends of Constantine, like Alec and Sasha Danes. Any one of them could've sent me that knife, but it wasn't Thane. You have to believe me. He wouldn't do that. He's a good guy. He recently fired half his board from All Heart Tech because he'd found out they had a plot to frame me. If you ask him, he can give you their names."

Officer Kevin nodded and returned to Thane. She spun around, wringing her hands. This time, both officers surrounded him. They stayed with him for a while. Every few words he said was copied down into a notepad.

Finally, Officer Kevin returned. "We have a list of suspects. We're going to leave now with the box and the knife. I'm giving you one more chance to signal me."

She stared with wide eyes. "I swear I'm safe with him."

"Very well." He faced his partner. "Let's go."

While Officer Wolfgang collected the box and the knife, Officer Kevin said, "If we find anything, we'll call you. And if anything else ever happens, call us directly." He handed her a business card from his pocket.

She took it. "Thank you."

With a nod, they left.

Letty quickly shut and locked the door.

Thane still stood by her bedroom. "They thought I was a suspect." His voice was soft, beaten. He inclined his head toward the counter where the box and knife had sat. "They thought I had done that."

"I'm so sorry." Halfway in her living room, she

came to a halt because of the hurt on Thane's face. "I told them that anyone who knew Canmore would do that, but I didn't have a chance to say you wouldn't, that you're the exception. They jumped to conclusions when they heard your name, and I'm so sorry for that. I told the officer that you wouldn't do that. I said I'm safe with you."

Hearing that, Thane closed the distance between them. He held her tight, and she clutched him in return.

"When I saw that officer in your doorway, it shaved off a few years off my life."

"I'm sorry. I called the cops right away. I should've called you, too. My mind went blank. I panicked."

Cradling her face with his hands, he tilted her head back and kissed her softly. "I'm just glad you're okay."

When his lips came back to hers, she opened her mouth, accepting him. His kiss weakened her knees. She shifted back to nestle her head in the crook of his neck. His warmth, his scent, his arms...they all comforted her.

"I saw how they reacted to your last name," she whispered. "I didn't like it."

His embrace tightened a fraction.

"Constantine did wrong. Not you. You shouldn't have to suffer for his crimes just because you're his son, because you have his name." She shut her eyes. "I remember how I reacted when I saw your name on your credit card, and I'm so sorry for that."

"No, Letty." He inched her back to gaze into her eyes. "You don't have to apologize for that. You had every right to react to my name."

She shook her head, still not liking it, because she knew how it pained him to be compared to that monster, to be put in the same boat as him. Before she could say more, though, Thane silenced her with a kiss. She sank into it.

"I mean it, Letty," he said against her lips. "Don't apologize to me. Please."

Forehead to forehead, she nodded. "Okay."

"Come on. I just want to hold you right now." He led her to the couch where he held her in his arms.

"Do you...do you think it could've been Jessalyn?"

Thane's arms stiffened. "I don't know, but if she did, I'll find out."

She picked at her fingernails. "Tomorrow is your big day. You should probably go home so you can get decent rest and get ready properly."

"After someone left that package, I don't want to leave you alone, but if you'd rather that I not be here, that's okay."

She sat forward to face him. "I'd like you to stay, but I don't think I'm ready to..."

"I'll sleep on the couch."

"My couch isn't very comfortable."

He smiled. "It's fine."

She wanted to get up the nerve to ask him to sleep in her bed, just sleep, nothing else, but she didn't want to rush things. What they had was already so powerful that she thought it would be best not to increase the tempo. Not yet.

"I have clean gym clothes in my car I was planning to leave at All Heart Tech—"

"You have a gym at All Heart Tech?"

"For employees who need an energy boost. It's better than a two-o'clock caffeine boost."

"Hm. I would've thought you'd have a private gym in your penthouse."

"I do, but I'm at work more." He tilted his head and studied her a moment. "If you want me to stay, I can get my bag."

"I want you to stay."

Thane carried in a small duffel and the bag of leftovers from lunch. "I dropped our dinner in the hallway when I saw the cop at your door. Fortunately, they're in containers."

They ate, and then he changed into dark gray joggers and a white T-shirt. She cleared her throat when he stepped out of her bathroom. Damn he looked sexy. Now more than ever his long limbs were prominent. The fabric was form-fitting, too, tempting her imagination. He made joggers look good. Sinfully good.

They stood a few feet apart, watching each other silently.

She swallowed. "Um. Goodnight."

"Night."

She kissed his cheek. "See you in the morning." And then she escaped to her room. On the other side of the door, she pressed her back to it. *Don't think about his body. Don't think about his body. Don't think about his body.*

She was thinking about his body.

14

Thane

earing a light gray suit, crisp white shirt, and dark purple tie, Thane sat at a panel with members of his team responsible for the software they'd be unveiling in a matter of moments on stage. First up, an exclusive meet and greet with the press before the shareholder's meeting. The press room was packed with technology journalists and columnists from around the world, as well as reporters Thane didn't recognize.

When asked who had a question, everyone in the room raised their hands. "If you have a question pertaining to Letty Remis in any way shape or form, lower your hand," Thane instructed.

Half the room lowered their hands.

"That's what I thought. We're here to talk about

technology, people." He scanned the front row where he requested the young and marginalized reporters to sit. Most top brass wouldn't call on them; he was not your typical CEO.

Directly across from him sat a reporter with a beard who wore hot pink stilettos that matched the nails framing a rose gold tablet. Thane read the name tag pinned to a black blouse: Jay (he, they). "Jay, go ahead."

Jay's eyes widened for a split second before he straightened. Thane answered their question and then called on India, a Black woman, who sat next to them. Their questions were far more professional than what the veterans had been shouting.

For thirty minutes, he talked about their newest software for cyber security, without giving it all away, since that's what the presentation on stage would do. He and his team also discussed what this software meant for All Heart Tech and how it'd influence the tech world. Questions about All Heart Tech buying out a small tech company came next, and Thane explained how they would be taking over their software and giving them much-needed upgrades. Then someone asked about the future of All Heart Tech, and Thane revealed how they'd be expanding in every department in order to provide people with what they need, starting with app development. He hoped to create more apps that would assist women and children experiencing abuse.

Journalists leaned forward, stretching their recorders and cell phones closer. They were literally on the edges of their seats.

"I've been a domestic and child abuse awareness advocate my whole life. These are two areas where I am most passionate. We have a few apps in mind. One we hope to release in a few months."

He couldn't say more than that, but the app would let women dealing with domestic violence put out a simple message in a nondescript app that would look like nothing more than a chatroom about beauty and cosmetics. When a woman asked to know more about handmade soaps in the chatroom, the workers behind the app, monitoring it at all hours, would know to contact her safely through the app's messaging system, kept private with password protection, for daily checkups. When a woman asked about *buying* homemade soaps, the workers would know immediately to send the police to her, using the address the woman provided during sign-up.

He hoped the app would save lives.

"Because of Letty?" someone asked.

His gaze flicked to the reporter who'd asked. "Because of my father."

Cameras clicked furiously.

Yes, he did come up with the idea because of Letty. Or, more precisely, Charm and her mother. An app like this could've gotten the two of them away from his father. An app like this could've saved Carmen's life.

"That's all the time we have today," Thane said. "I hope you enjoy the presentation." He stood while buttoning his jacket, and his team followed him out of the press room.

Backstage of the packed auditorium, he stood with

Letty. In the past, he'd never had someone waiting for him backstage during a shareholders meeting, watching him present the latest device or software from All Heart Tech. He liked having her there.

"You're going to be brilliant," Letty said. "You *are* brilliant."

"Thanks."

On stage, the presenter announced his name. The shareholders broke into applause, and he headed onto the stage, but then he whirled around, grabbed Letty's face, and planted a kiss on her mouth. She stared dreamy-eyed while the auditorium full of people echoed with applause and whistles.

"I needed that," he said before striding onto the stage, brimming with confidence.

He executed the presentation flawlessly, describing each element and feature of the software and detailing how it edged out all the cyber security software currently on the market. A laptop hooked up to a projector was rolled out onto the stage, and he demonstrated exactly how the software attacked cyber assaults. Pretending to be a cyber attacker, he attempted to hack into All Heart Tech's system. The moment he tried, the software knocked him back. When he sought another way into the system, through a backdoor, the software caught him there, barring him access. He ran through a couple more scenarios, and the software effectively shut him down each time.

"See that? I know how this software works, and helped to create it, but I can't even break into my own system."

The shareholders applauded.

He moved out from behind the laptop and was closing his presentation when a voice shouted, "Traitor!"

Thane's gaze snapped to the floor between the rows of seats. Sasha ran toward the stage. She lifted her arm and threw something. The glint of silver caught in the stage's bright lights, and he jerked his body to the side to dodge it. A clattering sound drew his gaze to the floor behind him, where a large butcher's knife had fallen. It was exactly like the one someone had left at Letty's apartment.

Panicked screams lifted as the audience scurried for the exits, pushing and shoving. The people in the front rows ducked to the ground as security tackled Sasha. They wrenched her arms behind her back and slapped handcuffs onto her wrists.

At the same time, more security rushed onto the stage, including Abbot. They surrounded Thane and rushed him backstage where Letty instantly grabbed him. He embraced her in return.

"I'm okay. It missed me," he said with his cheek pressed to her hair.

She inched back. "What was it?"

"A knife."

Her eyes widened. "Like…"

He nodded.

"Oh my God." She clutched him again. After a moment, she shifted back and studied his left jacket sleeve. Her fingers touched the fabric. "Your sleeve is cut."

He noticed a slit in the thick fibers. "It's fine. It didn't cut me."

She pulled back her fingers; they were stained with blood. "Yes, it did."

Frowning, he peeled off his jacket. The white sleeve had a cut through it, and the fabric was soaked with blood. He blinked in surprise. "I didn't even feel it."

Abbot raised his radio. "We need a medic now!"

15

Letty

Thane shook his head. "I'll be fine."

Letty couldn't believe how calm he was being. "You're bleeding."

Rebekah rushed over to them. "We need to get Thane out of here. The press is swarming. The medics will meet us in his office."

The three of them with Abbot, and as many security personnel as could fit into the elevator, rode up to the top floor. By the time the door slid shut, blood dripped from Thane's fingertips. Letty held his hand, catching the blood that splattered onto the floor of the elevator. "Holy shit, Thane, you're really bleeding."

"Small scratches can do that."

He was trying to reassure her that he was okay, but it wasn't working. She fingered the tear in his sleeve and ripped it down to his wrist. His arm was streaked with blood, and more gushed from a four-inch-long cut on the side of his shoulder. Looking at the security in the elevator, she found the one who held Thane's jacket. She yanked the purple silk square from the breast pocket and use it to apply pressure to the cut. While holding the silk square in place, she prayed none of his arteries had been nicked.

The elevator door opened onto the top floor, and everyone hurried into Thane's office. The whole way, Letty kept her hand plastered to his injury. Everyone was talking at once, frantic. Their boss had just been attacked in front of a room full of journalists. No one was okay, especially not Letty, but she forced herself to remain steady. Even when his blood soaked through the silk square and was warm against her fingers.

Thane sat on the edge of his desk as chaos unfolded around them.

Abbot entered the office. "The medics are on their way up."

Rebekah came over to them. "We need to cut away his shirt."

While Letty kept firm pressure on the laceration, Rebekah sliced the shirt from Thane's body with scissors. She peeled it away and dropped it to the floor. Letty stared at it. The bright, wet redness of blood stared up at her. Then Rebekah placed the trashcan from behind Thane's desk onto the floor beside his feet. The blood dripping off his fingers landed on discarded pieces of paper in the plastic bin.

"Letty."

Her gaze lifted to his.

He opened his mouth to say something, but two paramedics came in right then.

"We've got it from here," a medic said to Letty.

She backed away.

From several feet away, she watched one of the medics apply a thick wad of gauze to the laceration in Thane's arm, while the other medic opened a bag of medical supplies and readied a syringe of saline with a splash cap. When the bleeding lessened, they squirted the saline into the wound, irrigating it so they could better see what they were dealing with.

Was an artery damaged? Would he need stitches?

Letty took another step back as her grasp on control slipped. She lifted her hands toward her face but froze when she saw they were covered with blood. Her breath caught in her chest, as if her lungs had been snatched from her body. Suddenly, her hands were the tiny hands of a child, and it wasn't Thane's blood, but Constantine's blood. Memories slammed into her—the fear she'd felt that night, the weight of the butcher's knife in her hand, the impact of the blade plunging into Constantine's chest, and his blood squirting onto her hands.

With a frantic blink, the vision snapped away. Now her hands were back to normal, but still covered in blood. Thane's blood.

Rebekah's hand curled around her arm. "Come on, dear, let's get you cleaned up." She ushered Letty into the bathroom, shut the door, and twisted the faucet handle.

Letty stood in front of the counter, hands over the

sink, staring at the flow of water coming from the faucet.

"It's okay." Rebekah guided Letty's hands to the stream of water. Then she squirted foaming soap onto Letty's hands and washed away the blood.

The sink filled with blood-tainted water. Letty watched red droplets splash onto the white porcelain. Her mind fractured, taking her back to when she'd washed the blood off her hands in her neighbor's house, where Constantine had chased her. She'd been a child covered in a grown man's blood. The look of it and the feel of it had terrified her. She hadn't known that would happen. Hadn't known so much blood could come out of a person.

Gradually, the water lightened to pink as Rebekah washed more and more of the blood off Letty's hands. The sink gurgled loudly as it drank it up—water, blood, and soap. Letty didn't move a fraction.

"This isn't the first time I've had Canmore blood on my hands," she whispered.

"Don't think that," Rebekah said in a soothing tone. "This is different."

"Yes, it is. It's Thane's blood this time."

"No, dear, you didn't do anything to Thane. You didn't do this."

Tears slithered down Letty's cheeks. "But I did kill his father."

Rebekah squirted two more pumps of foaming soap onto Letty's hands. "That wasn't your fault, either. That was self-defense. And Thane will be okay."

Letty shook her head. There was no way he'd be okay with her in his life. She peered at her hands. The blood was gone now, but she could still feel it. His blood was there, forever staining her hands.

"Is there rubbing alcohol?"

While Rebekah hunted through the cabinet under the sink, Letty yanked the faucet handle to its hottest setting. Rebekah stood with a bottle in her hands.

"Splash some on my hands."

Rebekah doused her palms with rubbing alcohol.

"More." She flipped her hands over, and Rebekah complied by pouring more of it over the backs of Letty's hands. With the strong smell of alcohol in her nostrils, making her lightheaded, she dove her hands under the running water again.

Steam lifted.

Her skin became bright pink.

Rebekah gasped and wrenched off the water. "That's enough."

Hands raised, Letty stumbled back and collapsed into a chair. The stinging of her hands shot her back to the moment. Her vision blurred with tears. She would start sobbing any second, and she didn't want Thane to hear that.

"T-towel," she stuttered. "S-small t-towel."

Rebekah passed her a hand towel.

Letty balled it up and held it to her mouth to muffle her weeping.

Rebekah knelt beside her. "He's okay, and you're okay." She rubbed Letty's back.

The comforting contact only broke Letty more, and she sobbed harder. Sasha had gone after Thane because of her, and Letty would never forget that. Her chest constricted, and her throat tightened. She tried to breathe, but only ended up hyperventilating. Frightened, she dropped the towel to her lap. "I c-c-can't b-breathe."

16

Thane

T hane kept glancing at the closed bathroom door, wondering what was taking so long. He didn't like the look on Letty's face when Rebekah had ushered her in there to clean her hands. Letty had been pale. Too pale. And there was a horrified, haunted look in her eyes that plunged his heart to his gut.

The medic irrigating his laceration inspected it. "You're going to need sutures to stop the bleeding. We should bring you to the emergency department."

He shook his head. "I'm not going to the hospital just for stitches."

"Then I can do it here, with your permission. I'm trained in giving sutures on scene."

"Do it."

The medic inserted a needle around the laceration in several places to numb it with anesthesia, then they draped Thane's arm with a sterile blue cloth, and began stitching the laceration closed right there in his office.

The bathroom door opened, and Rebekah came out. She scurried straight to the other medic and whispered something. Without a word, the medic picked up their bag of equipment and followed Rebekah into the bathroom.

Thane tensed. What the hell is going on? His heart raced harder and faster the longer the three of them were in there. He couldn't even feel the needle piercing his flesh and tugging the sides of the laceration together. All he felt was concern.

For Letty.

Minutes lasted forever, and he didn't know what was happening behind the closed bathroom door. He couldn't hear a thing.

Finally, the door opened again.

Rebekah squeezed out, not so much as giving him a glimpse of Letty. She shut the door behind her and hustled to the coffee table without glancing at him. She filled a glass of water. When she was rushing back to the bathroom, with the water sloshing, he pushed off the edge of his desk.

"Sir, you can't move," the medic said.

Gritting his teeth, Thane stayed in place, but he called out Rebekah's name. "What's happening? Tell me."

Rebekah sighed. "Letty had a panic attack. The medic is giving her oxygen and monitoring her." She lifted the glass of water. "I have to give this to her."

Before leaving, she squeezed his good shoulder.

With no other choice, he watched Rebekah enclose herself into the bathroom with Letty and the medic. If he weren't getting stitches at this very moment, Thane would've gone right in there and wrapped Letty in his arms. He'd assure her that everything was okay, and he'd stay until she felt better. But he couldn't even fucking move.

The medic took extra care in suturing him. Any other time, he would've appreciated that, but not now when he'd prefer the task done quickly.

Several minutes later, the bathroom door opened.

This time, the paramedic exited.

Thane addressed the medic. "Is she okay?"

"She's better now. That kind of reaction is normal."

Thane peered at the door. Nothing was normal about this. Most people in a situation like this didn't have to deal with severe PTSD from their childhood.

The medic working on stitching him up finally snipped the sutures and wrapped his arm with elastic wrap.

He shifted when the door opened once more.

Rebekah had an arm around Letty, supporting her. Letty's gaze met his, and then it lowered to the floor. He looked, too, and saw his bloody shirt in tatters.

"Excuse me," Thane said, speaking under his breath to one of the medics. "Can you pick up my shirt and throw it away, please?"

"Sure." The medic discarded the ruined shirt out of sight.

"Thank you."

"No problem."

Rebekah escorted Letty to the small couch where they sat side by side. She rubbed Letty's arms and whispered something. Letty nodded in response and hugged herself around her middle, but she didn't look at him.

He swallowed.

When the medics packed up their things and left, Thane pushed off his desk. "Thank you, everyone, for everything, but...can you give us some privacy?"

His security team filed out, followed by Abbot and Rebekah, who shut the door. Instead of going directly to Letty as he wanted to do, he walked to his armoire, opened the door, and slipped a white button-up shirt from a hanger. He didn't want Letty to see his wound, even if it was bandaged. Except, pulling on a shirt wasn't so easy now with the stitches protesting any movement.

Letty rose. "I'll help." She moved behind him and held his shirt so he could get his hands into the sleeves. Then she eased it up, over the layers of bandages, and onto his shoulders. She came around to stand in front of him. Silently, she buttoned his shirt.

He studied her. Her face was still pale, and she had yet to meet his eye. "Letty, look at me."

"I can't button your shirt if I look at you."

He caught her fingers with his right hand, brushing them away from the buttons. Then he lifted her chin so she'd meet his gaze. He stared into her eyes and saw redness from crying. "I'm okay."

As soon as he said that, fresh tears bloomed in her eyes.

He looped his right arm around her shoulders and pulled her to him. She slipped her arms around his waist, holding him tightly. They stood like that for a long time. Even when a knock sounded on the door, they didn't part.

The door cracked open. Over the top of Letty's head, he saw Rebekah peering inside. "I'm so sorry to disturb you, but there's a ton of media downstairs. Security is having trouble getting them to leave."

"Have them moved to the press room. Tell them I'll come down shortly to give a statement about what happened. If they ask, say I'm perfectly fine."

Rebekah nodded and ducked out.

Thane rubbed Letty's back. "I have to neutralize this before it blows up."

Letty nodded against his good shoulder. Then she backed away. "Do you, um, need my help tucking in your shirt?"

His lips twitched. "I'll manage." In the bathroom, he did manage, but not without a bunch of squirming. It wasn't perfect, but a jacket would hide that. Except, he couldn't shift his left arm back enough to get it on. He exited the bathroom. "I actually do need your help with this." He held up the jacket.

Letty slid the jacket up his arms. Then she positioned it into place on his shoulders, fixed the collar, and buttoned it. "How fortunate that you had a light gray suit jacket in your office."

"Think they'll notice that it's not the same one I was wearing earlier?"

"I doubt it." She ran her fingers along the lapel and then over his shoulders to smooth it out. "Looks good."

Then she settled her hand over his left shoulder, above the bandages. "Does it hurt?"

"They numbed it."

She pressed her lips to his. "You should go."

He stepped out of his office and paused in front of Rebekah's desk.

Rebekah scanned him. "You don't even look like anything happened."

"Good, because that's what I'm going to tell them." He glanced at his closed office door. "Can you do me a favor? Can you keep Letty company until I return?"

"Of course."

"Thank you."

He made his way to the press room where there was standing room only as journalists who'd attended the launch volleyed for space with reporters from major networks. As soon as he stepped inside the room, they erupted into questions. Their voices shouting to be heard deafened him.

To silence them, he held up a hand.

After a handful of seconds, they quieted.

"I understand you all want to know what happened. I can tell you that Sasha Danes, the wife of a former board member of All Heart Tech, Alec Danes, carried out an attempt to cause me harm, but she was unsuccessful."

"Why'd she call you a traitor?" someone shouted.

"I imagine it has to do with the fact that I fired her husband."

"Why'd you fire Mr. Danes?" someone else wanted to know.

"That is private business information that I am not willing to divulge now or at any time." Because it had to do with Letty, and if they knew that, they'd be chopping at the bit to know more. About her. About her past. About the two of them.

"She threw a knife at you. Did you get hurt?"

"I did not. I have good reflexes."

"Paramedics came," someone else said from the back of the room.

"A precaution from my security team."

"They were here a long time for a precaution," another reporter pointed out.

Thane's lips quirked. Can't get anything past a journalist.

"We decided to play a video game while waiting for all of you to arrive."

That response had many of them laughing.

"Which video game?"

"Minecraft."

They asked him question after question for fifteen minutes. Each one meant to try to get him to trip up and reveal something he didn't want to share. They'd often circle back to a previous question, phrasing it in a slightly different way, or digging further in the hopes of uncovering the truth. Thane'd had plenty of practice with the media and knew how to skirt around what they wanted to know and what he didn't want to tell them. He was also good at changing the line of questioning smoothly away from areas he wanted to avoid, without them even noticing.

When answering their questions exhausted him, he held up his right hand again. "Let's not forget that today was about the launch of game-changing cyber security software. Perhaps after this I should think more about knife attacks instead of cyberattacks." He smiled. "If you'll excuse me, I have a lot of work to do. Thank you."

Raised voices and questions followed him as he left the press room. He rode the elevator—now free of blood—straight to the top floor. When he stepped off, he found Rebekah sitting behind her desk. His heart sank.

"Did she leave?"

"No, she's still in there. She looked tired, so I had her rest on the couch. She's asleep."

Thane eased his door open to see Letty curled up on the couch beneath the blanket that was usually draped over the back. He closed the door quietly and approached her. Her hands were tucked beneath the pillow, hugging it to her cheek. Curls had slithered over her forehead and cheek. He itched to brush them aside, but she appeared so peaceful that he didn't want to wake her.

To let her sleep, he went behind his desk to work.

17

Letty

Letty cracked open her eyelids. She frowned, not sure of where she was. After a moment, she recognized Thane's office, and then everything that happened flooded back. Her gaze flicked around the room, searching for him. He sat behind his desk, with his jacket off, writing with pen and paper.

She sat up, pulling the blanket from her legs. "You should've woken me when you came back."

He lowered the pen. "You looked too peaceful to wake."

She rubbed her eyes. "How long was I asleep?"

"Two hours."

She blinked. "Okay, yeah, you definitely should've woken me up."

He smiled but didn't say anything.

She tilted her head, amazed. "You were cut by a flying knife and got stitches. And what do you do? You go back to work."

He glanced at the paper in front of him. "Just notes. Nothing strenuous."

"Still. You said you hadn't even felt the knife cut you."

"And I didn't. Let's not talk about that." Standing, he held out his right hand. She took it, and he drew her to a stand. "I'm ready to go home." He trailed a finger along her jawline. "Do you want to come home with me? To my place?"

Her heart rate kicked up at his question. She'd never been to his penthouse. In her mind, that was the next level up in their relationship, a sign that things were progressing, which she was finally ready for.

"I'll come home with you."

After locking his office, Rebekah held up an orange prescription bottle. "I had pain meds filled." When he didn't reach out to take it, she sighed and directed her gaze toward Letty. "Will you be staying with him tonight?"

Letty's cheeks burned. "Yes."

Rebekah held out the bottle. "Make sure he takes these."

Letty accepted them. "I will."

In the elevator, Thane said, "You don't have to do that. You're not my nurse. I'm good."

Letty eyed him, and said one word, "Stitches." Then she shook the bottle. "You will take these, whether you like it or not."

He flashed a grin. "Yes, ma'am."

Abbot drove them to Thane's penthouse.

During the drive, Letty checked the messages on her phone. Lydia and Yawanda had sent her several frantic texts while she'd been knocked out from her adrenaline let-down. She opened up the texts sent from her mom first.

—The knife attack is all over the news. What's happening? Are the police there? Are you at the police station? The hospital?—

—I've watched the clip over a dozen times. In slow-mo. It looks like the knife came really close to Thane's arm. Is he hurt?—

—Letty, what the hell is happening?! Call me when you get this!—

—Okay. I saw Thane's press conference after the attack. He's alive. That's good.—

—But he's wearing a different jacket. The blade cut it, didn't it? Did it cut him, too?—

Letty swallowed. Her mom had the eyes of a cop, made to pick up the slightest detail change. It hadn't helped that her mom had watched the clip obsessively, probably with her nose practically touching the screen. Hopefully no one else had paid as much attention to the clip as her mom.

She sent off a fast text to bring her mom some

relief.

—We're okay. Promise.—

Then she typed out a longer reply, detailing everything that had gone down.

—I would've texted you sooner, but everything happened so fast. My head was spinning, and then I had a panic attack. My phone was on silent. I laid down during Thane's press conference and fell asleep. I'm SO sorry for worrying you. I don't like to do that. But we're okay.—

The messages updated with "seen" immediately. Her mom replied back.

—Thank goodness. Do you need me to come? I can get the next flight out.—

Letty embraced her phone to her chest, hugging it to her heart a moment. Then she texted:

—I appreciate that so much, but everything is okay now.—

They sent messages back and forth.

—How are you feeling after your panic attack?—

—Worn out.—

—*If you need me for anything, let me know. I will drop everything to be there for you. For you and Thane.*—

Letty's eyes misted.

—*I know. I love you, Mom.* 🍥—

—*I love you*, sweetie.—

Letty closed the conversation with her mom to pull up Yawanda's.

—*OMG. OMG. I saw the news. Is Thane okay?*—

—*Dude, is Thane okay??? Are YOU okay???*—

—*I don't even care that I am covering the shop alone, but I do care that you're not responding. WHAT THE HELL?!*—

Letty grimaced. *I'm not a good friend or boss.*
She sent a text to Yawanda.

—*I'm SO sorry for not responding sooner. My phone was on silent because of the event and then after everything that happened, the adrenaline let-down knocked me off my feet. I feel asleep. I just woke up. I'm okay. Thane's okay. I'm soooo sorry for worrying you and for not texting you and for being a shitty boss and not coming back to the shop. More, for being a shitty friend.*—

As soon as her message status showed it was sent, the bubble with the three dots popped up. The fact that Yawanda had been waiting by her phone for a response doubled Letty's guilt.

Yawanda's reply appeared.

—*THANK THE LORD.* 🙏🙏🙏 🙏🙏🙏 *I'm glad that you both are okay. That was some crazy shit, girl. But you're not a shitty boss. I've had plenty of shitty bosses, and you are not one of them. And you're not a shitty friend either, just a little forgetful. I get that you're going through a lot. I don't blame you for any of it. And if I have to cover for you at work because of it, I've got you.* 👊—

Her words made Letty's heart smile.

—*Thank you for being so awesome.* 👊—

Yawanda replied back with: 😈

Smiling, Letty tucked her phone into her purse. Ringer on.

They arrived at Thane's building and rode the private elevator, which required a keypad code to access it. Letty's mouth became dry when the elevator opened to his penthouse. She had been right in assuming his place would be much larger than her apartment. His penthouse could hold ten of her apartments in one gulp.

The décor was modern with clean lines and not many decorations, aside from a few expensive-looking paintings. Not like her apartment, which was homely and probably frumpy to someone accustomed to this. Her flat screen TV was an infant compared to his, and his couch could definitely fit a full-sized person, unlike her loveseat. Two people, in fact, since he had a blue-gray, suede sectional. The kitchen was massive with a dozen white drawers and cabinets. Marble tops—the same blue-gray of the couch—gleamed along with chrome appliances.

Letty gaped at her surroundings. *Holy shit.* Her feet froze just beyond the elevator.

Thane peered at her. "Don't let it intimidate you." He held out his hand. "It's just where I eat and sleep. And occasionally workout."

For a place where he *just* ate and slept, it was rather grand. Never-the-less, she clasped his hand and let him draw her inside.

"I'm going to change, and then we can figure out what to have for dinner." He waved his hand. "I know it's a bit obnoxious, but please make yourself at home."

He headed down the hall toward where she assumed his bedroom was located. A moment later, he returned in faded jeans and a plain white T-shirt. She bit the inside of her cheek, because damn! Jeans hung just right on him.

"How does pizza sound?"

"Great," she managed.

They ate a large, hand-tossed, thin crust cheese pizza while sitting at the counter. Thane was shutting the cardboard box when his cell phone sounded. He checked it, read the incoming text, and laughed out loud. "People really do have a thing for shock and gore. That was Rebekah. Sales on our cyber security software have been astronomical."

"What'd you say in response?"

He rotated his phone toward her to show her the thumbs-up emoji he'd sent.

"That's a lot of excitement for astronomical sales."

"I've had enough excitement for today, so..." He grinned. "Do you want to watch an action movie with me?"

She burst out laughing and gave him a thumbs-up. Lounging on his couch, he switched on his TV and loaded a streaming service. She sat beside him. After a few minutes of scrolling, they settled on an action movie neither of them had seen yet. Thane started the movie, but before the company intros even ended, he hit pause.

"Would you mind sitting on my other side?"

"Sure." She stood and sat on his right side.

As soon as she lowered onto the cushion, he resumed the movie. Then he lifted his right arm and wound it around her shoulders to draw her close. "That's better."

Smiling, she curled her legs beneath her, leaned into his side, and rested her head on his good shoulder. She even stretched her arm across his abdomen and curled her hand around his ribs to hold onto him.

"Even better," he muttered.

Halfway through the movie, though, he fell asleep. She picked up the remote from the cushion beside him and paused the movie. Then she shifted back to study his face. Her heart pitched, and her stomach clenched. There was no logical explanation for why he could be so damn sexy. Maybe this was proof that God was a woman, after all. Or at least a being who could appreciate a sexy body regardless of gender.

She trailed the tip of her finger down the length of his throat and over his Adam's apple. He released a small groan that vibrated against the pad of her finger. The sensation made her smile. His eyelids stayed closed, though, so she moved her finger to his jawline and followed it to his chin. Another groan sounded, which prompted her to trail soft kisses along his jaw.

"I like that even more," he mumbled.

She shifted back, and his eyelids fluttered open. Creases between his brows and red lightning bolts crisscrossing the whites of his eyes told her he wasn't only tired but in pain. "You should go to bed."

"Mm." He closed his eyes again.

When he didn't budge, she kissed his jaw again. This time, though, her lips weren't feather-light. She planted quick kisses on his skin, hoping to pry him awake.

He turned his head, and her lips landed smack dab on his mouth.

She moved back with a laugh. "Come on," she said. "I'll tuck you in."

"That sounds good."

Shaking her head, she leant him a hand. At the end of the hallway, she found his bedroom, with a king-sized bed of blacks and grays and blue-gray walls. Thane lowered onto the left side of the bed. She snapped back to reality and stepped into the adjoining bathroom, where she tried not to stare as she filled a glass of water, but she noted the large, enclosed shower and huge tub.

With water in hand, she came back out and sat next to him, trying to not think about the fact that she was sitting on his bed. "Take this." She dumped two pills into the cap of the prescription bottle.

He eyed them.

"Down the hatch."

Now he eyed her.

She pushed them closer. "They'll help."

Sighing, he picked up the cap. He popped them into his mouth, accepted the glass, and knocked them back. She set the glass on the black nightstand beside the pill bottle. When she stood, Thane folded the covers back and turned so that he lay on his good arm. She tucked him in.

"You can ask Abbot to drive you home," he said as she moved around his bed.

Without a word, she pulled back the covers on the other side and climbed in. Facing him, she settled her head on the extra set of pillows. "I thought I might stay here."

He stared a moment before his eyelids drifted shut. His lips quirked, and he whispered, "Better and better."

Letty opened her eyes when sunlight filtered through the blinds, lighting up the room. Thane lay on his back, sound asleep. Not wanting to wake him, she slithered out and tiptoed into the kitchen. She discovered the single-cup coffeemaker on the counter beside the refrigerator, but she had no idea where to find the pods of coffee grounds.

Opening the cabinet above the coffeemaker, she found the mugs and chose two. Then she opened the drawer beneath the appliance, hoping to unearth the coffee. A tray of utensils sparkled up in the early morning light. One by one she searched each drawer and cabinet. Maybe he was out and needed to buy more. Standing in the middle of the kitchen, she scanned the area for a place she hadn't checked.

"I thought you left."

She whirled around to see Thane standing behind her. He still wore the jeans and T-shirt from yesterday, although they were a little wrinkled. Even rumpled from sleep, though, he looked cute as hell.

"I wanted to make coffee, but I don't know where the coffee is."

"Here." He opened the pantry door and removed two plastic pods of coffee grounds from a glass canister. Then he prepped the coffeemaker.

"How's your arm?"

"Mm."

She pursed her lips. "You need to take more pain meds, don't you?"

He kissed her. "That's all I need."

"My lips aren't pain meds," she mumbled against his mouth.

"I beg to differ." He kissed her again.

She laid a hand on his chest. "Seriously, though. Pain meds."

He faced the coffeemaker as it gurgled and braced his right hand on the counter.

"I don't like to take pain meds. Growing up, my mom was addicted to them. She started after a doctor prescribed them to her because of injuries that my father had inflicted."

"I'm sorry." She stroked his back. "But taking pain meds for actual pain is okay. You're strong, but you shouldn't have to suffer." She stepped into his bedroom and came back with the pain meds. "Take these. For me," she added when he let out a groan. "I don't like to see you in pain."

"Okay." He held out his hand, and she shook out two.

She watched him take them with a swallow of coffee. "I wish I didn't have to leave, but I need to go home to get ready for work."

"There's going to be more paparazzi downstairs than usual because of what happened," Thane said. "I'll ask Abbot to drive you home. The windows are tinted. They won't see you."

"I appreciate that. Thank you." At the elevator, she kissed his cheek. "I'll see you later." She pointed a finger. "And take it easy."

"I will. I promise."

Letty showered, changed, and walked to work. She really hoped Thane was taking it easy as he said he would. At least he could do a lot of work remotely from his penthouse using a laptop, but if he kept up with the pain meds as needed throughout the day, they could make him groggy. She wanted him to rest, but he was used to working and doing whatever needed to be done, so she didn't have much faith that he'd be kicking back and relaxing.

Recalling the laceration and the feel of his blood on her hands tightened her throat. She pushed it down. At least it had only nicked the side of his arm. He hadn't been stabbed. And, although he'd required stitches, none of his arteries had been compromised. She was thankful for that. All of it. But now he had stitches and would bear a scar because a deranged woman thought he was a traitor for being in a relationship with Letty. She hated that she was the reason for the attack.

In an attempt to shove those thoughts aside, she focused her mind on the man in question, which, of course, conjured images of him in his jeans, him asleep in bed, and then the memory of how him in his cotton joggers blazed to the front. She imagined what he'd look like without that layer of cotton. It wasn't hard to accomplish.

Oh geez. Her cheeks flamed, so she waved her hand in front of her face to cool the flush. She'd never wondered what someone looked like naked before. Not until Thane. For that, she felt horrible, like one of those women who sought him for his body and his money, as if he was a prize to be collected.

Still, she couldn't stop herself from wondering, from imagining. What would it be like to touch his bare chest? To clutch his bare back?

When he'd been shirtless in his office, while the medics tended to the laceration, she'd glimpsed his golden-brown skin, his defined abs, his muscles, and cuts in his abdomen that led to intriguing places. Leaning against his desk, ankles crossed, even with blood streaking down his arm, he'd been sexy. She didn't like that, either. He'd been wounded, bleeding, and beneath everything she'd been going through, her mind had made a note and taken a mental picture of how sexy he'd appeared in that moment.

Letty shook her head. *I'm no better than those lustful women.*

She stepped up to her shop door. At eyelevel, she found a tiny plastic bag taped to the glass. Sunlight glinted on something inside it. She squinted her eyelids at the small object, trying to make out what it was, and when she did, her blood ran cold.

Hands shaking, she ripped it off the glass. Then she peered up and down the sidewalk.

The person who'd left that for her could be out there, watching. She didn't see anyone paying her attention, though, so she unlocked the door and shut it at her back.

Yawanda wasn't there yet. Alone, Letty floored it to the backroom where she felt safe, where no one could see her. Her palm was sweating when she lifted her hand. Inside the plastic bag was a sterling silver charm of a knife with an oxidized handle, like a butcher's knife. Whoever left it likely thought it was a clever play on her given name. They couldn't know that Letty'd had a charm bracelet that she'd lost in the woods that night she fled from Constantine. They couldn't know charms had been her mother's precious gift to her. No one could know that a charm could nauseate her with horrible memories. No one.

Whoever left the charm thought they were clever. That was it, but hopefully they weren't clever enough.

She accessed the footage from her security camera. Gripping the mouse, she fast-forwarded until she caught sight of someone at her door after midnight. Her index finger jerked, and she paused the feed. Even with the camera showing the culprit up close, she couldn't see the bastard's face because they wore night vision goggles and a black covering over their face. So...clever enough.

"Damn it." Whoever was doing this was one step ahead.

She dug her phone out of her purse. It took her a couple of tries to get a good picture of the charm because her hands were shaking so much. Once one came out clear, she sent it to Thane with a text that said: *Someone left this for me.*

His reply came seconds later. *Where?*

Taped to my shop's door. Security camera showed a person with their face covered.

The sound of a key slipping into the door handle of the backdoor had Letty stashing her phone in her purse.

"Hey," Yawanda said. "How are you and Thane holding up?"

"Good. Everything is good...considering." She slipped the charm into her pocket, not wanting to alarm Yawanda. Whoever left the charm was after Letty, not Yawanda, and Letty planned to keep it that way.

While Yawanda worked in the back, Letty covered the front. After what happened yesterday, there were more people in there than the past few days. The gawkers had petered out, but now they were back in full force. Thane was right; people sure did like shock and gore. They were drawn to blood.

Someone placed a ring on the glass countertop. As Letty rang it up, the customer said, "You know that woman attacked him because of you, right?"

Letty didn't look at the customer as she placed the ring in a box and slipped that box into a bag. "Have a good day." She passed the bag across the counter.

"Uh huh." A hand jerked the bag out of Letty's fingers.

Letty did her best to be friendly to the customers while avoiding eye contact. They knew. Each and every one of them knew that yesterday's events transpired because of her. And they knew. They all knew that she felt guilt over that, which was why every single one of them wanted to rub her nose in it.

She let them.

One by one, she provided customer service to people with scorns, who shook their heads, who whispered or spat that she was no good for Thane, didn't belong with him, wouldn't get away with ruining the Canmore name, would never, ever be one of them.

She let them.

"You better watch your back," one of them threatened.

"Canmore loyalty runs deep," another hissed.

"That knife should've been thrown at you, not him," someone claimed.

She agreed. One hundred percent, she agreed.

"Why don't you just leave?" someone asked before stomping out of the shop.

Why didn't she leave?

"We're not going to let you get away with this."

She was aware of that.

"The next knife will be for you."

Letty's gaze snapped up at that, and she met the eyes of the woman who'd said those words. It was Sasha Danes, coming back to taunt her some more.

Why isn't she in jail?! She should be locked up forever, but she had the money to stay out of jail. No doubt she, or her husband, had posted bail immediately.

Letty steeled her spine. "You're not welcome in my shop. Leave now or I'll call the cops and tell them you threatened me."

Sasha cackled. "As if they'd believe you."

"They will when I show them the video of what you just said to me." Letty pointed at the security camera over her shoulder. "That is just one of the new cameras I installed after my shop was vandalized."

Sasha glared at the camera.

"Leave now and don't ever step foot in my shop again."

Sasha's glare lowered to Letty. "You have some nerve."

Letty nodded. "Yes, I do."

Sneering, Sasha marched out the door.

Letty returned to working the cash register. Now aware of the security camera, the rest of the customers bit their tongues and kept their remarks and judgements to themselves.

She let them.

Yawanda came over to her an hour after opening and whispered in her ear, "You have to take care of something in the backroom. I'll cover things here."

Letty nodded. When she stepped into the backroom, she gasped. She shut the door before anyone could walk by and peek in after her. "What are you doing here? Is Abbot with you?"

Thane stood before her, seemingly taller than usual. "Where's the charm?"

She removed it from her pocket and handed it to him.

"Did you call the cops?"

"No. I called you, and then I opened the shop."

"Good." He closed a fist around the charm. "I'll handle this." With that vow, he spun on his heel and shoved open the backdoor.

After a stunned moment, she raced after him into the back-parking lot. "Thane!"

But he was already in his car, peeling out of there.

18

Thane

*T*hane's tires shredded the gravel leading to Canmore Estate. He shoved his car into park and slammed the door shut. Then he raced up the stairs two at a time to the front door. Using the copy of the key in his possession, he let himself in. Seething inside, vibrating with anger, he stormed to Jessalyn's quarters. He found her lounging on a chaise in her private library.

Jessalyn lowered the book she'd been reading. "Why, hello, little bro."

"Did you do this?" He tossed the charm bag at her.

She flinched when it landed on her opened book. Pursing her lips, she plucked it up. After a moment, she burst with laughter. "Oh, this is clever. I like it." She directed her smile at him. "By your anger, I assume this was sent to Letty? Well, I hate to burst your bubble, but I didn't do it." She flung it back.

The bag hit him in the middle of his chest, and he caught it with his hand before it could fall to the floor. "But you know who did, don't you?"

"Think again. Not everything that happens to Letty is because of me." She tilted her head and pointed at his left shoulder. "Looks like you lied when you said you weren't hurt. Wasn't it your left shoulder the knife sailed past?"

Was that concern he detected in her eyes? In her voice?

"Did you have something to do with *that*, sis?"

Her mouth popped open. She clamped it shut, and then she said, "If you think I would do anything to hurt you, you clearly have no idea who I am."

"No, I don't. The sister I used to know wouldn't have paid someone to stalk a woman for twenty-three years."

Jessalyn rolled her eyes. "You really need to get over that."

"I'm not going to unless you change."

"This is who I've always been!" She flung her book aside. "It's not my fault you were blind to it. And now you're blind to her."

He inhaled in an attempt to calm his anger. "I'm going to tell you this once and only once. I'm in love with her."

Jessalyn's eyes widened.

"What you do to her, you do to me. So as long as you keep this shit up, I don't want anything to do with you. Until you change, you're not my sister. I'm done."

He left her looking as though he'd shot her in the chest.

When the clock showed it was after closing hours, Thane called Letty. She answered immediately and asked, "What'd you do?"

"I confronted my sister."

A stretch of silence followed his statement.

"What happened?" she finally asked.

"She said the charm wasn't from her, and she doesn't know who did it."

"Do you believe her?"

He ran his hand over his head. "I can't trust her. I know that for a fact, but I don't think she was lying." Another length of silence resumed until he struck up the courage to say this next part. "I want you to stay with me."

"What do you mean?"

"Here. At my penthouse. I want you to move in. Temporarily. Until this is resolved. Someone left a package at your apartment and now this at your shop. I'd feel better if you were close, if I knew you were safe."

More silence.

He paced. "It's your choice, of course. I won't force you."

Startling silence.

His heart raced. "Are you still there?"

"Yeah." Her voice was a rasp.

He shut his eyelids and pressed a fist to his forehead. Damn it, he'd screwed up. Asking someone to move in so soon, even temporarily, was a fatal error. "If you don't like that, I can ask Abbot to post outside your apartment while you're there."

"Abbot is *your* bodyguard. Not mine."

"But he'd do it. If I asked."

Silence returned. Then—

"Okay."

His feet stopped pacing, and his eyelids flipped open. "What?"

"I said 'okay.' I'll stay with you."

He stared up at the ceiling, saying a quiet prayer of thanks.

"Do you want me to stay tonight?" Her question brought him back to earth.

"I'd like that." He'd like that very much. "I can send Abbot to pick you up. From now on, I'd like him to drive you to and from work. If you agree to that. Even if you stayed at your place, I wouldn't feel comfortable with you walking by yourself when anyone could come up behind you and…" His voice trailed off. He couldn't say what he was thinking. That someone could stab her in the back and leave her on the sidewalk, bleeding to death.

"I'm afraid having Abbot drive me around will spoil me, but I'll agree to that."

"Abbot can be there in twenty minutes. Pack enough clothes to last a week."

Another long silence.

"Okay."

"If you don't want to do this, you don't have to, Letty."

"No, I do…I want to be close to you. It's just…"

"Fast?"

"That and…intense. What I feel for you is intense."

His heart picked up speed. "I know what you mean."

The buzz of silence returned.

"I'll let you go so you can get ready," he finally said.

"See you soon."

They hung up, and Thane said another prayer of thanks for the fact that he would be seeing her soon and that she'd be staying the night again. She'd be staying for a while.

When she arrived, though, she clutched her bag, looking nervous. He stole the bag from her hands, set it on the floor, and drew her in for a kiss. He kissed her until she melted, until her muscles became liquid and she leaned into him. Feeling her relax against him helped to dissolve some of his own stress.

"Do you want to help me cook dinner?"

She lifted a brow. "You cook?"

He smirked. "I do."

Together, they made lobster mac and cheese with sautéed asparagus and glazed carrots on the side. Then they finished the movie they'd started the night before. Having Letty in his arms made it difficult to concentrate, but at least he didn't fall asleep again.

Come time for bed, the tension returned. He let her change first, and he couldn't stop his smile when he saw her in plaid pajama shorts and a matching short-sleeve top. This was the first time he'd seen the skin of her legs above her knees. The urge to caress her legs made his hands warm as if they were on fire.

She came to a halt. "What?" Peering down at herself, she shifted her hand to the bottom of her shorts and tugged on them.

"Nothing. You just look incredibly cute in pajamas. That's all." It was more than that. Far more, but he couldn't say that without making her even more uncomfortable. "Is it okay if I sleep shirtless?"

Pink blazed across her cheeks. She nodded.

In the bathroom, he changed into black cotton pants and unwound the elastic wrap from his arm. Then he peeled off the gauze, which tugged at a few of the stitches. The four inches of skin held together by surgical thread was still red, spotted with blackened dried blood. He taped the edges of a large non-stick bandage in place. With that done, he exited the bathroom to find Letty already beneath the covers on the right side of the bed, sitting up, with her back against the headboard. Seeing her there caused his insides to clench with desire.

He stepped around to the left side of the bed and sat. Because he wasn't exhausted as he had been last night, or groggy from pain meds, this moment was fraught with a ton of sexual tension that stole his breath. He faced her, and his gaze lowered to her left sleeve. The end of a vertical scar peeked out from beneath the cotton. She'd never worn short sleeves around him before, so he'd never caught a glimpse of her scar.

"Can I see it?" he asked.

She covered her shoulder with her hand. A moment later, she stared into his eyes. Finally, she nodded and lowered her hand.

Getting that confirmation, he slid across the mattress. While watching her face, which she'd turned away, he lifted the sleeve to her shoulder. Once the sleeve no longer covered her skin, he directed his gaze toward her arm. He froze. The vertical scar was about five inches long and a gentle pink-ish white. He swallowed, unable to imagine how much pain a break that resulted in this would've caused a child.

His gaze flicked from her face to the scar, wondering how she'd react if he touched it. Being as tentative as possible, he skimmed the tips of his fingers down the length of the scar. Her shoulder lifted slightly at the contact, but she didn't tell him to stop, didn't pull away.

He brushed the side of his thumb against the top of the scar, feeling its smooth texture and the hardened line from where her flesh had been stitched back together. The urge to kiss her scar overpowered him, and he bent his neck toward it. He planted kisses down the length of it.

Letty's hand came up and molded to his face. The kiss she gave him was all heat and passion and sent electricity through his body.

"I didn't mean for that to go this way," he mumbled against her lips.

"Then you probably shouldn't kiss my scar again."

He chuckled. "I'm sorry. I couldn't resist. I'll behave. I promise." To prove it, he shifted back to a safe distance.

She lowered her shirt sleeve, and he realized they both had a scar in the same place now. Fate couldn't get any more twisted than that, but he didn't dare bring it up to Letty, because she had just crawled over to him. Like a dream, she fell asleep in his arms.

Relishing having her in his bed, in his embrace, he

rifted asleep, too. Mere hours later, though, he jarred awake when Letty let out a scream.

Fear spiked in him. His heart shot up to his throat as it pounded dangerously hard and fast. Letty tossed and turned beside him, throwing her arms and kicking her legs, as if she were fleeing an invisible assailant. The realization that she was probably escaping his father in her mind was like a vise around his throat. He yearned to snatch her out of that nightmare, but not just Letty...Charm. He wished he could scoop that little girl right out of her subconscious, out of Constantine's path, and hug her, keep her safe from the monster that had sought to hurt her.

"Letty, baby, wake up." He grasped her shoulders.

She screamed again

"Letty, Letty, please wake up."

She fought even harder.

Against him. And that had his blood running cold.

19

Letty

Hands swallowed her shoulders, holding her down, but she wouldn't be stilled. If she did, Constantine would kill her. She had to get him off. Using all her strength, she shoved Constantine's body off her. Then she launched on top of him and struck her hand down fast, plunging the knife into his heart.

"Letty, it's Thane. Look at me, baby. Look at me."

Thane's voice dropped Letty from her nightmare as if she were free falling from a broken harness. She blinked through the fog of her dream. Constantine's face, shocked from the blade sinking into his chest and his eyes wide with death, transformed into Thane's face. With the dream still clinging to her mind, she stared, frowning. Then her gaze lowered to her hand, which was balled into a white-knuckled fist over his heart. The sting on the side of her hand told her there'd been an impact, and a hard one. She peered from him and back to her hand, connecting the dots.

Gasping, she unclenched her hand and scrambled off him. "I stabbed you."

"No." Thane sat up. "You didn't."

Backing away, horrified at what she'd done, she nodded. "Yes, yes, I did. In my dream, I stabbed Constantine." She lifted her right hand, the one that had been over his heart. "And I stabbed you."

Thane followed her, moving cautiously. "It was a dream."

She pointed a finger, wanting him to stay away. "It was real. What I dreamt had happened. What I did to him, I had done to you." On the other side of the bed now, she backed toward the wall.

He kept coming. "You didn't do anything to me. I'm fine."

Pressing her back to the wall, with tears expanding over her eyes, she held up her hands to stop him from coming any closer. "I'm a danger to you."

"Don't say that. No, you're not."

"Yes, I am, Thane." Her voice choked, and fat tears plunged down her cheeks. She slid against the wall to the floor.

He lowered to his knees a few feet from her.

"Sasha called you a traitor because of me. She threw a knife at you because of me. You were cut and bleeding because of me."

He reached out to her, to touch her ankle, but she tugged her foot away.

"Don't touch me, Thane. Don't...don't..."

"Okay." He held up his hands. "I won't. I promise."

She sucked in a shaky breath. "What if I had slept walked and gotten a knife from the kitchen? I could've killed you."

"You wouldn't do that."

"You don't know that, Thane!" She covered her face. "If I hurt you, I'll never forgive myself."

"You won't hurt me, and I won't ever hurt you."

She spoke behind her hands, not having the strength to look when she said, "I shouldn't be around you. I shouldn't have come here. You'd be safer if I was gone."

"Letty, please don't do this." The heartbreak in his voice killed her.

She was killing herself.

She lowered her hands to see devastation marring his face. "I don't want to do this." Her voice was thick with tears. "But I can't trust myself. During a night terror, I could hit you. I could grab something." She shook her head, dislodging more tears. "I can't..."

"I can help you with your night terrors. They don't scare me."

"They should."

Her gaze lowered to his arm. Red stained the white bandage on his shoulder. Her heart plummeted to the pit of her stomach. "You're bleeding."

He checked his shoulder. "It's okay. I'll take care of this. I'll be right back."

When he disappeared into the bathroom, Letty didn't waste a second. She grabbed her sneakers from her duffel bag, shoved her feet into them, sans socks, and yanked a sweatshirt over her head. Then she snatched up her purse, leaving her bag because it'd slow her down, and bolted.

She was jabbing the button for the elevator when she heard him say, "It's okay, Letty, a stitch popped. That's—"

The elevator dinged.

"Letty!"

She dove into the elevator, hit the button, and dropped to the floor behind the panel, because she couldn't see him and didn't want him to see her.

"Letty, please don't go." His voice was close, but he wasn't coming in after her. Nor was he stopping the door from closing. As soon as it did, she broke down crying.

She stayed there, huddled on the floor, until the elevator stopped. Then she pushed to her feet. When the door opened on the floor directly below Thane's, her breath fled from her lungs.

Abbot stood there. He wore a white T-shirt and jeans, and he clasped his hands in front of him. His expression was unreadable. He placed a hand on the elevator door to keep it from closing. Was he going to bring her back?

"It's okay. Thane called. There's paparazzi outside. I can escort you to the underground parking garage and to the car so they won't see you."

Wordlessly, she nodded and stepped back to let him enter. The ride down was awkward. There could be no mistaking that something was wrong, not with her red eyes. Not with the tears wet on her cheeks. Not with the fact that it was the middle of the night and she wore pajama shorts. But he didn't say anything else. Nor did he look at her. He was respectful of her privacy and ever professional. That made her want to cry even more.

He led her to the car and held the back door open for her before getting behind the wheel. Even though the paparazzi couldn't see her, she still sank low in her seat.

They were on the road, driving away from the building, when her cell phone rang.

She knew without looking it was Thane, but she looked, and she answered it. "Hello?"

"Please tell me you accepted Abbot's offer to drive you home."

"I did."

Neither of them said anything for a while, but she couldn't stay silent. "I'm not leaving to hurt you, Thane. I don't want to hurt you." She slammed her hand over her mouth to muffle a sob as it broke from her throat.

Discreetly, Abbot pushed a button and had the black partition rising to divide them and give her privacy. Even so, she still didn't remove her hand, because she didn't want Thane to hear her sobbing, although he could tell. Without a doubt.

"Then why are you leaving? You don't have to leave."

She breathed in and out a few times to get herself under control. "To protect you," she finally managed. "I have to stay away from you. Not forever. Just until things calm down." When Constantine's friends stopped harassing her. When things stopped showing up at her apartment and shop. When she could trust herself.

"Letty, you could stay away for a year, and whenever you come back to me, it'll all blow up again and will be ten times worse because of the time gap. But, please, God, don't do that to me. Don't stay away for a year."

Letty sobbed harder, because she knew he was right, but running was all she could think of doing. She couldn't fight, so she chose flight. She also wept because of his plea. His plea absolutely shattered her.

"I won't," she whispered. "I won't be gone that long. I couldn't because...because I...I care about you...need you...want you..."

"Then please come back."

Every time he said "please," he fractured her resolve that much more.

"I can't." She dashed away her tears. "But I won't be gone forever. I promise."

The car pulled into the back-parking lot to her apartment complex.

"I have to go." She sucked in a shuttering breath. "Bye."

"Letty, wait—"

Hating herself, she ended the call.

20

Thane

*N*umb, Thane stood in his bedroom, not knowing what to do. After a moment, he opened his closet. The dresses she'd hung in there earlier still hung on hangers. Her duffle bag sat beside the bed, unzipped, showing a few pairs of shoes and folded pajamas. In his bathroom, her bottle of perfume sat on the white countertop.

He paced into the living room and stared at the cold elevator door. His heart sank. He turned his back to it.

"Let her go," he whispered and put his hands to his head. "Just let her go. Let her go, Thane. Let her go." His pleads became increasingly desperate as his emotions ravaged his insides.

He understood why she ran, but damn, it tore him

apart. His throat tightened as if a vise had closed around his neck, choking him. After all the times he'd seen his father corner his mother, yank her arm when she tried to run past him, strangle her wrists as she writhed from his harsh hold, and stand firm in a doorway with his arms crossed so she couldn't leave, Thane was torn. He didn't want Letty to go, but he also didn't want to do something his father would've done to keep his mother from fleeing.

He lowered onto a stool at the kitchen counter and held his head in his hands. "Let her go, let her go, let her go," he repeated. "Let her, let her, let her…" Tears pressed against the backs of his eyelids.

He loved her, though. He loved her, and he couldn't let it end this way.

"Fuck it." He shoved off the stool. In his bedroom, he yanked a sweatshirt over his head, tugged on sneakers, and then snatched up his keys.

His foot shoved down on the gas pedal as he raced to her apartment. He didn't quite know what he'd do once he got there. If he had to talk to her through the closed door again, he would. If he had to sleep in the hallway, he would. He'd sleep there every night, to make sure she was safe.

He zoomed into the back-parking lot of her apartment complex. Then he ran up the stairs. At her door, he knocked gently. Standing perfectly still, he strained his ears and searched for a sign that she was there.

Please come to the door, baby. Please.

But she didn't come.

He knocked again. "Letty?"

Tentatively, he wrapped his fingers around the doorknob and attempted to turn it, but it was locked. He closed his eyes, unsure of what to do. When another minute crawled by, he dug out his phone and texted Abbot.

A reply came immediately.

—I dropped off Letty fifteen minutes ago. —

Thane stashed his phone in his pocket. "Letty, please, I just want to talk. You don't have to be scared of me, of you, of us. We can deal with this together. You and me, baby. You and me."

He held his breath as his heart pounded. He prayed she'd come to the door, say something, anything. She didn't even have to open it, although his arms ached to wrap around her, comfort her. He wanted to convince her that everything would be okay, that he trusted her, but she didn't come to the door or say a word.

He lightly tapped a knuckle on the door, losing confidence.

"She's not there."

Thane jumped and whirled toward an elderly woman, who stood in the dim hallway a few paces away.

She wore a floral mumu, fuzzy slippers, and curlers in her hair. "I'm Ida. I live next door. Letty came to my door and asked me to watch her apartment while she's gone."

"What do you mean? Where'd she go?"

"To JFK airport."

Thane's body went ice-cold. He hadn't thought

she'd go to such drastic lengths to get away. "Did she say where she's going?"

"Georgia to visit her mom for the weekend."

"Thank you." Thane ran past her and clambered down the stairs.

At the airport, he set his ID and credit card on the counter and pushed both toward the employee. "I need a ticket to Georgia. Any city." He just needed a ticket to get in and find Letty. The ticket wasn't important.

The employee passed him a ticket to Savanah. He grabbed it and hurried to the security checkpoint where he ripped off his shoes and dropped his wallet, phone, and keys into a bucket. He stood, trying not to vibrate anxiously while the guard waved a wand over him after he'd stepped through a full-body scan.

The guard waved him ahead, and Thane grabbed up his possessions. After putting his shoes back on, he ran through the airport toward the terminal for his flight, hoping Letty would be somewhere near there. Every seating area he passed, his gaze sought her.

He was getting close to his terminal when he spotted her. His feet came to an abrupt halt, and his heart plunged to his colon. She dropped onto a chair against the back wall in front of him, sitting sideways, with her knees to her chest and her arms wrapped around her legs. She was crying. Right there in the airport, she was crying. He stepped back toward a pillar, not wanting her to notice him.

Seeing her like that ripped him to shreds. This wasn't easy for her, either, and yet, she was still leaving. He wanted to sit in the chair beside her and hold her, whisper in her ear, but he didn't budge from where he stood. Something about how broken she looked immobilized him. She obviously thought leaving was the right thing to do, no matter how much it hurt her to do it. Because of that, he had to let her go. Still, he couldn't unstick his feet from that spot.

Defeated, he leaned his shoulder against the pillar and watched her cry. She swiped the cuffs of her sweater against her cheeks, and he swallowed down the lump clogging his own throat. Never did he want to see her suffering like this. And all because she'd had a dream of his father. The monster. The demon. The devil. To this day the bastard continued to cause her harm, and it sickened and enraged Thane.

A young person walking in front of him glanced at Letty and then did a double take. A cell phone appeared.

From where Thane stood, he watched the camera app open on the screen. He moved quickly and stuck his hand out in front of the phone, blocking the lens' view of Letty. The camera flashed a photo of his palm.

The kid jolted. Their eyes widened with recognition.

"I'll pay you two hundred dollars to not take a picture of her and to leave her alone. It's more than what you would've gotten for that photo from a tabloid."

The kid mulled it over a minute before agreeing.

Thane selected two one-hundred-dollar bills from his wallet.

The kid stuffed them in a pocket and scurried away.

Thane didn't want to leave, yet, so he shifted behind the pillar and leaned his back to it. He stayed like that for a long time, waiting in excruciating pain.

Finally, a flight attendant announced that the flight to Atlanta, Georgia was boarding. Shoulders low, he peered around the pillar to see Letty pulling her small suitcase to the opened door. She handed her boarding pass to the flight attendant, took it back, and then began walking down the corridor to the plane that would take her away. States away.

He shut his eyes. *Let her go. Let her go. Let her go.* Inhaling deeply, he took a step and then another and another, heading for the exit.

He was letting her go.

Thane dragged himself out of his car and to the elevator in his building. He felt as though he'd gone a round with a champion boxer and had lost. Miserably.

Abbot stood outside the elevator, waiting.

Thane didn't say a word to him but slipped his key into the slot to summon the elevator. He didn't so much as meet Abbot's eye. When the elevator door opened, Thane started to take a step inside, but Abbot's hand on his arm halted him.

"What's that?" He plucked at the sleeve of Thane's sweatshirt.

He looked. A small, dark, wet spot had leaked through the fibers of cotton.

"Blood," he said, flat and uncaring. "Mine."

Abbot's face hardened. "What?"

"I popped a stitch." He tried to board the elevator, but Abbot's hand became firm.

"You need to get that checked out. I'm taking you to the Emergency Room."

Thane faced him, not in the mood.

Abbot glared back, daring him to object. "You may have me in height, but I have you in weight. I will throw you over my shoulder and toss you into the SUV if I have to."

Abbot's threat wasn't necessary, though. He didn't have any fight left in him. That champion boxer had beat the shit out of him and left him for dead in the middle of the ring. That champion boxer was Letty. So, he turned right around and climbed into the passenger's seat. He even buckled himself in.

A moment later, they were on their way to the hospital. Thane stared out the side window, looking but not seeing.

Was this what being in shock felt like?

Was this despair?

Heartbreak?

Surrender?

Failure?

It was all of those. And so much more.

"Do you want to talk about it?"

He didn't. If he talked about it, he'd realize that this wasn't a bad dream as he continued to hope it was. Any minute he could wake up and find that he'd dreamt the worst-case scenario. Letty would be sleeping soundlessly beside him. No night terrors to rob her of her sleep and steal her away.

Even so, he needed to talk to someone. He couldn't keep his misery bottled up inside, eating away at him like hydrochloric acid. "She left. She left the state." And saying that hurt like hell. His chest ached, as if someone had plunged their hand into his chest cavity and was squeezing his heart, seeing how much pressure it could withstand before exploding.

"What happened?"

Car lights streak past the window.

"She had a nightmare. I tried to calm her, but that only made things worse. She shoved me onto my back and hit me." He dug his own fist to his chest. "Right here. She thought I was Constantine."

"Shit," Abbot hissed. "Man, you couldn't have known but—"

Thane whipped around. "But what?"

Abbot shook his head. "Night terrors are the worst. I used to get them a lot after I came back from my deployment to the Middle East. The thing with night terrors is that it's better to let them play out. Waking someone up in the middle of a night terror will cause them to lash out and defend themselves. All they'll see when they open their eyes is whatever they'd been dreaming about or having a flashback for."

"Fuck." Thane ran his hands over his head. "So, it's my fault this happened? If I had left her alone, she wouldn't have attacked me. She wouldn't have left."

"You can't think that."

"Can't I? I woke her up, and she thought I was my father." He shook his head as the horror of that clenched his throat, his heart, his very soul. "She looked at me and saw *him*." The person Thane had tried so desperately to not resemblance.

The monster.

The murderer.

Constantine Canmore.

"This isn't your fault, Thane. And it's not her fault,

either. She can't control when a night terror will come or how she'll react to it. And you wanting to wake her up to get her out of that nightmare as fast as possible is a natural thing for a loved one to do. Neither of you could've known this would happen. You're not to blame."

Except blame riddled his body like bullet holes. "What she did to *him* in her dream, she had reenacted with me, and it freaked her out. She's scared that she'll sleep walk and get a knife and..." His voice trailed off as his throat closed, cutting off his words. He swallowed and cleared his throat, but his words still came out hoarse with emotions. "Nothing I said helped. She doesn't want to be anywhere near me."

Abbot nodded, his jaw tense. "I get it. When I first came back from the Middle East, I was staying with my brother Kahlil. Like you, he also didn't know what to do when I had a night terror and woke me when I was screaming, shouting orders to my men, watching them die all over again." His hands tightened on the steering wheel. "By the time I came to, I had my hands around my brother's throat. If I hadn't come back to reality when I did, I would've killed him. In the morning, I packed up my duffel bag and moved out. I didn't feel safe to stay with anyone, so I went to the VA and they found me an emergency shelter and then temporary housing. What I did to my brother weighed on me for a long time, though."

Thane regarded Abbot; a Black man who had fought for a country who often viewed Black men as weapons and dangerous at a very young age; a veteran who had fought for everyone's freedom even when he and other Black and brown people were denied the same equal rights at every level; a bodyguard who'd throw himself in front of Thane and take a bullet for him out of duty and loyalty and friendship; a man he admired.

"Do you still have night terrors?"

Abbot stopped at a red light. "Not so much anymore. The last one might've been six months ago. Sometimes, they're triggered by something. I still fucking hate The Fourth and New Year's Eve, but I've learned how to lessen those triggers. Like with noise canceling headphones on top of earplugs. I also have techniques to combat my sleep terrors. I noticed a pattern. They all happened around three o'clock in the morning, so I set my alarm for a quarter to. When it goes off, I turn on my light and sit up for five minutes before lying back down. It works."

The light changed to green.

"But I was having terrors every single night. That may not work for Letty." He glanced at Thane. "There are things she could do, and that you could do."

Thane nodded. He'd do anything.

"If she's afraid of sleep walking while she's in the middle of a night terror, you could hide all the knives before bed. I'd advise locking them up, because if she knows where they're hidden, her subconscious will know that information and she could still retrieve one."

"I have a safe for my gun."

Abbot nodded. "That'd work. You can tell her about it, but tell her for her safety she can't know the code. And I don't know what Letty is doing or has tried, but meditating before bed helps a lot." He cast an eye at

Thane. "Yes, I meditate."

Thane held up a hand. "No, judgements." He'd be a hypocrite for judging a veteran for mediating for their wellbeing, especially since he did it several times a week. "I meditate between meetings, a CEO trick."

Abbot drove into the parking lot outside the Emergency Room. "You good?"

Thane nodded. "Yeah. Thanks for all that."

"No problem."

Everything Abbot had told him repeated in his head while he waited to be called back. A nurse removed the gauze he'd placed over his sutures and cleaned it. Then a doctor replaced the stitch that had popped and checked the others.

"You need to be more careful."

Thane only nodded. No point in explaining what had happened.

With orders not to lift anything and a sling to limit his mobility that Thane definitely was not going to use, he and Abbot left the Emergency Room. The drive back to his penthouse was quiet.

In the underground parking lot, Abbot switched off the SUV. "Thane."

He met Abbot's eye.

"The best thing you can do for Letty is to be there when she's ready."

Thane shifted away, but he had to express his deepest dread out loud. "I'm afraid she won't ever come back."

"She will." Abbot's voice was firm, one-hundred percent positive.

But Thane wasn't as confident.

21

Letty

*L*etty cried off and on during the flight. By the time the plane landed, two hours later, her body felt ravaged, depleted, utterly wrecked. She rolled her suitcase behind her and dropped into the first available chair in the terminal. Her hands shook as she dug out her cellphone, powered it on, and navigated to her contacts.

"No," Yawanda grumbled when she answered.

"I'm sorry for waking you so early."

"Letty?" Yawanda cleared her throat. "What's going on?"

Letty hated that she was that person…the one who always brought drama, so whenever they called or texted, you instinctively asked, "What now?"

"Something happened last night, and I had to leave.

I boarded a flight to Georgia."

"Is your mom okay?"

"Yeah. She doesn't even know I'm here."

"Did something happen with Thane?"

Letty swallowed. "I'm not ready to talk about it."

Understanding softened Yawanda's voice. "Okay."

"I'll do all the office work remotely. If you need extra help with the front while I'm gone, we can hire someone temporarily." Yawanda's cousin, Kalisha, was always looking for side jobs to pay her way through beauty school. They often hired her on as a seasonal helper during the holiday rush. "Is Kalisha still looking for work?"

"My cuz is always looking for that bank. I'll give her a ring, and don't you worry about anything. I know the shop like the back of my hand. Just focus on yourself."

"Thank you. For everything. While we're at it, you're getting a raise."

"But we're both making the same amount of money."

"And?"

"And our hourly wage is damn nice. No other assistant manager at a gift shop is making as much as I am."

"I repeat…and? You're going to be running things for a while. Alone. Even if Kalisha is there. You'll also be dealing with paparazzi and everyone looking for gossip."

"You mean the nosy, rich white people who need to get a life?"

"Precisely."

Yawanda sighed. "All right. I'll accept a raise while you're gone. How long will that be exactly?"

"I don't know." Although she'd told Ida that she was going away for the weekend, she no longer believed that would be enough time to get her head on straight. "In the meantime, I'll handle all the office work and we'll talk every day. Okay?"

"Okay."

Before they hung up, Yawanda added, "Good luck."

"You, too."

Letty ended the call and requested a ride-sharing service. Then she sat silently in the backseat of a car from the airport to Covington, where Lydia lived, where her birth mother had died, where it had all begun. She decided against calling Lydia because if she heard her mom's voice, she'd break down in front of a stranger. She wanted to wait until she could hold her mom and cry on her shoulder.

The sun had risen above the tree line and the sky had lightened by the time she arrived. Gripping the handle to her rolling suitcase, she stood on the porch to the home that had become her refuge after foster case. She knocked but didn't have to wait long.

Lydia came to the door a moment later. When she saw Letty, surprise and happiness blossomed across her face. "Letty! I had no idea you were coming."

Seeing the woman who had saved her life caused fresh tears to zip down her cheeks and her lungs to quiver. She couldn't hold anything in anymore. She wept.

"Oh, Letty. Letty." Lydia gathered her close.

"What's wrong? What happened?" She rubbed Letty's back in a soothing manner as if she were seven years old again. And in that instance, she was. She was that little girl again.

Lydia ushered her inside and sat her on the couch. For several minutes, she allowed Letty to cry in her arms and offered the comfort that only a mom could give.

Finally, Letty eased back and accepted a box of tissues. She ripped out a couple and used them to mop up her tears.

Lydia laid a hand on her knee. "This is because of Thane, isn't it?"

"But not how you think. He didn't hurt me. He didn't abuse me in any way." She explained what had happened and why she was so afraid. When she finished, the two tissues she'd used to clean away her tears were worn and falling apart.

"You're in love with him, aren't you?"

"Yes," she whispered as her throat tightened. "Yes, I am." She shook her head. "But that's unthinkable. Right? We haven't known each other long, haven't been together long."

"I know couples who got engaged or married after just one month, and they've been happily married for twenty or thirty plus years. Time has nothing to do with it."

"No one wants us together."

"Screw them. They don't decide. You do. He does. Not them." Lydia jabbed a finger to emphasis each of her points.

"But it's weird, isn't it, given what happened? My

mom. His father."

"Admittedly, it is a bit bizarre, but the two of you are connected in ways that none of us will ever understand. That is powerful."

Letty ducked her head and dabbed at her eyes. "I can't be around him right now. There's too much happening. The two of us being together is causing my enemies to target him. And I can't handle that. Mess with me, fine, but don't go after him. Not him." She stabbed her finger into her chest. "Not for what I did."

Lydia embraced her. "It's not all your fault. You're innocent. You have always been innocent."

Those words only made her cry harder.

When she controlled herself again, Lydia pulled her back and swiped her cheeks. "If you love him, and if he loves you, you'll get through this. But you'll stay here until you feel strong again, until you're ready to go back. Why don't you take a bath while I cook something to eat?"

Letty nodded. "Okay."

She soaked in a tub of hot water and bubbles, bathing her face to wash away the residue of so many tears shed. Then she changed into a pair of fuzzy pajama bottoms and a baggy T-shirt that she'd packed. Since she'd left her toiletries and cosmetics in Thane's bathroom, she borrowed Lydia's deodorant; she'd go out to get the things she needed later.

The kitchen smelled like bacon, hash browns, and eggs when she stepped into it. Her stomach growled with hunger. A glass of orange juice waited for her on the counter. She picked it up and chugged half of it. The sweetness filled her and helped to calm the dizzy feeling dominating her head.

"I used your deodorant."

Lydia peered over her shoulder. "Ew."

Letty rolled her eyes, and Lydia laughed.

When she finished cooking, she set a full plate in front of Letty, complete with sliced and buttered toast and a few strawberries. Letty smiled at the breakfast, and she ate every bite, filling up the void inside her that had been left empty when she ran onto the elevator, when she packed her suitcase, when she strapped into that airplane seat.

"Feeling better?"

"A little."

Lydia eyed her. "You should lay down. See if you can get some rest. You look tired."

"I feel tired."

"Go on back. I'll wake you in a few hours."

Letty shuffled down the hallway and stepped into her childhood bedroom. The yellow walls welcomed her. She glanced around the space where she'd grown up. It was as she remembered it with the patchwork quilt, the pink stuffed flamingo, the bookcase of L. Frank Baum books and other fantasies like *Into the Land of the Unicorns* and *So You Want to Be a Wizard*, and the tower of CD cases from Backstreet Boys to The Carpenters. This spot had been her retreat, her fortress, her place of solitude. She'd navigated childhood and adolescence in that room.

Lying on the bed, beneath the quilt, hugging the flamingo to her chest, she squeezed her eyes shut. In her mind's eye, she couldn't erase Thane's face. She fell into a fitful sleep while thinking about him.

What was supposed to be a weekend escape became a week. And then a second. And then a third. The day came when Letty couldn't avoid it anymore. She had to go back to where it all began—to her childhood home where Letty's world had crumbled.

She borrowed Lydia's car but didn't tell her where she was going. If she had, Lydia would've asked to come, too, but she had to do this alone. She'd been alone that night, so she had to be alone again.

While she drove, she thought back on her childhood home. It had been a small trailer, painted a pale yellow with lavender trim and a white door. She'd been five years old when her mom had redecorated it and let Letty choose the paint colors. Yellow had always been Letty's favorite color, so she picked a swatch of the prettiest yellow she could find. Then her mom showed her samples that would go with that shade of yellow, and Letty picked a soft shade of purple. Her mom bought the paint cans that day, and they painted the trailer together.

Letty drove down the winding dirt road toward where the trailer had sat in the woods, surrounded by pine trees and palmetto bushes. The closer she got to it, the more her hands froze on the steering wheel, the more her palms and underarms perspired, the more her mouth went dry, the more her heart pounded. She hadn't gone back there since the police had taken her away, and she had never thought she'd return.

Dirt floated into the air behind the car, looking like

a dust storm blocking her way from turning around and escaping. Except, she didn't want to turn back now. She wanted to face this head-on. Otherwise, she feared she'd never move forward. For Thane, for the two of them to have any hope, she had to do this.

She maneuvered the car around the final curve. "What the—" She slowed the car to a stop and gaped at what she saw. Gone was the yellow and purple trailer. Gone was the tiny cement driveway. Gone was any proof that a home had stood there, that a crime had happened there, for in its place was a garden.

Amazed, she shoved the car in park and climbed out.

Lush green grass replaced the lot. Stepping stones with sparkling glass to look like butterflies and dragonflies created a path through the garden. She followed them past pink rose bushes and potted daisies. Hand over her heart, she gazed around in awe. Bonsai trees trimmed to perfection were placed in beautiful displays with statues of angels surrounded by clusters of marigolds.

Butterflies fluttered above soft pink snapdragons, and bright yellow daffodils erupted from the ground around birdbaths. She passed rows of sweet peas and inhaled their yummy scent that reminded her of being a child, because sweet pea perfume had been her mom's preferred scent.

Throat clenching with memories, Letty continued on through the garden. She found a small pond with lily pads floating on the surface and fat koi fish swimming lazily above smooth river rocks. Sunlight reflected off the water, and a fragrant breeze made her curls dance.

She followed the stepping stones beyond the koi pond to the heart of the garden where a bench sat among daylilies in yellow, orange, pink, and purple.

Beside the bench, she found a plaque, held up by a sturdy pole. Golden letters engraved on the plaque spelled out:

For Carmen Ambrosia
And Charm Ambrosia

She skimmed her fingers over their names. Then she peered around at the majestic garden, unbelieving that this was here for them. The darkness of what had transpired in this very spot had been cleared away and replaced with beauty. It no longer bore any resemblance to a place of fear. It didn't look like a crime scene.

She sat on the bench. Eyes closed, she inhaled the clean air, the sweet fragrance of flowers, the crispness of greenery, and the earthiness of dirt. Peace descended over her. She stayed there for a long time, listening to birds and watching butterflies flit from bloom to bloom. This garden was everything she hadn't had when she was growing up with Constantine. This garden was full of tranquility and love and happiness. This garden didn't have a drop of Constantine in it. She saw her mom in the angels' faces. And she saw herself in the flowers' heads.

After a while, she made her way back to the car. She paused at the driver's side door and glanced toward the woods, the same woods she'd torn through to escape Constantine's murderous hands.

Swallowing, she dropped her keys back into her

purse.

I have to…

And with a few steps, she entered the woods.

Chills raked her spine. She wrapped her arms around herself to fend of the fear from that night that swooped around her, smothering her. The woods were full of shadows. The sun came down in streams through the trees' branches, but not enough to light up the ground. Pine needles and pinecones crunched under her sneakers, reminding her of how her tiny feet had been cut up after her frantic trek. She headed in the direction of the Anderson home.

Every step increased her anxiety.

On the other side of the woods, she'd left her childhood behind; she'd killed someone. Shivers shook her body. Her throat constricted. Part of her begged for her to turn back to safety, but she couldn't stop her feet from moving forward.

The terror she'd felt that night dropped onto her, making her knees buckle. She tripped and caught herself on the trunk of a tree. Her heart raced. The sound of Constantine shouting her name returned to her, as if he were in these very woods with her now, chasing her, hunting her.

She broke into a run.

Desperation had her throwing herself through overgrown brush just as it had that night. If thorns scratched her, she didn't feel them. Going into those woods alone had been a mistake. Eyes blurring with tears, she pushed her legs to go faster. Had the run felt this long that night? How had she managed it so young? So small? And considerably slower? An angel must've been by her side, lending a wing to carry her faster. Or perhaps it had been her mom, taking her away so she wouldn't share the same fate.

Right when panic set in, Letty burst out of the woods to discover a two-story building where the Anderson home used to stand. She halted and blinked at it in wonder. Curious, and panting for breath, she circled around a white picket fence toward a wooden sign. Growing at the base of the sign were blue morning glories that matched the dark blue paint of the letters spelling the business's name—All Heart Sanctuary for Women and Children.

She plastered a hand to her mouth.

All Heart.

Thane.

He had built a home for families escaping domestic violence on the very spot where she'd killed Constantine in self-defense. And he'd had a peaceful garden planted at the sight of her mother's murder. He'd never told her. Would he have?

Tears zipped down her cheeks.

Thane really was all heart.

Gripping her purse, she walked up to the door of the sanctuary and knocked.

22

Thane

One month became two months.

To keep himself busy, Thane focused on work more than ever before. He stayed in his office hours after everyone else left for the day. Several times, he slept there, bending his body into uncomfortable positions on the loveseat. He had to do something so he wouldn't think about Letty all hours of the day and night, but, of course, that was exactly what he ended up doing when he decided to push the launch for the domestic abuse chatroom app.

Every day, he worked with his team to fine-tune the logo's design, the app's pages, beta test it, and run security checks. Doing that, though, kept Letty on the front of his mind, because he was doing it for her. Not to mention how the paparazzi wouldn't let him forget that she was gone. They'd long since noticed her absence and hounded him outside his penthouse and All Heart Tech around the clock.

Time dragged on, but before he knew it, it was time to launch the app. He sat behind a mike at a long table. His team sat on either side of him and a room full of tech journalists occupied the seating spread out in front of him.

One by one, he answered their questions, like what inspired him to create this app, what it meant to him to be a domestic violence awareness advocate, and what else All Heart Tech would do for women and children experiencing abuse.

"What would your father think about this app?" someone asked.

Thane's lips lifted in a dangerous smile. "We all know who my father was and what he'd done. He never would've allowed Canmore Tech to come out with an app like this, because it's an app that would've taken away his control. That's why Canmore Tech no longer exists and All Heart Tech does. When I renamed the company and rebranded it, it wasn't a publicity stunt or to merely distance myself or the company from him. This company *is* all heart. We will continue to do things like this because we *have* heart."

Many of them nodded approvingly while taking notes.

"You fired five members of your board a few months ago. Was that because those former board members were all from the Canmore Tech era?"

"Partly. Information came to me that revealed they didn't harbor my morals. Everyone who works for All

Heart Tech has to represent the brand, not only in what they do at work but also in their personal lives. My employees have the drive to do good."

"Is that why you fired your sister?"

His lips twitched. "No comment."

Several of them chuckled at that.

Directly across from him a reporter with a beard, wearing hot pink stilettos and matching nails raised their hand.

Thane nodded. "Go ahead, Jay."

"This app will help many women who feel trapped and afraid to leave. What would you like to say to them?"

"You're not alone. All Heart Tech is here for you. We're listening. We care. We will do whatever we can."

Beside Jay, India, a Black woman with a small afro, asked, "The app's name has been closely guarded by your company. Well, it's launch day, so you have to tell us.

What is this app called?"

"Letty's Corner."

Silence.

Every journalist and cameraperson in that room didn't say a word for several seconds. When their surprise faded, cameras clicked in a frenzy. Journalists shoved their recorders forward and shouted questions all at once.

"What does that name mean to you?" India called out.

"It means I'm in her corner. I am in her mother's corner. I am in the corner of every woman and child experiencing domestic abuse." He tapped his index finger against the surface of the table each time for emphasis. "Every member of my team who helped to make this app a reality is in their corner. They paid attention, asked the right questions, and came up with the right ideas. The staff who will be monitoring the app behind the scenes are in their corner, too. We stand behind the victims of domestic violence and child abuse. We stand beside them. We stand in front of them, like shields." He paused. "I stand behind, beside, and in front of Letty. I'm in her corner and always will be."

More questions.

"That's all the time we have," he said and rose to his feet.

Their questions followed him out the door.

"Does Letty know about this app?"

"What does she say about it?"

"Have you talked to her?"

No, I haven't. And I may never have the chance to talk to her again.

The door closed, silencing their intruding voices.

23

Letty

"What are you doing?" Lydia asked, with her hands planted on her hips.

Letty frowned at the bowl of cereal in front of her and waved her spoon in the air. "Isn't that obvious?"

"I mean, what are you doing in general. It's been two months, Letty."

Letty's throat tightened. She set the spoon in the bowl, submerging it in almond milk. "I know how long it's been, and you said I could stay here as long as I needed."

"I did say that, and I meant it, but, sweetie, yesterday I caught you staring at a picture of Thane on your phone and you looked so damn heartbroken, but the thing is...Thane is still there. Waiting for you. He didn't go anywhere. You did. And I understand why you did. You were terrified, and after everything that happened, you had every right to be. Meeting Thane, falling in love with him, and these people harassing you brought up a lot of trauma that triggered your night terror and activated your fight-or-flight defense. Fleeing is a valid reaction. And everything you've felt and all your reasons for leaving when you did are also valid, but at this point, you're only hurting yourself and Thane unnecessarily."

Tears crowded in her eyes. "I hate that I'm hurting him."

"I know you do." Lydia walked around the table, put an arm around Letty's shoulders, and gave her an affectionate squeeze. "I know that you never intended to cause him pain, and I believe he knows that, too. The fact that he hasn't been calling you or texting you says that he respects the decision you made and cares about your wellbeing. Speaking of which, I've watched you over the past two months. You've done so much healing. You faced your demons by going back to your childhood home, you've talked to a therapist, and you've procrastinated by volunteering every day at All Heart Sanctuary. But you can't keep your life on pause anymore. It's time for you to make another decision. Will you go back to New York to be with Thane or to end things?" She lowered her head and rested her chin on Letty's shoulder. "We both know which of those options you want to do. You're just scared to do it."

"I am scared." Tears streamed down her cheeks. A drop fell off her jaw and landed in her cereal. She pushed the bowl away. "I love him so much but a knife was thrown at him because we were together, and I attacked him in my sleep, and it's been two months. We hadn't even been together that long. What if he met someone else?"

"You know he hasn't." Lydia rotated Letty around to face her. "No more 'buts.' Ands. You love Thane so much *and*...fill in the blank."

"I love Thane so much and..." She paused. "...and I miss him."

Her mom nodded. "Keep going."

"I love him so much and hate that strangers think they have a say over whether or not we should be together."

"I fucking hate that, too. More. What else?"

"I love him so much and hate that Constantine is still hurting us from beyond the grave by creeping into my dreams."

"The asshole needs to be exercised."

The corners of Letty's lips twitched and stilled. Looking her mom in the eye, she said, "I love Thane so much, and it doesn't matter anymore who his father is because Thane is his own person. Thane is everything his father wasn't and nothing his father was. I love him for him."

"Good. Don't stop."

"I love Thane so much, and I believe he loves me, too."

"Fact."

Letty laughed. "I love him so much, and I want to tell him that. I love him so much and want to spend the rest of my life with him. I love him so much and was foolish to stay away for as long as I have. I love him so much and want to see him. Today. I love him so much and won't let anyone or anything drive me away ever again."

Her mom beamed as her eyes misted. "That's my girl. So, what are you going to do?"

"I'm going to get the first flight back to New York."

"And?"

"And I'm going back to Thane."

"And?"

"And I'm going to tell him I'm sorry and that I love him and that I'm here to stay."

Her mom extracted a silver credit card from her back pocket and held it up triumphantly. "We'll redeem my air miles.

Letty arrived in New York at five o'clock after catching the first available flight. In the airport, she sat in a chair and called Yawanda, just as she had done when she'd landed in Georgia. Yawanda answered with a happy greeting.

"I'm back," Letty blurted.

There was a pause and then, "Back-back?"

"Back-back. I'm in JFK."

"Holy shit."

"Yeah."

"This is sudden. This morning you didn't say anything about coming back today."

"This morning, I didn't know I *was* coming back today."

"So, what made you hop on a plane?"

"Thane. I came back for Thane."

Yawanda hooted. The snapping of her fingers came through the phone. "Yas, girl! It's about damn time!"

"I came back for the shop, too, of course."

"Shoot. Forget the shop. Go get your man!"

Letty laughed, but it died quickly. "I'm nervous."

"Of course, you are. I would be, too, but Thane has been a saint. That man has superhero patience. Don't let him wait another minute longer."

"Okay. I'm going." She stood and gripped the handle to her rolling luggage.

"Letty, before you go…"

"Yeah?"

"I'm glad you're back."

"Me, too."

Letty hailed a cab to All Heart Tech, figuring Thane hadn't left work for the night.

Security did a double take when she walked in. She gave a small nod and continued to the elevators, glad that she had clearance so Thane didn't have to be tipped off of her arrival. That didn't stop her nerves from being a jumbled mess, though.

A figure appeared beside her as she pressed the button to summon the elevator. "Damn." Abbot grinned at her.

"Hey," she said.

"You're a sight for sore eyes, Letty. Does he know you're here?"

"Not yet."

"And I repeat…*damn*." Abbot let out a laugh. "You're answering his prayers right now." He lifted his balled fist. "Welcome back."

She tapped her fist to his. "Thanks."

The elevator whisked her up to the top floor. When it opened, Rebekah gasped. She sprang out of her chair, hurried around her desk, and gathered Letty in a tight hug. "I knew you'd return. I knew it."

Letty nudged her chin at the door to Thane's office. "Is he in there?"

"Yes. Everyone has left for the day. I'll go, too, so the two of you can have privacy." She powered off her computer and snatched up her purse. "Have a good night, Letty."

"You, too, Rebekah."

She waited until the elevator's doors closed before approaching Thane's door. Her pulse was frantic with anticipation, her knees weak. She sucked in a shaky breath. Then she raised her hand and knocked.

24

Thane

Thane stared out the window at the city sparkling with the glow of lights. All the reports for the app ran through his mind. He thought about the number of downloads, the number of people who were already using it to save themselves, and considered what All Heart Tech could do next.

A knock sounded.

A second later, his door opened.

He didn't turn. "You can go home, Rebekah. I'll see you tomorrow."

Rebekah's reply didn't come, though. A voice he'd dreamt about for two months spoke instead. "It's me, Thane. It's Letty."

He stopped breathing.

Please let it be true. Please don't let it be a cruel

hallucination from exhaustion. He turned slowly, not wanting to come face to face with his empty office, but there Letty stood. Magnificent. Gorgeous. Real. She wore a pink dress with quarter sleeves that skimmed her knees, and she never looked more beautiful.

Unfortunately, all Thane could do was stare, unmoving, in shock, afraid that if he so much as breathed, she'd vanish.

Letty smiled, but he couldn't get his body to do a damn thing.

"Hi," she said.

He couldn't get his mouth to form a response.

She approached him, and still his body was paralyzed. A couple of feet away, she came to a stop. "I should've called. I shouldn't have just shown up, but I wanted to surprise you." Her head tipped to the side. A curl slid over her cheek.

His hands twitched.

A sign of life. That was good.

"Although, I hadn't expected this." She shifted back. *No.*

"Thane, I really need you to do or say something, because first and foremost, I came back for you. Over my shop. Over my friends. Over my apartment. I came back *for you.*"

Her words unstuck him. He launched forward, closed the distance between them in two strides, and grabbed her into a kiss. "Don't ever leave again," he said against her lips.

She grasped his shoulders. "I won't, I won't, I won't—"

He crushed his mouth to hers again, taking her vow

into him.

She pressed into him. *My God, the feel of her body, her scent.* How he'd missed her scent. Having it on his pillow, while it had sustained him, didn't equate, not when her skin gave the perfume a scent that was uniquely her.

Letty inched back. "I love you. I love you so much."

Her claim staggered him, and he cupped her face. "I love you, too. Loving you was instantaneous. Natural. Total."

Their kisses became increasingly more passionate with each second that passed. He lowered his hands from her face, stroked his palms down her arms, and then clasped her waist. While their lips were locked, he let his hands reacquaint themselves with her shape. Slowly, he moved his hands to her back, up and down. Finally, he molded his hands to her butt and yanked her even closer.

Letty moaned and shuddered. "Make love with me."

He leaned back to gaze into her eyes.

"Please, Thane. During the flight and car ride here, I was thinking about you and this moment and imagining what could happen...what I want to happen. Make love with me. Please."

The moment she said the second "please," he swept her into his arms and set her on his desk. He cradled the back of her head with one hand and stamped his mouth over hers. She responded to his hunger with an appetite just as fierce. He stroked his tongue against hers, needing to fill himself with her taste, her heat. She hooked her legs around him and drew him close. His thighs dug into the edge of the desk.

"This would be easier with a bed."

Breathless, she met his eyes. "There's absolutely

nothing wrong with this desk."

Needing to feel her skin, he slipped a hand beneath the skirt of her dress and caressed her thigh. A small sound escaped her, and her hips pivoted against him. The contact ignited him everywhere.

He slid his hand higher up her thigh to her hip, where he worked his fingers beneath the band of her panties. With his hand plastered to her hip, he could feel even more her excited movement when she rocked her hips forward again.

Thane paused. "Are you sure about this?"

She met his eye. "Yes. I want you. All of you."

His jaw clenched. Her words stirred his already raging libido. "A couple of months ago I had myself tested. I'm negative for everything, but the papers are at my penthouse."

Her fingers contracted on his. "That's okay. I believe you. I have papers at home, too. They're almost a year old, but I haven't been with anyone in…let's just say a long time. I haven't wanted anyone. No one but you." Her mouth fastened to his.

A groan broke from his throat. He slipped her panties down her legs and dropped them to the floor at his feet. Then he lifted her off the desk and carried her to the love seat where she straddled his lap.

As their tongues glided together, he reached for the zipper at her back. Gradually, he lowered the zipper a few links at a time. Once the zipper was as low as it would go, he slipped his hand beneath the warm fabric. His fingers brushed over her spine and soft skin, but then he felt the slightly-raised and shiny-smooth texture of a scar. When he shifted his fingers, he found another thin mark.

He leaned back, disconnecting their kiss, and continued to feel her back, pausing when his fingers met with yet another piece of evidence from past hurts.

She lowered her gaze. "Those are my scars. From Alec's riding crop."

"Stand for me."

She complied. With his hands on her hips, he guided her around. Still sitting, he parted the sides of her dress to expose her back. Several pale pink scars marred her skin. They were thin and widened at one end where the keeper, a leather tongue, had met her skin. Keepers were supposed to prevent the rod from marking horses, but Alec must've used so much force that the keeper couldn't do its job. Both the keeper and the rod had made contact with her back, cutting her skin.

"May I touch them?"

Her voice was a whisper. "Yes."

He skimmed his fingers over each one. Five. Then he kissed them. "I'm never going to let anyone hurt you like this again." It was a promise that he'd sacrifice his own life to ensure.

Letty rotated. She curled her hands over his shoulders, pushed him back, and then climbed atop his lap again.

Needs swelled inside him. He slipped his hands beneath the fabric of her dress, and she shivered against him. The action had him going hard. When she rubbed against the bulge in his pants, a rumble clawed up his throat. Her hand slid down his chest and unzipped his pants, unleashing him to his full capacity. She leveled up over him, but he gripped her hips to still her. "I don't have a condom."

She grazed his bottom lip with her thumb. "It's okay.

I track my cycle. I'm past ovulation. And I want you. Like this."

Her hand closed around him, stroked.

He squeezed his eyelids shut and touched his forehead to hers.

"I want you like this inside me."

He clenched his jaw, nodded; he wanted that, too.

She guided him into her, and my God, it nearly shattered him right then. She moved slowly at first, rocking, rubbing, building up the sensation until the pleasure grew to the point where neither of them could endure that tempo anymore. Her hips moved faster and faster. Overcome, she threw her head back and arched her body. He wrapped his arms around her, supporting her. She gripped his shoulders, anchoring herself, while her hips became a frenzy of movements.

What she was doing was so intense that he was paralyzed beneath her. All he could do was hold on and enjoy it. Damn did he enjoy it. He reveled in her passion, both the passion she gave herself and what she gave him.

Before he could warn her, he came. Even while his body purged his lust into her, he reacted quickly. He slipped one hand between them, found her clitoris, and rubbed it. Letty bent backward even more. Small breaths fluttered from her opened mouth. The sensations were so great that she was holding her breath. Her hips and abdomen quivered again and again. Warm liquid squirted onto his finger. She sang out several times in a row before her body became fluid, and she collapsed onto him, sated.

He kissed her shoulder.

"Mm."

He rubbed her back. "Are you okay?"

"Mm-hm."

He smiled and dropped another kiss onto her shoulder. "I love you, Letty."

She eased back to gaze into his eyes. "I love you, too."

God, he'd been yearning to hear her say that for so long. He didn't want this moment to end, and he was glad when it didn't.

They cuddled on the love seat, whispering for hours. It felt so good to have her in his arms, to hear her voice, to smell her hair, her skin, and the scent of her cum. He inhaled deeply and trailed his fingers up between her thighs. She parted her legs for him, but his skimming fingers halted at the apex of her legs. A whimper left her, and he hardened. Just like that.

He scooped her up into his arms and stood.

She let out a small gasp. "Where are you taking me?"

"To my shower."

Water pulsed down on them as they kissed and sucked each other's lips. Once they were dripping and warm, he coaxed her onto the wide, waist-high ledge for bottles of shampoo and bodywash. He squirted a dollop of his own bodywash into his palm, worked it into a lather between his hands, and then smoothed the soap over Letty's shoulders and down her arms to her hands. He rubbed her breasts until her chest was covered with a blanket of velvety bubbles. Between the tips of his fingers, he rolled her hard, taut nipples to the sound of Letty's breathy sighs. She leaned her head against the damp tile, and his hands journeyed lower. When they brushed her navel, she inhaled.

Smirking, Thane squirted more bodywash into his

palm and lowered his hands to her right ankle. He worked the soap over her shin and then massaged her thigh, kneading it sensually. Just when she was humming, he switched to her other leg, starting once again at her ankle. He purposefully gave her left thigh a little more attention, moving higher and higher. His fingertips skated between her legs, and she parted her thighs once more. Still, he postponed what she wanted. When she captured her bottom lip with her teeth, he stroked his bubble-slicked fingers over her pussy.

Letty moaned.

He massaged every centimeter of her, memorizing, enticing. Then he focused on her clitoris. One finger, two fingers. Small circles, bigger circles. Clockwise, counterclockwise. Up and down. Side to side. Diagonally.

"Like that," she panted. "Like that."

He'd found the ticket—two fingers, diagonally, fast and hard.

She came with a cry that echoed in the shower.

He lifted the showerhead and sprayed the streams of water over her, washing away the bubbles. Her breathing returned to normal, but the heat in her eyes hadn't diminished. Standing before him, she took the showerhead and directed the beads to course down his body. The warm water loosened his tensed muscles, but the moment she soaped his chest, he became rigid with desire.

She made circles over his chest and abdomen, as if she were waxing on and waxing off. He closed his eyes to enjoy the feel of her lathered hands exploring him. She soaped his back and buttocks, making his dick jerk. Then her fingers were mixing bubbles with the hair on his thighs. He groaned.

Her fingers curled around him, and he inhaled sharply between his teeth. The feel of her hand, the sleekness of the bubbles, and the heat of the water excited him beyond reason. Letty pressed her naked body into his side. He looped an arm around her hips, holding her close while his blood roared. With sure strokes, she encouraged him to glorious climax that was like a surge.

Letty hosed off his body, sending the remnants of bubbles from his body down the drain. After he turned off the faucet, he tied a towel around his hips and bundled Letty in another towel.

As soon as they dried off and dressed, he drove Letty home to his penthouse and carried her to the bed—*their* bed—where they put their mouths on each other, but they stopped before they came, edging each other to excruciating pleasure. Only when he was inside her, stroking deep, sinking thoroughly, with the two of them clutching each other, moaning and gasping, did they drive each other over the brink again.

25

Letty

*I*n the morning, Letty slipped from the bed, cracked open the closet to find her dresses still there, removed the white dress with black and yellow flowers, and tiptoed into the bathroom. Seeing her cosmetics where she'd left them was like a jab to her heart. She showered fast, brushed her teeth, applied a bit of makeup, and fixed her hair. When she came out, Thane sat with his back against the headboard.

"Did I wake you? I tried to be quiet."

He shook his head. "I woke when I realized the bed was empty." He glanced over at the spot where she'd been sleeping. "I thought I'd dreamt last night."

Shaking her head, she went to him and cupped a hand to the side of his face. "It was real. Every beautiful, satisfying moment of it."

He angled his head and kissed the palm of her hand.

"I'm going to start the coffee. I know where everything is. Take your time." She kissed him before leaving.

The sound of the shower running came to her as she prepared the coffee maker. She didn't know what to make for breakfast, so she popped halved bagels into the toaster and located a container of cream cheese. She was plopping a small handful of rinsed blueberries on their plates with sliced strawberries when Thane wrapped his arms around her waist. His face nuzzled her neck, and he kissed her skin there, igniting her nerve endings.

"You smell so good," he whispered.

"That reminds me...why do the pillows on your bed smell like my perfume?"

"Because I missed you. Because I sprayed them with your perfume. Because I'm a sentimental fool."

She faced him. "I really hurt you, didn't I? I didn't want to or mean to, but I did."

"That's in the past. You're in my arms now."

She didn't speak.

Although he wore dress pants and a belt, he was shirtless. Her gaze lowered to his bare shoulder. She traced the scar on his shoulder with the tip of her finger.

He caught her chin with his fingers. "I researched PTSD night terrors. I made a mistake by touching you and trying to wake you. I'm not supposed to interfere but wait it out. I know that now."

His words struck her; he really did want to take

care of her, but he also thought what had happened had been his fault. She looped her arms around his neck and settled her head in the crook of his shoulder. "The most important thing is that I want you there once my night terrors release me. I don't want anyone else there but you."

He held her close. "I will always be there. Always."

She touched her lips to his and said, "We should eat something. Re-fuel and all that, so we can indulge in each other tonight. In your bed."

"Sounds like a plan."

They ate side by side at the counter.

Letty enjoyed being close to him like this again. It felt normal. Natural. Real. And she didn't want to give it up for anything.

When Letty entered her shop, Yawanda spun around. Her crochet locs spread out like a fan. She scanned Letty from head to toe. "You've got the sex glow written all. Over. You." She snapped her fingers with each word. "You and Thane did the nasty all night long, didn't you?"

Letty grimaced. "'Did the nasty,' really?" She thought about the hours in his office and then in his bed. Her cheeks warmed. "Actually, that term is accurate. So, yeah, we did."

Yawanda laughed. "Yes, you did!" She propped herself on the counter. "Now spill. Thane…give me all the juicy details. And don't skip the *juice*."

Letty shook her head. "I am most definitely

skipping the juice, whatever that means, but I can tell you that whatever your dirty mind has conjured is one hundred percent accurate."

"I had a feeling he wouldn't disappoint. He can't hide it with those suits. They actually make it worse."

They do.

"Okay. I need to get to work or else I'll start having some inappropriate thoughts about your boyfriend." Yawanda paused. "Oops. Too late."

"I'll give you a free pass this once."

Letty peered around the shop, realizing right then how much she'd missed it. It was her home. More so than her apartment. "How has it been inside the shop lately?"

"Pretty quiet with you gone. For a while, it was busier than ever while everyone flocked here to see if you were really gone, but after a couple of weeks, that died down. The paparazzi had also returned in force. Once they realized you weren't around, though, they abandoned their posts. Sales are back to normal. Pre-Thane normal."

Pre-Thane sales had been good, so that didn't bother Letty.

A few minutes after opening the shop, a customer came in. Their neck swiveled around when they spotted Letty behind the counter. They dug through a designer bag and removed a matching phone case. Manicured nails tapped on the device. Then they angled it toward Letty. A tap later and a photo had been captured of her.

Yawanda propped her hands on her hips. "Do I have to explain the 'no cell phone' rule inside this shop?"

The customer dropped the phone into their bag. With a sniff, they spun on their heel to face a display of scarves hanging from an antique coat rack.

While Letty checked out the customer's purchase of a vintage silk scarf, she wondered who they'd sent that text to. Sasha? Jessalyn?

Thirty minutes later, her question was answered when a rapping sound came from the shop window. A paparazzo stood there wearing a black T-shirt with a logo stamped across his chest. As soon as she faced the window, he lifted his camera and clicked away on the hammer.

"Letty, where have you been? Did you break up with Thane? What's going on?"

Hands in fists, Yawanda marched up to the window. "This is a business establishment. We're working in here and providing a peaceful atmosphere for our customers, so I know you're not shouting questions at my best friend!"

"Sorry, Miss Yawanda."

Yawanda returned to the counter.

Letty tilted her head. "Miss Yawanda?"

"While you were gone, I had to deal with them. Let's just say they got to know my name and learned how to show some respect."

Letty grinned. "That's my girl."

The news of Letty's return spread quickly.

Two hours later, the shop was packed. They might've been there for the scoop and to get a good look, but they were still customers. Letty rang up their purchases and offered assistance when they had questions about an item or asked her for something specific. She was walking past the counter after helping a customer test an antique gramophone when her eye caught something. Her feet stilled, and her gaze surveyed the opened jewelry box on the counter. She shifted aside a few of the larger pieces but didn't see it.

"Hey, Yawanda, did you sell the gold locket?"

Yawanda handed a small bag to a customer. "The one with the single diamond and star engraving? Yeah. Last month, I think."

Letty's heart fractured at that news. She'd always wanted to be there when it was sold, to see who the new owner would be. She supposed it was a good thing she hadn't been there, though. It would've been hard for her to part with it.

At lunch time, Letty and Yawanda took turns eating in the backroom. Letty told Yawanda to go first and to take her time. While Yawanda ate, Letty manned the front by herself. Fortunately, Sasha never showed her face. If she did, Letty was prepared to call the cops. Jessalyn didn't show up, either. Letty wasn't sure if Thane's sister had ever stepped foot inside Let It Charm You or if Jessalyn thought the shop was beneath her and wouldn't dare sink so low as to step a stiletto on Let It Charm You's floor. Even with their absence, Letty had her hands full.

No one asked her prying questions.

No one spat rude remarks.

No one attempted to capture an image of her on their phones.

But it was clear why they were there. As soon as they entered the shop, their greedy gazes latched onto her.

Chrys Fey

Yeah, she thought, *it's me. I'm not hiding anymore.*

She was so over hiding her love from the world that she asked Thane to have dinner. Out in public. In front of prying eyes.

Letty studied the dresses hanging in her closet. She had many options to wear on their public dinner date. One by one she pushed aside hangers until she came across one that had her smirking. It was red. Bright, vixen red. A seductress' red. If strangers were going to scrutinize her and call her a gold-digging tramp, she might as well should take a page from Scarlett O'Hara's book and look the part. The quarter sleeves were lace. The hem came a few inches above her knee, and a strip of lace to match the sleeves extended the rest of the way to cover her knees. A scoop neck didn't offer a glimpse of her beasts, but the dress clung to every curve. She added black heels and red lipstick to complete the look.

When she stepped out of the bedroom to where Thane waited in her apartment, he turned and froze. "You look stunning." He tilted his head as she continued to walk toward him. "Actually, you're bewitching."

She smiled.

"Enticing," he added.

She stopped in front of him. He wore a black three-piece suit with a silk shawl lapel, a white shirt, and a black bow tie. She trailed her fingers down the shawl lapel. "Enticing is a good word," she said. "So is magnetic. And mouthwatering."

He skimmed a finger along her jawline. "Check and check." His gaze lowered, and he ran a hand down her left sleeve. "Do all your clothes cover your scar?"

"The ones I wear out?" She nodded. "I never wanted anyone to see it, the thing that links me to my past, to that little girl. Plus, it's not exactly cute."

He curled a finger under her chin. "Every part of you is beautiful."

"You're biased."

"Never."

She laughed. "So, where are we going for dinner?"

"I got us a reservation at a restaurant where all the rich and famous dine. You did say you wanted to give them a show, didn't you?"

"I did. How'd you get a reservation on such short notice, though?"

He shrugged. "Gave my name."

"Ah. The perks of being Thane Canmore."

He looped his arms around her, pulled her close, and nibbled on her bottom lip. "This is a perk of being me. I get to kiss you whenever I want."

"Yes, you do," she muttered against his mouth. "But if you do too much of it, we'll

be late for the reservation."

"They'd still give us a table," he said against her lips.

"Mm." She indulged in his kiss a moment before shifting away. "Abbot is waiting. I don't want to give him any ideas about what we're doing if we come down an hour past when we're supposed to."

Thane laced his fingers with hers. "All right. Let's go." He kissed the back of her hand. "I *am* starving." The wink he gave her told her he wasn't talking about food.

Thirty minutes later, they arrived at a restaurant that Letty had only dreamed of eating at. A massive chandelier hung from the ceiling, and the maître d' stood beneath it at an ornate podium. She scanned the gold-edged pages in a thick book laid out before her. "Welcome to The Ruby Spoon, Mr. Canmore." She glanced at Letty, and confusion drifted over her face, causing crinkles between her brows as she debated how to address Letty. "And...guest."

"Ms. Remis," Thane corrected.

The maître d's cheeks seared pink. "Yes, of course. My apologies, Ms. Remis."

Letty shook her head. "That's okay."

"We have a special table for you. Our best table. I hope it is to your satisfaction." She guided them through the dining room, past countless tables where elegantly dressed patrons sat, eating from sterling silver forks and sipping champagne from crystal flutes. Their gazes lifted and latched onto Letty. She felt their judgement and had a feeling what they must be thinking.

She doesn't belong here.

She's not one of us.

She shouldn't be with him.

Who does she think she is?

Her heart raced, and she gripped Thane's arm. He reacted quickly and laid his other hand over hers. Then he dipped his head and whispered, "It's okay, baby."

She forced herself to breathe.

At the back of the dining space, they were presented with a single table set on a platform four steps above the dining floor, elevating it above all the rest. It sat in a nook with three angled windows that provided a stunning view of the city and the evening sky. Thane pulled out the chair for her, and she sat, thankful to not be on her shaky legs anymore. The walk to the table had been a real test. If it hadn't been for Thane, she either would've frozen up or tripped and fallen flat on her face.

The maître d' handed them menus. "If there is anything you need, please let us know."

"We will. Thank you."

All Letty could do was smile.

The maître d' bowed her head before excusing herself.

"Are you okay?" The concern in Thane's voice practically embraced her.

She glanced to her right, where the entire dining room was laid out before her and countless gazes were trained in their direction. "All this table is missing is a spotlight. Oh, wait." She peered up at three small lights shining down on them.

"We can go to another table. Or to another restaurant. Just say the word."

"No." She reached across the table and touched his hand. "I'll be fine."

He lifted her hand, kissed her fingers. "If, at anytime, you want to leave, let me know."

She nodded. "Why exactly is this table set up on a pedestal of sorts?"

"Because it's for the best."

"Like?"

"The president."

"The president of what?"

"The United States."

She blinked.

"Or Oprah. Or Common. Or Justin Timberlake. Or Kim K."

"And do you know all these influential people?"

"All but Kim."

"I'm a bit relieved about that."

He chuckled. "But I do know Khloe."

She nodded. "I'm okay with that."

They read over their menus. The prices were astronomical and made her throat tighten at the mere thought of dropping that much cash on a single meal. Her eyes widened when she saw the cost of a single Kobe beef steak that was covered in edible 24K gold. "What exactly does edible gold taste like?"

"You can order it and find out."

"I'll pass." She returned to her menu and mumbled under her breath, "The last thing people need is for their shit to be gold."

That had Thane bursting with laughter.

Several people faced them.

Her cheeks flamed. "Ssh."

Also on the menu was a pizza that cost even more than the Kobe beef steak, because not only did it have edible 24K gold but caviar and shaved truffles. A burger wasn't just a burger here, either, but included lobster and foie gras. Even a Philly Cheesesteak had foie gras in it. It seemed everything was either topped with caviar or a gold leaf, or both. Even their vanilla ice cream sundaes! Nachos were elevated to the tastes of the rich and famous, too, with a pound of crab meat, and yes, caviar. Grilled cheese, too, thanks to bread made with

Dom Perignon and normal butter swapped out for white truffle butter. She scanned the appetizers, but they weren't any better, including oyster pie. Gold-dusted chicken wings, tacos with tequila salsa, and lobster Frittatas. The options were more than daunting. They were ridiculous.

"I should've considered the menu before bringing you here. You look like you might faint or throw up."

She peered at Thane. "I think I'm in shock."

"We really can go somewhere else. I still love McDonalds."

"Next time. I think…I think I'll go with the crab cake." The crab cake was made with blue king crab, black truffles, Irish oysters, and topped with a teaspoon of golden caviar. At least it wasn't dusted with gold or platinum.

Thane lifted his hand in the air, and a moment later, a waiter stepped up to get their order. "The crab cake for Ms. Remis, and I'll take the A5 Wagyu Steak."

"And to drink?"

"A bottle of Dom Perignon."

"Very good, sir." The waiter left.

"The bill is going to be huge," she said.

"Don't even worry about that." He reached for her, and she stretched her arm out. He cupped her hand in his. With his fingers, he traced the thin bones on the back of her hand, giving her chills. "I know this restaurant makes you uncomfortable, but I want to give you things you've never had or experienced before."

"You're already doing that."

He gazed into her eyes.

"By loving me, you're already doing that."

He inhaled.

"I never accepted love before you. I never felt loved before you. I never *loved* before you. That means more to me than edible gold. *You* mean more to me."

His chest heaved. "Goddamn I want to kiss you." His voice was deep with lust, and his eyes were opaque in the intimate lighting.

The waiter came, popped a bottle of Dom, and filled their glasses.

She sipped. *So, this is what being rich tastes like?* It wasn't bad.

Thane set his glass down. "Still...what are things you've always wanted to do?"

She thought a moment. "Travel. I'd love to travel with you."

The lighting sparkled in his eyes. "Where'd you like to go?"

"Ireland, Scotland, New Zealand, Venice, South Africa, India, Egypt, Bali." She grinned from ear to ear. "Everywhere. I've dreamt about traveling the world." She stared into his eyes. "And I'd go anywhere with you."

"What else have you dreamt about?"

She knew what he was doing; he wanted to know her dreams, because he

wanted to give them to her. Her pulse raced. She swallowed and spoke from her heart. "See the Northern Lights, go on a safari and see elephants and lions in person, see the Grand Canyon, whale watch, sleep under the stars, go skinny dipping, or, better yet, go skinny dipping, make love under the stars, and then sleep under those same stars, in that order." She didn't break eye contact, because what she wanted to say next were her deepest desire. "Get married. Honeymoon in an amazing location. And have a baby. More, if kids are in the cards."

Thane's Adam's apple bobbed. "We can do that. We can do it all."

Her heart skipped a beat. "Thane…"

The waiter stepped up to their table right then, halting the words in her throat. He set their plates down and bowed before leaving. For the rest of dinner, they discussed lighter topics, but she couldn't get his comment out of her head.

We can do it all.

That held so many possibilities. That held a lifetime of promise. She wanted that. More than anything.

After they finished eating and drinking Dom, Thane paid the bill, making sure she didn't catch a glimpse of it, and then he escorted her outside. While they waited for the valet, they stood at the curb. She faced Thane, twined her arms around his neck, and kissed him. In front of everyone, and she didn't care.

He held her hips and leaned closer, but she shifted back to say, "What you said in there…that we can do it all. Did you mean that?"

Forehead to forehead, he said, "I always mean what I say."

She moved her hands to his face and pressed her lips to his, needing to taste, kiss, draw that vow inside her. The valet drove their car up beside them, and she stepped away reluctantly. At the penthouse, though, they picked up right where they had left off.

The next day, there was a picture of the two of them in a passionate lip lock on the cover of every tabloid and every celebrity news show.

John and Miranda, two hosts for a talk show, were arguing over their opinions on a relationship that should not be any of their business.

"I don't get how a man could want to bang the woman who killed his father," John said.

Letty winced at his use of the word "bang."

"She was a child," Miranda pointed out.

"Child, teenager, woman. It doesn't matter. She killed his father."

"In self-defense."

John scoffed.

"Everyone seems to forget what kind of man Constantine was. That happens when someone dies. But he was not a sweet, doting man. He was harsh. He abused his first wife, his son, and his second wife—"

"Speculation."

Miranda eyed him. "There's plenty of stories and images out there that say otherwise. Everyone keeps asking why is Thane with her? But I think, why *can't* he be with her? Why can't the two of them find happiness with each other? Thane has not been shy about his distain toward his deceased father and what kind of man Constantine was when he was alive. When you hear him talk, it's clear that there was no love between father and son." She pointed at the image of Thane and Letty in an intimate embrace behind her. "These two have been through things that no one could understand.

Somehow, they found each other after all these years. We may never know how that happened, and we don't need to know. Somehow, they fell in love, and no one has the right to say a damn thing about it. It's no one else's business."

"Damn straight," Letty said and shut off the TV. She popped off the couch, spun toward the kitchen, and froze when she saw Thane standing in the hallway. "Did you hear all that?"

He nodded. "We'll hear more of that for a while yet, and it'll get brought up during every important milestone in our relationship. When we marry..." He stepped toward her. "When we have our first child..." Another step. "Every anniversary. We won't ever escape it."

"Then we'll just have to ignore it."

He caressed her arms. "I'll cover your ears, if you cover mine."

She cupped her hands over his ears. "Done."

26

Thane

*T*hane was happier than he had been in a very long time, and it was all because of Letty. He wanted so much with her, and he believed it was all within his grasp.

Rebekah smiled when he stepped off the elevator. "To see the happiness written all over you these past two days..." Tears glistened beneath the lenses of her glasses. "It makes me so happy to see the life back in your eyes."

A small sob broke from her, and Thane wrapped her up in his arms.

"It broke my heart to see you so heartbroken."

"I'm sorry."

"I never had any children, but you're mine." She clutched him. "You're mine."

His arms tightened around her. "I am," he whispered in her ear. "I am *your* son."

She let out another sob.

He stroked her back. "Ssh." Even as he soothed the one true mother he'd had, he struggled to hold it together himself. Rebekah had been a rock. A beckon. A constant source of comfort and love when he needed it as a kid. She'd been there for him, and with him, through it all. She had remained a rock, a beckon, a source of comfort and love for him as an adult, too. Rebekah was his mother in every sense of the word, and he was proud and honored to be her child. Biology had nothing to do with it. Look at what biology had given him.

He hugged Rebekah until she was ready to end the embrace and stepped back.

Tears wet her cheeks. He removed her glasses carefully, freed his pocket square, and used it to wipe the tears from her cheeks.

She let out a laugh. "Thank you."

"No, thank you. You've been the best mother I ever could've asked for."

She snatched the pocket square. "Don't. You're going to have me blubbering again."

He squeezed her elbow. "I just needed to say that."

"Me, too. I've never said it out loud...how I've viewed you as my son ever since you were a child. It feels good to own that."

He kissed her forehead. "Same."

"Okay." Clearing her throat, she slipped her glasses back on. "So, how's Letty?"

"She's..." He gazed off and smiled like a fool.

"That look says it all."

Beaming, he said, "She's...everything. Everything good and beautiful and..."

Rebekah nodded. "That's exactly what all women want to hear." She tilted her head. "Did you tell her?"

"Tell her that she's everything?"

"No. That you love her."

"I did, but she told me she loves me first."

Rebekah sighed. "She's come a long way. I can tell. You did that."

He shook his head.

"Don't deny it. You did."

"*We* did," he corrected.

"You're right. I pray for only the best for the two of you."

"Thank you. We need it, because...well, we're a long way from things being quiet in our lives. Who knows what Constantine's lackeys have in store for her? They could have worse things planned. They could do something irreparable that'll break us apart for good. That is, after all, their goal."

"Fuck them," Rebekah spat.

Thane blinked. Never had he heard Rebekah drop the f-bomb. And he loved it! He felt like applauding. "I've never heard you curse before."

"Just because you've never heard it doesn't mean I never curse, and those bastards bring it out in me."

"I can see that."

"Vile language aside, you know I'm right."

"I do, and I share your sentiments. Vile language and all."

"Make sure Letty knows that no matter what they

do, you will always love her, and none of it is her fault."

"I'll do my best."

"I know you will. She couldn't have fallen in love with a better man."

"I appreciate that." Even though a part of him wondered if it was true. Would there ever come a day when he didn't doubt himself because of whose seed he came from?

Throughout the rest of the day, the need to see Letty became fierce. He was gearing up to leave minutes before five o'clock when Rebekah's voice came on the intercom. "A messenger is here with an envelope for you. Security checked him and the package."

Thane compressed the speaker button. "Send him in."

A moment later, a man wearing a hoodie clomped into his office. "Are you Thane Canmore?"

He stood. "I am."

The messenger held out a Manila envelope. When Thane closed his fingers around the other end, the man said, "You've been served."

Rebekah joined him when the messenger left. "What is it?"

Thane ripped open the envelope and worked out a stack of papers. He scanned it. A sneer manifested on his face. "Alec Danes is suing me for wrongful termination and assault." He lifted his gaze to Rebekah.

"That look is a dangerous one."

He could feel it. The rage. Simmering. Searing. "I don't know what you mean."

That rage came to a boil later at his penthouse when Letty showed him a package she'd found at her apartment when Abbot drove her there to check her mail before work. Inside a Manilla envelope was a single slip of paper and a tiny plastic bag. The note read: *You should've stayed gone*. And the three charms spelled out 'Dad.'

In the next instant, he whipped around, snatched up his keys from the counter, and marched toward the elevator.

"Thane! Don't. Please."

The elevator door opened, and he stepped in.

She jumped in, too.

"You're not coming with me," he said as the door slid into place.

"Thane, please come back to the penthouse. You might make things worse by confronting her."

"She needs to learn it's in her best interest to leave you alone." The elevator dinged, and the door whisked open. He hit the button for the penthouse, stepped out, and then blocked her way off.

"Seriously?"

"It's for your own safety." He kept his arms up and his hands braced on the outside of the elevator until the metal door cut them off.

His fury grew while he fought traffic all the way to Southampton. Vibrating with anger, he marched into Canmore mansion and toward Jessalyn's quarters.

A voice calling out to him had him pulling to a sudden stop.

His mother stood inside the sitting room. She wore black pants, a silk blouse, and tweed jacket. A string of pearls adorned her light brown neck. For the first time in his life, she appeared sober. Even after her other rehab stays, she'd be high or drunk by the time her chauffer brought her home.

"Mom." His temper dissolved at the sight of her. He met her in the living room and wrapped his arms around her. She didn't smell like booze but Chanel No 5. He leaned back and placed a hand on her cheek. "You look good."

"I feel good." She held his hand. "Come sit with me." She perched on the edge of the couch, angled toward him, and crossed her ankles. Her gaze lowered to her hands, placed elegantly on her lap. "In rehab, I faced many things, none of it pretty." She inhaled. "And I have to apologize to you." Her gaze lifted then, and her eyes were clear without the tell-tale signs of addiction. "I wasn't a good mother to you or Jessalyn. I was too concerned with what I wanted to worry about what my children deserved. You deserved a mother who was sober and present and strong. Instead, you got a mother who was sick and selfish and weak. I wish I had stood up to Constantine and taken you and Jessalyn away before it got as bad as it did. You never should've heard or seen the things you did. I hate what I put you both through, but more so for what I put *you* through." She squeezed his hands with thin, long fingers. "You were only being a good son, and I pushed you away." Tears swam over her eyes, and emotions choked her voice.

"Mom." He held her close. "You were sick. Nothing that happened was your fault. It was his fault. All of it."

"But having me for a mother just made things worse, and I'm so sorry." Her shoulders bounced up and down.

"Ssh." He rubbed her back. "It's okay now, Mom. It's okay."

After a moment, she eased back, sniffling.

"How long have you been home?"

"Since yesterday. I planned to call you today." She paused. "You know the rehab facility doesn't have any TVs and forbids social media to help us recover in peace?"

He nodded.

"Well, I've been out of the loop. This morning, though, I caught something on the news about you dating a woman named Letty."

Inside, he winced, but outside he remained immobile.

"They did a whole piece about it, detailing what they know about your relationship, when it started, what's happened since, and how odd it all is." Her finely arched brow lifted ever-so-slightly. "She was the little girl who…" Her words trailed off, as if voicing exactly who that little girl was and what she did was too much.

"Yes."

"How in the world did that happen?"

Thane told her everything.

She sat silently for a while, staring off at nothing in particular. Finally, she faced him. "I can't say I approve."

He figured as much.

"But I would like to meet her."

He hadn't expected that. "Really?"

"If you love her, I would like to meet her before your wedding day."

He grinned at that. "We're not there yet."

"Seeing how happy you are when you talk about her, I imagine it won't be long. How about we have dinner, just the three of us, this Sunday?"

"I don't know if that'd work. Letty is still traumatized by everything that happened. After Jess's treatment of her, she might be reluctant."

"I can understand that. Tell her that the dinner will be a safe space. I won't mention Constantine or anything that happened. I promise." She inhaled and exhaled. "This is important to me. My therapist says putting the past in the past and atoning for my faults will be healing. It's not just you and Jessalyn, but Letty, too. Jess doesn't have to be there, if that'd make her more comfortable."

He picked up her hand and kissed it. "Thanks, Mom. I'll ask. Speaking of Jess, I came here to talk to her. Do you mind?"

"Not at all. I think I'll go rest my eyes for a bit."

When they stood, Thane gave her another hug. "I missed you."

"I missed you, too." She laid a hand against his cheek. "It's nice seeing you truly happy for once. Let me know about dinner."

"I will."

He watched her head upstairs, amazed at her recovery. Everything he'd said to Rebekah was true; she was his mom in every way. He'd meant what he'd said to his mother, too. She was his mother, for better or

Chrys Fey

for worse. Right now, there was a chance for the better. Hoping for that, he made his way to Jessalyn's quarters.

Jess sat on the terrace. A large, white hat shaded her face. She had a glass of red wine in her hand. When he stepped up to her, she tilted her head back to see him beneath the wide brim. "Ah, little brother. What can I do for you this fine evening?"

"You can stop lying to me."

"Have I been?" She sipped her wine.

He squatted next to her lounge chair to look her in the eye and held up the plastic bag. The charms reflected in the dark frames of her sunglasses.

"I didn't do that."

"Excuse me if I don't take you for your word anymore."

She ripped off her sunglasses, revealing pink-streaked eyes. "I. Didn't. Do. It."

He lowered his hand, concern flitting through him. "How much have you had to drink?"

"Oh, seriously? I'm not drunk. I just have a lot on my mind." She shoved to her bare feet. "Damn, be the daughter of an alcoholic and addict and you can't ever cry or have a glass of wine." She stepped up to the terrace's railing and poured the rest of her wine over the side. "There. Happy?" Then she let the glass slip from her fingers. Seconds later, it shattered on the concrete below. She leaned against the rail now, arms crossed, eyeing him. There was too much bitterness there. Far too much.

Thane rose slowly to his feet, prepared to lunge if she teetered backward or tried to pitch herself over the ledge next.

"Someone is framing me so you'll look a different way. And who better to frame than the person who has had it out for Ch-Letty from the beginning? But I haven't done any of the things you believe I have."

"Okay." He inched closer. "Who knows about your vendetta against her?"

"My PI, anyone who was around after Daddy's death, and anyone who might've heard us arguing about her, like Rebekah."

"Rebekah wouldn't do such a thing."

"But it's so easy to believe that I would?" She smirked now. "Of course, it would. I'm as manipulative as him. As cunning. As arrogant. As self-centered. As malicious."

Thane frowned. "Who?"

"Daddy." She glanced over her shoulder, down at the shards of glass and spilled wine. "He didn't get a son like him, but he got a daughter." Her gaze ticked back to him. "That's why he loved me more. He saw himself in me." She eyed him up and down. "You? You had been his greatest disappointment."

That didn't sting. Not one bit. What did bother him was the look in her eyes.

"I've never heard you talk like this. What's brought this on? Mom?"

She let out a snort. "It would be so easy to blame her, but no." She moved away from the rail, much to Thane's relief, and plopped onto the lounge chair. "You have."

"Me?"

"Yeah, you." She removed the hat from her head and fluffed her blonde hair. Then she set the hat on her knees and plucked at the bow's black, silk ribbon. "You thought I was working with Daddy's friends, but I never did. I certainly wouldn't work with the man who'd raped me."

That was like a punch to the gut. Thane's heart sank, and his throat tightened. He dropped to his knees in front of her. "Who?"

"Alec."

"When?"

Jessalyn's gaze met his, and a small smile without an ounce of sarcasm lifted her lips. "Do you remember our last holiday party at Canmore Tech with Daddy?"

He nodded, already hating what she would share.

"Alec gave me a pearl he'd found in an oyster. Then, when we were taking the group photo, you stood to my right, and he and Daddy stood behind me to my left. While the pictures were being taken, Alec stuck his hand under my dress and grabbed my bare ass. I tried to get away without making it obvious."

Thane recalled how Jessalyn had bumped into him during the photos. He'd had no idea. Goddamn it, he hadn't known.

"I could feel his fingers. He almost..." She stopped. "But the photographer finished and I left before he could. I escaped to the bathroom, and he followed me inside."

Thane sat back on his heels and covered his face with his hands.

"He locked the door and cornered me between the stalls."

Horror roped through Thane.

"He said that I was his Christmas present. That

he'd bought me."

Thane's hands fell from his face.

"He gave Daddy one hundred thousand dollars."

Numb. Numb from his brain to his toes. Numb in his heart. All he could do was sit there and stare at his sister.

"He raped me right there, up against the stall. From that first time to when Daddy died, Alec raped me a total of ten times. And he paid Daddy for each...transaction."

Thane shook his head from side to side. Not because he didn't believe her, but because it was too much. Constantine had sold his own daughter to a rapist.

What Jessalyn said next, she said slowly, word by word. "One hundred thousand dollars. Ten times. That's one million dollars." The corners of her lips tugged into a dangerous sneer at the irony, at the cruelty. "That's how much Daddy had left me in his will. He'd given me the exact dollar amount Alec had paid him."

Thane swallowed.

"You can see it in the photo, where his hand is, how my skirt is ruffled up in the back. And in that photo, in that fucking photo, Daddy has his arm around Alec's shoulders, and they're grinning in the exact same way. Moments after they had struck their deal."

Breathing hurt. Thane's lungs felt like fire, as if his heart was surrounded by an inferno. Anger seared through him with grief and the fierce urge to protect his sister.

"Why didn't you tell me?"

"You were twelve. What could you have done?"

"I could've punched him in the balls."

Jessalyn let out a laugh. "It's not funny, I know. But it is."

Thane waited for her to stop laughing before saying, "If I had known, I wouldn't have let him run the company until I was eighteen. You and I may be different, and we may not always get along, but you're my sister. You know I don't stand for shit like that. I would've had your back. Protected you. Fought with you to get him sentenced."

"He's too powerful."

"Powerful men go to prison."

"Not for long. They get out. They all do."

Thane's heart tore. Jessalyn had been sexually assaulted at a young age by their father's best friend, and Thane had had no idea. All these years. He felt as though he'd failed her. But someone else had failed her first, in an even more gross and unspeakable way. "How could you love Dad after that? How could you have had his back all this time?"

She shoved her sunglasses onto her face and pushed them up the bridge of her nose, hiding her eyes. "You wouldn't understand."

"Help me to."

"I can't."

Thane badly wanted to understand, but he respected her right to not share more than what she'd already told him. He stayed there, though, kneeling on the ground, unable to move. If she had told him what had happened when they were kids, he would've stood up for her, and he would've paid for it. His father would have beaten him black and blue for defending Jessalyn, but Thane still would've done it. Even risking death, he would've done it.

"He loved me more."

Jessalyn's whisper broke through his tortured thoughts.

"He never hurt me like he did you or Mama."

"Yes, he did, Jess." What he said next, he said softly. "He just used someone else to do it."

A tear slipped out from beneath a dark lens.

"Jess." He reached out, but she shrank back, so he lowered his hand.

"Just go," she whispered.

He wanted to stay, to comfort her, but she didn't want that, so he pushed to his feet. At the door, he paused and glanced back. She turned her head away. Heart clenching in his chest, he stepped over the threshold. With each step, his heart shattered more. She'd carried that secret for twenty-three years. Held it inside herself. Let it weigh her down. Darken her soul and her heart. For twenty-three years.

Some carried it longer. Some never shared it. Society didn't make it easy for them to come forward, to report the crime, to tell anyone.

Twenty-three damn years!

He changed direction and stomped into the sitting room where he'd talked with his mother. His glare swept over the framed photos above the fireplace until he found the one he was looking for. Right there, in the middle of the lineup, in a platinum frame, was the last Christmas photo he and Jessalyn had taken with Constantine at Canmore Tech. He picked it up. In the front row, he stood beside Jessalyn, who leaned into him, and just behind her towered Alec and their father, grinning like sharks. Alec's right hand was directly behind Jessalyn's hip, and the back of her skirt was bunched up.

Thane's hands shook.

His breathing quickened.

His lungs trembled when he attempted to take a deep breath.

Rage seared through him.

"That son-of-a-bitch."

The memory of that night, a moment he usually didn't recall, rushed back.

"Time for the group photo!"

More like it was time for everyone to pretend they were happy working for Constantine Canmore. Sighing, Thane joined Jessalyn in the front row where the kids lined up. Jessalyn stood to his left, fixing her hair. Constantine and Alec stood behind them, also to Thane's left. At least this time his father wouldn't have his hand on Thane's shoulder, squeezing, bruising, demanding him to be better, stand taller, look like "you're Goddamn fucking happy to be a Canmore."

The photographer instructed everyone to smile.

Thane plastered on a fake smile that he hoped would pass his father's inspection later. Jessalyn bumped into him, and he shifted to the side but kept his gaze straight ahead. The sooner this stupid picture was taken, the sooner he could sneak off.

"Smile. One, two, three."

Flash.

"Perfect."

Jessalyn broke away from the group first, nearly plowing him over. He glanced in her direction to see her heading for the hallway where the bathrooms were. Probably had to pee. The teens had likely been sneaking alcohol. They'd been known to sneak flasks full of whatever liquor their parents had at home.

The longer the party wore on, the more his father drank, and he wasn't the only one. All the teens were drunk and several of them were making out. Thane still didn't see Jessalyn anywhere. Where was she? He peered around. Should he look for her?

He left his table and headed toward the hall, but before he could take five steps, Jessalyn hustled down the hall and back into the main room. She quickly rejoined her friends and snagged a flask from one of their hands. As she chugged it, Thane shook his head. Typical Jess.

At the end of the party, Thane stood on the sidewalk in front of their car while Constantine whispered in Jessalyn's ear. After a moment, he kissed her on the top of her head. She slid into the backseat of the car, and their father shifted to him. He clamped a hand on Thane's shoulder, bent forward, and hissed into his ear. "I expect you to do better next time." His gripped tightened. "Be. My. Son."

I am your son. For better or for worse.

"Yes, sir," he whispered.

Constantine released him, and Thane climbed into the car. As soon as his father couldn't see him anymore, Thane slumped and sighed in relief.

Beside him, Jessalyn was uncharacteristically

quiet. She had her arms crossed in front of her while she stared out the window.

"Are you okay?"

She didn't look at him. "Fine."

Nothing at all had been fine, but he hadn't seen it. He hadn't known.

Seeing red, Thane slammed the frame into the mantlepiece. Glass broke. He hit it again and again until the glass rained to the floor at his feet and the frame dented. Then he ripped out the photo. With the punch of a button, he had a fire roaring. He tossed the photo into the fire and watched it burn with a great deal of satisfaction, but it didn't lessen his anger.

Movement out of the corner of his eye caught his attention. Jessalyn stood there, staring into the fire. The sunglasses were gone.

Moments passed. Finally, she peered at him. "If you ever see Alec again, give him this." She approached Thane and held out her closed fist. He opened his hand, and something small and warm plopped onto his palm—the pearl.

"And this." She passed him a small piece of paper next.

He unfolded it to find a check written out to Alec for one million dollars. On the "For" line she'd penned: *What you paid my father so you could rape me.*

Twenty-three years and she hadn't spent a penny of that money? He couldn't say he blamed her, but before he'd learned the truth about it, he'd assumed she'd blown through it.

"Jess."

Suddenly, her composure shattered, and she threw her arms around him. He stuffed the pearl and the check into his pocket and held her close while she wept on his shoulder. He cradled her as he had when they'd found out Constantine was dead and she'd been overcome with grief. But this was worse.

"I've got you," he whispered. "I won't let him or anyone hurt you again."

His words only made her sob harder.

Thane stayed, giving her the security and comfort that she'd never received from their father. Eventually, she passed out from sheer exhaustion. Her face was puffy and red from crying. Her lashes were still wet and clumped together. But she appeared to have found a bit of peace in unconsciousness.

He spread a throw blanket over her, being careful not to wake her. She looked so fragile, not like the unbreakable, stuck-up, harsh sister he'd known his whole life. Perhaps that had been a shell she'd fashioned in order to survive being a Canmore. It was clearer now more than ever that he hadn't been the only one damaged by their childhood. He'd assumed Jessalyn had gotten out unscathed, even relished being a Canmore. How wrong he'd been.

27

Letty

*L*etty rode the elevator up to Thane's penthouse. Not that she really had any choice, stuck in the elevator and all. But when it opened, instead of going back down to the garage, she walked into the penthouse and hunted down her cell phone. She rang Thane, but he didn't answer. Considering he was driving, and driving while angry, she didn't blame him for not answering. Even using the dash speaker phone option would've added another distraction. So, she sent him a text.

—Please call me as soon as you can. Before you do anything. Please.—

She paced the length of the penthouse while biting

her nails and eyeing the text messaging app, hoping to see those three little dots manifest to indicate Thane was responding, but those three little dots never showed themselves.

Thane never texted her back. She didn't think that'd happen, and it didn't make her feel good. Thane could be doing anything, and anything could be happening to him, and she had no idea. Panic squeezed her throat.

Her feet hurt from her constant pacing. To relieve them, she plopped down on the edge of the couch, ready to take action the moment her phone notified her of a text or call, or if Thane came home. But after a half an hour of sitting there, tense, she curled up in a corner of the couch. If only she had her weighted blanket. That might help to calm her. The next time she stopped at her apartment, she would grab it. More and more of her things were winding up at Thane's. It really was becoming her home, and she liked that. She liked it even more when she wasn't there alone, frantic and wondering what Thane was doing.

She rested her head on the couch's arm. With the TV off and the room growing darker, her eyelids lowered. Gripping her cell phone, she dozed in a half-aware state so when the elevator sounded sometime later, she sprang off the couch. Her heart pounded with adrenaline.

"Thane?"

She stomped toward the elevator. "If you ever do that again—" The rest of her tirade faded on the tip of her tongue at the sight of Thane leaning against the wall, with his head bent and his hands holding his head.

Worry spiked in her like a fever. She rushed to him and placed her hands on either side of his ribs. "Thane?" He didn't raise his head, so she lifted her right hand to his neck. "What happened?" She ducked her head to try to see his face.

Exhaling, he dropped his hands to his sides. Then he rested the back of his head against the wall. His eyes were closed. "It wasn't Jess."

Letty frowned. "The charms?"

He gave a small nod. "It wasn't her."

"How do you know?"

He opened his eyes, but he wasn't looking at her. His gaze was pinned to the ceiling. "She told me…" He swallowed. "Shit." Tears brimmed in his eyes.

"Here. Come here." She led him to the counter and pulled out one of the stools. "Sit down." As soon as he lowered onto the stool, she touched his cheek. "Do you need something?"

His arms snaked around her waist. He tucked her between his legs and held her close. "This. Just this," he whispered with his forehead in the crook of her neck.

She cupped the back of his head with one hand and stroked the spot between his tense shoulder blades with the other. The need to comfort him overwhelmed her. From all the times she had wanted and needed comforting, she knew not to back away or let go until he did. And she didn't ask him again to tell her what was wrong; he would tell her when he was ready.

She closed her eyes and focused on sending Thane her love through their embrace. Every time his lungs expanded, she inhaled. Then they exhaled together.

"Alec raped her."

Thane's statement stiffened Letty's spine.

"My father arranged it."

Her eyelids sprang open as horror surged through her like magma.

"Alec paid him. Ten times."

Letty's chest tightened.

"When my father died, it ended."

Her stomach churned.

"And he willed her the money."

Finally, Thane inched back. He didn't meet her eye, though, but kept his gaze lowered. "My father hurt her. More than she knows. More than she is capable of admitting." He met Letty's eye now. "Jess told me all that when I confronted her about the charms. There was something off about her. Something...scary. *She* scared me. I was afraid she would harm herself. I stayed until she fell asleep, but I shouldn't have left. What if she wakes up and does something?"

He started to get to his feet.

"Thane, take a minute." She grasped his arms. "Do you really think she'll harm herself?"

He raked his hands over his head. "I don't know."

"Is there someone we can call to check on her?"

"The staff. Ms. Rawlings has run the house since we were kids. She'll know what to do."

"Okay. Give her a call."

Thane slipped his phone from his pocket. He made a few taps and then lifted it to his ear. After a moment, "Hey, Ms. Rawlings. It's Thane. Can you do me a favor? Can you check on Jess for me?"

He gave Letty a nod before falling into silence. She held his hand while they waited. He studied their interlocked fingers. She stared at them, too. Their hands fit together perfectly. She'd never enjoyed handholding. In the past, with other men, it'd felt restraining, restrictive. Now, with Thane, it felt nice. More than nice. Revitalizing. Rejuvenating. She welcomed the contact. Enjoyed it. Wanted more of it.

Thane let out a sigh. "Good. Can you check on her hourly for me? Let me know if anything happens? Thank you. I appreciate it. Bye."

He set his phone on the counter and continued looking at their joined hands. She wondered what he saw. Did he see possibilities? Did he see a future he didn't want to release? She hoped so.

"My mom would like to meet you."

She jolted. "At…at rehab?"

"No, she's home. I saw her before Jess. She apologized for the past and expressed wanting to have you over for dinner."

Letty shook her head. "There's no way your mom could want to ever see me after…after I…"

Thane tucked one of her curls behind her ear. "She does." He trailed the side of his thumb down her cheek. "She wants to get to know the woman I love."

Her face scorched as if on fire. She loved hearing that, but the idea of meeting his mother, Constantine's first wife, filled her with anxiety. "I…I don't think I'm ready for that."

He lifted one of her hands to his lips and kissed her fingers. "I understand. I don't want you to do anything you're not ready to do."

That right there was one of the reasons why she

loved him. He didn't push her, didn't force her to do anything she didn't want to do.

"Is there anything I can do for *you*? Or Jess?"

"I'm okay. As for Jess, I don't...I don't know."

"I disagree. You're not okay. You heard about horrendous things someone you care about had to endure. You're in pain. What do you need?" She'd give him whatever it was he required—time alone, another hug, comfort food, a long shower, a strong drink, or just talk. He had offered her comfort whenever she needed it, without fail, without hesitating, so she wanted to do the same for him.

A breath left him. "I need..." She remained silent, letting him process his thoughts. After a moment, he tilted his head. His brows lowered. He peered toward his cell phone. "I need to call my attorney."

28

Thane

*I*n the conference room at All Heart Tech, Thane sat across from Alec and his attorney, Uri Von Dickerson, the same man who had handled all of Constantine's legal matters. Uri had a face of sharp angles and a bony nose, short blonde hair, and wore a black trench coat. Seeing Alec's smug face—as smug as Uri's—sent Thane's blood broiling. All he could imagine was wailing his fist into that bastard's face again and again. He wouldn't stop. Nothing could make him stop.

"We've been notified about the countersuing measure that Mr. Canmore has taken up against my client's wrongful termination and assault lawsuit. What was it for? One dollar?" Uri scoffed. "Quite bold of you. Sounds like you think you've already won."

"We have evidence," Abigail, Thane's attorney said. "And it is quite damning."

"Then let's see it." Uri held out his hand.

Abigail slid a folder across the table.

Uri's attorney opened it and scanned the document inside. Then he passed it to Alec, whose jaw tensed while he read the evidence of his mistreatment of Letty, the same piece of paper Thane had shown Alec before firing him.

Seconds passed.

Uri leaned over and whispered in Alec's ear.

Alec whispered something back.

Uri folded his hands on the tabletop. "My client has agreed to drop the lawsuit."

"Wonderful," Abigail said. "As soon as we confirm the lawsuit is dropped, we will drop our lawsuit, but this"—she snatched the document back—"is ours."

Thane, however, continued to glare at Alec, because he wasn't done yet. "Give us the room. I have something to say to Alec."

Abigail leaned toward him. "Are you sure?"

He gave a terse nod.

She nodded back and stood.

When the door closed behind their attorneys, Alec had the nerve to sneer. "What? Going to chastise me again for whipping that little bitch?"

Thane's hands flexed. How he wanted them around Alec's neck. Instead, he removed something from his pocket and flicked it over the table. A rolling sound filled the air, and Alec caught the pearl before it could sail over the edge of the table and land in his lap. "Remember that?" Thane asked, keeping his voice level, calm.

"I do." Alec held it between his thumb and forefinger while he admired it. Then he showed his teeth at Thane. "I had sucked on this pearl before I gave it to your sister."

Thane's jaw ticked.

"How sentimental of her to keep it all these years."

"There was something else she kept." Thane tossed the folded check at Alec. It landed on the table with a soft snap of paper.

Alec plucked it up and unfolded it. His gaze scanned the check. A laugh erupted from him. "Is she giving me a refund?" He slipped the check and the pearl into his jacket pocket. "It's nice to get my money back after all these years. I guess you could say they were all freebies."

Thane pushed to his feet, shoving the chair back.

Alec sprang to his feet in reaction. "What? Going to hit me again?"

"I'll do more than that." Never taking his eyes off Alec, he stalked to the corner of the table, yearning to get close enough to get his hands on the bastard.

Alec backed away quickly, maintaining that distance. "The first deal...at the Christmas party...you were right there."

Hands clenched, Thane stepped around the first corner.

"You heard your father telling me his plans about Charm once she became of age."

Thane's chest rose and fell as his rage battered against his insides, fighting to get free, thirsty to be unleashed. He stepped around the second corner as Alec backed toward the opposite end of the table.

"If you had stuck around, you would've heard him offering Jessalyn to me. He'd seen how I'd been eyeing her for the past year." He licked his lips. "Practically salivating. Damn, your sister sure matured quickly, and nicely."

Thane lunged.

Alec skirted around to the other side. "Your father saw a way to profit off that. A hundred thousand dollars for me to fuck her. A bargain, I thought, and after the first time, I was right. I had to have more, so I was a repeat customer, completely satisfied with my purchase."

Blood pounded in Thane's ears. His heartrate hammered at every pulse point. Fury scorched his veins. His breathing became ragged. He came to the chair where Alec had been sitting during the meeting.

On the other side of the table, Alec stood across from him. "She uses the word 'rape,' but she enjoyed it. Each and every time. I made sure of that." His lips lifted in a sneer. "I made sure she enjoyed it."

Thane flung the chair backward and leapt onto the table. He slid across it and had one hand around the lapel of Alec's jacket and his other hand cocked to slam it into Alec's face when the door flew open. Abbot and another member of their security team grabbed Thane and yanked him back, preventing him from doing anything more. Two other security officers restrained Alec and wrestled him out of the conference room.

Thane fought against the hands holding him and managed to get through the doorway.

Rebekah stood a few paces away, gripping her

headset in one hand. "Escort Mr. Danes off the premise," she said. "He's not allowed back on this property."

Security walked Alec toward the elevator banks.

A ding sounded, and one of the elevator doors opened.

Letty stepped out.

No.

She peered around in confusion at the commotion. Then her gaze found Alec, and she backed into Rebekah's desk.

"Ah. If it isn't, little Charm." Alec stopped in front of her, resisting the guards who struggled to get him to move. "Look at how you've grown."

Thane made to charge at Alec, but the hands gripping him tightened.

Rebekah rushed over and placed herself between Letty and Alec.

Alec shot a look over his shoulder at Thane. "I would've outbid them all."

In one quick motion, Thane dropped down and twisted, breaking the hold Abbot and the other guard had on him. He was halfway to Alec when his arms were caught from behind, halting him. Unable to do more, he spit curses at Alec. He didn't even know what was coming out of his mouth because he couldn't hear himself. Threats of violence, surely. It didn't matter what he was saying, though; all he could hear was Alec's laughter.

The guards wrangled Alec onto the elevator. Before the door slid shut, he shouted, "Way more than one mill."

The door closed.

All became silent.

Seething inside, Thane eyed Abbot. "Let. Go."

Abbot released him immediately.

He tugged his jacket back into place. "I need a minute." Without so much as glancing at Letty, he headed for his office, stepped inside, and shut the door with deliberate calm. There was so much fury beneath the surface that he was afraid of what would happen if anyone came close to him right now. Especially Letty.

He dug his fists into the top of his desk and leaned against it. His heart rammed against his ribs and breastbone. Each breath he purged from his lungs was like exhaling fire. Every single muscle in his body was tensed, ready for a fight. He clamped his eyelids shut and clenched his jaw in a desperate attempt at seizing control.

A gentle tapping at the door made him jolt.

Before he could tell whomever it was to leave, the door opened.

"It's me." Letty's voice made his body tense even more.

The door clicked shut.

He unclenched his jaw enough to say, "Letty, you can't be around me right now. I'm not safe. I don't want to hurt you."

Dear God, he didn't want to cause her any harm.

"You're not going to hurt me." Her voice was closer.

"Letty, please, go. There's so much anger inside me right now. I'm afraid I'm going to snap, and if that happens, I may not be aware of what I do."

He'd never forgive himself if he caused her pain.

"Then wail on a couch cushion or go to your private gym. Do something to let it out. It's not healthy to keep all that rage bottled up. That's how people *do* snap."

She was behind him now. Too close. Didn't she realize the danger she was putting herself in by getting that close?

"I have to calm down a little first."

"I can help."

He shook his head.

"I'm going to put my hands on your back on the count of three. One…two…three…" Her hands flatted to the middle of his back, one on either side of his spine. His muscles contracted at the touch, and her hands flinched.

He bent his neck. "I felt that, Letty. You're scared of me."

"No, I'm not." She moved her hands up his back and then down. Gentle, soothing strokes. "Take a deep breath with me. Inhale."

He sucked in a lungful of oxygen as her hands roamed up his back.

"Exhale."

Her hands slid back down.

She did that two more times. "Feeling any better?"

He opened his eyes. His heartrate had slowed. "A bit."

Her hands slipped up his back again, and her fingers applied slight pressure to his neck. They prodded away the stiffness. Along his shoulders now, her hands kneaded his rock-hard muscles. He let his eyelids drift shut while he melted beneath her attentive hands. They wrapped around his right arm and stroked him from shoulder to wrist. At his hand, still balled into a fist, she paused. Her fingers circled around his fist, and she made as if to lift it. He relaxed, allowing her to hold his hand in hers. She rubbed her thumb in circles over his knuckles and the bones in his hand. When she finished, she moved around to the other side and did the same thing with his left hand.

"Turn around."

He did, and leaned back against his desk.

She placed his hands on her hips, forcing him to keep them relaxed. He studied her face. No fear. No anxiety. But perhaps traces of worry. She raised her hands to his face and probed the tips of her fingers into his rigid jaw. He carried a lot of tension there, as if all the tension she'd massaged away had diverted to his jaw.

She brushed her lips over his. "Unclench your jaw. Open your mouth."

He eased his mouth open. In response, she kissed him tenderly. With their lips locked in a sweet embrace, she circled her fingertips into the joints that connected his jaw to his cheekbone. That tender spot was sore from gritting his teeth.

"Better," she said between his lips.

Her fingers journeyed along his cheeks to his temple, where they massaged away more strain. Then over his forehead, where his very skin felt bruised. She lowered her hands back to his shoulders and searched his eyes.

"You have the magic touch," he said.

"When I was little, after I'd have a night terror, I'd be so tense that I couldn't sleep. My mom, Lydia, would calm me with her loving touch and turn me into putty. Then I'd sleep the rest of the night soundlessly."

"Well, thank you for doing that for me."

"Any time." She moved her hands to his elbows. "But it might be a good idea that we go home. You still have anger inside that needs to come out."

He did. No matter how great her touch, it hadn't driven away his emotions. And he didn't want to erupt. One word from anyone could set him off. He wasn't safe.

"All right. Let's go home."

29

Letty

*L*etty busied herself in the kitchen making lunch while Thane beat his pent-up aggression into a punching bag in his private gym. She made enough for both of them, planning to wrap Thane's up until he emerged from the gym.

The thumps of Thane attacking the punching bag met her ears. She knew he was purging a lot, more than he'd want to admit. No doubt he blamed himself for not seeing it, not realizing that Constantine would've found another way to abuse Jessalyn that didn't involve his own fists.

Blame.

Guilt.

Shame.

But not only that. Thane carried so much. So much that he did not cause but which he couldn't escape, couldn't shed, couldn't forget.

His mother's alcohol and drug abuse.

Every single childhood fight that left her bleeding, bruised, and beaten.

His sister's rapes. Ten. An unspeakable number. Just one was one too many.

Every time he'd seen Alec after that Christmas party, through his youth and then at All Heart Tech. All the times he'd trusted the man. Each time they'd shaken hands.

Hatred.

Wrath.

Vengeance.

Then there was Constantine, the mountain among giants. Thane carried all of Constantine's crimes; the sins of a father piled atop an innocent son's back.

A 9 iron to the face.

Letty's broken arm.

Thousands of pills and bottles of booze consumed by his mother.

Ten rapes and one million dollars.

The murder of Letty's mom.

Crime after crime. Sin upon sin. Weighing him down, crushing him.

Letty paused while prepping a Greek salad she was pairing with grilled lemon chicken. The sounds of impact had ceased. She waited, with her fingers on a piece of romaine lettuce, paused in the act of breaking the leaf into small chunks. Her ears strained. She held her breath, waiting to hear if the thumps would pick back up again.

A door closed.

She tilted her head.

Water coursing through pipes told her Thane was taking a shower.

She resumed her task. While listening to the water flowing, she sliced the grilled chicken into neat strips. On large, shallow bowls heaping with Greek salad, she laid the chicken pieces on top. She retrieved two forks and then stood there, wringing her hands. Should she wait for him? Would he even want to eat? Surely after going at the punching bag like that he'd be starving. She checked the time on her phone. He'd been in there for over an hour, without so much as pausing to get a gulp of water. Not only starving, but she expected him to be exhausted, too.

At the fridge, she got out a bottle of water, which she set next to his plate.

Deciding to wait, she set to work washing the pan and utensils she'd dirtied.

Thane entered as she placed the scrubbed and rinsed cutting board on the drying rack. He went straight to the drink cart between the kitchen and living room. Crystal clinked when he lifted a stopper. Whiskey splashed into a glass. He took a swallow before bringing it to the counter.

"I made lunch, if you're hungry."

"Thanks, but this is all I want." He sat on a stool and wrapped his hands around the glass.

Her eyelids widened. "Thane." She hurried around the counter and caught his left hand in hers. His knuckles were swollen and colored with red and purple bruises. His right hand, his dominate hand, looked worse. "You didn't wear gloves."

"I needed to feel the punching bag," he said and lifted the whiskey to his lips.

"Do you have an ice pack?"

He didn't answer right away as he eyed his bruised knuckles with a bland expression.

"Thane."

"Under the bathroom sink."

She found an old-fashioned ice pack under the bathroom sink next to a first aid kit. At least she didn't need that; his knuckles hadn't split. In the kitchen, she unscrewed the cap and filled the bag with cubes. Then she sat on the stool beside Thane. "Hand."

He switched the glass to his left hand and held out his right. She cupped his hand in her lap and settled the ice pack over his damaged knuckles. When she did that, he shifted toward her on the stool, but he didn't say a word. His gaze fell on the ice pack and his hand in her lap. He didn't move his fingers at all. She worried that hitting the punching bag hadn't been enough.

"You should've worn gloves. Your hands are important." She paused while she adjusted the ice pack to get the side of his final knuckle, by his pinky finger. "At work, you're going to have a hard time typing and holding a screw driver. And at home, you're not going to be able to hold my hand."

He lifted his left hand and placed his fingers under her chin. "Nothing will stop me from holding your hand."

"It'll hurt."

"I'll endure it."

She tore her gaze from his.

In her lap, his fingertips skimmed over her thigh and cotton skirt, and then they closed, ever-so-slightly, around her hand. "See?"

She applied the same amount of pressure in return.

"I like hearing you call my penthouse home," he said.

She licked her lips. "Well, it is my home now. I mean...I am living here." She shifted the ice pack again. "At least until my apartment is safe."

"I'd like you to live here permanently, but that's up to you, of course."

She opened her mouth to say she wanted that, too, but his cell phone buzzed.

"Can you get that for me?"

She placed the ice pack on the counter, stood, and retrieved his phone from the other side of the counter. "It's a text from Rebekah."

"You can read it. My passcode is five-three-eight-nine."

She tapped in the passcode and opened the messaging app. "Rebekah says, 'What do you want me to do with the recording?'" Letty stiffened and faced Thane. "What recording?"

"Before Alec and his attorney came, I had activated the speaker connected to Rebekah's desk. She recorded the entire thing. She heard everything that was said, which is how she got security in there before I could hit the bastard."

Letty's heart pounded. "What do you want me to tell her?"

"I have to talk to Jessalyn first. I don't want to do

something she wouldn't want."

She typed out the reply and sent it. Back on the stool, she swapped his phone for the ice pack. "Other hand."

He twisted on the stool so she could reach his left hand. While icing his swollen, bruised knuckles, she replayed what she'd seen transpire at All Heart Tech. Alec's leering look and eyes dripping with sexual innuendo blazed through her mind.

"What did Alec mean when he said he would've outbid them all?"

Thane's body became rigid. "Nothing."

"He wouldn't have said it if it was nothing. You wouldn't have reacted the way you did if it was nothing. Tell me. Please."

Thane drained the last of his whiskey. "My father...my father said when you came of age, he planned to give you to the highest bidder."

Letty swallowed. Constantine had intended to do to her what he'd done to his own daughter. It shouldn't surprise her; the man was evil incarnate, but it sent ripples of shock and revulsion through her.

"If I had known...if I had realized..."

She plopped the ice pack on the counter and cupped Thane's face with her hands. "None of this is your fault. None of it. You were a child. You couldn't have known, couldn't have done anything about it. You didn't do anything wrong." She kissed his brow. "Please accept that." She leaned back to peer into his eyes. "You're beating yourself up for not protecting us back then, but you did what you could when you yourself needed protection." She laid her forehead to his and whispered, "And you're protecting us now."

Thane roped his arms around her waist.

"Thank you for protecting us."

He dropped his forehead to her shoulder.

"Thank you for fighting for us."

A hot tear landed on her collarbone.

"Thank you for being you."

Letty iced Thane's hands, made sure he ate, and then headed back to work when he laid down to rest. Yawanda smirked at her when she came in. "You had a long lunch. Got in a quickie, did you?"

Letty shot a look around the shop. A customer browsed the shelves not too far away. "Ssh. And my tardiness is not because of what you think."

"Uh huh."

"It's not."

Yawanda only snickered. Better to let her believe she and Thane had engaged in a quickie in his office than to explain what had actually happened. Yawanda didn't have to worry about Letty any more than she already did.

Letty returned to work, hoping that Thane had fallen asleep. The customer strolled through the shop leisurely, examining each and every item, so Letty scanned through a catalogue and mark pages. Anything she considered buying for her shop, she had her customers in mind. What would they like? What did she need to add to her collection that other gift shops and antique stores nearby did not have?

She finished flipping through the catalogue, excited

about a few pieces within those pages that she would purchase as soon as she could. The customer still explored the displays. In a wicker basket on the customer's arm rested the brass unicorn figurine and a vintage Enid Collins handbag. Letty smiled; glad those pieces would be going to a new home. The fact they were going together, although they weren't a pair, was even better.

The customer paused at the counter and checked out the jewelry there. A chuckle came from their lips when they examined the vintage button necklace Letty had displayed on a necklace holder. "Oh, that's fun."

Letty beamed. "It is, and it'll look great with that Enid Collins handbag. Would you like to see what it'd look like on?"

"Oh, yes."

Letty unhooked it from the mannequin and moved around the counter. As she looped it around her customer's neck, the bell at the door jingled. She clasped the necklace and glanced over her shoulder at someone standing with their back to Letty, inspecting the vintage hats that customers usually cleared out leading up to the Kentucky Derby. "Welcome to the shop," Letty called out. "If you need anything, please let me know."

The head of honey hair fashioned into a chignon nodded but didn't turn around.

Letty picked up the antique sterling silver handheld mirror that she kept on the counter just for this purpose and held it up for her customer. "What do you think?"

"I think I must have it." Thin fingers trailed through the buttons. They tinkled together before settling back into place. "I'll have to wear this out of the shop."

"And everyone who sees it will be jealous."

Letty rang up the statue, purse, and necklace. She included a black velvet box for the necklace to be stored in when not in use and added rose-scented tissue paper to the purse. "Thank you for coming to Let It Charm You. Please come again."

"I have a feeling I will."

Letty's gaze shifted to the person who'd come in while she'd been busy. She stopped breathing. That person was Thane's sister.

Letty didn't move, and neither did Jessalyn. They stood on either side of the counter, watching each other as if eyeing a rattlesnake that was shaking its tail in warning of an impending attack. Letty started breathing again, fast and shallow. *What do you want*? She would've ask Jessalyn that, but she couldn't get her lips to move. It was as if she was paralyzed by the endless possibilities of what Jessalyn could say or do.

What do you want? She didn't take her gaze off Jessalyn. When was she going to do what she came here to do? Why prolong it? Did she get a kick out of Letty's discomfort? *WHAT DO YOU WANT*?! Her mind shouted it, but she still couldn't fucking move.

"Do you love my brother?" Jessalyn asked, without so much as changing her facial expression or posture. Not even her stare had altered.

"Yes," Letty said on a breath, also not daring to look away.

"I thought so." Jessalyn stepped closer and laid her purse on the counter. She peered at her hands.

Letty's brows lowered a fraction.

"I want to apologize for how I've treated you. For what I said to you when I saw you at All Heart Tech, for telling a paparazzo about you, and…for hiring a PI to spy on you. I…I've been messed up ever since…" She cleared her throat. "Because of Thane and *you*"—she met Letty's eye—"I'm now realizing how messed up." Just as quickly, she looked away again. "I don't expect you to accept my apology, but I had to say it anyway. Part of healing and all that." She removed her purse from the counter. "When you tell Thane about this, tell him I said he's not like them. He's good. Through and through."

"I have told him that," Letty said. "But I think he'd like hearing it from you."

Jessalyn paused. "There's a lot I need to say to him, but I don't know how."

Letty glanced at a notepad with her shop's logo on it. "When Thane had to tell me things that he couldn't tell me in person, he wrote me a letter." She picked up the notepad and a pen. "Write it all down, and then when you're ready, give it to him."

Jessalyn didn't move.

"I know it would mean a lot to him."

That had Jessalyn reaching out to take the notepad and pen. "Thanks." She turned to leave.

"I do," Letty said, stopping Jessalyn short.

She glanced over her shoulder.

"Accept your apology," Letty added. "I do."

Jessalyn nodded. Then she left.

Letty collapsed onto her stool and flattened a hand to her chest where her heart beat frantically. Never did she expect to have an encounter like that with Thane's sister, but it'd happened, and she'd survived it. They both had. Perhaps she would also survive dinner with Thane's mom. It was worth considering.

She stared at the door. Would Jessalyn write Thane a letter? Would she give it to him if she did? Letty had no way of knowing, but she decided not to tell Thane about this. It wasn't for her to tell Thane, but for Jessalyn. Letty owed her that much.

30

Thane

wo days later, Thane's knuckles were still a mean red and purple. His fingers were stiff and ached when he stretched them, but he still typed on his keyboard, he still picked up screw drivers to tinker away at devices, and he still held Letty's hand. He wouldn't let anything stop him from doing that, as he swore.

He arrived at All Heart Tech, ready to dive into work. Rebekah already occupied her desk. She gave him a strained smile. Was she still upset about what happened the other day? He didn't blame her. Perhaps he should pull her aside, see if she was okay.

"I have something for you." She picked up a small, thick envelope from her desk. "Jessalyn was waiting outside when I arrived."

Thane took the envelope. On the front, Jessalyn had neatly scrawled out his name in cursive letters. The envelope felt heavy. "Thanks." He brought it into his office. On the other side of the door, he ripped into it and removed the folded stationary. When he flipped the stack open, his heart tripped in his chest. The logo for Letty's shop stared back. Jessalyn had been there. When? Why hadn't Letty said something?

His eager gaze read the opening to Jessalyn's letter.

Hey Little Brother,

I assume you noticed where this stationary came from. I visited Letty at her shop and apologized. Then I told her to tell you something...something I haven't had the strength to tell you all these years. Actually, there's a lot I haven't had the strength to tell you, but I'm working up to that. First things first, though...

I told Letty to tell you that you aren't like Constantine or Alec, that you're good through and through, because you are. She said she has told you and I should tell you myself. She's not wrong. I should've been telling you this every single day since our childhoods. I should've told you until it sank in, until you believed it.

You are the best man I know.

I can sit here and say that Mama and Daddy hadn't been good parents to us, but I hadn't been a good sister to you. You tried, though. You tried to be a good brother to me. Except, I wouldn't let you. I pushed you away. A part of me used to think, "How could he not be like them? He has to be like them." So, I treated you as though it'd be inevitable. But you're not, Thane. You never have been, and you never will be. I need you to believe that now, especially before I tell you more. You are what all men should be. I'm realizing this now, after being hurt repeatedly by men. Men who tainted my vision when I looked at you, so that all I saw was them. THEM.

You. Are. NOT. Like. Them.

I hope I'm not too late in telling you that.

Thane side-stepped to the wall and leaned against it, needing its support. He shifted the first sheet to the back of the pile to read the second page.

I'm taking a deep breath as I write this. So, stop reading and take a deep breath with me.

He did. For good measure, he took two more as Letty had instructed him. Then he continued reading.

You had asked me to help you to understand how I could still have Daddy's back after everything he had done to me, how I could still love him. Well, I'm going to do my best to explain that. It's not going to be easy. For either of us.

Thane's hands tightened, digging his fingers into the layers of paper.

The night of the Christmas party, after Alec did what he did to me, Daddy kissed me on my temple and whispered in my ear, "The things that matter the most to me are worth money, and you matter a great deal to me." My twisted mind morphed his words into meaning that he sold my body to his best friend because he loved me... because I was special.

Devastated by her words, Thane slid down the wall to the floor and clamped his eyelids shut. He could hear

Chrys Fey

his father's voice saying those words, manipulating a young woman who'd just been violated and traumatized into believing whatever he wanted her to. Constantine had known how to use people, especially his own family.

It has taken me all these years in therapy—and seeing you and Letty (hearing you say that you're in love with her)—to realize just how screwed up I am because of him. I spent weeks after the Christmas party repeating over and over again, "Daddy loves me more than Thane and Mama. I mean more to him. I'm worth more."

Then came the second time, and I thought for sure that meant I was even more valuable to Daddy than I'd thought. Each time. More and more. I convinced myself that I was his treasure that he only trusted to one man, his best friend, his right hand. Who better? And that I wasn't being taken against my will for nothing. The fact that Daddy wouldn't accept nothing less than what I was worth proved Daddy's words to be true. I meant a great deal to him. I mattered the most in his world.

Thane shook his head from side to side as tears

328

built in his eyes. His sister had been taken advantage of in the most horrible way possible, and Constantine had made her believe it was all done out of love. Jessalyn had a warped sense of the word—of the emotion—her whole life. How had she accepted love since their father's death and the contract between him and her rapist had expired? It was common for women to accept the love they thought they deserved based on what they received when they were young and impressionable, also based on how their mothers were treated. And Jessalyn had experienced both. God, he prayed it wasn't too late.

When Daddy died, I mourned for him and his lost love. I mourned that I was suddenly worthless, because how could I be worth anything to anyone when the one person who claimed I was as important to him as his one true love—money—was dead? I would never be anything again. I wouldn't be worth a damn thing. Not a cent.

Then came the reading of the will. Daddy willed me every dollar he'd ever earned from Alec. What could that mean if money was his true love? What could it mean that the money he'd collected for selling my body, because I meant a great deal to him, was being given back to me? It meant it was a lie. All of it. But thinking that was too much, so I changed my internal dialogue. I forced myself to believe he did it because he respected me. He'd collected that money not for himself as I had first thought, but for me. That was how much he loved me.

How wrong I had been. How stupid. How naïve. How desperate.

You fighting for Letty and the love the two of you have forced me to realize the truth. It's hard to swallow. Still. You see, when we last spoke and I told you about Alec, I was still lying to myself. I had said that Daddy loved me more than you and Mom, but that was not only a lie I had said to you but one I was struggling to not say to myself. And I'd fallen for it again in that moment. The truth was...that million dollars had been a snub at me. A joke. He hadn't loved me more. I dare say he might've loved me less. I wasn't a daughter but an object, one whose value hadn't meant a damn thing.

Watching you defend Letty again and again proved to me that real men don't do what Alec or

Daddy did. Thank you for being a good example, my only example, of how real men treat women.

From the bottom of my heart, thank you, little brother.

Jess

P.S. if you call me after reading this, do not take offense when I let your call roll to voicemail. I'm not strong enough to talk to you, yet, but I love you.

Thane dropped the letter to the floor beside him. He extracted his phone from his pocket with a shaking hand. Even though she said she wouldn't answer, he still called her. He wanted her to hear his voice when he said the things she needed to hear. As she promised, his call rolled to voicemail.

He waited for the beep. "I love you, too, Jess. I always have, and I always will."

He inhaled again.

"I have to tell you something, though...I recorded Alec when he and his attorney were here. I have his confession about everything he did to you, but I won't do anything with it unless you give me your permission. Whatever you decide, I will honor that."

He laid his fist against his forehead. "And, Jess, I am so sorry for telling you that you aren't my sister and that I was done. I was upset, but that's no excuse. You are my sister no matter what. I will always be here for you. Remember that."

He hung up as his throat tightened and laid his phone atop the letter. Then he buried his face in his hands and unleashed the tears he'd been holding back for days.

31

Letty

*L*etty enjoyed going to All Heart Tech to have lunch with Thane. She looked forward to it every day. This time, when she stepped off the elevator, chaos wasn't unfolding in the hall. All was quiet.

"Hey, Rebekah."

Except, instead of the usual smile Rebekah aimed at her, concern was etched there, drawing deep lines into her face. She removed her headset and hopped to her feet. "I think something's wrong."

"What do you mean?"

Rebekah glanced at Thane's closed office door. "Jessalyn left a letter for Thane. He went in, and he hasn't come back out. He hasn't even turned on the lights."

Letty peered at the door. No light seeped through the cracks or between the drawn blinds blocking the windows.

"He didn't have any meetings this morning, so I gave him privacy, but it's strange for him to not head down to the labs each morning to check on the progress of what's in development or to roll up his own sleeves."

Letty touched Rebekah's hand. "I'll check on him."

Rebekah nodded. "Let me know if there's anything I can do. He…he's like a son to me. He *is* my son."

"I will." Letty knocked softly on the door and listened. Nothing. He didn't say to come in or go away. She twisted the doorknob. It wasn't locked, so she eased it open.

The office was cloaked in darkness. Light didn't even glow from the computer screen. She opened the door wider. He wasn't stretched out on the loveseat. The bathroom door was open, and the light off. Her gaze shot around the space, searching for him. Rebekah had said he hadn't come out. If that was true, then where was he? The blinds still covered the panes. Wind didn't rustle them from an opened window.

She stepped over the threshold, worried that he was unconscious behind his desk or in the bathroom. As she entered, her gaze fell to the floor. She jumped in surprise when she saw him sitting up against the wall beside the door.

"Thane." She shut the door quickly, lowered to the floor, and touched his arms, which were crossed over his knees, propping up his head. He didn't look up. "Thane. Look at me."

He raised his head. His eyes were red. Tears had

left wet paths down his cheeks. He shook his head while peering at her, and fresh tears bloomed in his eyes.

She swiped them away when they fell. "What happened?"

His jaw ticked, and he shook his head again. "If he were still alive, I'd kill him myself."

Constantine. His name blazed through her mind like a massive asteroid about to demolish Earth. Her gaze found the letter pinned beneath Thane's phone. Whatever Jessalyn had told Thane must've been far worse than Letty had imagined.

She nodded, knowing he meant what he'd said with every fiber of his being. He would've preferred to have done it himself, to have saved her from having to do it, to have saved Jessalyn.

"I could've snuck into my parents' suite when they were going at it one night. We had plenty of hunting rifles. I could've gotten one and done it then, ended it once and for all. I wish…" His voice caught.

"Ssh." She kissed his forehead. "Sit with me." On her feet, she held out her hands.

He took them and stood. On the loveseat, he leaned forward with his elbows on his knees and raked his hands over his face. "He'd ruined her," he said, his voice muffled against his palms. "He ruined his own daughter." He dropped his hands. "I can't imagine how a man could do that to his own daughter."

"Of course, you can't. You don't have an abusive bone in your body."

His eyes were drawn when he met her gaze. "You can still say that after I just admitted to wanting to kill him myself? Abuse is violent treatment to *any* person regardless of gender. How can I not have an abusive bone in my body when I fantasize about murdering my dead father?"

"Because you have a *humane* bone in your body, a *protective* bone, a *loving* bone." She lifted his left hand and brushed a kiss over his bruised knuckles. Then she cradled his hand in her lap. "What you wish you could do, you wish because your loved ones had been abused, time and time again. You want to erase that pain from existence. That's love, Thane."

He met her eye.

"Everyone wishes for the opportunity to make the people who hurt their loved ones pay. You're not evil for thinking that. It's normal. It comes out of love."

"I failed her."

"No. No, you didn't. You loved her, even when she made it hard. That is not failure. Jessalyn is blessed to have you for a brother. Your mother is blessed to have you for a son. And I am blessed to have you for..." She paused, considering the best word to use. He was her boyfriend, but that didn't sound strong enough for what he was to her. Lover didn't quite cut it, either.

Thane angled his head toward her, waiting.

"...my soulmate."

He bent his neck, and she kissed his temple, his cheek, the corner of his mouth. He moved his head and teased her lips with his. His kiss was faint, as if he kissed her delicately. She returned the soft pressure and linked her fingers loosely with his in her lap, conscious of hurting him with the contact. She parted her lips enough to mold them tenderly around his top lip. A light kiss. A soothing touch. She dipped her head to do the same to his bottom lip. Then she eased back so only the top-most, sensitive layer of skin of their mouths touched. It couldn't be called a kiss. There was no pressure to it what-so-ever, but it was staggeringly strong.

Thane's fingers cupped her chin, and he inched forward to take her lips fully, but the kiss was restrained. The contact was careful, cautious, considerate. She kissed him back in the exact same way he wanted to kiss her in that moment. Their lips fondled each other's so sweetly that it stole her breath. It reminded her of the first kiss they'd shared after their first, official date. Damn this man knew how to kiss with all his emotions and it sent her heart racing.

Thane pulled his lips from hers, but not all the way. His breath tickled them. After a brief moment, he returned, and the tip of his tongue teased her. She widened her mouth, granting him access, and her tongue met his in a silky greeting. Just as before, the kiss remained tentative. Still, with his tongue gliding against hers, as if savoring a sensual taste of a decadent fruit, it was powerful. She gave a satisfied sigh. Once she did, he broke the contact completely.

Disappointment fluttered through her body, but then he shifted on the couch so he sat sideways, and said, "Cuddle here with me."

She slipped off her heels, made a bridge over his lap with her legs, and nestled into his side. He held her in his arms. After a moment, he kissed the top of her head and stroked his hand up and down her arm, where her scar hid beneath a quarter-sleeve.

"This always helps," he murmured.

She smiled, liking that she could comfort him in this way.

They lay like that for some time, breathing together, feeling each other's beating hearts, soaking up each other's body heat. She didn't know what time it was—if her lunch break was about to end or had already ended—but she didn't want to leave his arms. However long he needed her, she'd be there. And if he needed her in his arms, she'd give him that. Any time of the day or night. Whenever he required it; she'd hold him, and she'd let him hold her.

His phone released a chime. Her gaze lowered to it and its glowing screen.

"I should check that," he said.

"I'll get it for you."

He didn't release her, though.

She stroked his right arm from wrist to shoulder, but she didn't move to leave.

Finally, he released her. She sat forward, twisted around, and laid a kiss on his cheek before getting up and walking across the floor, bare-footed. She scooped up the phone and pressed the home button to see the notification. Her stomach clenched.

"It's Jessalyn."

He turned his body so he sat straight. "What does it say?"

She read the text that showed in its entirety on the lock screen. The message had her heart pounding for a vastly different reason than a moment ago. She studied Thane, who was clasping his hands together and eyeing the floor. Then she read him Jessalyn's words. "'Do it.'"

Thane lifted his head. He stared. A nod of his head later and he was on his feet. He headed for the bathroom. The light flashed on. Water ran in the faucet. When he came back out, a new look had taken over him—determination.

He held out his hand, and she placed his phone on his palm. His mouth twitched. "I meant your hand." He slipped his phone into his pocket. With his hand back out, she laid hers in his. "Come with me to the police station?"

"Of course."

Hand in hand, they exited his office.

He paused at Rebekah's desk. "I need that recording now."

Rebekah unlocked the top drawer of her desk. From a discreet cardboard jewelry box, she removed a USB drive and held it out to Thane.

A few hours later, cops arrested Alec Danes.

32

Thane

A week later, all the news could talk about was Alec and his charges of multiple counts of rape and child abuse. Speculation circled while the police kept the victims' names under wraps, but they all assumed that Letty was the victim of both heinous crimes. Reporters and paparazzi returned with a vengeance to catch a glimpse of her, to snap pics, shout questions; as if that was any way to treat a survivor of abuse. That was a perfect example of how demented the media and society were to victims, and Thane hated them for it. No matter what he did or said, they wouldn't back down now.

In the face of all that, Letty exuded a superhuman grace that Thane admired. She kept her head high and ignored them, even when it brought back her night terrors.

Her whimpers woke Thane in the middle of the night.

He flipped on the light and winced from the brightness. On his side, he faced her. She lay on her back with a pained expression on her face. Her body flinched.

"Letty." He reached out to touch her but stopped himself. *You're not supposed to wake her.*

She let out a cry and jolted in her sleep.

Inside, Thane cursed. He yearned to take her into his arms, soothe her, whisper comforting words into her ear, but that wouldn't help her. *After*, he told himself. *I can do it after.* Right now, the night terror had to come to an end on its own, or she had to break free from it by herself. *You're stronger than whatever you're seeing, Letty. You're stronger than your memories.*

But she let out a yelp, and the bed shook from her spasm. Another cry left her lips. She rolled into a ball and raised her arms to either side of her head. Sobs broke from her body.

Thane hovered his hands over her. His heart sank. Seeing her like that and not being able to do a damn thing about it was killing him.

Again and again her body flinched, as if hits rained upon it.

Please wake up, Letty. When she let out a scream, he changed his prayer. *Please let her go.*

She jerked so hard that her eyelids sprang open.

Thane held his breath.

Shivering and gasping, she blinked. Her gaze landed on him. "Thane?"

"Yeah, baby, I'm here." He scooped her into his arms. "You're safe."

She clung to him.

"Was it my father?"

She shook her head against his shoulder. "Alec and his riding crop."

Gut twisting, he settled a hand to her back to stroke away the bad memories, but her back tensed, and she recoiled from the touch. He snatched his hand away. "I'm sorry."

"No. No. It's a reflex, a defense mechanism. You can put your hand back. It's okay."

He did so gradually, as if her body would shatter if he touched her too quickly, too much. His palm settled on her back delicately. When she didn't shy away from his touch but actually relaxed even more, he moved his hand in small circles.

"Ever since he beat me with that riding crop, noises at night, or even my pajamas shifting against my skin, makes my back tense. It's not you."

He dropped a kiss to the top of her head and continued to rub her back. "Is there anything I can do?"

"This is good." She rested her head on his shoulder. "This is enough."

Hearing her say that conjured a surge of love. He held her until she fell asleep in his arms. The fact that she could do that, and it had been easy for her to do so from the beginning, never ceased to amaze him. He settled her onto the mattress and laid her head on the pillow. Watching her sleep, he skimmed his fingers through her curls. Everything about her was beautiful.

"God, I love you, Letty," he whispered. "I'm going

to keep you safe, and I'm going to love you with everything I have in me."

Although she wasn't awake to hear his words, he meant to keep that vow forever. For the rest of his life and whatever came after.

In the morning, Letty didn't bare a sign of her night terror. She looked as radiant as ever, but the night terrors must've taken a toll on her. If they did, they were internal, and she was keeping it that way.

Thane fixed his cup of coffee and carried it to the counter. When all of this was over, he planned to take Letty far away from here.

His cell phone sounded. He glanced at it while reaching for a slice of toast. His arm froze. He hadn't heard from Jessalyn since her text telling him to, "Do it." Now a new text from her waited.

—I should've done this sooner. Turn on the news.—

He sprang off his stool. In a few long strides, he was at the coffee table. He snatched up the remote and jabbed the on button.

"What's going on?" Letty asked, joining his side.

"I don't know."

He changed the channel to the news. His spine snapped straight when he saw Jessalyn on the screen, standing in front of All Heart Tech.

"Thank you for coming to my impromptu press conference. I called you all here today to tell you something. Last week, Alec Danes was arrested and charged with rape and child abuse. There's been a lot of rumors since then. Well, I'm here to lay those rumors to rest. Alec raped me when I was fifteen years old."

Gasps exploded in the air.

"He raped me ten times."

Reporters shouted questions.

"And that's why he was arrested."

"What about the child abuse charges?" someone called out.

"You don't think raping a minor is child abuse?" She arched a brow. "That's all I have to say. Now leave Letty Remis alone. If you want to bug anyone, bug me. Strike that. Don't harass victims. Harass their abusers." Then she spun on her heel and walked into All Heart Tech.

Thane switched off the TV.

"She's brave," Letty whispered.

Braver than either of them knew.

"I have to get to All Heart Tech."

Letty nodded. "Tell her I said thank you."

"I will. You should stay away today, though."

"That's okay. I'll see you tonight." She kissed his cheek. "Now, go to your sister."

He hurried to All Heart Tech and rushed to the top floor.

Jessalyn sat in one of the chairs outside his office.

She stood. "Did you see it?"

Nodding, he came up to her and wrapped her in a hug.

"I'm going to make you proud of me yet," she said.

He tightened his hold. "I already am."

When she withdrew, he kissed her forehead. She squirmed and glanced at her feet, clearly not used to affection like that. Readjusting the strap to her purse, she backed away. Her reaction told him just how much he'd failed her. Her flippant attitude when they were kids had rubbed Thane the wrong way, forcing him to retreat. That had been the wrong course of action. Instead, he should've been chipping away at her hard exterior to show her that all women should be respected and treated right, including her. Especially her. Perhaps if he had, she would've changed sooner and had a chance. Letty said it wasn't his fault, but he'd never stop blaming himself.

"What happened to your hands?"

Thane peeked at them. His knuckles weren't swollen anymore, but they were still discolored with browns and yellows and greens. He shrugged. "A boxing accident."

She lifted a brow. "Well, in the footage of Alec getting hauled into the police department, he didn't have black eyes, so you didn't get them that way."

I wish I had.

She toyed with the strap of her purse again. "What a coincidence that the paparazzi were there at the right time to film that, isn't it?" She gave Thane a sly smile.

He grinned and let out a small, breathy laugh. He hadn't even thought about how the paparazzi knew. "The best coincidence."

She winked her thick, black lashes.

"Come on in." He held out his hand to her, letting her enter his office.

She plopped onto one of the chairs in front of his

desk, and he claimed the other. "It's weird to be back here."

Thane grimaced. "I shouldn't have fired you."

Jessalyn sent him a stern look. "Yes, you should have. I was being a bitch, and you did the right thing. If you hadn't fired me, none of this would've come to be."

"Still…if you want your job back, it's yours."

"No." She wrapped her purse strap around her hand. "Although All Heart Tech is different from Canmore Tech, and I had steered clear of Alec, this place…it's not a good place for me. Too much darkness. I think it's about time I did my own thing. I'm not quite sure what that'll be yet." She bit her bottom lip. "Actually, I've been thinking about helping victims…survivors…like me."

A swell of pride rushed through Thane. "That's great. If you need me for anything, let me know."

She smiled. "If I didn't know better, I'd think you were my older brother."

"Older or younger, brothers should always look out for their sisters."

"And sisters should always look out for their brothers. That's what I was trying to do when I…" She stopped. He knew exactly what she was talking about without her having to voice it. "But I took it too far. I did what Daddy would've done." Her head tipped back, and she cast her gaze to the ceiling. "He's too much a part of me. It's going to take me a long time to undo what he'd done and unlearn what I thought was right."

"You're strong. You're smart. You're resilient. You didn't get those things from him. You gave them to yourself."

Tears swam in her eyes. "Damn it, Thane, don't make me cry. I have a full face of makeup on for the cameras and don't want to ruin it."

"Sorry."

Taking a deep breath, she rose to her feet. "I should probably get going anyway." At the door, she paused. "Oh, but before I forget, Mom wanted me to remind you that she's still extending that dinner invitation."

Right. He'd forgotten about that.

"What dinner invitation is she talking about?"

"She wants to meet Letty."

Jessalyn's eyebrows shot up her forehead. "Seriously?"

He nodded.

"Whoa. I never expected that."

"She's doing better after her recent stay at rehab."

"It appears that way, anyway." She shrugged a shoulder when he squinted at her. "Old habits die hard. If you say she's doing better, I'll take your word for it. I just can't help but believe that it's all a farce. I have separate mommy issues that I'll have to deal with at another time. My daddy issues are taking up all my energy at the moment."

Thane could understand that.

"Would you like to come to the dinner?"

She burst with laughter. "Sorry, little brother, but you're on your own with that one. When it happens, though, tell me so I can wish you luck."

He chuckled, too. "Thanks." He gave her a small hug.

Chin lifted, she stepped onto the elevator, ready to face the cameras downstairs.

Yes, Thane was proud of her. More than she knew.

At the end of the work day, he left early so he would be there by the time Letty closed the shop. He parked in the back and rapped on the door.

Letty opened it. "This is a surprise." Her hands curled in the lapels of his jacket, and she leaned into him. Her warm, soft lips teased his. "But a welcome one." Lacing her fingers with his, she led him inside. "I'm glad you're here. I've already locked the shop. It'll just be a few more minutes, and then...I have to tell you something."

He tilted his head. "Are you okay?"

"Yeah." She held up a finger. "Hold on. I just need to empty the cash register."

He browsed the stands and shelves while she finished up. Whenever someone said they had to tell you something, was it possible not to think the worst? Was it possible not to struggle to breathe? Was it possible not to be afraid?

Her heels sounded as she left the backroom. "All right. I'm done."

He went to her and placed his hands on her hips. "I think I've thought of every possible scenario for the outcome of this moment. I didn't like any of them."

She smoothed his tie. "I don't think you've thought of this one."

His brows drew together. "If it's good news, then you're right, because I only considered the worst."

"It's not." She inhaled. The action was shaky. "If there's no more, then the charms weren't spelling Dad."

She dipped her hand into her pocket. Between her fingers dangled a tiny plastic bag with a sterling silver charm—an E. "They spell dead. But is that about Constantine, or is it aimed at me?"

Either way, Thane didn't like it. This was out of their hands now. This was an actual threat of violence against the love of his life. He couldn't let this stand any longer.

Wouldn't.

Once home, they called the cops who had responded to the call at Letty's apartment. Officer Wolfgang stood a few feet back, arms crossed while his partner asked them questions and wrote their answers in a notepad.

"Why didn't you notify us of the other charms when you got them?" Officer Kevin asked Letty.

She shrugged and glanced at Thane. "I don't know. I guess I didn't think there was anything you could do. Charms aren't dangerous."

Officer Kevin eyed them one at a time. "So, let me get this straight, after we responded to a knife being left at your house with a threatening message"—he checked his notes and then pinned Thane with his hard, cop stare—"Sasha Danes threw a knife at you during your presentation." That stare shifted back to Letty. "Following that incident, a knife charm was taped to your shop door. Is that correct?"

"Y-yes."

Thane glared at the cop, not appreciating how the man was intimating her.

"Then three more charms were delivered specifically to you, spelling out Dad."

She nodded.

The cop's eyes bore into Thane now. "Your father."

Thane met his glare straight on. "That's correct."

"You also assumed that your sister was the culprit behind them."

"At the time, but I no longer believe that."

"Right." The cop scribbled something in his notepad. "Ma'am, can you step over there with my partner so I can talk to Mr. Canmore alone?"

She fidgeted in place. "Why?"

"Just do what I say."

She flinched and hurried over to the other officer, but she kept a couple of feet between them. Her unease was evident. Her entire being pulsed with it.

"Mr. Canmore, I need you to turn your back on Ms. Remis."

He compiled.

"I have responded to many domestic violence calls, Mr. Canmore. I can see when a woman is terrified."

"Of course, she's terrified. Someone sent her a knife and charms that spell out dead. You think she shouldn't be afraid by that?"

"I think someone is having fun scaring her."

Thane scowled. *Well, no shit, Sherlock.*

"I don't know if Sasha Danes throwing a knife at you is connected to the rest or not. If it is, I'm inclined to think it was a diversion, to make it seem as though you were also in danger, but you never were, now were you?"

What the hell is he trying to say?

"You reacted pretty quickly to that knife being

thrown at you and managed to avoid a serious injury, as if you anticipated it—"

Thane's breathing became erratic. *Son-of-a-bitch.*

"Whether or not your so-called attack is really connected to what's going on with Ms. Remis, my thoughts are the same, suspects tend to do things to redirect suspicion. Or they use other people to do it. Like Sasha Danes."

Thane fought to keep calm, but his insides boiled. *This cop on a power trip thinks I'm behind everything.* And there would be nothing Thane could say that'd change his mind.

"When I watch Ms. Remis with you, I see all the classic signs of abuse."

"She *was* abused," Thane hissed, stressing that the abuse was in the past.

But the cop continued as if Thane hadn't spoken. "She looks at you as if she's afraid to say the wrong thing. I noticed it when we were called to her apartment the first time."

Because she worried whatever she told you about me, you'd twist her words. Just as you're doing right now, you piece of shit.

"I've seen abused women swear up and down that their partners don't hurt them, and even point the blame somewhere else."

Thane's fingers curled into his palms.

"Victims have very specific ways of speaking without their voices. Sometimes, it's subconscious and they don't even know they're doing it, but they point us to their abusers. The easiest and safest way of doing that is with their eyes. When Ms. Remis told us about each incident, her eyes shifted to you every single time."

Officer Kevin tucked his notepad into his utility belt. His hand didn't lower to his side but settled over the compartment holding his handcuffs. "Mr. Canmore, how'd you bruise your hands?"

Thane didn't answer. If he opened his mouth now, he'd be charged with threatening a law enforcement officer.

Officer Kevin removed the cuffs. "Put your hands behind your head and turn around."

Without protest, Thane linked his hands and faced Letty.

"What are you doing?" Letty rushed forward, but Officer Wolfgang grabbed her. "Don't touch me. Get your hands off." She wrenched away.

"Ma'am, if you interfere, I will have to put you in cuffs." He had his handcuffs in his hands, ready to slap them on her wrists.

Thane's heart battered against his chest. "Letty, don't. I expected this."

Eyes wide, she shook her head. "No, you don't understand. You're reading into things. Thane's not behind any of this."

Officer Kevin pushed him forward. "Ma'am, let us do our job."

"You're not *doing it* right!"

Thane caught her eye. "Letty, it'll be fine."

Officer Kevin escorted him onto the elevator.

Letty attempted to board, but Officer Wolfgang held up a hand to stop her. "You won't be coming with us."

She stayed put, staring at Thane. "What do you want me to do?"

He met her eye. "Nothing."

33

Letty

etty jabbed the elevator button again and again. *Please, please hurry.* She had no idea what the cop had said to Thane, but the outcome couldn't have been further from what they should've done. Listen to her, for starters. How many times did she have to tell them that Thane would never hurt her? What did she have to do to convince them? Whatever it was, she'd do it.

She ran for her purse and dug through the contents for her cell phone. Hands shaking, she called Abbot. "It's Letty. Thane is being arrested." She pushed the elevator button several more times. "I need you to take me straight to the police department."

Before he could answer, she hung up and stabbed the button without pausing. Finally, the door opened.

Clutching her purse, she punched the button for the underground parking garage. The elevator opened on the floor below Thane's, and Abbot boarded. Neither of them said a word. In the garage, they raced to the SUV. She flung open the front passenger's door and jumped in.

Abbot stomped on the gas pedal. The SUV sped up the ramp and bounced onto the ground level. Then he whipped the wheel, guiding the vehicle onto the road between two cars.

Letty scanned the traffic. "There." She pointed at the police car three cars in front of them. Her heart sank knowing Thane sat in the back of that car, handcuffed. She took out her phone again to call Rebekah, but she didn't let the woman even get her greeting out. "Thane was arrested. I thought you should know, but I don't know if he'd want you to know. I don't know—"

"Slow down, honey. Tell me what happened."

The whole time she explained the situation, she kept her gaze pinned on that police car. "They must think he's behind it. Or that's he's abused me or something. Which he hasn't. He hasn't laid a finger on me in anger."

"I believe you. Thane would never do that."

"We're following the police car now. Should I call his attorney?"

"Did Thane say anything at all before he was arrested?"

"He said not to do anything."

"Then that's exactly what we're going to do."

Letty's eyelids widened. "What?!"

"Bringing his attorney into this could make him

look guilty. We don't want to do that."

No, we don't.

"Thane is smart. We have to trust he knows what he's doing."

"Okay."

"If you need me, I can be there as soon as possible."

"Okay."

"Everything will be fine."

Letty's throat tightened. She couldn't say "okay" again, so she hung up.

They pulled up to the front of the police department as the cops yanked Thane from the backseat. The SUV jolted to a stop with a squeal of brake pads. Thane peered at the SUV and shook his head. Letty reached for the door handle. A loud snap of the doors' locking mechanisms engaging filled the inside of the vehicle right as she yanked on the handle. Not fast enough, though. The door didn't open. Her gaze shot from the door to Abbot. "No. What are you doing?" She yanked on the door handle.

"I'm sorry, Letty."

She pried the button back, but not even that unlocked the door; Abbot was keeping the button compressed that kept her from leaving the car.

"Let me out!"

"I can't do that. He doesn't want you in there right now. Give it twenty minutes for them to get him in the back, and then we'll go in."

She watched the cops escort Thane into the department. When she lost sight of him, she smacked her hand against the dash. Abbot kept her in there for twenty minutes, and those twenty minutes were the longest of her life. The moment she heard the locking mechanism release, she tugged the door handle, sprang onto the sidewalk, and slammed the door behind her. She raced into the department to the front desk. "Thane Canmore was just brought in for questioning or something. I need to speak to the officers or investigators or whoever is with him. Please. It's urgent."

"What's your name?"

"Letty Remis. Tell them it's Letty Remis and that I'll answer whatever questions they have, but I'm not going to leave until they speak to me."

The officer moved to the side and picked up a phone.

"Thane wouldn't want you in an interrogation room." Abbot stood at her side.

"You don't have to be here with me."

"Yes, I do."

The officer returned. "Have a seat. Someone will come and get you soon."

Letty sat in a wooden chair across from the front desk, and Abbot occupied the one beside her. It became apparent after thirty minutes that "soon" did not in fact mean soon. It meant "eventually, maybe. If we feel like it."

Her foot bounced. She couldn't imagine what was going on in that interrogation room. What kinds of questions were they asking him? What were they claiming he did?

My fault. It's all my fault. Whatever reason the cops had seen fit to arrest Thane, she was positive it was because of her; because they thought she was the victim and he was the offender.

Stupid. I'm so stupid. She hunted down her phone again and called the one person she knew who would tell her the truth about what was happening.

"Hello?"

"Mom, I need your help. Can the police arrest you for assault without proof?"

There was a brief pause on the other line before Lydia said, "An officer can make an arrest without a warrant based on probable cause. In this case, it would be an assault-mandatory arrest. Whether an officer makes this arrest is up to what the specific officer believes, if they see certain factors. For instance, has an assault occurred that resulted in a bodily injury? If an officer believes physical action has been taken to cause another person physical pain or fear of imminent pain, they can arrest the person they believe to be the primary aggressor."

Letty put her hand to her head.

"The officer should also consider serious threats that result in fear or physical injury, as well as the history of domestic violence of each person involved."

Shit.

"An officer with probable cause can always make a discretionary arrest if they believe someone has committed or is committing a felony, and they will always harbor the intent to protect victims of domestic violence. They will note the victim's appearance and demeanor and emotional state of mind to determine these things, like if the victim expresses pain or fear or extreme nervousness aimed at the offender. Any one of these things could lead to the conclusion that arrest is required." Lydia took a breath. "Now that I've explained all that, explain to me why you needed to know that."

Letty told her the whole story.

"Why have you not told me any of this sooner? All of this started before you came here and, aside from the attack on Thane, you didn't say a word about the danger you both are in."

"I thought I could handle it."

"Letty." Her mom didn't say more than that. She didn't have to. The use of Letty's name said it all; her mom was disappointed in her, but also hurt that Letty hadn't come to her with this. She had been there when Letty was a child, and she still wanted to be there. "All right." Lydia exhaled. "Tell me. Do you have any visible bruises on your body that they could've mistaken as a result of assault?"

"No, but…"

"But what? Spill it, Letty."

"Thane's knuckles are all bruised."

"How'd he get those bruises?"

"Hitting a punching bag for an hour without gloves after hearing a man admit to raping his sister ten times when they were young."

Lydia was silent a moment, and then, "Fuck."

"It was his bruises, wasn't it?"

"Yes, but not by itself. Can you recall your demeanor in the presence of the cops?"

"I was scared…nervous. You know me, I'm not comfortable around cops, not after what I endured when I was seven."

"They misread your reaction as a sign of your emotional state because of Thane."

Letty squeezed her eyelids shut and shook her head. "How do I fix this?"

"Demand to speak to the investigators. If they believe this is a domestic violence case, you have the right to make a sworn victim statement. Remind them that they haven't taken any photographic evidence of you to support their claim that Thane's bruises were acquired through causing you bodily injuries. Their case doesn't hold up if they don't have connecting proof."

"I can do that."

"I know you can, but if you need me, I can be on the first flight out."

"Thanks, Mom. I'll update you as soon as I can." She ended the call and leapt to her feet. At the front desk, she glared into the officer's eyes. "Tell the investigators questioning Thane Canmore that I want to give my sworn victim statement."

Moments after that message was relied, a man in a suit retrieved her. "I'm Detective Engle. Come with me."

She followed him to a small room with a one-way mirror. Sitting at a metal table, her palms and armpits began to sweat.

The man who led her to the interrogation room sat in the only remaining chair beside another investigator, who wore a black blouse and pink lipstick.

The badge clipped to the blouse's crisp collar said Paige Delacruz. "We were told you wanted to give your sworn victim's statement," she said.

Letty nodded. "I do. Can I get pen and paper? I want to write it down."

Detective Delacruz nodded.

The other detective left.

Letty avoided the woman's gaze, although she could feel her studying her.

A moment later, Detective Engle returned and slid a legal pad and a pen toward Letty. She wrote out each word with considerable care and thought. Her so-called victim's statement was a summary of her relationship with Thane. She detailed how he'd only treated her with kindness and respect from the start. She explained how he'd protected her from paparazzi, his sister, her past. Most of what she wrote was probably too personal for a statement that did not involve assault, but since she didn't have any abuse to describe, she figured she'd replace that with embarrassing romantic details.

At the end, she wrote, "Thane Canmore has never abused me. I have never felt threatened by him. I feel safe in his presence." She signed her statement before pushing it to the middle of the table.

Delacruz read it first. Then she passed it to her partner, who dropped it to the table with a smack. "What the hell is this?"

"My written statement, although not for being a victim. And here's my oral statement. I, Letty Remis, have never been physically harmed by Thane Canmore. I have never been assaulted or abused by Thane Canmore. I have never feared bodily harm by Thane Canmore. I have—"

"We get it," Engle snapped.

"I will finish my oral statement uninterrupted,

thank you." She glared. "I have never been threatened with physical injury or death by Thane Canmore. I have never had a bruise or mark or scratch on my person put there by Thane Canmore. Whatever else you believe, it has never happened at the hands of Thane Canmore. Now, if you want to talk about real, not imagined abuse, I can tell you what I have experienced." She told them about her childhood broken arm, riding crop beatings, and starvation. "My medical records and foster care records will attest to all that."

"We read the arresting officers' reports. They described you as being agitated, fearful, and nervous," Delacruz said.

"Of course, I was. Cops do that to me. I've been like that around cops ever since…ever since I killed Constantine Canmore in self-defense when I was seven. I was in an interrogation room for hours, terrified after what I'd just done and seen and heard. Add in that I was surrounded by and questioned by strangers, most of them men, then you can understand why I am agitated, fearful, and nervous around law enforcement."

"They also said you looked at Thane out of apparent fear before answering any of their questions. Why were you scared to answer their questions in front of Thane?"

"I wasn't scared, not how you think." She sighed. "I worry about him. What's happening to me pains him because he wants to protect me. He hates that he doesn't know who's doing these things to me. He hates that it's linked to his father. If you know anything about the Canmores, then you know that Thane hates everything about his father and what his father stood for."

Engle crossed his arms. "How did Thane get the bruises on his hands?"

"Boxing. But not with a person. With a punching bag. He didn't wear any gloves. He went at it for an hour because he'd just helped to get a rapist's confession on tape. Not only that, but this same man was the one who'd beaten me with a riding crop. His name is Alec Danes. He was Constantine Canmore's best friend. He was arrested last week. Surely, you've heard about that. If you speak to the detective on that case, I'm sure you could listen to the recording. You'd hear what Alec said and how Thane reacted. You'd understand."

They studied her silently.

"Thane was arrested for suspected abuse, right? Well, there was none, so you can't hold him. I'm certainly not pressing charges, so you have to let him go."

Neither of them said a word to that.

"You have no proof of physical injury. I don't have a single mark on my body. I only have the scars from my childhood. Nothing new. Certainly, no bruises. You've seen Thane's hands. They're still bruised. If he'd hit me with his hands as you believe he had, I'd still bear the bruises, too."

Still, they did nothing.

"Please! I will strip to prove to you that I don't have any injuries." Desperate, she peered at Delacruz. "I will go to the women's bathroom with you and remove my clothing in front of you. I will do that. I will do that because Thane is innocent and I love him.

Please." Tears brewed in her eyes.

Delacruz exchanged a look with her partner.

Engle lifted his hands in a "whatever" gesture.

With a sigh, Delacruz shoved to her feet. "Let's go."

In the women's bathroom, Delacruz locked the door.

Letty stood in the middle of the tile and bright lights. Her body already shook.

"I don't wish to further traumatize a survivor of abuse," Delacruz said. "This would be easier if you were wearing a shirt and shorts. Just lift your skirt so I can see your thighs."

Letty lifted her skirt, being sure not to show her underwear.

"Turn."

Letty rotated around and lifted her skirt to her buttocks.

"Now, I have to see your back. Pull down your dress zipper."

She reached around and lowered the zipper all the way.

"I'm going to touch the sides of your dress so I can view your back."

"Okay."

A gentle movement of fabric told her Delacruz was examining her back.

"You're going to have to draw your arms through the sleeves and lower the front."

She tugged the sleeves down her arms. Without so much as pausing, she exposed her chest and ribs. At least she wore a bra.

"Okay. You can fix your dress now."

Letty covered herself and rezipped her dress. "Can I…can I have a minute?"

Delacruz inclined her head. "I'll wait outside the door."

As soon as she left, Letty gripped the counter. Her legs wobbled. Her stomach squirmed. She thought she might throw up. Her vision doubled, and her body flushed with heat—a panic attack. She'd had them before.

She tore off a sheet of brown paper towels, wet them, and patted her forehead and the back of her neck. Focusing on her breathing, she recited the poem "Hope" by Emily Dickinson over and over again. It was the one thing that could snap her out of panic's clutches. After several minutes, her heart rate returned to normal, her knees stopped quivering, the burn left her skin, and her vision cleared. She opened the bathroom door to find Delacruz posted there as she said she would be.

Instead of bringing her back to the interrogation room, she led her to the front desk where Abbot still waited.

Letty faced Delacruz. "I don't understand."

"We're done questioning you."

"What about Thane?"

"We have one more piece of evidence to review."

With that, she left.

Letty resumed her seat, prepared to sit there all night.

34

Thane

The handcuffs clanked against the metal table when Thane shifted. They hadn't removed the cuffs, not while they questioned him for nearly an hour or when they left forty minutes ago according to the clock on the wall. He had no idea what they were doing. Nothing he'd said had convinced the two investigators of his innocence. Were they getting ready to book him? If they did, he couldn't blame them. With everything the officers had written in their reports, everything he'd been told, he looked guilty as hell.

The door opened.

Detective Delacruz came in. "Hands." He lifted his hands off the table, and she unlocked the cuffs. "You're free to go. You're lucky to have someone like Ms. Remis in your corner."

He gaped. "You were questioning her this whole time?"

"We weren't questioning her more than she was handing us our asses." Delacruz held the door open. "She's waiting for you."

With his jacket draped over his arm, he walked to the front of the department. He paused when he saw Letty sitting in a chair beside Abbot. Her neck was bent, and her hands were clasped on her knees as if she were praying.

"Letty."

Her head snapped up. "Thane!" She popped to her feet, dashed forward, and threw her arms around him.

He enclosed her into a hug and rested his cheek atop her head. The scent of her shampoo and perfume filled him. He drew the scents into his lungs; they smelled like freedom, and that freedom was pure love. "Let's go home," he whispered.

In the backseat of the SUV, Letty curled against his body. Her fingers skimmed against the skin of his wrists, where the cuffs had dug into him, leaving red marks.

He moved his hands, putting one hand on her hip and the other on her knee. "Detective Delacruz hinted that I was being released because of what you did." He glanced at her head of curls. "What did you do?"

"I told them I wanted to give my victim's statement, and I did, minus the victim part. Then I...I stripped in the women's bathroom in front of Delacruz to prove I didn't have any bruises on my body."

Thane shut his eyes. "You shouldn't have had to do that. I wouldn't have wanted you to go through that."

"I know you wouldn't have, but I had to, and I don't regret it."

Thane held her closer, cherishing her love. "Thank you."

In the morning, he stepped out of the shower and knotted a towel at his hips. Letty's whispers met his ears through the bathroom door.

"We got in late last night."

He paused with his hand on the door handle.

"He's okay. I think. He's home anyway, but I don't know how okay he really is."

He turned the handle and opened the door.

Letty sat on the edge of the bed. "I have to go, Mom. I love you, too."

She hung up, set her phone where she had been sitting, and made her way to him. "My mom was calling to check in. She was worried about us."

"I'd love to meet your mom."

"She'd love that, too. In fact, she said she has a vacation coming up soon."

"She's welcome here any time." He lifted Letty's hand and kissed it. "I heard what you said to her...I *am* okay."

Letty titled her head.

"I will be."

She cupped his right hand in hers, lifted it to her lips, and kissed each of his bruised knuckles. His stomach clenched, not out of desire but in self-loathing.

Hearing what the officers believed he'd done to her had twisted his gut. How many others thought he had lured Letty to him as his father had lured her mother? How many wondered if he mistreated Letty in the same ways, or even worse ways?

A vicious, vindictive, violent cycle.

The spawn of a demon picking up where his father had left off.

He grimaced. "Letty..."

She picked up his other hand and did the same thing; kissed every inch of his bruised skin. Then she flattened her palms to his chest and laid her lips over his heart.

This time, the clenching in his gut was purely desire. "Letty."

She drew him over to the bed. "I want to make love to you. Do you want to make love to me? If that's not what you want right now, I won't force you. I won't do that."

No, she wouldn't. She wouldn't take his erection to mean he wanted to have sex just because he couldn't control a part of his anatomy. But he did. He did want to make love to her, wanted to feel her body accepting him and her love enveloping him. After yesterday, he needed it as much as breath.

"Yes." His voice was strained. "I do."

She pressed her lips to his. While kissing him, she freed the towel from his hips and dropped it to the floor. Then she pushed him onto the bed.

"Lay down."

He swung his legs onto the bed and stretched out

on his back, ready and needing her to take full control in this moment.

Letty hitched her dress up to her thighs. Her hands disappeared under the skirt, and then she worked her panties down her legs. When they fell around her ankles, she lifted her feet out of them. He hardened even more.

She climbed onto the bed and straddled him. Her skirt pooled around her thighs, covering them. Slowly, she sank onto him, letting him fill her.

He screwed his eyelids shut and clenched his hips, keeping them from lifting and his penis from impaling her. A groan ripped from him. He tossed his head back and wound his hands in the bed sheets as she lowered even more. It felt good. Too damn good. So good, it was damn-near painful. She settled completely over him and paused.

A breath hissed out of him.

She didn't move, allowing his libido to calm a fraction. He pried his eyelids open to see her studying him. Then she worked his hands free from the bed sheet and held them to her hips. She nodded, telling him she was ready, if he was.

He nodded, too.

The significance that she was keeping his hands on her after everything that'd happened, everything he'd been accused of, didn't escape his notice. He started to take his hands away when he realized his fingertips were digging into her flesh, but she held his hands firmly in place.

She ground against him in deep, long strokes. "I love you."

A moan escaped him.

"I love you," she repeated.

His hips pistoned.

"I love you."

His body reacted again. It was her words, her sentiment that had the pleasure he felt exploding like fireworks throughout his body.

"I—" She gasped. "Love."

He groaned and pumped his hips.

"Yes."

His gaze feasted on her as she arched her back.

Her lips parted ever-so-slightly, and a soft sound came from her vocal cords. That soft sound became louder and higher pitched. She wasn't speaking anymore, but in his head, he could hear her saying, "Love. Yes. Love."

His own inner voice joined hers. *Love. Yes. Fuck, yes.*

Their moans blended.

Letty melted when she came, and he let himself go with a final, *loveyesfuckyes*.

Letty lay beside him, with her right leg draped across him.

He turned onto his side, and she hooked her leg more securely over him. The skirt of her dress still concealed them. He gazed into her eyes. "I love you, too." He nearly added "fuck yes."

She kissed him. "I think I know something else that'll lift your spirits."

"You lifted my spirits pretty well a moment ago, but what else do you got?"

"I'd like to meet your mom. I'm ready for that

dinner."

He pushed onto his elbow. "You really want to meet my mom? Doing it too soon could be triggering."

"Doing it at any time could be triggering, but with you there, I'll make it through."

"I'll be by your side the entire time. How soon are you thinking?"

"As soon as possible so I don't lose the nerve."

"Sunday?"

"Sunday."

Three days later, Letty stood in Thane's bedroom, wearing a lavender and white dress with quarter sleeves. Her hands shook while she attempted to hook a silver chain around her neck with a single imitation diamond. He brushed her fingers aside and hooked the clasp.

"You look beautiful." He planted a kiss to the side of her neck.

Taking a deep breath, she placed the tips of her fingers around the diamond.

His hands molded gently to her hips. "How are you feeling?"

"Nervous...scared."

"You don't have to be scared. I'll be right there the entire time."

"I know. It's just...it's just that I'll be where *he* used to live."

"Oh, shit, I didn't even think about that." He laid his forehead against her shoulder. "We can go to a restaurant instead. That might be better anyway."

"But public."

"Right."

"It's okay. I'll be fine."

He kissed her shoulder through the cotton. "If you're not at any time, you can tell me. Or give me a sign."

She rotated in his arms. "A sign like what? It has to be something your mom won't suspect."

"Hmm." His gaze lowered. "How about if you hide your necklace beneath your collar, I'll know to bring you home right away."

"That sounds good."

He framed her face with his hands and kissed her softly. "Are you ready to go?"

She nodded.

Because they were still taking precautions, Abbot drove them to Canmore Estate. During the drive, Thane held Letty's hand. Every once in a while, he lifted it and placed a kiss to her palm, the back of her hand, or her fingers.

Just inside the gate, Abbot slowed the SUV to a halt.

Thane stroked Letty's knuckles. "Are you sure about this? You can change your mind. Even now."

"It's too late for that. I'm sure they're making dinner already."

"Actually, I'm making dinner."

"Really?"

"I like to cook, and I thought if you helped me in the kitchen, it'd give you a reprieve from my mother."

She smiled now. "Thank you for thinking of that, but I'm okay." She gripped his hand. "Let's go."

Thane and Abbot exchanged looks in the rearview mirror. Then Abbot lifted his foot off the brake and eased the car to the front steps. Thane leaned forward and clapped a hand to Abbot's shoulder. "Are you sure you don't want to join us?"

Abbot let out a boisterous laugh. "I'm sure your mother would love having the help at the dinner table."

"Ouch," Thane said.

"That's what I am to her. Besides that, she scares the shit out of me. I've met her a handful of times, and that was enough for me. I'll stay here."

"I'll make you a plate."

"Appreciate it."

Thane climbed out of the SUV and held Letty's hand as she stepped down. He continued to grasp her hand as they made their way up the steps to the door.

"Abbott is an ex-marine. If he's is scared of her..." Letty's voice trailed off.

Thane exhaled through his nose in a soft laugh. "He was exaggerating."

Sort of.

Rather than enter with his key, he thought tipping his mother off on their arrival would be best. The doorbell trilled throughout the mansion when he pressed the button.

The door opened to his mother. She wore black slacks with perfect creases and a white, silk blouse with a bow. A strand of pearls adorned her bronze throat.

"Letty, this is my mom, Emma. Mom, this is Letty, the woman I love."

"Hello, Letty," Emma said. "It's nice to finally meet you."

Letty's voice shook. "You-you too."

In the sitting room, Thane watched Letty out of the corner of his eye. She sat stiffly beside him on the couch, gripping a cup of tea. Damn this wasn't a good idea. He shouldn't have believed everything would be fine. Here she was, sitting across from his mother, looking as though she wanted to run. *Fuck. She's actually shivering.* He didn't want to let go of her hand, but he did want to secure a supportive arm around her. To placate his urges, he shifted closer, pressing his leg to hers.

His mother noticed. Her gaze flashed to him and then to Letty. "So, Letty, tell me about yourself."

Letty swallowed. "I own an antique shop, Let It Charm You."

"Is that a play on your name? Or...names? Letty and Charm?"

Letty's cheeks flushed. "Y-yes, it is."

"Interesting." His mother sipped jasmine tea sweetened with honey. "How long have you lived in New York City?"

"Five years."

"That long? It's a wonder that the two of you hadn't run into each other sooner."

Thane smiled. "We ran into each other at the perfect time."

Letty blushed.

"It seems so. That's good. For the both of you."

Thane appreciated that his mother could say that.

"My son has expressed his love for you." Emma pinned her gaze to Letty. "Do you love my son in return?"

Letty's hand became sweaty in his. "Yes, ma'am, I do. Very much."

"Oh, please call me Emma." She placed her tea cup in its saucer. "Do you want to have children?"

Letty sputtered up the tea she'd been sipping and quickly placed the cup and saucer on the coffee table. She picked up a napkin and dabbed at her chin.

Thane eyed his mother.

"Don't give me that look, Thane. You're my only son." She turned her attention back to Letty. "He's my only son, you see, my only chance for grandkids."

"No, I'm not. Jessalyn could very well have kids."

His mother scoffed. "She's made it clear she doesn't want kids. I doubt she'll ever get married. I dare say she's damaged."

Letty flinched at that, and Thane stiffened. He had to actively make sure he wasn't giving Letty's hand a death grip.

"Jess. Is. *Not*. Damaged."

"You know what I mean. She's not marriage material. Or mother material for that fact."

Neither were you, he almost said.

Letty laid her other hand on his knee. The feel of her hand, the weight and warmth, reminded Thane of her technique to encourage peace. He inhaled, held it, exhaled. He was not going to fall for his mother's bait. No matter what she said.

"Children. Yes? No?"

His mother's words had him snapping back to the moment. Maybe he'd been too quick to believe his mother wouldn't get the best of him.

"This is something Letty and I should talk about.

Alone." He emphasized that last word, glaring at his mother, hoping she got the hint.

"I'm your mother, and one day, I may be Letty's mother-in-law. I would like to be close enough to Letty to have these conversations."

Letty squirmed uncomfortably. Red streaks splashed across her face.

"That would be nice, Mom, but this is a little too personal too soon."

"Fine." His mother sighed, deflating.

"No, actually, it's...it's okay," Letty said. "Um. I hadn't wanted to have kids because of what I'd gone through in foster care. It made me not want to bring another child into a world that could treat children like that, but"—she stole a peek at Thane—"since falling in love..." She inhaled. "...I have a new dream that involves kids."

"With Thane?"

"Yes," Letty whispered.

Thane's chest rose and fell. Her honesty stirred his passion. If they were alone, he'd drag her to him and kiss her with everything he had in him. But he couldn't do that in front of his mother. He wanted to marry Letty. Today. Tomorrow. Yesterday. And, yes, he wanted to have kids. They'd raise their children how they should've been raised, cocooning them in love and safety. They'd be the best damn parents.

"When do the two of you intend to marry?"

"All right, Mom. That's enough personal inquiries for now. I'm going to start dinner. Letty, would you like to help me?"

"I would love to."

Holding her hand, he stood and drew her to her feet. In the kitchen, with the doors shut, he hugged Letty to himself. "I'm sorry about all that."

"It's okay." She flattened her palms to his back. "I would rather have her ask me questions about grandkids than...that night."

He inched back and cupped her face with his hands. His kiss was thorough as his tongue stroked, seeking her unique flavor. Her moan ignited his urges from a roaring fireplace to a bonfire. Wishing they were home so they could postpone dinner in favor of delicious love making, he stepped back. "We should start cooking." He pried his hands from her body. Otherwise, he'd never stop touching and kissing her.

While Thane seasoned pureed cauliflower with rosemary and garlic, he couldn't get their future out of his head. How he yearned for the future to begin right now, right this second. "So...how many kids do you want?"

"I don't know. I've actually thought about fostering kids." She tossed orzo and chickpeas into baby spinach leaves. "Would that be something you'd be interested in?"

"Absolutely. Foster kids need love and support, too. We could give foster kids a very good home, the one they deserve."

Letty slipped her arms around him. "Thank you for being the kind of person who understands that. And thank you for being the person I can dream with."

He kissed her temple. "We'll do more than dream."

"Yes, we will." She stepped back and surveyed the kitchen. "What's next?"

"I need to get the filet mignon in the oven."

While the beef cooked, they worked on the finishing touches of the dishes. This dinner may end up being a nightmare, but at least the food would be good.

Thane's cell phone sounded. He removed it from his pocket. "It's Jess. She's probably checking to see how the dinner is going. Could you let my mom know it'll just be a couple of minutes?"

"Sure."

The door swung closed behind Letty.

Thane swiped his finger across his phone's screen and lifted it to his ear. "Hey, Jess. Don't worry. We're all surviving the dinner so far."

"She has Letty's bracelet!"

Frowning, Thane untied the apron he'd been wearing around his waist. "What bracelet? What are you talking about?"

"I opened Mom's safe deposit box, looking for Grandma's ruby and diamond necklace that she always swore she didn't have—"

"How'd you get access to her safe deposit box?"

"I know someone at the bank. We both know that I do shady shit!"

"Okay. Calm down." He bundled up the apron and set it on the counter.

Letty rejoined him in the kitchen. "What's going on?" she mouthed.

He shrugged.

"I found Grandma's necklace *and* Letty's charm bracelet," Jess shouted. "I read about it in the police report. She'd described each charm. She'd lost it in the woods when she was seven, and Mom has it! It's in my fucking hand!"

Thane braced a hand on the counter. "What?"

"Mom was there, Thane! She was there that night! How else could she have it?"

Thane's heart rate became erratic. Fear was a strong tonic in his belly. His entire body went cold.

"Are you listening to me, Thane? Mom was there! She could've been in on it with Daddy. You have to get Letty out of there. Now!"

The cold that was taking over his body disappeared in a wave of searing heat. "Fuck." He spun around and met his mother's eyes a second before piercing pain speared him in his abdomen. He stared at the knife in his mother's hand.

The phone slipped from his fingers. It hit the floor, and the screen shattered into a cobweb of cracks.

A scream filled the kitchen.

His mother yanked the knife out of his abdomen.

Blood spread across his shirt.

His legs gave out, and he fell.

That scream filled his ears and his heart. That scream belonged to Letty.

35

Letty

etty dropped to her knees. Blood poured from the stab wound in Thane's abdomen. Her heart raced with fear, choking her. Her hands shook when she grasped his shoulders. He leaned against the warm oven door. His mouth was open in shock. He wasn't looking at her but at his mother, who was wiping her fingerprints off the knife with a handkerchief. The woman could very well stab Letty in the back or the side of the neck, but all Letty cared about in that moment was Thane, who was bleeding out right in front of her eyes. "You need to lay flat." She managed to maneuver him from the sitting position to a prone one.

The bottoms of his shoes slid over the tile, pulling his legs straight. "L-Letty." His voice was a rasp. "Run.

Go."

"I'm not leaving you." She yanked off the hand towel that draped over the oven's handle and pressed it to Thane's wound. *Stop the bleeding. Gotta stop the bleeding.*

"That's it, dear," Emma said. "Get his blood all over you. That'll help my story."

The knife was no longer in Emma's hand. Now, she held a gun, which she pointed at Letty's head.

Letty flinched, but she didn't stop applying pressure to Thane's wound. Her gaze flicked from him to Emma to the floor. The knife, coated with Thane's blood, was right next to her foot. No doubt, Emma wanted it to look as though Letty had stabbed Thane. And she had no doubt that the gun was meant to make it look as though Letty had taken her own life after killing Thane. Then Emma would fake a survival story, maybe even fake injuries that she'd claim Letty had inflicted on her. Forever after, Emma would be hailed as the lone survivor of a twisted mother-daughter murderous scheme.

What would Emma do about Jessalyn, though? Jessalyn knew everything.

Letty searched the floor for Thane's phone. The screen was black, lifeless.

Thane's fingers fluttering over hers made her jump. She peered back.

His face was pale. Too pale. His lips were turning a faint purple. "I...love you."

Fat, hot tears ballooned in Letty's eyes.

Emma's laughter stopped her from replying. "And that will make this a tragic tale. The son of Constantine

Canmore loses his life to the woman who'd conspired to kill his father, a woman he was fooled into believing loved him. A murderous scheme twenty-three years in the making. People will talk about this forever."

Thane's eyelids lowered.

Blood soaked through the hand towel.

Stay with me, Thane. Stay awake.

The click of heels on tile had Letty looking up to see Emma standing over her. She stared down the barrel of the petite handgun into Emma's hate-filled eyes.

"This is for Constantine."

Letty's gaze fell to Thane.

Through slits between his heavy eyelids, he stared. His lips trembled open, but only breath came out.

I know. I love you, too.

She closed her eyes.

Ready.

Accepting.

Surrendering.

Bang.

She jerked.

Bang.

Her eyelids flew open.

The gun pressing against her temple clattered to the tile.

Emma crumpled to her knees. Her back slammed into the floor, and her skull made a sickening crack against the tile. She stared blankly up at the ceiling.

Abbot stood in the doorway, pointing his gun at Emma. Ears ringing, Letty gaped. She watched him move as if in slow motion. He slipped his gun into a holster at his belt—did he always have that?—and rushed over to them. His mouth moved. What did he say? He slid into position on the other side of Thane.

"I've got it." His voice penetrated the buzzing in her ears. He moved her hands out of the way and took her place.

She crawled to Thane's head. Hands on either side of his face, she bent forward, locking gazes with him, even as his eyelids drifted shut. "Please don't leave me," she whispered. "I need you. I love you. Please don't die on me."

His eyelids descended

"Thane, please. Please stay."

But he didn't open his eyes again.

Paramedics came and rushed Thane to the hospital. She joined them, and Abbot stayed behind to talk to the police. When they arrived, surgeons ran Thane into an operating room. Now Letty sat in a chair, dazed and alone.

A nurse soon approached her.

No, the blood wasn't hers. No, she wasn't hurt. No, she wasn't okay.

"Is there someone you can call?"

"Yes."

She called Jessalyn, Rebekah, Lydia, and Yawanda.

Twenty minutes later, Jessalyn scurried into the waiting room. She scanned the room, spotted Letty, and hurried over. "Any news?"

Letty shook her head.

"I didn't think she'd hurt him," Jessalyn muttered as she lowered onto the chair beside Letty. "Not Thane.

He was her favorite."

Silence descended among them.

Letty and Thane had discussed their future together, a future that may never happen. They may never get their happy ending. They'd had it for a moment, but their happiness hadn't been meant to last.

But she'd always love him. Even in death, she'd always love him.

She swiped the tears from her cheeks. Tears that wouldn't stop coming.

No. Their lives couldn't end up like this after everything they'd been through. This couldn't be their ending. No way. They'd survived so goddamn much and had found each other. Roadblocks and hardships had plagued their relationship until they finally made it past those struggles to the place where they'd been able to dream. They weren't going to be robbed of that already.

Thane is strong. He will pull through. She had to believe that.

"He won't die," Jessalyn stated, as if she'd heard Letty's thoughts. "He won't." She met Letty's eye. "He won't let anything take him away from you."

"Us," Letty corrected. Then she held out her hand to Jessalyn.

After a moment's hesitancy, Jessalyn clasped her hand to Letty's. Soon, Yawanda and Rebekah joined them, and they formed a chain of support.

Hours later, the surgeon came out.

They leapt to their feet together, still gripping each other's hands.

"Thane pulled through the surgery just fine."

Letty laid her free hand to her chest. "Thank God. Can we see him?"

"Only two of you."

Rebekah waved her and Jessalyn on. "I'll see him after."

The nurse led them to the ICU.

Thane looked so fragile in the hospital bed, in a thin gown, with tubes and wires connected to him, pumping saline and drugs into his system and monitoring his vitals. The coloring of his face was still pale, and dark circles surrounded his eyes from blood loss and trauma, but his lips weren't blue anymore. That was good.

Jessalyn gave Letty a little shove. "Go to him. Talk to him. I'll be outside." She released Letty's hand, backed out the door, and shut it.

Letty approached the bed slowly. The sound of the heart monitor beeping made her heart sink. Thane was magnanimous, but here he was in a hospital bed, post-surgery, with stitches closing up the damage done by a knife at the hands of his own mother. Letty carefully laid her hand over his wrist, not wanting to disturb the IV in the back of his hand. The blood pressure cuff around his arm suddenly inflated, making her jump. She let out a nervous breath.

"Thane." She touched his brow. "Can you hear me?"

He didn't stir.

She bent forward to kiss his brow. "I'm right here, and I'm not going anywhere."

His chest continued to rise and fall rhythmically.

She leaned down so her mouth was close to his ear.

"Thank you for not leaving me, but you have to wake up now."

His lashes didn't so much as flutter.

"Open your eyes." She skimmed her fingers over his forehead then down his cheek. "Please."

The blood pressure cuff and heart monitor responded to her request, not Thane. He didn't open his eyes. He didn't shift in place. He didn't groan in his sleep. But he did breathe. She watched the steady rise and fall of his chest and counted each of his breaths, letting them reassure her that he was okay and would continue to be okay.

She lowered into the chair beside his bed. Exhausted from fear and worry, she rested her head beside his hand. "I love you." And she let her eyelids fall.

36

Thane

*P*enetrating through the fog of pain and drug-induced unconsciousness was like swimming through pudding. Thane was aware of struggling to come to, but the power of the anesthesia and pain medication was too great. He managed to open his eyelids to see blue-gray walls and his legs and feet covered by a white, cotton blanket before unconsciousness yanked his eyelids shut again.

Time was unknowable in this state. He could've lost hours or mere seconds; he didn't know, but he woke up sometime later. Lying there, he forced his eyelids open.

A TV hoisted to the opposite wall.

A small side table with a plastic container for water.

His eyelids descended again before he could see more, but he could put the pieces together. He was in the hospital. Based on how he felt and his battle with staying wake, he'd had some kind of surgery.

The memory of his mother stabbing him in the stomach blazed through his mind. The shock. The searing sensation. Once more, he saw her hand wrapped around the knife's handle and the blade buried deep in his flesh.

A butcher's knife, just like the one Letty had used to defend herself with, identical to the one Sasha had thrown at him and someone had left at Letty's door.

My mother stabbed me. She wanted to kill me. She wanted to frame Letty. She wanted to frame and *kill Letty.*

He pried his eyelids open. "Letty." Her name came out on a weak breath.

Movement to his left.

Letty raised her head from the mattress. Her curls were in a disarray. The blanket, and possibly wires connected to his body, had created lines on her cheek. "Thane, oh thank God." She planted kisses over his face. "I love you. I love you so much." When she withdrew, she cupped his face and touched their foreheads together. "You're okay. The surgery was successful. The blade missed everything vital. You're okay."

He lifted his hands and held her. "Are you? Okay, I mean?"

"Abbot heard my screams. He came in before your mom could..." She sat back to look him in the eye. Her eyes were puffy and streaked with red lightning bolts.

"Abbot had no choice. He—"

"Ssh. You don't have to say more." He already knew. Deep down, he knew, and he didn't want Letty to have to tell him the details.

"If it weren't for him, neither of us would be here."

"Don't think about that now. Come here."

Avoiding his IV and all the tubing, she climbed onto the bed beside him, laid her head on his shoulder, and stretched her arm across his chest, far from his stitches.

He lifted his hand to her face, traced his thumb along her jawline, and played with the ends of her hair. For as long as he could, he resisted the lure of the pain meds and residual anesthesia, but they eventually won out. He slept with Letty in his arms, right where she was meant to be.

Thane came to again to find Jessalyn sitting beside his bed.

"Hey, little brother." Her normally cool façade crumbled and she bent forward, burying her face in her hands. A sob broke free, and her shoulders shook as she wept.

"Hey, hey, hey," he said. "I'm okay."

Shaking her head from side to side, Jessalyn scrubbed the heels of her hands over her face, which was bare of makeup, a rare occurrence for his sister who believed no one but herself should see her nude face. She didn't even have on sunglasses to hide her tear-ravaged eyes.

"Jess. Come here."

She didn't budge from the chair.

"Jess, I want a hug."

She let out a whimper before popping to her feet and lunging toward him.

"Careful. I have stitches."

She jolted to a halt. A small laugh broke free. He was sure that if he weren't lying in a hospital bed, she would've smacked his shoulder. Instead, she bent over him and commenced to cry *on* his shoulder.

"She's dead. They're both dead. And you almost died, too. I would've been all alone." She blubbered out each word. "I can't believe...I can't believe that..."

"I know, Jess. I know." He rubbed her back in small circles. "But you're not alone."

Jessalyn sucked down mouthfuls of oxygen between sobs. She sniveled loudly and shifted back. Tears streamed down her cheeks. She swiped her hand under her nose. "Do you need anything? Ice chips? More pain meds?"

"I'm okay right now." Through the haze of pain and medication, he gazed around the room. "Where's Letty?"

"Her mom arrived from the airport an hour ago and convinced her to go home to shower, change, and rest."

"Good." He shifted on the bed, but the movement caused a sharp stab of pain in his gut. Wincing, he inhaled and exhaled slowly until the pain dissipated. "I do need your help with something, though."

"Anything."

After Jessalyn left, Thane drifted off.

Sometime later, he cracked his eyelids open to see Letty now sat in the chair.

"Hey," he whispered.

She set aside the magazine she'd been flipping through. On the edge of her seat, she held his left hand in both of hers. "Hey."

"Did you eat?"

She smiled. "Still protective, even in a hospital bed."

"Of course."

"Yes, I did eat."

"Good."

She pointed to the side table. "You actually have a lunch tray, too. Unfortunately, it's soft food. Pureed vegetable soup and vanilla custard. On the plus side, there's a roll, which may be hard by now. And the soup may also be cold, but I'm sure they can reheat it for you. Are you hungry?" She started around the hospital bed toward the tray of food.

Although he *was* hungry, he'd noticed the duffel bag he'd asked Jessalyn to pack sitting on the counter. He could wait for food, because what was in that bag was more important. "First, can you open that bag for me? I asked Jess to pack a few things."

"Sure." She stepped up to the counter. "What do you need? A jacket? Socks?" She slid down the zipper and parted the sides. As soon as she did, she froze. "Oh my God." Her voice came out on a breath. She bent forward. Her hands disappeared into the duffel. When she straightened her back and turned, she held the Reuge music box to her chest.

Wide eyes. Gaping mouth. Pink cheeks. She stared in utter shock.

"Jess left the hospital to buy it for me…for you."

She continued to gawk. "Why?"

"Open it."

With the music box sitting on the bed next to his shin, she lifted the lid. Inside was a thick envelope. "Another letter?"

He didn't respond but watched her open the envelope and peer inside it. She stamped her hand over her mouth. Her voice was muffled beneath her hand when she said, "I can't believe..." She lowered her hand. "Thane."

The surprise and love scrawled across her face made him smile.

In her fingers she held the gold locket with the single diamond in a star engraving. Eyes closed, she pressed the locket to her chest. After a moment, she opened her eyes and gazed at him with so much love that his heart stuttered. "How?"

"I asked Rebekah to buy it when you were in Georgia." He lifted his hand. "Let me see it."

She laid the locket in the middle of his palm.

Although he was weak, he pinched the chain between his fingers. "This isn't traditional, but"—he held up the locket—"will you marry me?"

Letty's breath fluttered from her lips. "Is that the drugs talking?"

He chuckled, which immediately had him grimacing. *Shit. Laughing bad. Very bad.* He lowered his hands to his lap. "No, baby, this isn't the drugs talking. This is me. I'd been waiting for the perfect moment to give it to you and propose. Although, I didn't imagine it happening like this, but this is what I want. More than anything. Life is fleeting, and I don't want to spend another moment of my life without being your husband."

She rubbed her hand over her chest, as if to keep her heart from flying away. Quiet tears continued to leak down her cheeks.

"Letty Remis, will you marry me?"

"Yes." She cupped his face with her hands and kissed him. "Yes, yes, yes," she said with their lips still locked.

He attempted to hook the necklace around her neck but had a hard time doing it with his shaking fingers, so she did it for him. The locket was where it belonged, dangling from her beautiful neck and resting above her heart; her heart that she had opened for him, her heart that beat with their love, her heart that he occupied, and he would never take that for granted. For the rest of his life, he'd prove he was worthy of that space.

Letty was his beginning and his forever.

She was his angel...his everything...his charm.

Epilogue

Letty

The investigation into Emma led police to question everyone in the old Canmore circle and to acquire countless search and seizure warrants. There were two people who knew all of Emma's secrets—Sasha Danes and Astrid Cabot.

According to them, Emma had killed Letty's mom and had wanted to kill Letty, too, because Emma had wanted Constantine to come crawling back. She'd made up the story about the ten million dollars and had destroyed Constantine's will to make everyone believe her lies about Letty's mom. In rehab, she'd orchestrated the foster homes that tormented Letty to get what revenge she could on the little brat who had gotten away. Then, twenty-three years later, they told her about Thane and Letty dating, a nasty reminder of her loss. And her failure.

From rehab again, she talked Sasha and Astrid into carrying out her wishes to split Letty and Thane apart. She wasn't about to let the daughter of the woman who stole Constantine from her take another Canmore. They hadn't known she planned to kill Thane, but they speculated that it was because Thane had gotten in the way. She'd told them many times that she'd never wanted kids anyway, so it probably hadn't mattered.

Although brutal, knowing the truth opened the door to Letty, Thane, and Jessalyn finally healing. Slowly and painfully, but they'd had each other.

Seven months later, Letty and Thane got married and traveled the world on a honeymoon tour. Their final stop was Ireland where they rented a house for the month, surrounded by a lush, green landscape. The cottage was next to a pond that they had just frolicked in, naked. Wet and cool, they made love on a blanket spread out over the ground, beneath the stars. Now they lay in each other's arms, bathed in moonlight and the sheen of love-making sweat. A perfect date. A perfect night with Thane. A perfect end to their honeymoon.

Letty's hand rested on Thane's abdomen, right over his scar. "These past few months were amazing. Thank you for giving them to me."

Thane kissed her temple. "I'll give you everything and anything."

She believed him. "You know...I've been thinking about names."

"Names for what?"

"Our kids."

He shifted so that he lay on his side. "Are you trying to tell me you're pregnant?"

"I…um…I don't know. My period is a few days late, but that could just be from all the traveling and excitement."

"But it could be because…"

"Yes, and we definitely did have a lot of unprotected sex while I was ovulating." She studied him. "Would you be okay if I was pregnant now?"

"Are you kidding?"

"Nope. No. Not kidding."

He kissed her forehead. "I'd be beyond happy. So, what names have you been considering for our kids?"

She stamped her lips together and shook her head.

"I'll tell you the names I thought of, if you agree to tell me yours."

She blinked. "You've thought of names?"

"Couldn't help it."

His enthusiasm for their future still made her breathless. "Okay. Deal. What names have you thought of?"

He skimmed his fingers down a lock of her hair. "Just one name, actually." He peered into her eyes. "Grace, after you." A smile touched his lips. "In a way. Or Gracen."

Her heart stuttered. "Grace?"

He twined his fingers with hers. "I scoured a thesaurus. Charm can mean trinket, or enchantment, or enchanting. And grace is a synonym for charm."

That made her smile. "Did I ever tell you that my mom named me Charm because when she first held me, I looked at her with the widest eyes and puckered my lips, and all the nurses gushed about how charming I was? It wasn't until I was four when my obsession with charms happened. My mom showed me a charm bracelet at a jewelry store we were browsing. From that moment on, I had thought all charms were made specially for me. After all, they were named after me. The next week, my mom gifted me with my own charm bracelet. Just one charm was on it at the time. A butterfly. But she bought me a new one whenever she could afford it."

"You've never told me that before. That's cute." He lifted her hand, kissed her fingers.

"So, Grace, huh?"

"Yeah. It could mean charm, or elegance, or a prayer…a blessing. You coming into my life was an answer to a prayer my heart had been begging for since I was a boy."

Her heart spun at that.

"Our love is a blessing that I am thankful for every minute of every day. We've had a lot of grace in our lives, I think. Working behind the scenes. Invisible. Without it, we may not be here right now. And our kids will bring even more grace into our lives."

She willed her eyes to stay dry. "You're good with words." He could speak and write his emotions better than she ever could. She admired that about him. "And names. You're great at coming up with names."

He was right, too. Everything he'd said. Their lives together, from the moment they'd run into each other, had been full of grace. Even when other people attempted to tear them apart, even when her own panic threatened their happiness, even when a knife almost ended Thane's life, grace had been a stronger force. Grace had had their backs and still did. It would be the perfect name for their first child.

Letty pressed her lips to Thane's, sealing all their hopes and dreams with a kiss. "Okay. Grace it is."

Chrys Fey

Bonus Content

Thane
12 Years Old

*T*hey were yelling again.

No, not just yelling. Screaming. Threatening. Attacking.

Thane stood in the hallway outside his parents' master suite. His heart raced. His knees wobbled. He hated it when his parents fought because it always came to physical blows. Blood and bruises. His mother sobbing, curled up on the floor.

He'd seen her crawl through shards of glass to her vanity where alcohol bottles and over a dozen orange and white prescription bottles sat. With shaking hands, she'd reach up, remove a flat mirror, lay it on the ground, bend over it, and inhale loudly through her nose. Then she'd fall backward atop the wreckage of their brawl. In seconds, she'd be unconscious, and Thane would tiptoe inside, stepping gingerly around the glass to get to her. He'd wipe away the blood from her bronze skin with his own T-shirt and smooth her dark brown hair. When she'd wake, she never knew he'd been there, comforting her. Instead, she'd pour herself a glass of vodka and down it with several white tablets. Those tablets always knocked her out until morning, when it would happen all over again.

Thane hated it when his parents fought. It made him feel weak. After all, what could he do? He was twelve years old and his father was a grown man. Still, he stood in the hallway, wishing for the strength to charge into their room and make his father stop.

Glass shattered.

"You bastard," his mother screamed. "You come back here to tell me you're getting married?"

More glass smashed.

Thane's brows lowered. Married? He hadn't even known Constantine was dating. His parents had been divorced for a year, but Constantine still owned the mansion, allowing his mother and sister and Thane to live there. Keeping the house was Constantine's way of keeping Thane's mother under his thumb for whatever Constantine may want from her—nightly visits and violent fights. If Constantine was getting married, would he kick them out or finally give the mansion to Thane's mother?

"Emma, calm down. You know how I get when you act like this."

"Fuck you!"

Something else broke.

"You're marrying some white trash from Georgia?!"

"Carmen Ambrosia is a better woman than you ever were."

His mother scoffed. "Better in bed."

A second later, a slap echoed out into the hall, and his mother let out a cry.

"Watch your mouth! She's a better woman and mother in every way. Just look at all this shit." The sound of plastic containers clattering against tile filled the hallway.

"I take all these because of you!"

Something hit the wall, followed by tiny plinks as a pill bottle exploded, sending tablets flying and bouncing on the floor.

"Why do you think I self-medicate with pills and vodka? Huh? It's you, Constantine! It's you! It's this! It's how you treat me!"

"How I treat you?" his father roared. "Want to see how I can treat you?" The closet door banged open. Metal clattered. His father's shoes stomped back out. "Want to see how I can treat you?!"

She released a high-pitched screech. All of a sudden, the bedroom door flew open. Thane's mother ran down the hall and right past him, as if he wasn't even there. Her hair was falling down from a lopsided bun, mascara streaked down her light brown cheeks, and her dark red lipstick was smudged around her mouth. Her dress tangled around her legs as she fled.

A second later, his father stormed out of the room, brandishing a 9 iron. His dark blond hair, usually

Chrys Fey

slicked to perfection, fell into his eyes. His face was splashed with red rage.

Fear shot through Thane. He stood his ground and clenched his fists at his sides. "Leave Mom alone!"

His father glared down at him, gripping the 9 iron. "What the hell did you say to me?"

Thane's knees shook. His stomach squirmed as if he'd throw up, but he straightened himself and glared his father in the eye. "I said to leave Mom alone!"

His father raised the 9 iron and swung it. Thane didn't have time to lift his arms in defense before the clubhead struck him in the face. His body slammed into the wall with the force, and he collapsed into a heap on the floor.

Thane woke in the ER with stitches and a large bandage over his jaw, a swollen face, and an IV in his hand. He felt sleepy and struggled to keep his eyes open. His older sister, Jessalyn, sat beside his hospital bed, popping a wad of bubble gum and flipping through a fashion magazine. His gaze shifted to the door, where his father stood talking to a police officer. From his coat pocket, his father removed his leather wallet. He flipped it open and ripped out several bills. His fingers folded them in half, and he discreetly passed them to the officer.

Another cop bought. His father probably owned all of them in the precinct now.

"You should've stayed out of it," Jessalyn said.

"He was going to hurt Mom."

"So, what?" She fluffed her honey-colored hair

404

with her hand. "They get into fights every day. It's better to ignore them."

Jessalyn may be able to ignore the abuse, but Thane couldn't. He couldn't put on blinders. He saw it all. Heard it all. Internalized it all.

"Did you know Dad's getting married?"

Jessalyn jolted. Her arched brows lowered over blue eyes that were so much like their father's. "What are you talking about?"

"That's what they were arguing about. Dad is getting married to someone named Carmen Ambrosia."

Jessalyn snorted. "What a stupid name."

"I think she has kids. Dad said she's a better mom."

"That wouldn't take much," Jessalyn mumbled.

Thane stared at his sister, unbelieving. "Why do you always take his side?"

Jessalyn slapped the magazine closed. "Because Mom is weak. She doesn't deserve Daddy. I'm glad he found another woman." Looking toward the door at their father, she shook her head. "I don't care that he's getting remarried, but her brats better not try to take Daddy away from us. You and me, I mean. He is *our* father. No one else's."

Thane eyed their father as he slapped the officer on the shoulder and laughed. He could be Jessalyn's father all she wanted, but as far as Thane was concerned, the less Thane saw of Constantine Canmore, the better.

Their father entered the hospital room while tucking his wallet back into his coat pocket. "Good, you're awake." He glanced at Jessalyn. "Jess, give us a minute."

Sighing, Jessalyn rose to her feet. She tossed the

magazine onto her chair and left the room. With her gone, Thane eyed his father, not trusting him.

His father braced his hands on the footboard at the end of the hospital bed and glared at Thane. "You were lucky," he growled. "It could've been far worse than six stitches and a light concussion. The next time you speak to me in that way, the next time you *get in* my way, you won't be as lucky." He moved around the edge of the bed. "Mark my words, boy." When he stepped closer, Thane pressed into the bed's guard rail. "I will beat you as I beat your mother." He leaned over Thane, putting one hand on the rail that Thane pressed his body into. "You have too much of your mother in you. If I have to, I will beat it out of you. I'll make you my son, yet." His eyes gleamed as he bent his neck closer. "Are you listening to me?"

Thane nodded.

"Good. I'm going to get you discharged, and then I'll drive you and your sister home." He spun on his heel and flung the curtain aside as he left.

Alone, Thane let the terror he'd felt form in his eyes and slither down his face. He didn't move as shame filled him, because the second his father had bent over him, he'd wet himself.

When they arrived home, their father didn't get out of his car. "I'm leaving for Georgia. When I get back, you'll have a stepmom. Now, get out."

Thane and Jessalyn climbed out. Their father didn't even wait to see them enter the house before he ordered his driver to bring him to the airport. Thane stepped into the house, still wearing the hospital bands on his arm. Gripping the banister for support, he ran up the stairs one at a time to the third floor. Cautiously, he headed for his parent's master suite. The door was shut. He gripped the handle in his hand and twisted it.

Unlocked. He pushed it away from the jamb and slipped inside.

One of the housekeepers must've been in there already, because the glass, the pill bottles, the tablets, and the spilled vodka had all been cleaned away. His mother lay in the bed, with the white, fluffy comforter tucked around her shoulders. Thane toed off his shoes, climbed onto the bed, and settled beside her. There were dark smudges around her eyes. Not bruises, thankfully, but signs of her fear, exhaustion, and drug use. He laid his hand gently over hers.

Her eyelids fluttered open, and she focused on him with amber-colored eyes. Her gaze shifted to the bandage on his jaw. "You're so stupid," she slurred.

Thane removed his hand. He stared, unblinking, until she closed her eyes. Even after her claim, he stayed there, protecting her. He'd always protect her.

Eventually, his own eyelids drifted shut. While his body relaxed, he thought about the woman in Georgia his father planned to marry. Did he treat her how he treated his mother? What about her kids? Did his father hurt them as he did Thane? Or did he dote on them as he did Jessalyn?

Selfishly, Thane hoped his father would stay in Georgia and never come back.

Charm
7 Years Old

"Charm, come inside."

Cupping wildflower buds in her hands, Charm tossed them into the air and twirled around, arms out. The charm bracelet at her wrist jingled as the flowers fell into her hair, swayed on the breeze, and landed at her feet. She liked to pretend they were fairies. Giggling, she ran barefooted through the patch of wildflowers growing next to their trailer. Her mom stood at the opened door and laughed when she saw Charm. The wind fluffed her black, curly hair from around her shoulders.

"Look at you. Flowers in your hair and dirt on your feet, like a proper woodland fairy." She tapped Charm's nose. "We're going to have company over for dinner. I made a bath for you so you can get all squeaky clean." She plucked a yellow flower from Charm's hair. "Why don't you save this one so you can tuck it behind your ear?"

Beaming, Charm took the flower and hopped inside.

"I'll lay out a dress for you to wear with your flower," her mom called out while Charm spun into the bathroom.

She removed her dirty play clothes and climbed into the bath. The bubbles rose up to her chest, and she had fun scooping handfuls of it to make Santa's beard on her face. By the time her mom came in to check on her there were no bubbles left on the surface of the water; they were all slicked over Charm's arms, head, and chest.

Her mom laughed. "Enough playtime, Charm." She held open a towel.

Charm stepped out of the bath. Bubbles trailed down her legs. Her mom wrapped her up in the towel, squishing the bubbles and making Charm giggle some more.

In her bedroom, she slipped on a pink dress with white and yellow daisies on it. Her mom sat on the edge of her bed, and Charm crossed her legs on the floor so her mom could brush her hair.

"Tonight is an important night. I want you to meet someone."

Charm bounced her legs up and down like a butterfly. "Who?"

"His name is Constantine. I've been seeing him for a couple of months now."

Charm frowned. "Seeing him?"

"Dating him."

"Oh."

"He's sweet and caring." Her mom paused while she ran the brush through Charm's curls. "He makes me laugh." She set the brush aside. "Stand up and turn around."

Charm did.

Smiling, her mom smoothed her hands down Charm's curls. Then she slipped the yellow wildflower behind Charm's ear. "Beautiful." When she held Charm's hands, the charms on her bracelet clinked together and emitted a sweet melody. "Honey, he's asked me to marry him, and I've said yes."

Charm blinked. "Oh."

She didn't know what else to say. For as long as she could remember, it had only been her and her mom; her dad had died before she was born. She had no idea what it was like to live in the same house as a man.

"This must seem sudden. I had wanted you to meet him sooner, but he lives in New York and runs an important company. He's always busy, but he's here on business and wants to meet you. Once you get to know him, you'll like him, too."

Charm nodded, wanting her mom to believe she was excited, but deep inside, she was sad. She didn't want anything to change.

While dinner cooked, her mom tidied up the house. She wore a long, black cotton dress with a pattern of flowers on it and itty-bitty buttons down the middle. It looked pretty with her black curls, olive skin, and red lipstick.

A knock at the door had her jumping. "He's here," she whispered. "Come here, sweetie." She held out her hand, and Charm took it.

Her mom inhaled before opening the door. A tall man stood there. He wore a dark suit that gleamed in the porch light. His shoulders were nearly as wide as the doorway, and his face had sharp angles as if someone had carved them out of stone, like one of those sculptures she'd seen in her mom's art books. On his wrist was the biggest watch Charm had ever seen. Her eyes widened. Were those diamonds?

"Constantine." Her mom kissed the man on the mouth.

Charm squirmed. Her face warmed with embarrassment.

"Come in."

The man entered their house, filling it with his presence. She blinked. Was he a giant?

"Constantine, this is my daughter, Charm." Her mom stroked a comforting hand down the back of her head. "Charm, this is Constantine. He's going to be your stepdad."

The man knelt down in front of her. "Hello, lil Charm."

"Hi," she whispered, wanting to hide.

He peered up at her mom. "Beautiful curls just like her mom." He settled his eyes on Charm again. They were blue, but not a peaceful blue. They were the color of the ocean during a storm. "But you don't have your mom's eyes."

Charm knew this. Her mom had kind brown eyes, and Charm had curious green eyes. At least, that's how her mom described them.

"She got her daddy's eyes."

The daddy she'd never met. She'd only seen

pictures of him. He had brown hair, fair skin, and green eyes. He seemed gentle.

She eyed the man in front of her, who did not look as though he could be gentle. He was too big. Far too big.

"How old are you?" he asked her.

She swallowed. "Seven."

"That's a good age. Plenty of time to learn yet." He winked one of those ocean-storm-blue eyes.

That wink made her uncomfortable. She stared down at his glossy shoes. Why were they so shiny? She could see herself on their surface.

"I have something for you." From the inside of his coat, he produced a small, light blue box with a white ribbon tied in a bow. Was he a magician then?

She peered up at her mom, who nodded. "Go ahead. You can open it."

Charm pulled on one of the ribbon's tails until it unraveled. The ribbon fell into a coil onto the floor. Carefully, she lifted the lid. Nestled inside the box was a silver charm in the shape of a heart.

"Your mom told me about your bracelet. I wanted to give you something to add to it."

Her mom laid a hand on his shoulder. "That was really sweet."

He stood. "I hope it's okay. I bought you a ring from Tiffany's, so I thought it only fitting that I got something for Charm, too."

"It's perfect." She leaned in and kissed him.

Charm studied the charm. A heart. She thought was it was funny. She'd heard of a broken heart before. In this moment, she finally knew what that meant. The charm might be whole, but her heart was not.

She stayed silent throughout dinner. When was he going to leave? Right after dessert? She hoped so, but after the dinner plates were cleared and dessert was served, the man stayed, sitting next to her mom on the couch, with his arm around her. Not even after he'd finished his coffee did he get up to leave.

Before Charm knew it, it was bedtime. She figured he'd go then, but he didn't. She changed into her cotton nightgown and shuffled to the living room where her mom was cuddled into the man's side, like how Charm usually snuggled up with her.

"Night, Mommy."

Her mom gave her a hug and kissed her cheek. "Night, sweetie."

Charm shifted to the man beside her. His blue eyes watched her. "Night, Con...Con..." She clamped her mouth shut; she couldn't remember his name.

"Constantine," her mom said with a laugh.

"It's okay. She can call me Con. It'll be our little thing." He gave Charm another wink. "Night, Charm. Sweet dreams."

She gave him a small smile before heading toward her bedroom. Before closing her door, she peeked back at them. They were connected by their lips. His hands roamed over her mom's body. One of them grabbed her breast. Charm quickly shut the door and scrambled onto her bed. Beneath the covers, she crossed her arms over her chest. Why would he do that? Why would he touch her mom there? It made her uncomfortable, and it was all she could see until she fell asleep.

Thane

Constantine returned Monday morning, not married as he said he would be. He came into the mansion smiling from ear to ear. Thane couldn't remember the last time he'd seen his father happy.

"Probably spent the weekend having sex with that gold digger," Jessalyn muttered into her slice of lightly buttered toast.

Thane glared. "How do you know she's a gold digger?"

"Oh, please." Jessalyn dropped the triangle of toast onto her porcelain plate and dusted the crumbs off her fingers. "Daddy is one of the richest men in America. He owns the best IT company in the world. Any woman around him is a gold digger."

"Including Mom?"

"Especially Mom."

Thane clenched his jaw. "You shouldn't talk about her like that."

Jessalyn rolled her eyes. "You should be taking notes, little bro. That's going to be you in a few years."

Thane shook his head and stared at his bowl of cereal. "I'm not going to be like him."

She snorted. "That's not going to stop the gold diggers from coming after you. Learn how to deal with them now before it's too late." She popped off her stool. "I'm going to my boyfriend's house." As she left the kitchen, Thane heard her say under her breath, "And make sure I don't become our mom."

It was the summer, so Jessalyn spent every day with her boyfriend. Thane usually stayed in his room, tinkering away at old computers, taking the motherboards apart and putting the pieces back together in different ways to see if he could create something new. He may not want to become his father, but he hoped to one day lead the tech industry into new and better places.

Thane was making his way up the stairs when his father came down. Instinctively, Thane edged to the side, out of his father's way.

"Get ready," Constantine barked. "You're coming with me to work. And take that goddamn bandage off."

"Yes, sir."

Thane wasn't supposed to remove the bandage yet, but he peeled it off to avoid his father's wrath. In his closet, he removed a dress shirt and a pair of slacks, knowing his father would want him to look presentable, like a little business man. He dressed in a light blue, button-up shirt that he tucked into black slacks and slipped on black shoes that he made sure weren't scuffed. Before a mirror, he eyed his reflection, looking right into his amber-colored eyes. At least he didn't look anything like his father. He had his mother's coloring, but he was a shade lighter because of his father. Perhaps that was why Constantine hated him so much. He'd wanted a clone of himself, but instead he'd gotten a son who took after his wife from a failed marriage.

Thane smoothed a brush over his shaved head. Inching closer, he inspected his jaw. The stitches resembled barbed wire, and there was a purple and red splotched bruise around it. Going farther out, the bruise was green and yellow. The people at Canmore Tech would notice, but they wouldn't say a word. They never did. Not when they saw bruises on his mom's neck and arms. Not when Thane couldn't rest his back against any chairs because of the welts on his back from his father's belt.

No, they wouldn't say or do a thing.

Thane trudged down the stairs to where his father waited. Constantine scrutinized him, nodded, and then went outside to the car waiting for them.

Canmore Tech was a skyscraper in the heart of New York City. It was tall, menacing. Like his father. Everyone they passed bowed their heads and greeted his father as if he were God, but God wouldn't beat his wife and child.

On the top floor, his assistant sprang out of her chair the moment the elevator doors opened and Constantine stepped out. "Mr. Canmore, your meeting with Tokyo App is confirmed. One hour."

"Fine," he barked. "Watch him." He tossed a look over his shoulder before flicking the door to his office shut behind him.

Rebekah, his father's first assistant who sat outside his door, studied Thane. She wore a tweed pencil skirt and jacket and rimless glasses. Her brunette hair was slicked into a high, tight bun. Her brows lowered. "What happened?" She held Thane's chin gingerly and inspected his stitches.

"I...sports."

She eyed him. "Which sport?"

"Golf. I was standing too close and took a club to the face."

At least it was mostly the truth.

She hissed between her teeth. "It looks painful."

"It's not bad."

She sighed. "You're strong." She glanced over her shoulder. "That'll help you."

Perhaps Thane had been wrong. One person at Canmore Tech cared. Rebekah always paid attention. She'd get him hot cocoa whenever she had to make a run to get his father coffee, made sure he had lunch, and kept him company. He'd tell her all about his school projects and show her his report cards proudly. It was Rebekah who he enjoyed seeing whenever he came to Canmore Tech. In many ways, she stepped in like a substitute mother.

"Why don't you go down to the labs and check out what they're working on?"

Thane smiled. All the real work in the company happened in the labs. Dozens of people tapped at keyboards, working on codes. Others used tiny tools to build prototypes they hoped would become the next big gadget to own. The lab was his heaven. He spent hours down there while the workers explained what certain sequences in codes meant and showed him how a single character difference could make the code work properly or ruin it completely.

Hours later, Rebekah fetched him before his father would want to leave, so when he exited his office a moment later, Thane was sitting in one of the chairs outside the door.

"How was he?" Constantine asked Rebekah.

"He was a delight."

His father grumbled something that Thane couldn't make out.

"Let's go," he shot at Thane and started toward the elevator.

Thane waved a hand at Rebekah. When he passed her, she tweaked his ear, making him smile. Yeah, at least he had her.

The moment they arrived home, all hell broke loose. They had no sooner stepped through the door when a crystal vase sailed through the air and smashed onto the tile at their feet.

Thane leapt back.

His mom ran at them. Her hair was stuck up in every direction. She still wore her nightgown and bathrobe, which flew behind her like a cape. With a shriek like a banshee, she was on his father, slapping him, scratching him.

"Get out of my house! Get out!"

His father caught her arms in his large hands and shook her. "I own this house!"

She squirmed to get free. The bathrobe fell off one of her shoulders.

"I didn't give you the house in our divorce settlement. I *let* you and the kids live here. What am I getting out of that arrangement, huh? Huh?!" He shook her violently. "What am I getting from you in return? What are you good for?"

His mother smiled like a hyena who'd just spotted the jugular of her prey. Her hand grabbed the crotch of his father's pants. "I know you like it rough."

Thane backed away. He didn't want to see this. He didn't want to hear it.

His mother pressed into Constantine, hiding what her hand was doing, but Constantine closed his eyes and leaned his head back, enjoying it.

"Can you be rough with Carmen? Because you can with me."

Constantine opened his eyes. "You want to have it out one more time? Fine. Have it your way." He tossed her over his shoulder and ran up the stairs, taking the steps two at a time. On the third floor, a door burst open as if kicked down. A moment later, it slammed shut.

House workers had congregated, with their mouths open. They stared up the stairs, and then one by one they all gaped at him. He spun away from them, flung open the door, and tore across the gravel driveway to the field beside their house. He ran hard and fast, desperate to get away, far away. When he couldn't run anymore, he dropped onto his knees, gasping for breath. Lungs shaking, he sobbed.

I'm not going to become him. I'm never going to become him.

He bent his neck, letting his tears fall to the ground.

Never. I won't be like him. Not like him.

He cried harder.

Not him. Not him.

He repeated that oath over and over again.

Thane didn't know how long he was out there, but by the time he came back, all of the lights had been switched off. He made his way up the stairs. At the top, he turned toward his room. A door opened at the opposite end, and his back became rigid. He gripped the banister. The sound of footsteps came up behind him. Spine stiff, he rotated.

His father held a leather duffel bag in his hand. "I'm going back to Georgia. I'll get a penthouse somewhere in the city when I can. I don't know when I'll be back." With that, he continued down the stairs and out the door.

As soon it closed, Thane smiled. "Good."

Charm

Charm had one thought when she saw Constantine sitting at their kitchen table the next morning. *Not him*. He'd been gone for one day and was back already. Dread filled her when she realized she wasn't going to get rid of him.

Two months later, her mom married Constantine in a small ceremony at the courthouse. They honeymooned for a week, during which time Charm stayed with their neighbors the Andersons, who lived on the other side of a stretch of woods from their trailer. No one else lived nearby.

When they came back home, her mom's skin was tan and she appeared happy, despite whatever awful things Constantine did to her at night, which caused frightening thumps, thuds, and thwacks. Her mom sounded desperate, shrieking and howling. And Constantine's demands and growls made Charm tremble in bed, wishing for it to stop.

The day after they returned, her mom had to go to

the store to restock the fridge and left Charm with Constantine. He occupied the kitchen table, gulping down coffee and tapping away at his laptop. Every once in a while, he barked orders at someone on the phone. Charm retreated outside to play, to get away from him.

She climbed onto the porch's wooden railing and balanced on the top. Pointing her toes, arms stretched, she pretended to be a gymnast on a balance beam. She lifted her arms above her head and pulled her shoulders back as she'd seen her favorite gymnasts do before performing. Then she tapped her toe to the beam a few times and inched away from the post at her back. Tiny step after tiny step, she made her way to the center, where she moved her arms up and down. A butterfly. A fairy. A princess. She was all things beautiful and graceful.

"Get off that!"

Constantine's shout made her jump. She waved her arms frantically to regain her balance. When she caught her footing, she shot a look toward the door. Constantine stood behind the screen, glaring. Shaking, she scooted toward the post at the other end of the rail so she could hold onto it while she climbed down. She'd taken a couple of tentative steps before Constantine shoved the screen door open. It banged against the house, and he plowed through the opening.

She froze.

"I said to get down!" His large hands came out and rammed into her stomach.

She didn't have time to scream. Her body hit the ground. Her fingers poked through soft dirt. Flowers cushioned most of her body, but her left arm struck the concrete edging around the flower bed, and she landed on her arm.

Pain.

Pain like she'd never felt before.

Pain that blinded her.

She let out a wail.

Hands snatched her off the ground, making her bawl even harder. Those hands. Those hands had pushed her. Those hands had hurt her.

Get them off.

Get them off!

All she could do was sob.

Those hands dropped her onto a leather chair. A moment later, an engine rumbled to life. She held her arm while the car swerved.

"Shut up!"

But she couldn't. She was terrified. In pain. She couldn't stop voicing that even if she had wanted to.

"Shut the fuck up!"

The order, the bad word, the way he shouted only made it worse.

All of a sudden, the car jerked to a stop, causing her to pitch forward and slam into the dash before falling backward onto the seat. Those hands grabbed her shoulders and shook her. Lightning shot down her arm to her fingertips.

"Stop crying!"

A hand clamped around her face. "Look at me." When she didn't, he jerked her head from side to side. "I said, look at me!"

She blinked away her tears and stared at Constantine. His face was red, as if he'd spent the whole day at the beach without sunblock.

"You're not going to tell anyone what happened. You fell on your own. Do you hear me? *You* fell. If you tell anyone I touched you, your mother will pay."

Fresh tears zipped down her cheeks.

"So what happened?"

His fingers dug into her cheeks.

"I fell," she whispered.

"Did I have anything to do with it?"

"No."

"Good girl." He removed his hands and maneuvered the car back onto the road. "If you pick back up with that crying, I will pull this car over again."

Cradling her arm, she pressed her body into the car door. Quiet tears escaped her eyes, mixing with the snot that continued to leak from her nose. She sniffled and held her breath. Not even sniffing was safe around Constantine.

In the ER, a kind, young doctor examined her, asking her to squeeze his thumb, but she couldn't. "Can you tell me how this happened, Charm?"

She kept her gaze down, feeling Constantine's glare on her. "I fell."

"How did you fall?"

Her voice was soft. "I was pretending I was on a balance beam."

"Apparently, she thinks she's a gymnast," Constantine said, and laughed.

She peeked at the doctor to see him smile at Constantine.

Right then, her mom rushed into the exam room. "Oh my gosh, Charm! I came as quickly as I could."

She kissed Charm's forehead. "What happened?"

"She was standing on the porch rail," Constantine said before Charm could form a response. "I told her to get down, but she wouldn't listen." He shook his head.

"Charm, sweetie, you need to listen to Constantine. He's your step-father now. He was only looking out for your safety."

He's lying, Mommy. He's lying. But she couldn't tell her mom that.

Her mom stepped back and faced the doctor. "Is it broken?"

"We're going to take her down to X-ray to determine that, but based on the bruising and swelling, I'm afraid it is."

The break in her humerus bone was so bad, in fact, that it required internal fixation with a metal plate and screws.

Charm woke from the surgery groggy and thirsty. Her arm was in a yellow cast.

She turned her head and came face to face with Constantine. Her mom was nowhere in sight.

Smirking, he leaned forward in his chair. "You'll think twice before disobeying me again, now won't you?"

She swallowed.

Yes, yes, she would.

Charm's cast was removed after Christmas. Constantine had been a constant presence in her life since she'd broken her arm. Each day became scarier than the last. Not only the monster sounds she heard at night, but fights during the day.

Then came the bruises.

On her mom's arms and wrists.

Her mom's legs.

Her mom's cheeks.

Around her mom's neck.

And then came the bruises on Charm's own arms from Constantine grabbing her and shaking her whenever she did something he didn't like, which was all the time. Daily. Sometimes hourly. Every time he grabbed her, she'd curl in on herself, afraid that the recently healed bone in her arm would snap like a dry spaghetti noddle. Every time he grabbed her, she couldn't stop the tears from forming.

If she left her coloring supplies and the picture she was working on out, grab and shake, while yelling for her to "pick up her crap."

If she accidentally spilled her drink, grab and shake, before throwing a towel at her and yelling for her to "clean this shit up."

If she did anything he didn't like, grab, shake, yell.

Grab.

Shake.

Yell.

Teachers noticed her bruises and how she was "withdrawing into herself," and they gave her notes to bring home. Her mom would cry after reading them. Eventually, Charm ripped up the notes so her mom wouldn't get so sad.

Every night, her mom hugged her tight, with tears in her eyes, and would say, "I love you. Always remember that. I love you, and I'm going to fix this. I promise."

Charm didn't know what that meant, but she trusted her mom. Keeping that vow in her heart, Charm drifted off to sleep, hoping her dreams would carry her to happier places where Constantine didn't exist and her mom was happy again.

Then one night, Charm woke to the sound of glass shattering...

Thane

A scream yanked Thane out of bed. He tossed back his comforter and dashed out of his room, barefooted, wearing cotton pajama bottoms and a plain white T-shirt.

Another ear-piercing scream.

Jessalyn!

He ran to her room and yanked open the door. Hands to her face, she was sitting up in bed. Sobbing sounds broke from her. Her entire body shook with the force of them.

"What is it? What's wrong?"

"D-Daddy was m-murdered."

Thane froze. "What are you talking about?"

"He was murdered! Everyone is calling. It's all over the news! They're calling to say how sorry they are."

Right then, her bedside phone rang. With a roar, she ripped the cord from the jack and chucked the phone across the room, where it hit the wall.

Thane picked up the remote from her bedside table, pointed it at the TV across from her bed, and pressed the on button. The black screen brightened. Colors and shapes formed. He switched it from MTV to a news channel. The breaking news banner at the bottom of the screen read: *Constantine Canmore Murdered Wife, Step-Daughter Killed Him In Self-Defense.*

Thane's jaw dropped.

It was true.

Their father was dead.

But there was more.

Their father was a murderer.

The news anchor shared the known details. There had been a domestic disturbance that was being described as a verbal fight that became deadly when Constantine shot Carmen Ambrosia, his wife of just three months, twice in the chest. Then he went after her daughter, seven-year-old Charm, who had escaped out her bedroom window and ran through the woods to a neighbor's house. Constantine had tracked her down there and attacked her. That was when she'd stabbed him, killing him.

"Where she found the knife isn't known at this time. The police chief is supposed to

make a statement soon."

"They're lying," Jessalyn screamed. "He didn't murder that trash!"

The news anchor paused in her report. "I'm getting word that Constantine's step-daughter is being escorted out of the police station. Let's go to our reporter, Chantelle Glover, live on the ground. Chantelle, what are you seeing and hearing?"

The image changed to show a reporter standing outside a police station. "Charm Ambrosia, the seven-year-old step-daughter of Constantine Canmore, should be exiting the police station at any moment. She has been in their custody since authorities showed up last night to a crime scene that spans two houses and the connecting woods. We're being told that they're taking her to a foster care facility because she has no living relatives who can take her in."

Activity behind the reporter caught the cameraperson's attention.

"There she is," the reporter said.

The cameraperson moved around her and zoomed in as three officers exited the police station. They shielded the little girl from the media. All Thane saw were her skinny, sun-tanned legs, patched up with elastic bandages; a pair of white tennis shoes; and the bottom of a frilly, pink nightgown. The officers ushered her into the back of an opened SUV with heavily tinted windows. One of the officers there climbed in and slammed the door shut, but as the little girl had clambered up into the vehicle, Thane had caught sight of a head of black curls.

The vehicle left right away, followed and led by two cars each. It was like a motorcade for the president, but this motorcade was meant to protect an innocent child who'd gone through an unspeakable ordeal.

Jessalyn threw her pillow at the TV. "She's lying! The little bitch is lying! Daddy didn't kill her mom. He wouldn't!"

Thane bit his tongue, knowing better than to challenge that in this moment. Instead, he sat on

Jessalyn's bed and wrapped his arms around her. She clutched him as she cried. Her tears wet his shirt, and he rubbed her back.

"She killed him! She killed Daddy!" Jessalyn choked on tears as she sobbed harder into his shoulder.

On the TV, a news helicopter followed the motorcade as if Charm was famous. Thane kept his gaze on the SUV and sent the little girl hiding in it his thoughts, "Thank you, Charm. Thank you."

She'd freed herself.

And she'd freed him.

Days later, with their mom home from a short stay at rehab, the three of them went to the office of their father's attorney to hear the reading of the will. Alec Danes and the other four members of Canmore Tech's board were in attendance. Everyone was silent while Uri Von Dickerson, Constantine's attorney and the executor of his will, opened a sealed envelope and extracted the documents. He cleared his throat.

"To you, Ms. Canmore, Constantine left the house."

After a pause, his mother exploded, "That's it? That's all I get?!"

The attorney cleared his throat again. "The house, everything in the house, and the land."

"What about his money? He has billions!"

Uri shook his head. "No. To you, he left the house and property."

"That bastard is abusing me even in death!"

No one said a thing to that. The board members

shuffled their feet and shifted awkwardly. They all knew, each and every one of them, what kind of man Constantine had been while he was alive. And they didn't care.

"To you, Miss Jessalyn, your father left one million dollars."

Jessalyn blinked. Her face paled. "What?"

"He left you one million dollars."

Red slashed across her cheeks.

One million dollars was barely a drop in the bucket in Constantine's bank account. Thane figured Jessalyn was insulted over the measly sum their father had bestowed on her. Probably expected a larger amount, just like their mother had.

"To you, Thane, your father left you five billion dollars."

Jessalyn's breath rushed out of her. "What?" Her voice was barely a whisper.

"And he also left you Canmore Tech."

Thane's head whipped around. "Me?"

"That's correct."

Alec stomped forward. "That's absurd! He's a child! He can't run a company."

"That's why Constantine wrote it into his will that the board would help Thane run the company until his eighteenth birthday, when he'll take over."

"Let me see that." Alec snatched the documents. Seething, his gaze scanned the will. When he found the part he was looking for, his fingers bent the papers. After a moment, his gaze flashed to Thane. "It's true."

Thane met Alec's eyes. He saw a man who felt as though he'd been robbed of what he thought he deserved. If Thane had to count on Alec and the rest of the men there to keep the company running smoothly and teach him the ropes, he'd have to give them something in return. "When I'm eighteen, I'll keep you and the current board members on as my board." He glanced at each of them before looking back at Alec. "I swear."

Alec nodded. "I hope you do."

Thane didn't hear any more of his father's will. He had six years to learn how to run a company, and in that time, he planned to learn how to do it right, how to treat his employees with respect, and what to do to take it out of his father's shadow, something he vowed to do for his mother, his sister, and himself.

Charm

hree years and six foster homes later, Charm was back in foster care after being in yet another abusive home. Each home left her even more deeply scarred and frightened and withdrawn than the last. The first home she'd ever been sent to belonged to a rich family who had a home not just in Georgia but New York, Florida, and California. She'd been intimidated by the three-story house, and by the couple. They wore crisp, spotless clothes and jewelry that sparkled. They eyed her in a way she didn't understand, with their faces screwed up, their eyes narrowed, and their lips tugged down at the corners. She quickly learned what their looks had meant, though, after the first time her foster father had whipped her back with a riding crop when she didn't call him "sir."

When the social worker assigned to her case, Ms. Snyder, came to check on her, Charm whispered to her what had been going on. Ms. Snyder gently lifted the back of Charm's shirt and inhaled. She immediately whisked Charm out of there, but the next home wasn't ideal, either. None of them were. Her final home, the sixth, had been with another rich family with a grand house. She wasn't whipped there. Rather, she was starved. One time when she talked back out of frustration, they sent her to bed without dinner, and they wouldn't let her have breakfast. The only food she had was at school during lunch because they'd drop her off too late to get a free breakfast. The punishment had gone on for four days and four nights because she wouldn't complete her chores properly due to fatigue. Finally, she collapsed in class, prompting the school to call the paramedics. Charm shared with them the truth, and she was taken, once again, back to foster care.

She'd been there for two weeks now. Her appetite had returned, and she felt better, but the fear of the next foster home never left her.

The day came when she was called to the head office, where she always received the news she'd be going to a new foster home. She braced herself. The seventh home just may be the one that broke her for good. Forever. Unrepairable.

Her case worker and the facility's CEO sat not with a couple as Charm was used to seeing but with one person.

The person sitting in the guest chair faced Charm. "Do you remember me?"

Charm started to shake her head but stopped. A snapshot from the past came to her. Brown hair in a ponytail with hints of red in the light. Hazel eyes. A caring smile. "Are you the cop…?"

Chrys Fey

The officer who had rescued her from that horrible night.

The officer who had wiped away her tears in the back of the squad car.

The officer who had shielded her from the press and held her the entire way to foster care.

"My name is Lydia Remis, and I want to be your foster mom."

Tears sprang to Charm's eyes while staring at the woman before her. She had wavy, shoulder-length hair. Creases formed at the corners of her hazel eyes when she smiled at Charm. "Would you like that?"

Charm nodded. "Yes, yes I would."

Lydia drove Charm to a homely home with white paint and purple shutters. Flowering bushes lined the driveway. A painted birdhouse dangled from a tree's branch out front. Along the windowsills sat flowerbeds where butterflies and bumblebees drifted from bloom to bloom. Charm's heart soared at seeing it. The little house was everything

she'd dreamed of since being taken from her home.

"It's not much," Lydia said, "but it's home."

Charm struggled not to smile, but her mouth stretched on its own. She wanted to say it was perfect, except the words got stuck in her throat.

Lydia led the way up the concrete sidewalk to a purple door. She opened it and said, "Welcome home, Charm."

Charm stepped inside. The surroundings were warm and comforting. A brown suede couch, a mixture of wooden furniture in all shades, a bookcase of books and another of VHS tapes, and lace curtains. Along

436

shelves and the tops of furniture were things she'd never seen before. They looked old, but pretty, and the air smelled like apple pie.

"I'll show you to your room."

Charm followed Lydia down a hallway to a room with a bed covered by a patchwork quilt. Resting against the pillows was a stuffed pink flamingo. "I don't know what you like, but we can get whatever you want, and we can even paint the room. Your choice of color. Or colors. We could paint each wall a different color."

Charm smiled.

"I want you to feel welcome here."

She already did.

"Would you like a snack? Something to eat?"

Charm nodded. She set her backpack on the floor. In the kitchen, she sat on a stool and watched while Lydia made her a grilled cheese sandwich. Everything about this home and Lydia was different from the previous six homes she'd been in. This home felt like it could be her permanent home, but she was too afraid to hope for that after everything she'd been through. Hope was a trap. Hope was dangerous. Hope was a weakness. If she hoped, she might find herself in a nightmare she couldn't escape.

Lydia placed a plate with the diagonally-sliced grilled cheese beside a can of ginger-ale. The smell of the melted cheese and butter and toasted bread made Charm's mouth water. She slid the plate closer.

"Thank you."

Lydia smiled. "You're welcome."

Charm lowered her gaze to the grilled cheese and

muttered again, "Thank you."

"You already said that, sweetie."

Charm shook her head. "Not for..." She lifted her head. "For fostering me."

Lydia lowered onto a chair. "I want to do more than foster you. I want to adopt you."

Charm's heart raced. "Why?"

The smile on Lydia's face softened. "Because ever since the day I had to leave you at that facility, I've thought about you. Every. Single. Day. The moment I opened my eyes in the morning, and while lying in bed trying to fall asleep. You were constantly on my mind." She laid a hand over Charm's. "I've loved you all this time. I had hoped you were okay...safe, but then something struck me a couple of weeks ago, a feeling that you weren't okay or safe or happy...that you needed me." Tears sprang to her eyes. "I called the facility, thinking I was crazy, but then I was told you had been removed from another horrible situation, and I blurted, 'I want her.' I've dreamt about the two of us being a family. One day, I hope you will see us that way."

Charm shifted away.

"Eat your grilled cheese," Lydia said after a moment, not pushing Charm to say anything she wasn't ready to say.

After finishing the grilled cheese, Charm ventured into the living room. She moved from shelf to shelf and furniture to furniture admiring what she saw. "You have a lot of cool things."

"Thank you. I like to go antiquing."

"What's that?"

"Antiquing? It's when you shop for antiques. Maybe we can go antiquing some time. Would you like that?"

Charm nodded. She really would, actually. She hadn't been to any stores in three years, and if antique shops had the kinds of things in it that Lydia's house did, then Charm had a feeling she'd love every second of it. Just exploring Lydia's house was fun. She paused in front of a gold-tinged sculpture of a naked woman, with her neck bent and her arms raised. From her hands draped what looked like a green blanket.

"What is that?"

"This is my favorite piece." Lydia joined her in front of the cabinet that housed the sculpture. "This is a bronze sculpture of Isis made by After Claire Colinet. The base is made of marble."

"Isis, the Egyptian goddess?"

"That's right."

Charm peered around at all the other antiques decorating the house. "Can you tell me about the others?"

Lydia beamed. "Of course."

Four months later, Charm stood before a judge, and beside Lydia. Today was adoption day, the day Charm and Lydia had been looking forward to for a long time.

Judge Justeen Goodwin smiled warmly at Charm. "I always like to ask the kids if they'd like to adopt the adults, instead of the other way around, since I believe a child's choice and decision is more important. So, Charm, would you like to adopt Officer Lydia Remis?"

Charm beamed. "Yes, I would."

Judge Goodwin nodded. "All right. I approve this adoption." She picked up her gavel.

"Wait!" Charm cleared her throat when Judge Goodwin raised a brow. "Can I change my name?"

"You can certainly take Remis as your last name now."

"No, I mean...can I also change my first name?"

Lydia laid a hand on her shoulder. "What do you mean, sweetie?"

"I...I don't want to be Charm anymore. I want to be someone else."

No more Charm.

No more foster homes.

No more abuse.

A fresh start.

A new home.

A new name.

She didn't hold any illusions that her memories would magically fade, that she

wouldn't have any more night terrors, or that something wouldn't call up her PTSD, but this was something she had to do. She needed to shed her old identity, say goodbye to Charm, the little girl people knew from the news, and discover who she really was.

"Have you thought of a name?" Lydia asked.

Charm bit her bottom lip. "The only name I've thought of is...yours."

"Aw, no." Lydia shook her head. "I appreciate that you want to be named after me, but you deserve your own name."

Charm peered at her feet. Lydia had been the one

who had saved her. She didn't know of any other name she wanted to be blessed with other than Lydia's.

"I have an idea. Sometimes my partner calls my Liddy, for short. I still think you should have a name that's unique to you, though, so what about Letty, with an e and two t's, instead?"

Letty.

Letty Remis.

A smile dawned on her face. "I like it." She faced the judge. "I want to change my name to Letty Remis."

Judge Goodwin nodded in approval. "It is nice to meet you, Letty Remis." She hit the gavel, making it official.

Outside the courthouse, her adoptive mom asked her what she wanted to do to celebrate. Her answer came right away. "Antiquing."

Thank you for reading Letty and Thane's story.

For deleted scenes, check out this link:

https://chrysfey.com/charm-deleted-scenes/

SCAN HERE

About the Author...

Chrys Fey is a disabled, tattooed author of books featuring heroines of steel. Her *Disaster Crimes* series is a unique blend of romance, disasters, and crimes, influenced by her own experiences with natural disasters. The conclusion of her series inspired her to create TheFightingChance.org, a resource for domestic violence survivors.

Fey got the idea for her first book when she was twelve and discovered a rusted screw with a crooked tip buried in grass. That screw was a key to an unknown world with an extraordinary character born in heaven. That story is *Heaven Born*, coming July 2026.

She is a fur baby mom of four rescued cats. For fun, she photographs antiques, makes playlists, and creates flip cup paintings of Avrianna's nebula. She loves Halloween, autumn, and gargoyles.

Website:
ChrysFey.com

Young & Hungry

Young
&
Hungry

Bryan Kromm

Flare Books/Catalyst Collaborative, El Paso, Texas

FLARE
BOOKS

Published by Flare Books and distributed through
Catalyst Collaborative, a division of Catalyst Press LLC.
For more information, please contact Jessica Powers at
catalystpressbooks@gmail.com.

Library of Congress Control Number: 2025936326

*Dedicated to the people that inspire me every day
to be a better person.*

PART 1

Chapter 1

The Boy in the Shadows' parents had always told him that from a young age, he had the ability to articulate. He could remember, even in his earlier days, his teachers praising him for "groundbreaking interpretations" of classical works—he was "enlightening" them, as if their roles were reversed. It pleased the boy to know that he was following in his parents' footsteps. They were both literary geniuses of their time and the boy was surrounded by people of high stature and class. It made him proud that he was emerging as an elite leader within the club. Famous people twice his age were coming up to him for direction, just like his teachers in earlier years. The boy thought he was special under such circumstances.

Comparatively, his parents grew up in poverty. His

mom, Sara, lived on a farm with three younger brothers. When her mom had passed away giving birth to the youngest, Sara was charged with cooking the meals and tending the house while the men worked the fields. Reading books was her escape from the harsh realities of her life—a teenaged girl forced to grow up too quick. School was no longer an option. She had dreams and goals, but she had a responsibility to her family now. Her father told her that reading was nonsense, and that books would fill her head with ideas that would only break her heart.

One day she came home from the store to find her father reading the newspaper, feet up on the ottoman, toasting them in front of the fireplace.

"I didn't expect you to be home from the field so early. I'll start supper right away," Sara said.

"Don't bother," he responded. "I made myself some toast and coffee."

"Fine then, I'll make some for the others anyway. You can join us later if you'd like."

"No, I'm good, but you should have plenty of time to prepare it now. I went ahead and discarded all of your books." He pointed to the blazing fire.

"What did you do that for?!" She gasped and ran over to the brick mantle to look.

"Things weren't getting done around here. Thought you might need some more free time."

Sara burst into tears and ran up the stairs to check the bookshelf in her room. Everything was gone. Even the books from her mother.

"You son of a bitch!" she cried down the staircase. "Some of those were given to me by Mom."

"Always told her those things were a waste of time," he hollered back. "They'll suck you in and break your heart. The boys will be back soon, better come down and fix them some supper."

"You can go to hell; they can fix their own!" she shouted and stormed back down the stairs and out the front door.

With time, Sara replenished her personal library. The episode of her father burning her books drove her even further away. As soon as her chores were done, she would sneak out to the barn and read. It turned into an obsession. The books took her to a different world, full of wonder and adventure. They created a life with a happy ending. There was always the guarantee that no matter how bad things seemed in the moment, they would always get better. She clung to the hope that one day life would be like that for her.

As for the Boy in the Shadows' father, Mark, his childhood was equally displeasing and traumatic. Although his family differed from Sara's in social status, his father and older brothers made life hard. Mark's father, a military general, knew only one thing—that there is life and there is death; that a mission succeeds or fails; and that failure costs lives. He raised his three boys under these guidelines. Mark's two older brothers thrived in that type of environment. They learned to do as they were told. In a way, this type of dictatorial

parenting eased their minds. They didn't have to think about anything, they just knew it had to get done—make your bed 0600, brush your teeth 0610, eat breakfast 0615. They'd suffer a great deal in life without routine. They developed a comfortability with predictability and structure. Naturally, they followed in their father's footsteps of service. As long as somebody created a plan for them, they were happy to follow orders and execute. It was a simple system and a life that worked for his brothers but not for Mark. He couldn't sit still and listen—his mind was always wandering, and he seemed aloof from an outsider's perspective. Internally, he was simply just curious about his world and wanted to understand how it all worked. The orders his father barked were always met with questions before they were obeyed.

"Make your bed 0600."

"Won't I be using it again tonight?"

"Brush your teeth 0610."

"Can't I brush them after breakfast?"

"Eat your breakfast 0615."

"But I'm not hungry."

Mark needed to know the reason before he did anything. He wanted to know the why. Adults struggled with Mark—they didn't have time to explain everything to him. Gradually, they developed a repulsion towards him and labeled him a nuisance. And because adults struggled with him, Mark struggled through childhood and into adolescence. His teachers couldn't teach him, and his parents couldn't parent him. After

his father felt that he had exhausted all his options to try and correct Mark's behavior (every punishment he could think of, that is), he sent Mark off to the most rigid boarding school he could find, one where even the orneriest kids came out straight as an arrow, boots laced, by the book.

Within a year, Mark was kicked out and sent home. Upon his arrival, he found an envelope of cash taped to the front door.

He read the note inside.

Mark, your mother and I have tried but it has become too much to bear. You can come back when you're a man.

Though Mark did not know it at the time, that moment ended up being the best thing that ever happened to him.

With the cash his parents left him, he bought a bus ticket to the furthest town he could. He got a room for a couple of nights at a small motel. When you're on your own, things become clearer—Mark learned about life or death right away. When something is told to you, it is not fully understood until it is experienced. His whys to his questions were answered through living. He was shaped by the invisible hand of human nature—survival—not by his father. His father's reasoning was, "This is the way we do it because this is the way it's always been done." People hit a crossroad at a certain point in their life—where they question everything they know because now it doesn't seem to make much sense. It is easier to get over these hurdles earlier in life than later, which is

why getting kicked out of the house was the best thing that happened to Mark. He was an answer seeker, and his parents were not answer givers. At the time, however, it was the hardest thing in life that he had been through. He picked up jobs around town and went through a period of trial and error. A kid without a diploma doesn't have the luxury of being too picky. There were plenty of opportunities in trades so that's where he started. He wasn't great with his hands, but he was a hard worker—his life depended on that. His bosses kept him around.

Mark had a hard time adapting to the people he worked for; as you can imagine for a kid who struggled with taking orders, working for anybody would be tough. This time, however, his survival depended on maintaining a job, which meant he had to take orders from people. Whenever he decided he was fed up and ready to move on, he had to make sure he had enough money saved to take that risk. In general, his decisions to quit various jobs came down to the direction the company needed to go and where he thought it was headed. He could have raised his concerns, but his conclusion was this: if you don't have a seat at the table or skin in the game, your opinions don't hold weight. For him, he knew that without an education, to be in important conversations, he would have to be loyal to the company for years, not just months. He needed to work for a business that was clear cut. One that was guided by natural order, not opinions. In all

his occupations, a company's trajectory relied on contracts and bids that he didn't have a say in. He needed a business model that was easily understood. What he needed was farming.

Chapter 2

Take care of the animals, grow the food, harvest the food, sell the food. Rinse and repeat. No decisions to be made. The owner owned the land, and Mark would work the land. Mother Nature decided the rest. At the time he started working on the farm, his future wife, Sara, had started creating her own stories. Reading books wasn't enough anymore. Somebody else told the story and dictated the ending. Her voice needed to be heard.

Over the years, she had developed friendships with people in local libraries and bookstores—when she was not doing chores, she was either in the barn reading or in these places searching for books. Sara shared her stories and exchanged them with other authors. In a way, her fantastical world of escape was becom-

ing a reality. Her future husband, Mark, finally started to enjoy his work. He knew what needed to get done each day and why. He learned through his failures. Plant a seed too deep and it won't grow; too shallow and it won't grow. Harvest something too early and it won't be ripe to eat; harvest something too late and it will rot. Nobody punished him, the consequence was evident—no food. He became a great farmhand and won the approval of Sara's father through his work.

Mark and Sara's romantic relationship budded the more they were around each other. There was an irrevocable connection when they looked into each other's eyes. They tried to find ways to spend more time together each day—he'd stay in to help with the dishes after meals, and she'd stay out to help him feed the animals. In these moments, they began to share their stories—his life without a childhood, kicked out and forced to grow up too fast, and her life without a mother, forced to grow up too fast.

As Sara's father grew older and her brothers married, it was inevitable that things were going to change. Her brothers were entrusted with the farm, and they now had wives to take care of the family. This left a snare in Mark and Sara's budding romance. They had to come up with a plan for their future together since there was no ownership stake in the farm for him and no more responsibility in the house for her.

Her writing had picked up some traction over the years, and the connections she made with the writing community presented opportunities. The local news-

paper had some openings, and since she had become good friends with the editor, she was offered a starter position posting short blurbs in the back sections. She took the job, and Mark agreed with Sara's father to continue helping on the farm until his sons were old enough to take over the responsibilities.

With her new job and no more ties to the farm, Sara moved into town with Mark, and they saved their money together. The goal was to save enough money to buy a plot of land once he was done helping the brothers tend the farm. Mark and Sara would live off the land and raise a family.

The growth of her career and the couple's savings blossomed. Her work was praised by her editor and was received well by the public—so much so that she quickly jumped from the back pages to the front cover. She was now getting the hottest leads and breaking the headlines. Financially, the promotion was a huge step towards their goal as a couple.

Internally, Sara felt that there was still a piece missing—she wasn't creating the stories, she was telling them. There wasn't any control over outcomes, plotlines, or characters. Those were already a part of the story. It was her job to weave the story pieces into something catchy and coherent. She wanted more ownership in the creation process. She wanted to feel like her work was her baby, not a stepchild.

She thought about this dilemma for quite some time. She still had those stories she had written in the barn from her earlier days. She thought that maybe if

they were developed into something more, she could start to shop them around. It helped that she was well-known in the community—her lifetime spent in local bookstores as a child, and now in the newsroom, created a network of people in her corner. She had an audience. She signed a small deal to sell some of her books at one of the bookstores, and thus began her new path as an author. She was now in total control of her work.

Although Sara didn't make any huge breakthroughs early on, she had some minor successes—just enough to keep her pushing along. With sustained effort over time, she gained notoriety.

Surprisingly, it was one of her earlier works that reemerged to capture the audience—sometimes the vigor of a young author takes time before it's appreciated. She would later concede that there was a ton of passion written in those earlier pages compared to her later works. For now, however, she felt like a much more polished writer and admired her current work over her previous attempts, even if they were garnering recognition. This big break was enough to catapult her into the limelight, earning the stage on a national level. Though it was a long time coming, it was certainly surreal to see her childhood escapes turned into something more.

Chapter 3

The fame and fortune brought unwanted attention and publicity. The couple's quiet, normal life became quite the opposite. They saw the worst in people—the ugly side of success. They no longer knew who their friends were. Even their families became harder to trust. They were suddenly the meal ticket for everyone who was struggling. They came to understand that the only relationship of true value they possessed was with each other.

Mark and Sara's goal of having a plot of land to raise a family wasn't a dream anymore, it was a necessity; they were no longer motivated by the excitement to achieve it but by the fear of what could happen if they didn't. If they didn't find a plot of land to live off, their privacy would be in jeopardy and their lives would forever be the epicenter of daily tabloids.

They packed their things and left home in search of what would later be dubbed Paradise Manor. They moved from town to town, exploring their options, staying a couple nights here and there, talking to locals, prospecting outskirts, and discussing ideas. They needed isolation, and fertile soil with a water source. They settled on a quiet place well out in the country, tucked away in the mountainside. They made sure the land they chose received plenty of rain and a healthy dose of sunshine. About a hundred acres in total, cloaked in trees and webbed with creeks. Spring water flowed in abundance. Vegetation sprouted in groves.

As they drove to the property, the dirt road winded and climbed through the woods into an everlasting tranquility. Time stood still when they were immersed in the landscape. Maybe it was because land is the timekeeper of the past and holds the future. When they immersed themselves in the land, they saw the bigger picture—they were observers of the natural world order. They came to understand that land had existed long before humans roamed, and it would exist long after they died. Take away all the nonsense that consumes people today—the pecking orders of society, the need for wealth and power—and let Mother Nature control the rest. If the world is a cruel place, let it be at the making of her hands. If protection of the youth is a concern, let the concern be raised by the dangers of animals or weather. Mark and Sara sought the need for isolation from the hand of man, not the hand of God, with hopes of a better future for their

children to come, a future free of the cruelties they experienced growing up.

When the purchase of the land was settled, Mark and Sara were finally at peace, in a home safe from the outside world. The chaos of their former life had subsided, and their dream life began. They rubbed off on each other. She learned how to cultivate the land from him, and he learned how to read and write from her. It was fun for them to share in their new successes and coach each other through challenges. Their relationship deepened.

With a lifetime of experience on the farm and in various trades, Mark had a lot of insights he could use to shed light on certain things. He recognized through reading and writing that there was still much unknown about the land and its cultivation, still much to learn about hard work and survival. His days with the outside were numbered and replaced by the in-doors. He had so much to tell other people. He had discovered the other side of his mind untapped. It was his turn to master academia—he wasn't a high school dropout anymore.

Like Sara, he started small and grew into becoming a notable author. He received recognition and noto-riety among working class men and women. He gave a voice to those that desperately needed to be heard. Mark was an underground hero in the making, con-tributing ideas that would shape the course of labor laws and the farming industry. Land protection and sustainability were foreign concepts until he penned

them. It also helped that he could reason and lobby with white collars—he knew how the land worked in harmony with the people. He knew the land because he lived it.

Sara's newfound love for cultivating the land grew too. She had a lifetime of introspection, reading books all those years indoors. Learning how to grow the land was her opportunity to be free and get her hands in the dirt. She finally had permission to sink her hands in the soil. She had the freedom to be the caregiver of the outdoors, freedom to watch something grow when it received love and care. Her efforts were rewarded. Growth was proof of her value—every seed that sprouted was saying thank you to her. She loved to watch things grow and flourish, knowing that she played a part in their success. Working outside was very much another escape she dreamed about when she was younger but was never allowed—the fresh air, the sunlight, the connection to the earth. She had mastered the indoors, now it was her chance to master the out. So much to learn, and the freedom to do it. Her writing days were replaced by this newfound freedom. She had her own triumphs—creating a meal from farm to table—growing the crops, harvesting them, storing the food, breeding the animals, growing them, butchering others. She learned the way everything worked in harmony with the soul, the way Mark described on his pages.

Both Mark and Sara became well-rounded over the years and had satisfied their itch for personal

growth. It was time to move on and think about the future. They had created a world stable enough to raise a child the way they wanted—the way a child deserved. They could now provide opportunities they never had growing up. The timing worked out where they would have just enough time to have a child before it was too late for her.

Nine months later, the Boy in the Shadows was brought to life.

Chapter 4

Provide him with protection and safety. Provide him with everything he needs and wants. Love him unconditionally. Praise him for all the good he does. Homeschool him. Grow his mind to become an intellect. Tell him to use his brain, not his hands. Only expose him to people we know and trust. These were Mark and Sara's guidelines to raising their boy.

The teachers they hired to come to the house were told they were working with a genius, after all, he came from a world-class couple in the literary world. According to his mom and dad, every word out of his mouth was "amazing" and every word written down was "incredible." If a teacher disagreed and saw his flaws, it didn't matter—his parents trumped any opinion a teacher had. The boy took his mistakes to

his parents, and they would reinforce him, undermining the teacher.

"Well, that teacher doesn't know what he is talking about, I think this is really good. It could be better than our work back in the day."

"You really think so?" The boy would start to smile.

"Of course it is, you think we'd ever lie to you?"

And then the boy would continue his ways, repeating small errors, and refuting any teacher's evidence to the contrary. Tough to do a job when the parents say otherwise. Some of the teachers quit, sickened by the immorality of the situation. Others stayed and played along—the money was too good to say otherwise. A few stood up to the couple. They were met with attacks on their character.

"I'm trying to teach your son. Let me do my job."

"No, what you're doing is crushing his hopes and dreams. A little white lie here and there is worth it if it sparks his confidence and passion. Stop critiquing him so harshly or we'll make it tough for you to find work in the future."

The teacher, at this point in the conversation, saw the writing on the wall. They concluded that it'd be irrational to sacrifice their reputation and career for one kid who would be okay in the end—there was enough wealth in the family for generations to come. He would live in a different stratosphere of society forever and always. And thus, the teachers would circle back to their original choices—take the pay and fake like the boy is doing well, or leave.

With the amount of time he spent inside and the amount of books at his disposal, the boy naturally gained intellect. He could recite facts like an encyclopedia. He could have sophisticated conversations and debates about things. He knew everything and he flaunted it too. His parents surrounded him with people that were agreeable—friends of theirs who had more important things to do than argue with teenagers. They smiled and listened. They retorted and allowed themselves to be refuted. Most of the time, the boy was just in his opinions—he had the depths of knowledge and information on his side. There was no sense in causing a scene if they were indeed factually wrong. They'd gracefully concede, removing themselves from the conversation with the boy.

The real issue their friends had with the boy was not his reading, comprehension, debate, or expertise. It was with his writing. The crux of the argument was this: his writing was a regurgitation of things already written. Ideas already brought to life. There wasn't any originality of thought within his writing. People didn't feel anything when they read his stuff. They didn't feel his life on the pages. There was nothing to connect them to the author. Nothing to make them feel like their voices were being heard. No story that excited and ignited passion. Nothing that could encapsulate a reader and take them to another world. Nothing to make a reader think about their life from a new lens.

Mark and Sara's friends refused to call the boy

an author because he didn't create; he repeated what others had already done.

Surely, the couple would have understood that. But they didn't. And, as expected, the couple protected their son.

Nobody was trying to pick sides; they were only raising concerns about the boy's future. A lifetime inside isn't good for the soul and isn't good for a writer. But their concerns were misinterpreted by Mark and Sara as "he can't do it." Nobody was allowed to tell Mark and Sara that their boy couldn't become a writer. Nobody was allowed to tell them that their boy needed to get out. They created a life to protect him and provide opportunity. They wanted to keep him away from the cruel people of the world. They wanted to give him a childhood better than theirs.

Curiously, Mark and Sara's own successes were due in part to the harsh realities and corrections that they experienced growing up. Furthermore, the love they shared together helped them persevere through hard times, and the connections they made with others fulfilled them. To isolate their child was to starve him from what he needed most: other people to share his journey with. Mark and Sara's life was a blueprint for their child to prosper, not a map that would lead him to eternal suffering. Yet they continued parenting their child with ignorance of their past.

Much like the teachers that stuck around, Mark and Sara's friends that stuck around were the ones who could live with sacrificing the boy's growth and

maturity to preserve friendship with the couple. The friends who stayed fed into the narrative that the boy was a genius. And the lie got bigger.

The peak of it all was when the time came to start publishing the boy's work. If his work was so great, according to his parents, then it was time to get it out there. His parents suggested that he start small—a couple pay-to-print magazines, something to test the waters and see how well he would be received by the public. The boy was skeptical at first—pay to print magazines were for vanity. He thought his work deserved more credit than that. His parents convinced him that it was better to generate interest first with some smaller works before jumping off the deep end; he had to develop a following before "going big." This is what his parents did when they first started. He did generate interest. Not because of his work, but because of his name. The second generation of Paradise writers—heir to the throne. Sir Paradise II, king of the castle. Next in line to rule the literary kingdom. Need it not be further mentioned that this was the deciding factor for every publishing magazine considering his junk—the family name. Companies could get paid handsomely by the family (triple the going rate) and generate some buzz. It was a bidding war for the rights to publish the boy's first ever piece.

After the publishing, the critics came to expose the truth. The boy was a phony. The parents' solution, as usual, was to throw money at the problem. "Either accept the cash and redact your statements or

we'll bury you and your reputation." They bought off a couple deadbeat critics to vouch for his piece—the ones who were willing to trade their reputation for a lump sum. Mark and Sara's wealth and power continued to speak all the way up the ladder. The boy's bigger works landed in bigger publishing houses. The couple went as far as to threaten to pull their own work from companies if they didn't bend the narrative to cater to the boy. All of this in an effort to protect their son. They wanted to maintain the illusion that he was a polished writer worthy of the highest praise. Nobody could say otherwise except the local joe schmo, whose opinion did not matter to the parents—the boy would never meet joe schmo. The boy would laugh in his face if he told him his writing wasn't good. What does joe schmo know about writing anyways? He's some dumb hick from the country who wouldn't know a good piece of literature if it smacked him upside the head.

Contrary to the family's beliefs about the boy's talents, sales didn't lie—joe schmo didn't buy. There were plenty of cop outs and excuses for the lack of numbers. The lie grew again and got bigger and bigger until it was too far gone. The damage was done. At some point, it became a reality. The lie became the life.

In his parents' eyes, they had done their job. The truth was they crippled him. The boy was spoon fed and sheltered from the outside. When his parents grew old and passed away, he was no longer protected. The truth came out in waves. One by one, compa-

nies pulled the plug. The show was over, and the boy was left with more questions than answers. For the first time in his life, he had no one to give him direction. His parents had left him with enough wealth to last a lifetime but no purpose—writing had been taken away from him. His parents' friends never stopped in to say hi anymore and he didn't have any of his own. He hired workers to do things for him because he didn't know how—chefs to cook, maids to clean, landscapers to tend the property.

This is how he lived the rest of the days, reading in the shadows while money took care of the rest.

Chapter 5

Over time, Paradise Manor turned into a fortress. His parents' stories about the outside made him paranoid. He did everything in his power to secure his isolation. He put up towering fences on the perimeter of the property, with cameras at every corner. New riverbeds and creeks were excavated to make the land difficult to navigate. Due to the redistribution of land and water, a bridge was built to get to the driveway. Beyond the bridge a little ways was the start of the property line, now bordered by fencing. On the outskirts, where the access road met the fencing, was a large heavy metal gate and its guard. The guard's job was to manage traffic in and out, and monitor the camera surveillance for trespassers. There was a reserve team of six ex-military men for emergency backup situations.

They were housed underground on the northwest side of the property. The boy paid them well and outfitted their quarters lavishly to ensure they were comfortable while "on duty." Two men in the barracks, two at home on-call and two off duty—that was their rotation. They were there to help the guard in the event of a security breech.

The irony was that the boy didn't draw any attention from the outside world. Paparazzi and trespassers were normal growing up because everybody wanted a glimpse of his parents. Their fame attracted the public eye. Now, there was nothing left to see. At the height of his parents' prestige, their hunting dogs sufficed to scare off any strangers (this was a bonus to their actual job of helping the couple hunt the land). The dogs died shortly after the parents did, and when they did, the boy felt that there were more reliable ways to ensure his safety. His security strategies and their implementation were obsessive. Sadly, nobody cared about the boy anymore. In fact, nobody even knew who he was. After the last of his contracts were pulled, the joke was over. He didn't fill the tabloids. He wasn't the brunt of comedy night shows. It was all over. Everybody had their fun while it lasted. The boy faded from memory. Questions of "whatever happened to" turned into "whether he ever was." Publishers buried his books deep in the archives. A dark spot on the couple's sterling reputation that could never be removed, but could be forgotten.

Part II

Chapter 6

Is it true that youth is wasted on the young? Or is it simply that youth is forgotten by the old?

Alfred felt that he was caught just in the nick of time, before jumping off the cliff of innocence and into the abyss of adulthood—before you find out how cruel the world can be. He maintained his optimism and youthful zeal for life well into his thirties. Nothing discouraged him. His salvation from the traps of knowledge and responsibility came at a price—because everyone around him matured, and he stayed the same, he had no connection with people his age. His intense focus on the things he did, often unconsciously ignoring others—like a child at play—was mistaken for pompousness. His well-mannered speech and proper attire, like a boy at prep school, was a confirmation of

his narcissism. His naivety, like the young who must put blind trust in the people that take care of them, was labeled as ignorance.

Beyond the price of not fitting in, Alfred's salvation from adulthood was, more gravely, costing him his life. He felt like he was a rock star, living his life in the fast lane, addicted to the finer things in life that could kill him if he overindulged. The difference between Alfred and a rock star was that he wasn't addicted to drugs or alcohol or money or fame, he was addicted to life itself. He completed bucket list items in half the time it should take a normal person. He had no fear, attacking everything with the same enthusiasm, optimism, and curiosity every day. Roadblocks for others were mere obstacles for him. He believed if somebody else could do it, so could he.

With the exponential speed of completed life achievements came the exponential decline in health. His joints creaked and cracked as he awoke in the morning. His face was weathered. His energy dropped quickly through the mid-morning, needing breaks for coffee and tea, followed by early afternoon naps. His balance and coordination were unreliable—he had to move at a snail's pace to prevent a fall. Most alarming was his heart—pain radiated every night, making it difficult to fall asleep. As his health continued to spiral, he thought of all the creative people who left this world too early; he thought of the amazing things they did in such a short amount of time and their future possibilities unrealized. Was he using up his

finite time on earth too quickly by living his life to the fullest every day? People use the span of their lives trying to figure it out. What if he had already figured it out at only thirty-five? The good lord wouldn't be so cruel as to take away the spoils of his life this early, would he?

Alfred thought of the Boy in the Shadows—a boy rumored to have lived his entire life within the confines of Paradise Manor. With the elaborate tales of sightings, and the disparity between these stories, it was hard to corroborate that anybody had seen the boy at all. In fact, it was widely speculated that Mr. and Mrs. Paradise had never had a son. After all, famous people don't have time to raise children. The mystery of the boy's existence had always intrigued Alfred and now seemed like the perfect time to fully investigate. Maybe the good lord would be so kind as to grant him one last wish on his bucket list before his time was up.

The tales growing up of medieval castles and dragons excited Alfred. Rumors about Paradise Manor spread like wildfire—barbed wire fences that sent electric shocks, watch towers with hidden snipers, rottweilers and pit bulls salivating to tear off a limb, sky high concrete walls, mountainous terrain with cougars and bears, white water rivers that carved through jagged rocks and boulders, sharks lurking in the depths— the list went on. Just getting in the front door seemed nearly impossible. Once you found a way to break in, there was more—lasers and ninjas and steel traps and anything else a young mind could conjure up.

Alfred had to assemble a team for the journey. He asked around to see who would be daring enough to join him. He had built up quite the reputation as a fearless renegade, always seeking to do things that had never been done before. He was often cited by the people of his generation as a hero. The population at large was either excited by his adventures or fearful of them. Some found them fruitless.

"That boy is always chasing something."

"He'll never be satisfied because he doesn't know what he wants."

"Be cautious of him, I fear he's going to run himself into the ground and drag you along with him."

"You can't always go go go. You have to stop and reflect. You have to think about what you're doing."

This was the advice and counsel from Jessica's parents—she was Alfred's first candidate evaluated to join his team. Jessica was an aspiring journalist familiar with the story of the Boy in the Shadows and his parents' legacy. She admired their work and wondered where the boy went wrong. Surely, he would have had access to the resources to become a fantastic author, she thought. And with the mentorship of two legends in the field, it should have been a guarantee that the boy would rise to the top—if she were a gambler, she would have doubled down on that. In any case, there was a story there that needed to be told. Something needed to be exposed. That excited her—breaking news on a never before told story. A "Whatever happened to?" Or a "How did a recipe for success turn

into such an utter failure? Where did they go wrong?"

Jessica was still green and finding her voice. She reported for the local news on occasion and wrote for the high school newspaper. Her potential was promising. She had a fire within her to know more—a thirst for knowledge and experience. There was a lot to learn in order to become successful. This adventure seemed like a great opportunity to hone her skills. She didn't believe in the speculation surrounding the dangers of this place but if there were any of it, it would be a great test to prove she could navigate hard-to-reach places for a story. There was nothing really to lose—it'd be a great experience even if it turned into a flop.

She had hunger and drive. Nothing was going to stop her from getting where she needed to go. She understood her parents' concerns about the adventure, but she evaluated it as an opportunity to grow. Her evaluation far outweighed her parents' opinions about it. There was a story there and she was going to get it.

Alfred went through the interview process with Jessica, judging the pros and cons. He liked her zeal and lust for a new adventure. He also thought that it would be good to have somebody report their findings. Her small size and stature were an issue—the physical environment would require some stamina and an expertise in navigating rough terrain. He contemplated whether he needed somebody to join at all. He had been many places and done many things but

never with someone. This posed new challenges and threatened the success of the mission. How would he deal with a fallen soldier? He reflected on some of his past experiences before coming to a final decision. The idea of telling a young mind "no" was something that he couldn't do. He had to keep Jessica's fire for adventure ignited. He agreed to bring her on to the team.

Jessica was elated at the opportunity. Now all she had to do was convince her parents that this was a good idea. The burning passion in her eyes said it all. The way she spoke about the future of her journalist career made it impossible for her parents to say no. They knew there was no real danger; driving up to Paradise Manor to interview a person who might not even exist is far from a life-or-death situation. They made one stipulation to the agreement—one of them would have to come with her. Alfred was too reckless, they concluded, to trust their daughter with him alone, traveling to an unknown place.

"Absolutely not. Alfred would never allow it. If one of you two joins us, the mission could be compromised!" Jessica yelled defensively.

"First of all, it's not a mission, stop calling it that. And second of all, Alfred is twice your age and doesn't have a life. He has had fifty different jobs and has traveled around the world at least twice while trying to figure out what to do with himself. We don't think you need to be alone with a person who doesn't know who he is and corrupts young minds with fantasies.

His parents are good people, we grew up together, but they opened up Pandora's box when they told him he could do anything or be anyone."

"What's so wrong with that? What's wrong with letting a kid dream? What's wrong with being told you can be anything?" Tears began to well in Jessica's eyes at this last conjecture.

"Nothing, sweetheart, but at some point in your life you have to choose and commit to something if you want to have success. Otherwise, you'll be a jack of all trades but a master of none. We aren't saying you can't go; we're just saying that you'd be better off accompanied by an adult."

Jessica wiped her eyes and thought for a moment.

"What about Uncle Bruce?"

Uncle Bruce was the fun uncle. He was the one who sparked Jessica's interest in journalism in the first place. He had stories of adventures and far-off places nobody had ever seen. He was an expedition-ist and an explorer. As a boy, he loved the outdoors and seeing new places. Animals and plants intrigued him. More specifically, interactions between the two—where organisms lived, how they survived, what other species they depended on, the climates that gave rise to certain things and fall to others. His domain of expertise became environmental sciences. With it came the necessity to learn how to navigate difficult and sometimes harsh environments—environments remote to the world and not meant for humans to roam.

At this point in his life, Bruce was over the hump and done with exploration. He had seen enough in his career, and as the years passed, his role shifted from explorer to consultant. He now shaped new companies and young minds. This was sufficient to serve his purpose nowadays. He loved exploring but he was older and didn't have the same vigor for it as in previous years. He felt like he had etched his place in the world of science and there was nothing left for him to give. His priorities shifted from proving himself to providing a life for his family. It wasn't about him and his ego anymore. It was about his children, and their children to come. It was about the new generation. It was about teaching. It was about creating a world that was better than he found it. It was about passing down his knowledge.

Uncle Bruce, Jessica's parents agreed, would be a fair compromise for the journey instead of them. At least they would have somebody they could trust accompanying the two kids on this absurd adventure. Convincing Uncle Bruce to join really wasn't that hard for Jessica since he was a bit of a pushover and had a soft spot for her—he was her godfather and he saw a lot of his younger self in her now. Moreover, helping a future adventurer find her niche was fulfilling for him. The harder part for Jessica was convincing Alfred.

"Why would we want some washed up old guy to join us? He's going to slow us down."

"He's not some washed up old guy. He's my uncle and I think he has a lot to offer our team. You said it

yourself; we need another member to help balance us out."

"Give me some time to consider it."

"If he's out, I'm out. My parents won't let me go without him."

It was true that they were going to need more help. Alfred couldn't hold Jessica's hand every step of the way. He needed another person he could rely on to carry some of the weight. Bruce had experience. Jessica was hungry but unproven. Bruce would be battle-tested—equipped to handle all types of situations. And if Jessica flaked, Bruce could take care of her, and Alfred could carry on with the mission alone. Alfred agreed to allow Bruce to join the team as long as Bruce agreed to train Jessica in terrain navigation. Bruce thought this was a silly suggestion, utterly ridiculous to put it plainly—they weren't embarking on a dangerous mission, they were driving somewhere to request an interview. An interview, Bruce might add, of a person who might not even exist. Nonetheless, Bruce agreed to do it for his goddaughter. It would be good for her to know things about difficult terrain for her career in the future.

Bruce invited Alfred to join Jessica in his three-month training program on outdoor navigation and safety; this included comprehensive coverage on free climbing and glacial terrains. Alfred chuckled and declined the invitation, almost insulted at the offer. He made sure his response conveyed the message, "Do you know who I am and what I've done?"

"Suit yourself," Uncle Bruce responded, shaking his head at Alfred's ignorance. *Mr. Know-It-All*, he thought.

Jessica loved training with her uncle. She learned so many new things, and so much of it would benefit her for her future career. She was amazed at all the small details. There were so many little things you needed to know to be an expert on exploration and navigation. The vastness of anything, frankly, takes a lot of time to study and understand. Uncle Bruce's years of experience came to life in those training sessions.

"Put your foot here not there," he'd command.

"Good, now look up and scan your surroundings," he'd continue.

He taught her to look for tree markings, soil compositions, rock scatter—stuff she never thought of but that made sense. The information she learned tied in with her experience—it was necessary to know these things in order to connect the why to her actions. Everything learned added to her direction and purpose. Learning with her uncle would get her where she needed to go—where she wanted to go.

The plan for the trip was to drive as close to Paradise Manor as possible and then hike in to request an interview. The access road had been blocked off for quite some time due to rain and snow. It was the change of seasons from winter to spring, creating muddy territory and precarious slides. Winding dirt roads need to be stable and dry for motorized vehicles

to drive. Bruce estimated it would take anywhere from four to six hours to make it to the gated entrance on foot. To do that type of trek out and back, with an interview sandwiched in the middle, wouldn't be feasible in a day. It was agreed that they would get a good chunk of the access road done, set up camp, complete the rest of the way to the gate, request an interview for the following morning, and return to camp to rest. Jessica liked the idea of having more time (if needed) to conduct the interview—sometimes people have a lot to say. She wanted to give the Boy in the Shadows the freedom to discuss things as thoroughly as he needed.

Everything for the expedition was set up and prepared by Bruce—equipment, provisions, time of departure, etcetera. Weather permitting, they would leave on a day's notice. Alfred was jacked up and ready to go. He loved adventures and doing new things. This adventure in particular felt like the pinnacle of his accomplishments—the mountaintop completed. After achieving this, he could rest easy, knowing that he lived his life to the fullest.

Jessica was nervous but also excited. There were a lot of unknowns, but she trusted her Uncle Bruce and knew that her experience in the newsroom and newspaper was meant for this—for the next step. For true journalism, chasing leads and breaking stories. Still, she didn't know what it would be like until she actually did it, and this caused her anxiety. The paradox was that the only way for her to overcome her anxieties was by exposing herself to them. She knew

that once she became comfortable being uncomfortable, soon what used to feel uncomfortable would feel comfortable. If she wanted to be a better journalist, she'd better practice journalism. It was nice to have her uncle as a safety net. If things went awry, Bruce would know what to do. Quietly, in her head, she thanked her parents for forcing her to invite her uncle on the trip.

Bruce was indifferent to the expedition. He was more or less just happy to share in the excitement with Jessica. He reminisced on his younger days when he was full of ambition and passion. He didn't approve of Alfred's zest for new things, but he admired his courage to chase them, no matter how ludicrous they seemed. Alfred the nomad, bouncing from idea to idea, place to place, job to job. He knew a lot about nothing. It was important to have the chase. Most are too paralyzed to move—they sit, they wait, and they ponder. They never do. It's better that way for them—it's more convenient to say, "I could've been" versus "I tried and failed." It's human nature to be terrified of potential—to fear investing a life into something and failing. Bruce contested that it feels better for most to not give it their best so they can bail themselves out—so they can say, "I could've been had I done more." That gives people hope to carry on. And then there are the few who say, "Why not?" or "Might as well" or "What's there to lose?" Bruce believed that people needed to give themselves the best chance to see what could happen. Then people could move on with their life, no longer living in past regrets. Bruce did it to the

best of his ability and didn't live in a world of "what-ifs." He had peace knowing that he gave everything he had; his path of all-in commitment turned him into a different person. Getting knocked down and getting back up time and time again molded him to handle hard things. It made him better at the next thing.

Alfred had the first piece to the puzzle—he had the dogged pursuit. And pursue he did, along with his new crew, to the mountaintop.

Chapter 7

It was a sunny day with clear skies—perfect for the drive to the access road. The pavement was warm and dry, as the tires guided them to a dirt cutout where the road to Paradise Manor began. They parked their car there and packed their hiking supplies for the long trek. They crossed the road closure sign and barricades. They exited the light and entered the shadows, leaving the world they knew in exchange for the world they didn't.

The access road was not as nice as the pavement driving in. A clear and sunny sky shining on a snow-covered dirt road can make boots feel heavy and footing unstable. Alfred slipped and fell more than once, kicking up chunks of mud. Jessica and her uncle chuckled at the "experienced adventurer." Jessica

and Bruce had no troubles navigating the terrain—they had been replicating these conditions for months in various areas around their town, practicing. They stopped chuckling when they sensed Alfred's frustration. His zest and excitement for the trip quickly fizzled out, but he was determined to finish the last thing on his bucket list.

As with all the things Alfred did, he made the concession that once it got hard, he would finish the task and move on. This trip became no different.

I finish everything I start. I ain't no quitter but man, do I hate this. This sucks. Who would want to do this all day? I could never. I'd lose my mind, Alfred thought.

Well ahead of Alfred, Jessica and Bruce had already set up camp. Bruce guessed they were probably another hour from the gates of Paradise Manor. They offered to wait until the next day to complete the walk but Alfred, to his credit, was determined to push on.

"Why are we stopping?" he asked in contention.

In reality, Alfred was fed up and already ready to get the trip over with. He was long past exhaustion, but he didn't want to admit it. Bruce knew it would've been better for Alfred's body to stop before things got worse, but they were in no real danger—they weren't committed to a multi-day hike with stages and base camps. Pushing through the pain was harmless, and in a cruel way, satisfying for Bruce—he enjoyed watching Mr. Know-It-All suffer.

You asked for it. You're the one who was too good to prepare like the rest of us, Bruce thought.

They carried on, Bruce and Jessica slowing their pace drastically to help drag along Alfred. As they approached the gates, the guard almost fell out of his chair. He squinted at the video surveillance and rubbed his eyes long and hard to make sure he wasn't asleep. Since the road closure, the guard hadn't seen a soul besides his coworkers. In fact, he couldn't remember a time when an unwelcome stranger roamed near the gates when the road was open. The avid outdoorsmen around the area had stopped coming long ago after continually being denied access to hunt the land. Stories of big game would remain a mystery and a temptation. What was inside those walls? The fencing and cameras served as enough of a deterrence. No point in risking an arrest for breaking and entering—there were plenty of places on the outskirts of the property with good hunting. If it lived on the inside of the walls, it probably lived on the outside too. The hunters would have to deal with the wonder of what could be.

After the initial shock of seeing not just one but three strangers approaching, the security guard felt a little relieved—he was finally in need to do his job.

"You guys must be lost; this is a no trespass zone. Private property." He pointed at the sign on the gate. "Can I help you find what you're looking for? Trailhead for Paradise Point is an hour and a half back the way you came. It's on the left-hand side with a green-arrowed sign."

"Oh, no, thank you. We appreciate the information, but we are looking for Paradise Manor."

"Well, you're in the right place, but like I said, nobody is allowed past the gates without authorized permission. Are you hunters? People come wandering around requesting to hunt on the land and offering money. Can't do that either. Plenty of places on the outskirts that have some good game though. I could tell you where they are?"

"No actually, we're hoping to speak with the resident of Paradise Manor. You see, I am an aspiring journalist, and me and my friends have come a long way to help shed light on this place. There have been rumors over the years that Mr. and Mrs. Paradise had a son who still lives on the property today."

"Sir Paradise II still lives on the property, yes, but he is very ill and doesn't accept visitors anymore. It would not be beneficial to his health at this point in time."

"Okay, well, is there maybe a phone number we can reach him at? Please sir, maybe you can call over to the residence and see if he'll have us. If not today on such short notice, then maybe tomorrow so he has time to prepare for guests. At least a conversation over the phone wouldn't hurt, would it?"

"Look it, I've been cordial, but don't test me. The answer is still no. Now, you can leave on your own, or I can help you."

"I don't really understand how a conversation on the phone or a phone number is going to make him sicker?"

"Do you normally make a habit of asking for per-

sonal information of people you don't know? The answer is still no."

Alfred had finally caught his breath. He gathered his bearings and released his frustrations.

"This is ridiculous. I didn't work my bag off, crawling through the mud for six hours, to be denied access by some third-rate doughnut boy. Let Mr. Paradise II decide who he wants to see or not."

Alfred walked aggressively toward the gates. The security guard drew his gun.

"Whoa whoa whoa!" Uncle Bruce interjected. "Nobody is dying on my watch to meet a has-been or never-was. Apologies for the brash young man. We appreciate your time; we'll be on our way now."

Bruce looked at Alfred and nodded at him to step away from the gate. Alfred obeyed the command and backed off. The security guard holstered his gun. Bruce tipped his cap to the guard, who smirked and spat on the ground in disgust. The group slowly turned and headed back to their camp.

Once out of the guard's earshot, Bruce snapped. "Are you two nuts?! You could've had us killed. I don't know about you, but I like my life!"

"Listen, if you didn't like the idea of the mission, then why'd you sign up? You have to be willing to die to accomplish the things I've accomplished!" Alfred responded.

"Do you know how ridiculous you sound? Stop calling this a mission. It's not. This is not life-or-death. This is just a silly escapade that I agreed to so that I

could protect my goddaughter from your stupidity. I'm most certainly not willing to die for this and I won't let you drag her with you! We're packing up tomorrow and heading back. You have your answer—he exists, and he doesn't want to talk. End of story."

Jessica listened intently to her uncle's harsh words. She didn't know what to think. She wasn't satisfied with the responses of the guard and knew that there was a story. And now with the proof of his existence, Mr. Paradise II needed to be questioned—it wasn't enough to know he was alive, she needed to know more. Why was he avoiding the public? Why all the privacy? Why all the walls? She disagreed that their journey was a "silly escapade." This meant something to her—this was journalism. There were inherent risks in the field. Sometimes it was life-or-death to get the truth. She needed to have skin in the game; that's what made it real. The good reporters were the ones who put their lives on the line and knew it was all-or-nothing.

It was hard for her to understand her uncle's perspective of the situation—that there was more to life than work. That once she established herself as a journalist, other things would become more important—her purpose would deepen. The "we" would outweigh the "me." Her purpose would not only deepen but it would change. Jessica hadn't realized yet that sometimes she wouldn't get the answers she wanted, and she would have to live with that. One thing Jessica understood was that her uncle

only wanted what was best for her. He was trying to protect her—a byproduct of love. She understood that. She also understood herself and knew that she was grown enough to take responsibility for her actions—to accept consequences. She needed to make her own choices and learn from them. Parents never let go; their kids break free. She calculated the risks before the eventual decision she would make.

There wasn't much talk among the group on the way back to camp—everything was already said. It wasn't until the campfire started that small talk was exchanged. Uncle Bruce's bottle of whiskey broke the ice and eased the tension as they passed it around. There wasn't a lot of substantial discussion about the day's events, but there were a lot of laughs, card games, and stories. Uncle Bruce took the camaraderie as a silent agreement that they had all moved on and forgotten about their disappointments. They would return home no worse for wear, and his trip, as far as he was concerned, would've been considered a success.

Alfred had not forgotten about what had happened and stewed about it all night, devising a plan. Everyone finished their night caps and put out the fire to settle in for the night.

Jessica awoke to a stir outside. Instinctively, she reached for the bear spray. It was still dark out—too hard to tell if it was late in the night or early in the morning. She paused for a moment and listened for another noise. It was the faint sound of a slow zipper.

The sound loosened her grip on the spray. The next sound she heard was familiar—the chainsaw snoring of her uncle.

Alfred's going back. I knew it! He can't go alone; he'll die out there, Jessica thought.

She quietly and efficiently collected her things. She thought of Uncle Bruce and wrote a note. She paused again and heard Alfred's footsteps towards the road.

"Go back. It's not safe," Alfred commanded Jessica, who was now following him down the road.

"Slow down, you're going to waste your energy. You're going too fast," she responded.

Alfred was sore from the hike yesterday, and the trot was more painful than the strength of his stubbornness—he slowed to a normal pace.

"You know you're not going alone," Jessica stated.

"I'm a big boy; don't need anybody's help," Alfred retorted.

"Well, good thing I'm a big girl and don't need anybody's help either," she continued. "Since we're headed in the same direction, may as well help each other."

Alfred walked for a couple more seconds while he contemplated how to respond.

"We need to figure out how to get past the guard," he conceded.

"Well, there's a camera down the main road that can spot us out a hundred yards. The guard will see us coming. We'll have to veer off the road to the right or the left and climb the fence."

"There are probably cameras on the fence line too. No matter what we do, as soon as we get close enough, the guard will spot us."

"If that's the case, then the furthest away we can get from either side of the gate, the better—by the time he sees us on video surveillance, he'll have to leave his post to come get us. If we can scale the fence quickly, we should have enough time to get to the house before he catches us. Once we're inside the house, it'll be harder for him to use his gun with Mr. Paradise II inside."

"Okay, let's cut off the road now."

They made their way through the pines. The woods were dense—moss and ferns cloaked the fallen trees, and orange and brown pine needles layered the forest floor. It felt like a trampoline to walk on, absorbing weight and pulsing you forward. The soft, spongy ground was a relief for Alfred who needed the extra comfort. Blisters had formed on Jessica's feet in her earlier training days but had since calloused over. She could withstand the hours on foot now.

Bruce woke up, probably from his own snoring, at the time that Jessica and Alfred had veered off trail. First light had just pierced the horizon. Bruce gathered himself in his tent. He stepped outside and noticed some of the group's gear missing. This raised some suspicion, and after relieving himself, he returned to investigate. It didn't take him long to find Jessica's note.

I'll come back if it gets too dangerous.

Bruce's heart jumped through his chest. He scrambled to process what was happening. He was running on foot before he could wrap his head around everything.

Jessica thought more about the plan as they walked through the forest.

"This isn't going to work," she finally said.

"What are you talking about?" Alfred spoke, irritated already from the day's hike on foot.

"The plan. It isn't going to work."

"What do you suggest we do?" He responded, starting to get angrier by the second.

"We need to split up. Think about it. If the guard leaves the gate unattended to find one of us, the other can waltz right in. If he stays at the gate, whoever climbs the fence has a free shot at the house untouched."

"You mean to tell me one of us has to go back to the main road after being off course for this long and approach the fence from the other side?"

"Yeah, I guess that's what it means," Jessica confirmed.

"Fine, but since this was your idea, you have to be the one that goes back."

"Okay, fair. I'll get to the road and find a hiding spot to watch what the guard does. You wait for me to get to the road, maybe like a half an hour, and then continue with the plan like we talked about—hop the fence and go for it."

And with that, Jessica made her way back to the

road. Once there, she continued off trail to the other side to avoid getting spotted too close to the gate. She found a hiding spot close enough to see the guard with binoculars but far enough away from the camera on the fence line. Now she sat watching and waiting. From an aerial view, the three drew an imaginary triangle—the security guard at the gate, Jessica and Alfred at the west and east sides of the property line. Bruce was on his way up the road, and, from a bird's eye view, the four of them started to shape a diamond as he travelled up the rear.

Just before Jessica was about to doze off from the quiet calmness of nature, a distant noise from the main road caught her attention. Uncle Bruce was huffing and puffing, chugging along as fast as he could. His adrenaline was surging, and, as out of shape as he was, there were no physical limits keeping him from getting to Jessica. There was a deeper force driving him that defied all laws of human nature— he could run forever if he had to save the life of his goddaughter. His eyes followed the footprints like a hawk. He stopped abruptly when he saw the two sets of footprints veer off course—one set to the left and the other set to the right.

Did the guard chase them off the road? There are no footprints leading from the gate to here, he couldn't have. They must have headed left and then decided to split up, taking the gamble that one would have to sacrifice for the other to get home free, Bruce thought.

Bruce decided he had to get to the guard before

the guard got to the kids—then he could reason with him, or in the worst case, disarm him before he shot anybody. He hadn't heard any shots yet, which meant he still had time. He continued straight ahead on the road, quickening his pace.

Jessica watched in panic as her uncle sprinted down the main road towards the gates. Her plan was compromised. The guard spotted Bruce.

Chapter 8

The guard was more alert today given the encounters of the day before. He had shared the story of yesterday's events with his co-workers. The ex-military men didn't fully believe him and thought that the guard was having a bit of fun, yanking their chain. They had continued their rounds of cards and whiskey well into the evening without thinking another second about it. Today, the guard recognized Bruce right away and stepped out with his gun pointed, cocked, and loaded.

"Where are the others?" the guard demanded.

Bruce kept his distance from the guard, his hands in the air. Sight of the guard's gun was a good thing— the kids were still safe.

"I don't know, they left this morning while I was

asleep. Please, I don't know where they are and I don't want them to get hurt," Bruce responded.

The guard wasn't buying Bruce's story.

"Stay right there," he commanded.

The guard backed slowly into his office to call dispatch. He kept Bruce within his line of fire. Before calling in backup, the guard glanced at the video cameras. Alfred was live, front and center, on one of the screens.

There was no way for Alfred to climb the fence, so he had to improvise. He spotted a couple of branches extending across the vertical plane of the property line. He had only climbed a tree once before in his life. He struggled his way up, branch by branch, until he found the one he wanted. He had never walked on a branch. The one he picked was too thin to support his weight. It snapped and he leapt off, the guard catching all the action on camera. With Alfred's feet and body worn down from grueling treks over the last day and a half, his right ankle broke on impact, unable to brace the landing. The guard slapped the red button in his office, activating the two ex-military men underground.

A little foggy from the night before and already starting the first cards and whiskey for the day, the two military men looked at each other as the red siren went off in their room. It was a look that asked, "Are you seeing the same thing I am, or am I still drunk from the night before?" After both of them confirmed that what they saw was indeed a reality, they strapped up and headed out.

Meanwhile, the guard went back and took care of Bruce.

"Get down on the ground, hands behind your head!" The guard began handcuffing him.

Jessica watched in fear as her uncle followed the orders. She had to make a decision. Turn herself in or continue with the mission. This was her chance; her uncle not in immediate danger and the guard distracted, it was now or never to get inside Paradise Manor. Risk herself for the story or turn herself in for safety? She kept out of sight and bolted for the fence line.

Faced with the same dilemma as Alfred, Jessica too made the same decision to climb a tree above the fence line. She, however, was better prepared for the task. She used the rope she brought from camp to help her up the tree, just as her uncle had taught her. When she was younger, she loved swinging from branches like Tarzan. When they would snap from her reckless play, she quickly learned which ones were better to swing from than others. Sometimes, she would snap the branches on purpose to practice her landings and impress her friends. Her favorite landing was the tuck and roll. Now, her playful techniques were instinct. She found the sturdiest branch and nimbly walked across it. She picked the best landing spot to perform a tuck and roll and then she jumped. The terrain was soggy. She made quite a splash when she landed. It would have been a zero on the Olympic dive score, but it was a ten out of ten given the situation—a little wet with a few scratches.

She landed on the southeast corner of the property. Alfred landed on the southwest. From her vantage point, she could see the two military men converging on Alfred's side.

The guard must have radioed Alfred's location after handcuffing Uncle Bruce, she thought.

If the terrain had been flat and dry, it would have taken thirty to forty-five seconds to sprint to the bridge that crossed the waterbed and lead to the front driveway. The terrain, however, wasn't flat and dry—it was littered with puddles and sink holes. A sprint would be risky in those conditions. Jessica moved briskly towards the waterbed in a crouched position. Alfred caught sight of the military men and dropped to a crawl through the mud towards the house. Jessica saw this and prayed Alfred would stay down and give in.

She made it to the waterbed and crossed the trench on the side of the bridge rather than the bridge itself to remain unseen. She made it to the other side of the trench and onto the neatly trimmed front yard. There was no hiding now—she took off in a dash around the back of the property. One of the military men turned on instinct and spotted her. Her hair flashed around the corner of the house, and he started in a mad scramble towards her. He screamed over the radio, "There's another one! There's another one! It's a girl! It's a girl!"

Alfred saw the commotion unfold. He eyed the front door within sprinting distance. With the two sharpshooters in range, he probably would have

thought twice before going for it. Now, with the other military man chasing Jessica, only one was standing in his way from completing the mission. Alfred stood up and began to sprint, slipping and stumbling through the mud and puddles, wheezing and wincing through his pain to get to his mountaintop—his lifelong list of achievements ready to be completed.

"Son, stop!" the military man shouted from a distance. Alfred kept going.

"Stop or I'll shoot!" Alfred kept running, feet now touching the bridge to the driveway.

The military man took one last inhale, to settle his heart and his hand. His vision was focused, crosshairs away from the vitals.

Arms are too close to the heart and lungs. Go for the legs. When's the last time you pulled a trigger on home soil? Never. Protect the man who pays you, he thought.

He pulled the trigger on exhale. Alfred dropped immediately, screaming in agony. His left calf was covered in blood. Chunks of his flesh spread across the front lawn. Alfred passed out at the sight.

Jessica entered the house through the back door and into the kitchen. There were no ninjas or steel traps, just books everywhere. Every nook and cranny were stuffed with leather and parchment. The walls had shelving built in to create more space for the books. There were no pictures of people in the house. No knick-knacks or crafts. No quilts or blankets. No toys of any sort. No paintings. Just books.

Jessica climbed up the spiral staircase and creaked

open the master bedroom. An old frail man with white strands of hair was sitting in a chair facing the fireplace. He was dressed in a silk robe. The chair he sat in had a tall, mahogany leather back. It was tough for her to see what the man was doing. She crept closer.

His nose was buried in the pages of a book twice the size of his head.

"Joy, is that you?" he hollered without looking. "Could you make me a cup of tea and a scone? I could use a midnight snack."

Jessica didn't remember seeing anyone in the house when she walked in, and it was midday according to the light shining through the bedroom windows. She approached the man. He gazed up at her with his pale blue eyes.

"Oh, Ms. Mackenzie, what a pleasure it is. I haven't seen you for years. Are you still teaching?"

Jessica froze, trying to think of what to say.

"Yes, Mr. Paradise II, I am," she stuttered to find the words.

"Ah, Sir Paradise II to you," he corrected her. "To what do I owe the pleasure?"

"Well," Jessica hesitated, "I'd like to ask you some questions about your work."

"Ah yes, all my pieces are quite wonderful, wouldn't you say? Now, which one would you like to discuss?"

She had to think on her feet. She read the stem of the book in his hands. *FARM OR FLEE by Paradise*.

"Farm or Flee," she responded.

"Now Ms. Mackenzie, did you come here to insult me, or talk about my writing? My mother was an extraordinary writer of her time, but her work is outdated and of sheer folly. I have created much more modern work that combines ideas and styles of the past, the present, and the future. Take for instance an excerpt from *Old Man and the Sun*. 'The sun beamed and hit his skin like a brick when he stepped outside, heavy and leaving his skin red on impact.' Metaphor, simile, diction—it all makes sense."

"Sir Paradise II, with all due respect, have you ever stepped outside and felt the sun?" Jessica questioned.

"What does that have to do with it?" he fired back.

"How about this? 'The man was chilled to his core from the shadows of the indoors. He stepped outside into the sun, and was immediately wrapped like a warm blanket, his soul finally free,'" she responded.

"Ms. Mackenzie, people pay me to write, and they pay you to teach. Can I help you with anything else, since it seems we have switched roles today? Or shall you show yourself out?"

"Yes, I have one more request." She mirrored his callousness.

"Well, make it good, it may be your last."

"Tell me why you think you're a better writer than me?"

Sir Paradise II laughed softly at this request.

"Is this the last question you ever want to ask me?"

"Yes, you won't see me again once you've answered."

He shook his head and began.

"It is because I have read every book ever written one hundred times over. I have taken this knowledge to design an intricate theory that can predict the most ideal ways to create masterful compositions."

"How come I've never heard of these 'masterful compositions?'"

"They are not meant for the general public. They are meant for elite minds that understand what great writing is and what it isn't."

"Okay, answer me this: say you read about something one hundred times and then you write about it yourself, how do you know it to be true?"

"It's the truth because the general consensus states it is. If one hundred people are coming to the same conclusion, then common sense says it's the truth."

"The general consensus does not account for every opinion, especially those that say otherwise. Theorize all you want, but a theory can always be refuted by one person who felt it differently than you. You don't know what it's like because you've never been through it—you don't know what you're actually writing about because you haven't experienced anything outside these four walls."

"I've written over a thousand times inside these walls. How's that for experience? How many times have you written?"

"Well then, I think you've answered my question thoroughly. Just as I suspected, Sir Paradise II: The Master Writer of Nothing. A true author has something to say about something."

They both turned at the sound of a creak in the floor. Jessica was unsure how long the military man had been standing in the room.

"Ma'am," he stated sternly, presenting the open handcuffs.

She took one last look at the old man before being escorted out. She felt sorry for him.

Chapter 9

Alfred was airlifted to the closest intensive care unit. He eventually passed away on the operating table. It was his heart that gave out. He became a local legend. Stories still circulate today about all the things he was rumored to accomplish in his life. Some say he lived it to the fullest—thirty-five years old, not a second wasted. Others say he lived it irrationally and brashly, his heart unable to keep up with his torrid pace.

The town erected a statue in loving memory of "The Man Who Did Everything." There has been much debate over whether Alfred lived a fulfilled life and what his purpose was. Some believe it was obvious that he did not know what he was chasing, while some believe he inspired others. There is no debating, however, that both Alfred and Sir Paradise II had one

thing in common—they died alone. They immersed themselves in their own version of darkness, void of any personal growth for they never had somebody beside them. Somebody to contradict them. Somebody to steer them in the right direction. Somebody to lean on. Somebody counting on them. Somebody to reciprocate a gesture of love. They never had somebody to connect with and not a soul could deny that.

Jessica became nationally recognized for the events that transpired at Paradise Manor. Nobody really knows the real story. Sir Paradise II was never found after their so-called encounter. Both the military men and the guard vanished as well. The property remains vacant, but the folklore carries on.

Whether the story was fabricated or not, Jessica and Uncle Bruce are its only survivors.

www.ingramcontent.com/pod-product-compliance
Lightning Source LLC
Chambersburg PA
CBHW031209260626
47169CB00004B/1304